Betray Her

Caroline England

PIATKUS

PIATKUS

First published in Great Britain in 2019 by Piatkus
This paperback edition published in 2020 by Piatkus

1 3 5 7 9 10 8 6 4 2

Copyright © Caroline England 2019

The moral right of the author has been asserted.

A CIP catalogue record for this book is available from the British Library.

ISBN 978-0-349-42280-0

Typeset in Garamond by M Rules
Printed and bound in Great Britain by Clays Ltd, Elcograf S.p.A.

Papers used by Piatkus are from well-managed forests
and other responsible sources.

Piatkus
An imprint of
Little, Brown Book Group
Carmelite House
50 Victoria Embankment
London EC4Y 0DZ

An Hachette UK Company
www.hachette.co.uk

www.littlebrown.co.uk

For Simon – 'solid as a brick' – like our dad.

PROLOGUE

The current glints and sparkles as she gazes. It has been a good outing: fresh air, camaraderie and fun. Freedom from the house, too. Her whole body a little weightless, she's contented, relaxed, happy. And high.

The rain-speckled wind strokes her cheeks. Closing her eyes, she breathes in the musky fragrances of the countryside surrounding her – woody pine and damp conifers, rotting moss and wet grass. The pristine and crisp smell of the river too. Save for the hum of falling water in the distance, it's silent.

She stretches and smiles. In this instant she has everything she wants; it's a moment to capture.

A sharp gust and she's teetering, then tumbling down. Oh my God, oh my God, she's slipped.

Instinctively holding out her arms, she gropes for something solid to protect herself from the fall. Nothing there but empty air, then the slap of the surface and shock of icy water. A powerless plunge into darkness hauls her down and down further. Liquid like bleach stings her nostrils, swamps her mouth, seals her throat.

Raw survival setting in, she pins her lips shut and tries not to inhale. Swim, she needs to swim, get back to the top. Kicking out her legs, she tries, then again. Futile, so fruitless. Boots too heavy, blazer leaden with water.

Weak, unduly weak. Paralysed limbs. Frozen flesh. No air left, no more room. A spasmodic breath and acid deep in her chest. So dark, very dark.

Inescapable tugging, insistent sucking, a swirl of murky depths.

The arms of the dead drag her in.

Pure and transparent, the blackness turns white. With it, realisation, as clear as the river.

She didn't trip; she was pushed.

Revenge, sweet revenge.

The friendship, the bonding. The smile, the pretence.

Cleverly biding her time.

And finally winning.

Part One

Part One

1

St Luke's – September 1988

It drizzled that first September day. Dad nearly missed the turning.

Quickly swerving to the left, he accelerated the Jag up a long and surprisingly modern driveway. 'Tennis courts, this must be it,' he said, his first words through the hour and fifteen-minute journey.

Mum was sitting next to Jo in the back. 'Looks nice, love,' she said.

Jo's new boater was still on her knee 'for safekeeping'. She looked at it doubtfully. What was it *for*?

Mum didn't seem to know either. 'Maybe you should put it on now, love,' she said.

The elastic snapping her neck, Jo pulled on the straw hat. It restricted her view, but that didn't matter; she hadn't been looking through the windows anyway, just at the back of her dad's black wavy hair and catching his sad eyes in the mirror.

Dad finally pulled up with a deep sigh. The car park was busy, large glossy vehicles lined in neat rows, their boots open. Girls were milling in grey suits or grey coats and grey socks, their hair tied in low bunches. They reminded Jo of the twins at her primary school whom no one could tell apart. The thought made her tummy turn.

Mum patted her knee. 'Are you ready, love?' she asked in a wheezy voice. Then Dad opened the door, holding out his rough hand to take hers, which wasn't like Dad at all.

Grown-ups with umbrellas were standing back from their car boots, watching men lug out brown and grey trunks and drop them on trollies with wheels. But Dad lifted Jo's trunk himself.

'I think it's this way, Stan,' Mum said, pointing to a sign with an arrow saying, 'Junior House'.

Jo wanted to stop and breathe. The leather smell of Dad's new car had made her feel sick all the long journey, and she'd been too hot in the thick coat, but she hadn't said anything. And suddenly they were here; time was going too fast. Dad was striding up a patchwork path, his rolled shirtsleeves showing the tight muscles in his forearms as he carried the trunk towards glossy black doors.

Feeling peculiar in her suit and grey belted overcoat, she clutched Mum's hand. Her stiff shirt collar and tie were almost making her gag. The boater felt funny as well, the elastic too tight beneath her chin, but at least it kept her newly blown hair neat and dry, holding off the wild frizzy mass which sprung up every morning.

Mum and Dad stopped. Adjusting her hat, she looked up. Made of dark greenish stone, the building was tall and old, not unlike a spooky Scooby-Doo haunted mansion. A woman with inky hair and a white face was standing at the door. Wearing a lilac jumper and matching cardigan, she was looking down from the top step with closed thin lips and a smile Jo wasn't sure of.

'Ah, the Wragg family. Welcome to Junior House,' she said in a posh, smooth voice. 'I'm Miss Smyth, Housemistress.' Her pale eyes rested on Jo and Jo *felt* them pierce her. 'You must be Joanna. You're from Barnsley, in Yorkshire, I believe.'

The woman's face was thin, nothing like Mrs Brown's nice, friendly dimples. In fact, she looked remarkably like the wicked housekeeper from an old black-and-white film Jo had watched with Mum only last week. Wondering how on earth the woman knew who they were, she turned to Dad, but his face was tight, his eyes fixed on the trunk.

Miss Smyth stood back and wafted an arm inside the building. 'Come through and see Joanna's dormitory and then quickly say your goodbyes.'

The woman said it in a sweet voice, but Jo thought it was crispy underneath. Still holding the trunk, Dad lifted his head and opened his mouth, but Miss Smyth interrupted. 'Thank you, Mr Wragg, but leave it there. The porters will deal with it.'

The boater at an angle, Jo followed, climbing the steps into what Mum would call a 'busy' room. An old piano stood at one end, a tall cupboard at the other; one wall had two small windows with orange curtains inside, the opposite was lined with rows of books. They were higgledy-piggledy, she noticed. At least she liked that.

'These are my rooms,' Miss Smyth said, gesturing to an opaque glass door on her left. Then, with her thin smile, she nodded to the hardbacks. 'This is the library, Joanna. I hear you like reading and we cater for all sorts, I'm sure you'll find something suitable and spend many enjoyable hours here.' She peered again at Jo. Her face was all powdery but the talcum didn't hide the funny lump at the side of her nose.

Dad's hands were in his pockets, surveying the room. Mum briefly took Jo's and gave it a squeeze. Jo just knew her mum wanted to mention the long list of classics she had already read, albeit the abridged versions, but it didn't do to brag and Miss Smyth was hurrying them along.

'This way, please.' Then, looking back with a sigh, 'Mr Wragg? This way, please. Joanna will sleep upstairs. To begin with at least.'

She led them along a musty corridor lined with wellington boots and large hooks. 'This is where we leave our cloaks,' she said. She picked one off and spread it out. Jo hoped hers was safely in her trunk. Ben had claimed it for this year's Halloween. ('All I need now is a broomstick and a hat!' he'd said with a suitable cackle.)

'Joanna? Are you listening?' Miss Smyth's gaze was still on her. 'I was explaining to your parents that we have the plain hoods for Junior House.' She leaned forward and showed Jo the hood buttons. She smelled of mothballs and a flowery aroma Jo couldn't quite place. 'Do you see? When you go into senior school, you just buy a new coloured hood. Depending on which House you choose.' Her eyes flicked to Mum, looking apologetic. 'Unless Joanna grows very tall, of course. But perhaps you could buy second-hand.' She gave Jo a little shove to the left. 'Up the stairs, dear, then your mother and father can bid you goodbye.'

Miss Smyth on her heels, Jo climbed the stairs.

'Here we are, Joanna,' she said with that smile when they reached the top. 'Home sweet home.'

Still worrying whether Ben had stolen her cloak, and what would happen if she grew very tall, Jo followed Miss Smyth into a cold and empty bedroom. She turned to her parents who hovered at the door, as though they were waiting for an invitation to come in.

The request didn't come, so Jo stepped out, dread slowly spreading from her chest, down her skinny legs to the tips of her toes.

'Time for goodbye, dear,' Miss Smyth said.

Dad wrapped her in his thick arms and held her ever so tightly. 'Bye then, love. Be a brave lass, just like your brothers.' He began to pull away, but Jo held on, suddenly realising she needed to remember his smell. Seeming to understand, he reached in his pocket and slipped his folded hanky in her palm.

Then Mum handed over the brown bag she'd been carrying,

cupped Jo's face and kissed her cheeks several times. Her eyes were like pebbles just plucked from the river. 'I'll write as soon as I'm home, love. It'll fly by. Just you see.'

Miss Smyth cleared her throat. Jo had forgotten she was there. 'The next new girl will be due any minute, Mrs Wragg. Let me show you down to the back entrance. You'll soon find your way to the car park.' She gave Jo a small push towards the bedroom. 'Off you go now, dear. Matron will be along soon.'

Alone in the room, Jo took off her hat, stared at the narrow bed, then rushed back to the landing. But Mum and Dad had gone, down the rickety stairs to the world outside, or to freedom, as she soon came to name it.

'Hello, I'm Catherine Bayden-Jones, but you can call me Kate. I'm from Barton in the Beans. That's in Leicestershire and I have two older sisters, Clare and Annabelle who are both in senior school. We each have a pony. Oh, and Daddy's much older than Mummy and his hair's growing thin. He was married before, but she died. Oh, don't you have strange hair?'

Still wearing her boater, they were Kate's first words to Jo in the small dormitory. She had arrived before Jo, emerging from the upstairs bathroom with a pink nose and a handkerchief (embroidered with tiny hearts, Jo noticed) not long after Jo's mum and dad had left.

Jo supposed that was how introductions were made and the room fell silent, Jo trying but failing to think of something to say, anything that would remotely match the splendour of Catherine Bayden-Jones's name, let alone her words and the way she pronounced them.

Kate and Jo had been allocated adjacent lockers in the cramped room, but the other girls hadn't arrived yet, so they sat dumbly at the end of their beds, their suit jackets still fastened. Kate kicked her (slightly) chubby legs against the thin mattress and Jo glanced around, wondering what they were supposed to do now. (Wait for Matron, Miss Smyth had said, though why they'd need a *nurse*, she had no idea. St Luke's was meant to give her 'the best education', not teach her how to wrap bandages. Besides, she knew how to do that already.)

Giving a little sniff as she peered, she tried to identify the smell. The pong of old things, she supposed. Which wasn't surprising. The room was pretty ancient, the white walls like painted sandpaper. Limp brown curtains hung each side of the old-fashioned windows. (*Sash*, Mrs Brown used to call them, a gentle word which sounded wrong for the monstrosity she now stared at. The prettier ones at her old school were 'painted shut'. She wondered if these would open; a vague notion of escape already there, despite the horizontal rods at the bottom.)

Feeling a shiver, Jo turned to her bed, wondering whether to put the grey overcoat back on. Like the one in her old classroom, there was a yellowing slatted radiator and a thick pipe up the wall, but she doubted they would be almost too hot to touch without gloves. This room was freezing, colder than outside. And yes, the smell was definitely fusty, nothing remotely like her modern warm bedroom at home.

From the alarming stories of boarding-school life told by her brothers in the holidays, Jo had expected military commands from Miss Smyth, but she'd only mentioned Matron. (Jo had the bossy *Matron* from an old film firmly in her mind. She'd watched it with Dad one Sunday afternoon and he'd chuckled the whole way through.) Were she and Catherine Bayden-Jones allowed to move, to look out of the barred window, let alone explore the garden outside? (Assuming there was one.) And what about their trunks? Could they go astray? Auntie Barbara had travelled to Torremolinos with two suitcases and come back with only one (and a Spanish man with too many teeth). Jo had preferred the suitcase.

She eyed up Kate. She was still kicking her heels silently and her slightly upturned nose made her look as posh as she sounded, but she seemed nice. Her boater had slipped to the back of her head like the hat of a friendly cowboy and there was no doubt in Jo's mind that she was pretty. She was plump (in a good way), had neat small teeth (not even approaching her *tombstones*) and dimples (like Mrs Brown – anything like Mrs Brown was a good thing); she had freckles and long golden hair in two plaits.

Jo looked down at her own scrawny frame. Her new school shoes were already scuffed (how had that happened? Mum had kept them off until the car), her knee-length socks were gathering at the ankle, and the thin legs protruding were bruised and brown from playing outside all summer. Noticing Kate's continued glances at her hair, she patted it. It had been cut too short and was waving in all the wrong directions already. She willed it to grow as long and as shiny as Kate's, preferably overnight.

'It's because my mum cut it yesterday,' she stated, picturing the dark chunks of hair on the kitchen lino. 'It gets all knotty, so Mum cuts it short.'

Kate leaned forward, her hands on her knees as she inspected the offending tresses at close quarters. 'How funny!' she said, suddenly brightening again. 'Mine gets a little knotty too but Mummy, whose name is Hilary by the way, sprays mine with a conditioner. It's called "No More Tears" and you squirt it on when it's wet and it works like magic!' She nodded, her face pinking with pleasure. 'I've brought some with me. It's in my trunk. I'll share it with you if you like.'

It was a defining moment for Joanna Wragg. Not only did Kate look and speak like a princess, she was friendly and kind and she was willing to be her friend. Jo didn't make close friends particularly easily, but once made, it was a friendship for life and she *never* let go.

'What's in that bag?' Kate asked politely, her gaze wide with interest.

Jo was surprised her new friend had seen it. Hoping it would be hidden from prying eyes, she had slotted the brown bag between her bed and the wall. It contained the china ornaments she'd selected with her mum's permission from the glass sideboard at home. She hadn't been able to decide between the calf and the baby donkey, so her mum had let her bring both.

She took a deep breath. Fearful she'd cry, she didn't want to peel back the crisp new tissue paper, nor look at her special mementoes of home so soon, but she recognised the need to reciprocate the offer of friendship.

With great care she unravelled her treasure. 'Oh!' Kate said, sitting back with surprise. 'Aren't they pretty?' Then, after a moment, with a small frown. 'Is that like bringing a teddy?'

Relieved she didn't have to explain, Jo nodded. She thought of letting Kate hold one, but large silent tears had spilt from her eyes, so she stood up and sat next to her, reaching over an arm without really touching. The lump which had clogged Jo's throat since leaving home seemed to expand unbearably but, even at eight years of age, she knew she needed to be strong for her new friend.

'Don't worry, I'll look after you, I promise. My name is Jo, by the way, short for Joanna.'

2

St Luke's

It was a funny money mix at St Luke's School, established wealth and *nouveau riche*.

'Well, it has to start somewhere, Dad. You wanted what was best for me and I'm doing the same for my lot,' Stan would argue with his father who'd 'still got coal in my nails. And in my heart,' and who fiercely objected to giving his grandchildren, 'bloody airs and graces'.

Surprising everyone, Stan had abandoned his job as a butcher and set up his own building business. It took several years to make it a success, but once the cash started to roll in from Wragg's Construction, he'd insisted on providing his sons with the best education that *Godspenny* could buy. It turned out this was best achieved by sending them to boarding school 'over the border'. Joyce had gone along with it on the surface, but Jo saw the devastation in her mum's face when her older brothers were sent away to school in their caps, blazers and short trousers. She was there too, the baby of the family, waving from the back seat of her parents' departing car, watching the boys until they disappeared from sight, but still picturing their tight faces and knowing how desperately hard it had been for them not to cry.

She understood her turn would come when she turned eight, but had no idea what a steep learning curve there would be once she was there. Her oldest brother Nigel had talked a *lot* about his school experiences (always doom and gloom, to put it mildly), and her next brother Ben a little (funny stories, mostly about food fights), but like a million other things in life, one couldn't *know* until one had experienced it oneself (she was already getting a handle on saying 'one').

During the first two weeks at St Luke's, she had been derided by teachers and pupils alike for her thick Yorkshire accent, for her unusual pronunciation of words and strange use of certain phrases. It didn't help that her school uniform and clothes were of just slightly inferior quality to those of the other girls ('Cole Brother's best, all the way from Sheffield, what's your problem, lass?' Granddad said when he heard her complain at half-term), that her hair had been cut short by her mother, or that she had arrived with bruised legs and arms from rough play through the summer.

But Joanna Wragg's worst mistake those few days was to reveal too much of herself, being overly honest about her roots, her home and her family. The description 'ragamuffin from Barnsley' was bad enough (Matron, naturally) but peer pressure was worse. The other girls in her form would point, giggle and whisper, 'Oh my God! Her daddy was a butcher!' 'Her uncle works down a mine!' 'She keeps her father's snotty handkerchief under her pillow!' 'Look at her dirty legs, I bet she smells too!' 'Can you believe that her own mother cuts her hair?' 'I can hardly understand a word she says!' 'She's so unbelievably common!'

Common as muck, Jo might have been, but she was tough,

she was clever and she knew to adapt. As young as she was, she understood that if you couldn't beat them, you joined them; you became one of the *twins* she'd seen that first day. So in just one short autumn half-term she transformed herself. She learned to speak like the girls from down south, adding an invisible letter 'r' after 'a', and lifted her nose like they did. ('Oh, you've become very hoity-toity, lass' – Granddad again.) She no longer called lunch 'dinner', nor the sofa a 'settee'. She ate 'tea' at four o'clock and 'dinner' at seven. When she was reprimanded by the teachers, she blocked out Mrs Brown's dimples and gritted her teeth to stop the tears. She brushed her hair ferociously until it grew long enough to tie in bunches and she vowed never, ever to reveal her true self to anyone again.

3

Peak District, present day – thirty years later

Jo gazed through the farmhouse window. The sky beyond the open shutters was teal blue, despite the late hour. All that remained of the food was the smell, peppery and sweet in the warm air.

'Jo? Hello?' Kate's eloquent tones punctured her thoughts.

'Oops, miles away.'

She shook herself back to Kate's beautiful kitchen, the timber purlins and exposed chimney-breast; the Georgian oak dresser, monastery table and *housekeeper's* larder cupboards. Pristine, polished, tasteful, much like her old friend.

'Sorry, what were you saying?'

Kate snapped open another bottle of Chablis. 'I was asking about ...' She lowered her voice theatrically. 'Men! Any good-looking suitors on the Manchester horizon?'

'As if I wouldn't have told you!' Shaking her head, Jo snorted. 'As it happens, I went swimming yesterday and balding overweight middle-aged business types were eyeing me up. Do I have a sign on my forehead saying *husband hunting*, or do I just look desperate?'

'Course not. It must be pheromones or some vibe showing you're ready to date.' Kate raised her pale eyebrows. 'You never know, Jo, it might even be because they think you're attractive.'

'A thoroughbred who needs to stop being lame and get back in the saddle?' She laughed. 'Horse analogy, just for you.'

'And duly appreciated.' Her eyes soft and concerned, Kate gazed for a moment. 'In all seriousness, Jo, it has been a long while. Don't you think it's—'

Surprised by the jolt of heartache, Jo reached for another jest. 'Don't get me wrong, I don't mind the odd lustful glance, but I'd prefer cute young men with more hair on their pates than their chests.' She grimaced at the image. 'Backs too, now I think of it.'

Kate cocked her head. 'Come on, Jo, be serious. Maybe it is time.' She turned to the opening door. 'Tom, finally! Tell Jo it's time.'

'Time for what?'

'To find someone new.' She flashed Jo a smile. 'Preferably not a balding and overweight middle-aged business type.'

Tom didn't reply. Instead he helped himself to a whisky and sat at the far end of the table.

Kate wafted her hand. 'Oh, don't glower at me, darling. She knows I only want what's best for her.' Her voice a little slurry, she grasped Jo's arm. 'Ignore him. You know I mean well, don't you, Jo? I'd hate you to be lonely for ever. Time to catch a handsome man while you're still young and gorgeous. Well, youngish.'

'Young*ish*! We're only in our thirties—'

'Nearer forty than thirty, Jo. Almost middle-aged!' Sitting back, Kate clapped her hands. 'And wouldn't it be fun to find you someone stinking rich? What did Hilary always tell us?'

Smiling despite the ridiculous gush of emotion, Jo pictured

Kate's glamorous mother. Her pearls of wisdom were legendary at St Luke's: 'You must marry well, girls!' being one of them.

Marry well. Kate had, of course. Tom. Tom Heath, whose steady stare she *was* trying to ignore.

Feeling unaccountably vulnerable, she clinked her friend's glass. 'Cheers to that! After all, it was rotten of Richard to desert me without wads of money. I would've suited being wealthy. A different man for every day of the week to see to my needs. You know, a spot of polishing here, a bit of scrubbing there, especially the loo. I hate cleaning toilets.'

Kate topped up her wine. 'Well, let's have a plan. If there isn't anyone fitting the Hilary criteria in Greater Manchester, we must hunt one down! I'm completely out of touch but I suppose it's the internet these days. Find your perfect match and all that. Sounds fun, Jo!'

'Hm . . .'

'Easy-peasy with these new apps, I'm told.'

Jo laughed wryly. She was pretty knowledgeable about dating apps as it happened, but only from research for a magazine article a few months back. 'OK. Which should we go for? Zoosk, Elite or Easyflirt? Or how about Coffee Meets Bagel?'

'Well, they all sound fabulous. So long as they're upmarket, of course.' Kate abruptly addressed Tom. 'What do you think? Are you still with us, darling? Should Jo try dating apps?'

Jo turned to her friend's husband, sitting in his usual place. Too broad for the spindled seat, he flexed his shoulders and stretched. He and Kate had plenty of comfortable chairs in their large home, in the conservatory, the lounge and the snug, but they sat around the old bench whenever Jo visited. The tradition had started two years ago – two long and short years ago – after Jo turned up unannounced to say, 'Richard's dead.'

His gaze still on her, Tom didn't smile. 'I'm still reeling from the shock of being . . . what was it? A fat, bald, middle-aged businessman,' he said dryly.

Jo touched his arm lightly before pulling away. 'Tom, you know very well that you're none of those things, except nearly middle-aged, as Kate has kindly put it, so stop digging for compliments.'

'A *businessman* too,' Kate pointed out. Her eyes sparkled with pride. 'My little investment. Aren't you, darling?'

Inwardly Jo winced. Tom's jaw had tightened. Though Kate was oblivious, her quip had irked him as usual. He stood up, the shrill scrape of heavy wood a reply. Turning his back, he topped up his whisky, then uncorked another bottle of red.

Kate's floaty voice pierced the dense lull. 'You still haven't said what you think Jo should do about finding herself a new man, Tom. Don't you have any eligible builders on your books? We could arrange a blind date!' She raised her empty glass. 'Let's toast to someone dishy. Dark and a *bit* hairy; designer stubble and all that. Your type. Am I right, Jo?' She laughed. 'A plasterer! Now that would be useful. Or how about a plumber? Plumbers always come in handy and I expect they would be good with a toilet brush too.'

His attention on the task, Tom didn't respond for a few beats. 'I think Jo should leave it to fate,' he said eventually. He swivelled to the creaking door. A blonde head appeared, followed by a yellow rabbit.

Alice stepped in, rubbing her eyes. 'I had a bad dream about a dragon blowing fire. Can Mummy sing me a song?'

Kate stood. 'Of course, my little darling.' Her knuckles white on the chair, she paused for a moment, then held out her hand. 'Just a very quick one, then sleep. Say goodnight to Daddy and Jo.'

Tom kissed his daughter's wispy hair and Jo lifted her palm. 'Night night, gorgeous girl.' Her diction felt heavy with wine. She tried to lighten it. 'We're having lots of fun tomorrow, I hope, Alice. Wake me up for a story!'

Kate turned before leaving. 'Back in five,' she said brightly. 'No more gossip allowed until my return!'

Sipping her drink, Jo smiled politely at Tom. She'd known him for twenty years, yet still felt awkward when alone with him. She'd first seen him laying bricks at her childhood home, one of a group of lads building a garage extension for her dad's vehicles. Handing over a stripy mug of tea made by her mum, she'd felt roused and uncertain and shy of his golden hair, chiselled looks and his white confident grin. But then he spoke. 'Thanks, love,' he said with a broad Yorkshire twang, the very accent she'd taken such pains to lose. That's when she realised he was Jimmy Heath's big brother. Little Jimmy from the village primary school, who'd smelt of poverty and piss at gym time.

Breaking her reverie, Tom moved towards her and topped up her wine.

'Thank you,' she said, stuck for other words and still jammed in the past.

Eventually forcing herself back, she glanced at Kate's husband. He had returned to his seat and was observing her, his gaze solid and unreadable. Quickly reverting to the rich vino, she squirmed inside. Bloody hell, she was blushing, that deep burning heat she'd hated as a girl. She stifled the snigger at her own discomfort. Perhaps Tom Heath was telepathic. Now that *would* be funny.

'What?' she asked with a small laugh.

'Do you really think you're ready to start dating again?'

The hilarity vanished. Tom never said much, so she deduced he was making a point. That it was too early to find someone new or perhaps she was betraying Richard by even joking about it. Playing with the stem of her glass, she stared at the light and dark shades of her distorted reflection. His simple query had made her feel defenceless and exposed. She didn't know why, but Tom had a way of asking her questions which demanded a considered and truthful response. She couldn't get away with the flippant or evasive reply she would have given Kate and her other friends.

'I don't know,' she replied slowly, trying to shape how she felt. 'But I'm bored so much of the time.' She shook her head, her thick mane falling forwards. 'No, it's not that. I'm busy with deadline after deadline, I go out, see friends, but ...' Catching another fragment of memory in the crystal, she turned it again, glad her hair was hiding her hot cheeks. 'At times life feels meaningless, empty. I need some purpose, some direction, I guess.'

'And you think a man in your life would give you direction?'

'I don't know,' she said again. She couldn't meet his eyes. 'Maybe if I'd had a child ...' she said quietly, before trailing off.

Tom dipped his head. 'Jo?'

Battling the sudden urge to cry, she stared at her hands. She was pissed, that was all – she *had* to get a grip. 'Oh, nothing. I'm blathering. Take no notice of me.'

She inhaled deeply. Tom was not, absolutely not, going to get under her skin. Lifting her chin, she met his relentless blue gaze. 'But if you have a handsome hottie who fancies a night of passionate sex, do let me know.'

He picked up his tumbler and sat back. 'I'm sure there'll be plenty of those on my books. I'll see what I can do.'

'What are you two plotting?'

The garbled query made her start. She hadn't heard Kate return to the room. Swaying slightly, she made her way around the table, then wagged her finger playfully. 'No gossip without me, I hope! You know we don't get any out here in the sticks. Save for the school run, I rely entirely on you for my six-monthly supply.'

Jo smiled. 'No scandal yet, but I'll see what I can rustle up for next time. Tom has promised to find me a few useful boys from his staff, all ready for action and mad for the attentions of a gorgeous *thoroughbred* woman,' she replied.

In her mind she could see precisely such a man, flaxen haired, bare chested and beautiful, staring at her intently from the roof of her father's garage.

4

Gazing at herself in the antique mirror, Jo cleaned her teeth. She loved staying in the spare bedroom at the farmhouse, or 'Jo's room', as Kate and Alice sweetly put it. Petersfield was no longer a working farm, but had been converted with taste (and reams of money, which of course always helped) into a sizeable, happy and comfortable home in the Peak District (only Kate could have found a village called *Hope*).

Unlike her own flat in Manchester, it was peaceful and quiet. Except for the sounds of the countryside, of course. The whoops of the owls and the sighs of the horses at night; the plaintive bleat of sheep and the wistful call of the cuckoos in the day. Though more subdued than the Barnsley landscape, they reminded Jo of her childhood, so she didn't count them as noise.

She took a sharp breath as she stared at her reflection. She could clearly picture Richard behind her, his gaze a deep pool of desire. Narrowing her eyes, she sighed. There it was; the weight of his arms around her waist, the trace of his kisses from her ear to her neck, from her neck to the hollow of her throat. Oh God, how he liked this mirror, his dark eyes watching her watching him as his palms cupped her sides, slowly caressing each rib with his thumbs before sliding his hands forward to circle her breasts, his fingers firm on her nipples. A strange, muted lovemaking; the silence had always turned them on.

Dropping her gaze, Jo shook her head. Her nose stung badly but she took a deep breath, willing the urge to cry away. There had been too many tears already; too much water. Two years had gone by and the yearning for him was still a gnarled knot in her chest. Before he died, she'd forgotten that old feeling of abandonment, but as soon as he'd gone, it came flooding back. It was the anguish she'd felt at the beginning of each term when her parents deserted her and her blue trunk to a dormitory full of chattering girls, but magnified, intense, unbearable. At school she'd known that eventually she'd be found, she'd see her parents again, she'd hold them and kiss them and *touch* them.

That's what she missed most, the corporeal human.

Staring at the trace of blood brightening the toothpaste bubbles, she contemplated Tom's question tonight. Impassively said, but loaded somehow. Would another man give her the direction she craved, the meaning for life? Could anyone fill Richard's shoes? She couldn't see herself falling in love with a guy and wanting to live with that same person day in and day out. She'd become too independent, too remote.

After a long year of grieving, and another of trying to find solid ground, she'd got to the stage where she wanted sex. Hard brutal sex, soft tender sex; anything more than a self-induced orgasm. It was younger men she was attracted to, the ones with short hair and firm bodies, guys who still retained that smug confidence about their own physical attraction. Before it was too late, the itch to feel captivating, beautiful and desirable was definitely there. But she didn't want anyone to get their trainers, let alone their slippers, under her table.

Leaning forward, she inspected the woman in the mirror, a complete person who didn't seem to be her. What would she look like in a dating app photograph? A polished boarding-school posh girl or a ragamuffin from Barnsley? A quirky and *youngish* (as Kate had put it) writer, or a sad, lonely widow? She twisted her dark hair into a bun at the top of her head before letting it fall around her sharp-boned face. Kate had always had the long mane when they were young; her hair was neither long nor golden blonde any more, but still it shone in its neat bob.

Lovely, kind Kate. Wanting so much for Jo to be happy.

Jo shrugged and sighed. She was having a getting-on-for-forty setback, that's all. She'd never join a dating site, let alone a blind set-up; it was all too contrived. Besides, she knew that her desire for rampant sex with a young god wasn't the whole story. It was that old chestnut of sexual desire and evolution she'd written about many times. Maternal instinct, genetic influences, biological compulsion, or whatever was supposed to be inbuilt. A baby, Richard's baby, her baby. Whether the longing was magnified because she'd been denied one, she didn't know. But that was the truth; she wanted a child.

Turning away from the sink, she flicked off the light and groped for the bed. Even now, the same thoughts plagued her in moments of solitude. What if she had taken Richard seriously? What if he had just gone to bed and rested? What if they hadn't walked so far? What if she had been carrying his baby?

Rancorous repeated *what ifs*; pointless and hopeless and bloody soul-destroying.

'Fuck off and leave me alone,' she said in a whisper.

Emerging louder than she'd intended, she held her breath. A floorboard was creaking on the landing. Someone else was still awake; surprisingly, given the amount of booze they'd all drunk. Or perhaps it was Richard, on a dash aboard the spirit train from

Manchester to Derbyshire, to reprimand her for so many things, her 'fuck off' included.

'Goodnight, Richard,' she said, just in case. Then she lifted the cold sheet and climbed into bed, drunk and teary, naked and alone.

Time passed but sleep didn't come. Jo lay awake, her body exhausted but her mind restless as she tuned into the sounds of the night (which *were* noisy, after all). She tried to dispel the rounds of her negative head-voice, the least of which was 'you'll look like shit in the morning'.

When the dawn chorus began, she climbed off the memory-foam mattress, watched the dent of her body disappear, then crept down the stripped wooden stairs to the kitchen. Hot milk was the thing. That's what her mum had always said when life went awry. 'Let me get you a glass of milk, love.' A cure for all maladies: sleeplessness, loose baby teeth, grazed knees. Death of husbands.

Watching the *watched pot* doing its thing, she cursed the Aga for its one-speed heat as she waited for boiling point. Silly though it was, she felt ridiculously nervous about being caught. Like at school, out of bounds. That heady mixture of excitement and fear.

Back in the spare room, the milk ruse nearly worked, sleep almost touching, time after time. But the masochistic head-voice continued to needle and prod, tormenting her as usual when her emotions were *live*: 'Is that a taste of metal in your mouth? Your tongue feels thick, your heart is beating fast. You can feel it coming, can't you, Jo? How will you cope? You'll make a fool of yourself if you're not very careful.'

5

A sudden pounce on the bed woke Jo with a jolt from her much-too-brief sleep. She peered at the culprit through sticky, sore eyes. It was Alice, of course, her blonde hair lit by the weak morning sunshine. Holding her baby doll under one arm and a book in the other, she was already yanking back the sheet and climbing in next to Jo.

Quickly reaching for a t-shirt, she noticed Tom at the door. His fair hair was tousled, his face apologetic. 'Sorry, Jo, she burst in before I could stop her. She knows she's meant to wait until eight o'clock.' He smiled wryly. 'And I guess even that's pretty early for a townie.'

Alice covered her mouth with her hand. 'But Mummy forgot to set the rabbit clock. So I didn't know the time,' she said, her smile beaming through her fingers.

Kissing Alice on the forehead, Jo pulled up the covers and settled the dolly in the crook of one arm. 'We can always have a nap later, can't we, Alice?' Then to Tom, still there. 'Don't worry. It's fine. Really.'

Raking back his fringe, he took a slow breath as though to speak, then turned away, closing the door quietly behind him.

Alice nestled on Jo's shoulder and opened her book. Then she closed it again and looked up. 'Mummy says you have known her since you were nearly as small as me and that you met at school,' she said, her pale eyes and pale skin giving her an ethereal, other-worldly appearance. 'She said that's where you lived all the time, even at night.'

Surprised Kate had mentioned it, Jo nodded. 'That's very true,' she replied.

'Like Harry and Hermione? Will you tell me a nice story about it?' Alice asked, her voice soft and appealing.

Feeling the usual surge of love for her goddaughter, Jo smiled as she studied her face. Alice had changed since her last visit. She supposed that's what growing kids did in six months. But this time her features were setting, no longer generic; at six years of age, she was becoming her own person.

'OK, a nice boarding-school story ... Hm, let me think,' Jo said thoughtfully.

Drinking in Alice's fresh soapy smell, a sudden urge to cry caught her. Children were so precious. How on earth had her mum simply handed her over to St Luke's aged only eight? And *nice* boarding-school stories. Were there any? Blinking away the burning sensation behind her eyes, she kissed Alice's fine hair. 'No magic, I'm afraid, but I'll tell you the adventures of our midnight feasts ...'

Stories, cuddles and a short nap accomplished, pangs of hunger brought Jo down to the warm kitchen eventually.

'Morning, Jo!' Kate said brightly. She was wearing smart ironed jeans, a crisp white blouse and flat sandals, as she always did. Her eyes were large and clear, showing no signs of tiredness or a hangover. Standing in front of the Aga, she was stirring something that looked worryingly like porridge with raisins.

'I hear Alice gave you an early morning call. Sorry about that. She gets so excited when you're here that she can't hold back. She doesn't realise normal human beings without horrible small people to wake them up at an unearthly hour like to sleep in a bit at the weekend.' She pecked Jo on the cheek. 'You look nice. Chic as usual. I like your t-shirt; khaki would look dreadful on me but it really suits your colouring. Did you sleep well?'

Jo nodded. 'Fine, thanks,' she said vaguely, desperate for a gallon of Yorkshire tea, but not the porridge and definitely not with raisins.

Pulling out a heavy chair, she sat at the table and suppressed a huge yawn. Then she mixed a smaller one with a sigh of pleasure – and relief – as she watched Kate don large padded mittens. Oven gloves meant freshly baked something. Jo should have known from the buttery whiff, but there was always a French patisserie type of aroma at the farmhouse.

Like Sa Pedrissa, she thought. She and Richard had holidayed at a boutique hotel in Majorca two years on the trot, much to her 'why on earth do people go to the same place twice?' surprise. They had booked for the hat-trick, but Richard had passed away by then.

She had taken to saying *passed away*. It didn't scare people off as effectively as *died suddenly* or, sometimes when the mood took her, *dropped dead*. These days she was making a positive effort not to scare people off.

Kate interrupted her reverie. 'Croissants, madame?' She slid them from the baking tray to an antique blue and white plate, the designer of which Jo should have been able to name, but couldn't.

'Oh, wonderful,' she replied, turning to her old friend.

Her face glowing with pleasure at her creation, Kate was smiling broadly. Definitely from scratch, Jo knew, not one of those Mr

Roly-Poly tins of puff pastry that her mum had astonishingly once bought from the local Co-op when she was small. How old was she then? Before St Luke's or after? The memory was still clear. After opening the can, she had carefully peeled off each doughy croissant under the watchful eye of her next brother, Ben, then he'd done the honours with a pastry brush and eggy milk. Ten long minutes of baking-time anticipation before they'd both taken a huge, too-hot bite. Pure heaven, those croissants had been at the time, but not a patch on Kate's.

Still warm to the touch, Jo popped one on her plate. 'Smells heavenly! You are an absolute star. You know how to spoil me.'

Her stomach groaning from both the hangover and hunger, she wondered how many she could eat without appearing like a *gros gourmand*, the title they had titteringly given to chubby girls at school, believing it to mean greedy pig.

But of course those jibes had been turned, dreadfully turned.

'Eat as many as you like, Jo. You never put on weight.'

Weight and eating problems. Jo pushed *that* memory away. 'And neither do you! Which is a miracle considering all the delicious food you create. I would be tempted to taste and to nibble.'

'Well, one must taste.'

'But not nibble.'

'Precisely!'

Briefly noting the 'home-grown and home-made' label on the jar, Jo spooned glossy jam on the side of her plate and Kate watched her eat.

It was funny how life worked out, Jo mused as she swallowed. Who would have put Kate down as the perfect hands-on mother and housewife? Save for deportment, elocution and drama, she'd been a duffer at school, hopeless at most things, cooking included.

'One would have expected you to be good at *something*, Kate Bayden-Jones,' the domestic science teacher would sigh as she scraped out yet another piece of eggshell from the curdled batter. Yet right from the start she took her role as Tom's new wife extremely seriously. Delighted to walk a traditional stay-at-home path, she baked on certain days, shopped, cleaned and gardened on others. Then, after several years of marriage, when Alice was born, she simply went up a notch to include all the parenting activities too. The feeding, the washing, the nappies, the toddler groups and kiddies parties; all the things that were supposed to be dreary. Yet still Kate had managed to look relaxed, bright and smiley.

'Just a tad annoying,' Jo used to confess to Richard. 'Much like this month's model on the front cover of *Good Housekeeping*.' Still, Kate had been great source material for articles; she still was. ('Are women really happier at home?' 'Is there such a thing as a feminist housewife?' she now sketched in her head.)

Kate's refined tones interrupted her reverie. 'Do you fancy going to the new Bridge Bar tonight for dinner? Alice has a party this afternoon and I've arranged a sleepover after it,' she said, watching as Jo failed to eat another croissant without spreading flakes of pastry around her vicinity like confetti.

Finishing her mouthful, Jo nodded. It was fabulous to be looked after and waited on, but only for so long. It was the same when she stayed for the weekend with her parents, Joyce and Stan. It was lovely initially, but her mother's constant hovering and her patient waiting for a request, like a silver-service waitress, began to get on her pip after the first few hours. Then she'd feel guilty for being snappy. She'd just got used to living alone, she supposed, to doing what she liked when she fancied; not having to worry about what other people wanted or needed.

'Just a selfish cow at heart, Rich,' she said inwardly.

Not mother material at all. Perhaps that was why . . .

She came back to Kate's expectant face. 'The new bar? Absolutely. Wild horses wouldn't stop me,' she replied. 'I hoped you'd suggest it – I've been looking forward to having a recce. Is Tom pleased with it?'

Tom's construction business had gone from strength to strength, the days of buying run-down terraced houses and tarting them up for resale were long gone. He had moved sideways, buying his first wine bar three years ago and adding new ones to his empire yearly.

Kate finally sat down and poured the strong tea. 'Bridge Bar *Dore*,' she said, smiling. 'The upmarket end of Sheffield, but of course! Yes, he is pleased. I'm so excited – we have a chain now!' She smoothed her neat hair. 'Only a fairly short one, admittedly, but still a chain.' She lifted her eyebrows. 'I don't like to get involved, but there was some bother over planning permission at one point. Tom was marvellous and sorted it out. All three have been unbelievably profitable, which is why he's looking to open a fourth soon. It means he isn't around as much as I'd like, but you can't have everything, can you? He's gone now to Lord-knows-where, but he'll give me a ring soon. He always does; you know how dependable he is.'

Nodding, Jo slurped her tea. 'He is.' Then, after a moment, 'Alice was asking about St Luke's earlier.'

'Oh, and what did you tell her?' Kate asked, her eyes averted as she tackled Jo's confetti with a dustpan and brush.

'Nothing much,' she replied.

Still astonished Kate had mentioned school to Alice at all, she gazed at her slim back. It wasn't something she liked to talk about, even after all this time, their days in Junior House especially. But Alice was an inquisitive child; she undoubtedly asked her mum all sorts of questions. 'Midnight feasts, actually,' she added.

Remembering the stark shock of being woken at midnight, the freezing dank dormitories and stolen grub, the pee-inducing excitement and fear of being caught, she smiled. Not that she put it to Alice in those terms. She had gone more for a *Worst Witch* mischief angle in bed this morning. 'She asked for a story, so I told her about eating sticky buns by torchlight! The feasts were actually good fun, weren't they?'

Kate sat down and snorted, but it was bitter, one only Jo would recognise. They sat in silence for several moments, then Kate relented with a small smile and held out her hand. 'Sorry, Jo, St Luke's was a long time ago now. I have a blessed life. I should just forget it and move on, shouldn't I?'

'Maybe,' Jo replied, too distracted to say more. Kate's sleeve had pulled up, exposing a nasty purpling bruise like a bracelet on her wrist.

Her friend's eyes followed hers. She pulled down the cuff and smiled brightly. 'The perils of horse riding,' she laughed.

6

The surprising heat was lifted by the breeze which gently whipped their faces. Kate and Jo strolled across the silent Derbyshire fields, the Labradors racing ahead as Petersfield shrank behind them. Alice, full of chatter after her nap, held Jo's hand tightly. She was a good little walker, considering her age. But it was hard to judge. Jo couldn't remember much about when she was that young. Life had started at eight, she and Kate 'born' that same bewildering September day.

Inhaling deeply, Jo took in the cheery smell of summer, that comforting aroma she always associated with home – sweet grasses, wild garlic and sheep dung. 'Where's Honey?' she asked, noticing for the first time that one of the yellow Labradors was missing.

Alice pulled the hair back from her solemn face, so like her father's. 'She's gone to heaven with her babies,' she replied.

Shocked at the news but not wanting to ask for graphic details in front of a child, she glanced at Kate, who nodded.

'Yes, Honey died. Out of the blue. Something she ate, according to the vet. Tom was devastated,' she said, shaking her head. 'Honey was his favourite and she was due her first litter. He was so excited to see the puppies. We all were.'

Feeling winded, Jo sniffed back a stab of grief. Like Richard; he'd taken her babies with him too. To heaven? Who knew?

Alice tugged her mum's hand. 'But you shouldn't have favourites. Should you, Mummy?'

Kate didn't reply. Her thoughts seemed elsewhere.

Favourites, Jo mused, Kate knew about that. Wanting to lighten the sudden gloom, she gently squeezed the tip of Alice's nose. 'Then it's a good job there's only you! Because you're my special girl of all time.' She pointed to a barn in the distance. 'See that big shed ahead? Race you there after I count to three.'

Darting off after 'three', Jo waited at the hut for Alice to catch up. Silly though it was at thirty-eight, she couldn't help feeling a smatter of pleasure. Alleluia! She could still sprint up a hill without looking like a completely unfit idiot. With a small frown marring her face, Kate joined them eventually. From the slight shake of her head, Jo finally twigged she should have let Alice win.

'Oops, sorry,' she breathed. 'Old habits die hard.'

Quietly competitive, her school reports had always said. And *still a dark horse* (that was Miss Arkwright, the one teacher she'd liked).

She turned to Alice. Her arms were folded, her face pink and sullen. Like a flash it reminded her of Kate as a child.

'Sorry, Alice,' she said. 'Did I mention that the winner has to buy an ice cream?' She gently scraped a handful of bleached grass under her chin, needing her forgiveness, just like she'd needed Kate's. 'A really big ice cream. How many scoops? Vanilla and strawberry—'

A reluctant smile. 'Mint chip too?'

'And chocolate strands if they have them . . . '

Walking along the path to the park, their easy chatter was interrupted by gelato and contemplation.

I should make more of an effort to exercise, Jo was musing. Get off my bum and walk, even run. That was the trouble with writing, it was an excuse to be lazy, to hide away in a hoodie and joggers all day.

'Unless I sit at the laptop and stare,' she always claimed, 'I won't be able to force out the drivel.' But that wasn't true. Like a long soak in the bath, ambling seemed to help creative thought – her mind was now racing with ideas for articles and angles, perhaps a short story or even a play. Pleased with the onslaught, she laughed. But where was a pen when you needed it?

The smile gradually waning, Jo shook her head. There was a time she grandly said, 'I'm writing a novel, actually,' when someone asked what she did for a living. Now she replied with a jaded wry smile. 'I'm a popular-science writer. Apparently.'

The novel, *the* novel was set in India and the African colonies. It had involved talking at length with Richard's father 'Abbu' (he was born in Bombay, but raised in Zanzibar – even the word sounded evocative), taking a trip to meet some of the family in Tanzania, as well as many hours of research. But the project had wavered and waned, even when Richard was alive. She used to wonder where that desire had gone, how it had evaporated so easily. But these days she didn't want to think about it at all, so she didn't. Besides, being a *popular-science writer* earned her a crust.

'Food and death mostly,' she replied when someone bravely enquired further about her jottings. 'Especially death.'

Sadly, it was true. Before Richard *dropped dead*, there had been many a time she'd visited bereaved relatives to delicately extract a story for a piece. The human tragedies were dreadful: children killed by a hit-and-run driver on their way to school; cot deaths, teenage suicide; toddlers who'd drowned in Grandma's pond. The suffering and heartbreak was painful to listen to and see, yet once she had left them, she shrugged it away and forgot it, indulging in a cheese-and-pickle sandwich for her lunch on the way home.

However much she'd cared, she hadn't cared enough.

Alice's high voice brought her back to the sunshine. 'Race you to the swings, Auntie Jo!'

The ice cream demolished, Alice was hurling herself forward, her thin blonde hair floating around her head like a dandelion clock. It brought back a St Luke's memory that Jo couldn't quite grasp. She smiled; Alice's enthusiasm for racing, for life, was infectious.

'Doesn't she ever run out of energy?' she asked Kate.

'Never!' Kate replied. 'Or chatter.' She looked sideways at Jo. 'Do you wish you'd had kids with Richard?'

It was a question she had asked before, and Jo's answer was the same. 'Not at all. You know me, Kate, I'm far too selfish for kids.'

Said, as always, without missing a beat.

Inwardly, she sighed. She was just like her parents, too bloody proud for her own good. Never admitting to any weaknesses or feelings. Stiff upper lip in the direst of times. Hating even to weep in front of someone else.

The photograph of her father and his seven knobbly-kneed siblings popped into her head. One at each end of the line, his parents were in it too, all suited and booted for church. Proper Methodists, deadly serious, with chins held high and shoes that shone. 'Poor but proud,' Richard said when he saw it.

Richard, Richard. The one exception. And he bloody well died.

Kate's clear voice was persisting. 'But don't you think you're missing out, Jo?' she asked, her eyes wide and innocent. 'If you never have at least one—'

'No, and anyway, Kate, you always said you didn't want children either. That Tom, darling Tom, was enough.'

She said it too sharply, she knew that. Kate had spoken without malice and now her expression was concerned and caring.

'You're right, I did, didn't I?' Then, after a moment, 'Funny how life turns out for the best. Look how lucky I am to have them both. Alice is just perfect, isn't she?' She lightly rubbed Jo's shoulder. 'I just worry about you, Jo, I want you to be happy.'

Jo took a breath. 'I am happy, Kate. Hunky-dory. No need for you to worry. Come on, let's catch up with Alice.'

Just like her bloody parents.

7

Jo pulled off Kate's old Hunters at the side door. They were green with the usual buckle, but they reminded her of something with a discordant note. Moor End, probably, though her mum never stretched to anything so grand. Black and basic wellies, usually a crusty cast-off from one of her brothers and inevitably too big. Did they wash them at an outdoor tap? Seemed pretty unlikely.

Shaking the prodding memory away, she stepped into the kitchen. Kate had replaced a virtually new double hob with an Aga a few years back. Jo had privately taken the piss ('perfect Aga saga life, Richard. Why am I surprised?'), but she had to admit its all-year sunny baked smell was consoling, somehow. Gentle, warm, familiar, safe. Like her childhood home, that singular aroma she could only dream about at eight years of age.

Still feeling a little guilty for snapping at Kate, she tried for jolly even though she could have fallen asleep standing. 'What should we wear tonight?' she asked. 'Shall we go glam and wow every-body? After all, I'll feel very important being associated with the owners, don't you know.' She looked at Alice and put a questioning finger to her mouth. 'I'll need a Very Important Person badge. V-I-P. Can you think of anyone who's brilliant at colouring with felt-tip pens?'

Alice dashed off with a squeal of delight but Kate sighed. 'I'll do my best, Jo, but you know me, I'm not really into clothes.' She suddenly smiled. 'Which is surprising really, considering Mother.'

Picturing Hilary's triple wardrobe, chock-a-block with an array of jaw-dropping outfits, Jo laughed. 'I know!' She slipped her arm through Kate's, pleased they were back in a comfortable zone. 'Remember how we used to dress up in her wonderful frocks? The ball gowns, cocktail dresses and fur? And her shoe collection! How many pairs did she have? There must have been seventy! I was so envious. Do you remember when I had to wear my Sunday dress for the Christmas party? The only girl in Junior House without home clothes because Mum hadn't packed me a party dress? It was a dull grey-blue with a tight collar and buttons at the back. What on earth were they made of?' She rubbed her arms. 'God, I can still feel it. Material like a carpet; it was so bloody itchy.'

Feeling a stab of guilt, she pictured her mum's crushed face when she'd complained in the holidays. 'Poor Mum; she followed the bloody *packing list* by the book. It wouldn't have occurred to her to slip one in the trunk. She probably only had one or two frocks herself.'

'Yes, but you made a joke of it, Jo. You threaded white paper through the neck and pretended to be the chaplain in drag. You were willing to make fun of yourself, you made everyone laugh. I never had that talent. I was far too nervous, too serious, too afraid.'

'But that was only later,' she wanted to correct Kate, but she'd already been spiky. She studied her friend's face, the pale skin smooth and clear without any trace of make-up. 'A sweetheart, you mean. My gorgeous bestie. Generous and giving and so very pretty.'

They stood in silence for a few moments, Jo trying but not

succeeding to stifle a yawn. She pictured the two of them that very first day. Kate polished and perfect and posh. Her quite the opposite. 'How did we ever become friends, Kate? Chalk and cheese we were, in so many ways.'

Kate nodded. 'And still are.' Then, after a moment, with a small tut. 'You're not hiding that yawning very successfully, Jo. I'm taking Alice to a party in a while. Have a long nap. *Like Sleeping Beauty*, as Alice would say.' She kissed Jo's cheek. 'We just need to find you a prince.'

'A plasterer-plumber prince!' Jo snorted. 'Knowing my luck I'm more likely to wake to Nick Bottom. But thank you, lovely friend, I'll give it a try.'

Waking with a jerk, Jo glanced at her watch.

'Sorry,' Tom said from the doorway. 'Just got in. I didn't know you were in here.' He folded his arms with no sign of moving. 'Was it a nice dream?'

Trying to shake the drowsiness from her head, she looked around the room. Bloody hell, how embarrassing. She'd come into the lounge to flick through the newspaper and must have fallen asleep. Caught napping on the sofa on a Saturday afternoon (not just a *settee*, but someone else's; her mum would be shocked)! Feeling sheepish, she lobbed a cushion in Tom's direction. 'I'll never know now you've woken me up!'

He leaned to one side to catch it. 'Well, it must've been nice because you were beaming. Maybe handsome young boys catering for your every need?' he said without smiling. 'Where is everybody?'

'Kate has taken Alice to a birthday party before her sleepover and I—'

'Thought you'd catch up on your sleep? Are you always awake at that time of night?' he asked.

41

'How do you know?'

He shrugged. 'I heard you.'

She felt the heat spreading. He was bloody doing it again, putting her on the spot.

Turning away from his gaze, she pulled up the soft throw. 'Sometimes,' she answered.

Absently staring at the leaded window, she thought back two years. Swamped with an overwhelming and icy feeling of abandonment, she drove along the black and winding Snake Pass from her flat to the farmhouse. God knows how she arrived in one piece, as she couldn't remember any part of the thirty-mile journey, just the sheer relief when the front door was answered after one soft knock. She'd been afraid she'd have to hammer to wake everyone up, make a scene and a fuss, the last thing she wanted.

Tom was there in a t-shirt and shorts. 'I heard your car,' he said, his eyes digging deep into hers. 'What's happened, Jo?'

'Richard is dead.'

He simply held her without saying a word, without even closing the door. It was exactly what she'd needed. No questions nor condolences, no tears, just the comfort of warm, solid flesh. It was only later, much later, she wondered why Tom was up in the early hours of the morning.

'Why don't you finish your novel? Wouldn't that give you purpose?' he now asked, still standing above her, holding the cushion to his chest like a shield.

The hot irritation rushed to her cheeks. 'You know perfectly well I haven't touched it since Richard died. It would be too emotional to go back to it, too . . . ' She grasped for a word to express how she felt. 'Personal,' she said, inadequately.

'And going out with other men wouldn't be personal?'

Throwing the blanket aside, she stood up and glared. Tom was making a point, she knew. It made her angry, bloody furious, that he assumed some entitlement to judge how she led her life. He wasn't her dad or her brother, for God's sake. Yet she was still compelled to justify herself, to explain how she felt.

'Look, Tom,' she said, trying to control the quaver in her hands and her voice. 'Not that it's any of your business, but writing my novel and loving Richard involved my heart and soul. If I did have it off with some man, it wouldn't. It would be just for the sex. Or maybe to feel attractive and desirable and bloody *wanted*. So the two things aren't remotely comparable. OK?'

Showing in his cheeks, Tom's jaw was tight. 'Just for sex.' He raised his eyebrows and snorted. 'Just for sex,' he repeated with a thin smile. 'Poor bloody sod, whoever he is.' He stared for a second longer before looking away. 'Last night you mentioned a child. Why didn't you have one with Richard?' he asked quietly.

Replaced with cold gloom, Jo's anger ebbed away. Throwing the newspaper aside, she brushed past his broad shoulder. At the door she stopped and blew out. Finally finding her voice, it emerged plummy and staccato. 'It wasn't for want of trying, Tom,' she replied.

8

Crossing another thorny (and identical) wooden stile, Jo began to wonder if she would ever find her way back to the farmhouse. All the sheep-shit fields (a Richard expression – he was a city boy, born and bred) of the Peak District looked the same. Though perhaps that was intentional. Didn't she read something about dry stone walls and *patterns*?

She stopped, turned her face towards the sun and felt the breeze rake her hair. The walk and the warmth had raised her spirits. They'd helped to structure her thoughts and rationalise her anger at Tom. And herself. Though she already knew. Tom had no bloody right to ask such personal questions, nor judge her choices. Querying about kids was absolutely out of order. And yet, and yet ... When it came to the novel, he'd reflected her own thoughts, daring to voice what no one else would. He was doing what Richard would have done if he'd been there, but in a different way – goading her into writing again. Not the freelance rubbish nor the women-looking-for-something books, but proper, serious writing.

'Come on, girl, off your fat arse and get to it!' Richard used to say when he caught her lazing at noon with a trashy thriller, or even worse, watching daytime TV.

'This is time out from my research. And my arse isn't fat, actually.'

'I know, it's pert and perfect, but that's no excuse.'

He'd given her the confidence, the courage and the financial support to leave the newspaper and to devote more time to the novel, but then something had happened, abruptly, surprising Jo with its ferocity.

'I want to try for a baby, Rich. I still love my project, but can you imagine having a little you and me in our lives? Writing and pregnancy is a perfect combination! What do you think, Rich? I want your babies and I want them now!'

She'd said it laughingly but it was true; the sudden desire and the need was as overwhelming as it was unexpected.

The smell of horse manure brought her back to the rugged countryside surrounding her. The tall grass in the next field seemed to be waving. It was as good as any other, so she ambled towards it, trying to avoid the clumps of dry heather and marsh thistles. And sheep-shit, of course.

She glanced at her watch. It was all very well basking in sunshine and memories, but she had to get back to Petersfield to make herself look half human for the planned trip into Sheffield. Astonishingly, two hours had flown by since she'd woken in the lounge. So fearful had she been of Tom seeing her in tears, she'd bolted from the farmhouse. For a woman who was never parted from her mobile, stomping off and heading towards the Peak District horizon without it was uncharacteristic, and certainly not the brightest of ideas.

Stopping again, she turned a quarter, then another. Scanning the peaks with a hand shading her eyes, a hint of panic started to root in her chest. *Win Hill* or *Losehill*, or another hill completely? To be honest, she had no idea.

A row of trees in the distance looked familiar. There was no obvious path across the cotton grasses and shrubs, but she spotted a gate in the high wall of the next field. Doggedly heading to the barrier, she climbed on to its metal bars, carefully lifting her leg high over the barbed wire at the top. She pulled her other foot. Oh shit, her sandal was stuck. Losing her balance, she fell against the metal, the sharp stab deep and quite painful.

Hitching across to the wall, she gingerly sat on its rough, jagged top and examined the wound on her inner thigh. For some minutes it bled, despite her attempts to stem it with an old tissue from the pocket of her shorts. From her high vantage she saw a solitary figure two or three pastures away. Like an omen, the sun had disappeared behind the sullen clouds and specks of rain danced on her bare arms.

Sitting on the stones for a while, she watched the walker draw nearer without any particular contemplation. Then a thought suddenly struck her. She was in the middle of nowhere. She was alone and vulnerable. Of course she bloody well knew that. But today she was *physically* alone and vulnerable, not properly dressed for a walk and without any means of calling for help. And the approaching stranger was a man, a man without a dog. She wished he had a dog. A pet gave a man a reason to walk all alone in the *middle of nowhere*.

She quickly slipped off the wall, a muddy patch below giving her a soft landing, but invading her sandals with a squelching sound. Getting lost had never been a problem as a child. She could walk for miles in the Yorkshire countryside, alone or with friends, and instinctively know the way home. But she was a city girl now, had been for an age.

'Fuck, Jo! Whatever happened to the girl from Barnsley?' she said out loud, the anxiety rising from her chest to her face as she tried to keep an eye on the walker while searching for a road in the distance, any road.

'My thoughts exactly.'

Jo snapped around to the voice. It was Tom. Thank God it was Tom! But her smile of relief was short-lived. His hands were on his hips, his jaw clenched, his frown deep.

'I was worried. You don't just walk off without telling anyone where you're going, Jo. You're alone and hardly dressed for a walk. I'm parked on a track, half a mile back. Follow me and keep up.'

With that he strode ahead, leaving Jo to negotiate the sheep-shit and thistles as swiftly as her muddy sandals would allow.

9

Her clear gaze sparkling with news from the party, Kate sat at the kitchen table and sipped her wine. 'So, yes, it was fun, but exhausting too. There's a little boy in Alice's class who's a maniac, but his mum is blind to it all.' Looking thoughtful, she paused for a moment. 'Or maybe she's just savvy. Lets the other mums sort out the mess and the tears. Mind you, there's a rumour flying around that she's having an affair. To be honest she's not my cup of tea, but even so, why would she do that? Why would any woman, when they've got what they want? A lovely husband and a precious child . . . '

Jo lifted her eyebrows. 'Or the child from hell.'

Kate's eyes widened. 'Oh, perhaps that's why. Poor little boy. But still, it isn't on when he repeatedly pulls Alice's hair.' She topped up Jo's glass. 'Sorry, Jo, mum talk! I forget that it's boring. Come upstairs and tell me all the gossip from the real world while I get ready. How is your American friend, the one who lives in an *apartment*, as opposed to a flat? She had another baby, didn't she?'

American friend. It's what Kate always called Judy. 'Judy's fine, thanks. Yes, a little girl called Evie—'

'And the German couple. She – what's her name again? Sorry, I always forget.'

Jo inwardly smiled. She always said that too. Lily was clearly not Kate's *cup of tea* either. 'Lily.'

'Of course, Lily. Did she have a boy or a girl?' Kate lifted her eyebrows. 'A beautiful blonde replicant like her parents, I expect.'

Jo groaned inwardly. *The Replicants*. She should never have told Kate the nickname her brother had given Lily and Noah. Both extremely fair, statuesque and with clipped accents, she could see where it came from, but being compared to a genetically engineered robot felt very wrong.

She turned her glass without replying. She didn't really want to talk about Lily and Noah. They'd had a boy, she knew, the 'new arrival' card was in a drawer somewhere in her flat. They were Richard's closest friends – hers too, of course, so she should've been in touch long ago. The child would be, what? Eighteen months old? Even more?

Pure jealousy really. Not something she was proud of.

Kate didn't seem to notice her lack of reply. 'The Replicants! Typical of Ben, he's so hilarious.' She suddenly put a hand to her mouth. 'Oh Lord. He doesn't have a nickname for Tom and me, does he?'

'Course not.'

'Thank goodness for that! How is he? Still like Peter Pan and breaking hearts wherever he goes?'

'He's great, thanks. Still living in Leeds and either turning up late or appearing at my flat when I least expect it.'

'And Nigel? Did you say he'd gone travelling?'

Jo thought of her oldest brother and rolled her eyes. 'Yup, he's on his *gap* year aged forty-two! I suppose he was brave to ditch the job in the face of Dad's disapproval. But to *find himself* is a joke. I don't think he'll find anyone remotely similar to *himself* in the world, let alone the Greek Isles.'

'You are mean, Jo! He's not that bad. Some women like the sensitive poetical type, I believe. He might even find a wife while he's there.' She studied Jo for a few seconds. 'I don't know why you have a downer on him these days. You used to have a massive soft spot for him at school.'

'Did I?'

'Well, you were proud as punch when Head Girl called you out and asked for a photograph. He was the heart-throb of that year's social! He's still not bad looking; the Wragg cheekbones and all that.' She smiled. 'Course Ben's handsome too. Though his poor face after that rugby match! Remember?'

Loveable, generous, brilliant Ben. 'Yes, of course.'

'Just goes to show how nature can work miracles. Come on, let's take the wine upstairs with us.'

Kate carried the bottle and Jo followed with the glasses, careful not to spill on the cream velvet carpet in Kate's fragrant bedroom. Still slightly stunned after the exerting walk to Tom's car, the first drink had already gone to her head, but Kate seemed to be full of nervous energy.

'Yes, we all want to strangle little Kieran. But you have to invite the whole class to birthday parties, otherwise there's trouble. One mum complained to the school, can you believe it, about the lack of a party invite. Then there's how much one should spend on the gift, whether it's acceptable to ask for money instead. Don't get me started on that.' She opened the large wardrobe and stared for a few moments. 'If I get ready now, then I'll have time to sort out the horses. Hm, what to choose?'

There were plenty of clothes in the closet, but Kate selected a knee-length black skirt and a silk blouse Jo had seen her wear a few times before. Sensible clothes, she supposed, the sort of clothes a busy mum – with horses – would wear.

Disappearing into her en-suite bathroom, Kate left the door

open a crack. 'Don't stop talking. I can listen and shower at the same time!' she called out. 'Did you enjoy your walk? I wondered where you were when I got back after dropping Alice off. Sweet of Tom to search you out. He's a darling, isn't he?'

Wondering where to sit, Jo chose the wicker chair next to the handsome four-poster bed. Conscious of making a dent in the cashmere throw, she looked around the newly painted bedroom. It was similar to Kate: neat, tidy, fresh looking. There was no trace of Tom.

Automatically sipping her wine, she thought of how ordered her bedroom in the flat was these days. Comparatively, at least. Richard was messy. Clumsy, chaotic and charming. She pictured him bending down to retrieve his bundle of papers from the grimy courtroom floor the day that they met, and she smiled at the image.

This is progress, she mused. Good progress. She could think of him and smile.

'Jo? Joanna Wragg!' Kate had popped her shower-capped head around the bathroom door. Reaching out a slim arm, she waved. 'Can you throw me some tights, please? They're in the top drawer. The far side. Hello? Joanna Wragg, are you listening?'

Her eyelids springing open, Jo stood to attention. Bloody hell, for a moment she'd been hurled straight from the courtroom to the classroom. *Joanna Wragg, are you listening?* Words yelled too often at St Luke's. Yet she'd survived. They both had, hadn't they?

'Sorry, miles away. Tights? OK, here we go. Barely Black or American Tan?'

Handing over both pairs, her eyes were again drawn to the bruise on Kate's bony wrist. Her shoulders were angular too. She wasn't nearly as scrawny as she had been at one time, but she was very thin. Still bodily shy too, rarely exposing bare arms or legs, even in this heat. Not at all like the guileless plump girl Jo had first met at school.

She went back to the dresser to close it, but her eyes caught a wooden item at the back. Quietly pulling the drawer out a little further, she ran her fingers over the decorated small casket. Another blast from the past! She'd been incredibly envious of Kate's *secret box* at school. She'd *so* wanted one for herself. Not only did it have Kate's name embellished in flowery handwriting on the lid, it had a key.

Pushing the drawer to, she sighed at the memory. A box with a key. That was precisely her, wasn't it? Locking the true Jo away; keeping a tight control on her emotions. Not just then, but now.

Reclaiming her cashmere crater, she gazed through the shuttered window as though it had bars. Why she still felt an urgent need to escape, she didn't know. It happened too often, that fluttering and tugging of memories which she never quite managed to catch. Wellies and running water, copper stones and dandelions.

'You and me. Friends for ever.'

Unsure whether Kate's voice was in the past or the present, Jo turned her head. Looking smart and polished, she had emerged from the bathroom and was observing her quizzically.

'Sorry, Kate. What did you say?'

'I asked what you were thinking about.'

'Right.' Surprised at the query, Jo tried to reach for the gossamer, but it floated away. She couldn't remember Kate asking that question before and it felt strangely invasive. Studying her face, she paused for a moment before answering with a smile. 'About how stealing Hilary's expensive face creams has paid dividends. I can't see even one line or wrinkle, Kate, it isn't fair!'

Kate smiled, a puff of pleasure, just like when she was young. 'Well, they say men should study their mother-in-law to see what their wife will look like in thirty years, don't they? So don't blame me, blame Mother! She's as glorious as ever, Jo. Auburn hair these days and of course the mandatory sunglasses. Asks after you every time we speak. Longs for you to visit.'

Thinking of her own mother's thick grey hair, Jo nodded. Joyce still had it set in rollers every two weeks at Pam's, the hairdresser's in their village. A map of fine wrinkles decorated the soft skin of *her* face. But Jo's thoughts were fond; she was lucky to have such a loving, solid, reliable mum, and she regretted what she called the 'missing years' when she hadn't fully realised it. Still, it wasn't something she wanted to share. 'Ah,' she said instead, pulling a wry face. 'No wonder Richard dropped dead on me! I suppose I'd better get out a trowel and start repairing the damage before you let me loose on the general public.'

An overwhelming weariness descending, she pulled herself out of the chair. Right now she'd like to jump in the car and drive back to her familiar little flat with its functional but cosy comforts.

However much she joked about it, the need for male company, any company for that matter, was pretty low on her list of priorities – it felt like too much effort. But then again, her first date night with Richard all those years ago had too. What had seemed a grand idea in court number two at ten o'clock in the morning had felt like a death sentence by eight. She had no idea why she'd said yes; she already had a good-looking boyfriend, and she'd barely noticed Richard in court for the two weeks previously, preferring to gaze at the aquiline nose of the haughty, but surprisingly attractive Crown Court judge (when she wasn't surreptitiously reading her book).

Still, he *was* husband material (as Hilary had always put it), so she went on the date. Turned out he was funny and charming and had an infectious smile.

She now glanced again at Kate, who returned the gaze with clear, guileless eyes. When she had first been introduced to Richard, she'd been slow to hide the surprise and was at pains to say later that he was funny and 'really, really lovely'. Jo had been angry when she saw her astonished look. Not everyone was as handsome as bloody Tom Heath. She'd wanted to explain that despite *marrying well*, there was friendship, happiness, contentment and love. But most of all about communication and connection. Though she hated the expression, they were *soul mates*. She could be honest and blunt, happy, angry, elated or sad. She could be 'a complete number one cow' (her words, not his) and he would just laugh and say, 'isn't everyone?' They complimented each other. But she didn't think Kate would understand. Besides, she would be horrified to discover she'd been inadvertently offensive.

With a last glance at the shuttered window, Jo stood. Stretching her arms, she jogged on the spot, the routine their history mistress had demanded of anyone who dared to yawn in the classroom. As much as she loved Kate, she'd never been completely honest with her and she felt a strange sense of guilt, as though she'd let her down somehow. But tonight she was going to throw off the rumination and make a big effort for her. She'd apply her brightest red lipstick and emerge from the haze, duly armed with frivolity, sarcasm and a brave face.

Which was, after all, what Jo Wragg did best.

10

St Luke's

The school day at St Luke's began with a cold abrupt start at seven o'clock.

'Everyone up. Make your beds!' Matron would roar as she pulled back the cotton sheets (though not entirely dissimilar to the person in *Carry On Matron*, Jo soon discovered this one had no medical qualifications and not even an ounce of TLC).

Kate's bed was next to the dormitory door so her bedding was pulled first. Once Jo had got used to not waking in her warm bedroom in Barnsley, it gave her enough warning to jump out before Matron could bustle to her bed. Though Jo couldn't say why, it seemed important to beat her. Remembering she was in prison was the hard part. After silently weeping into her dad's hanky before sleep, she would dream deeply until morning and for a moment on waking she'd think she was at home (a forerunner to the days, weeks and months after her future husband *dropped dead*).

Wearing their white vests and knickers in the chilly bathroom at the end of the landing, the girls would wash (sometimes) and clean their teeth (mostly, but one found it was easier just putting the blob of toothpaste directly in one's mouth when one's teeth were chattering). Then they'd dress as fast as they could to stave off the cold, fumbling with blouse buttons and ties, pleased to top it off with a warm grey cardigan and navy blazer. Thick grey knickers, too, on top of the white. Jo had been amazed when her mother had bought them from Cole Brothers. 'What the hell are these for?' Ben had laughed, holding them up high for the whole family to inspect.

'Go away, Little Ears,' Jo had said to Ben, pink-faced and angry.

'They were on the clothing list,' Joyce had replied, looking doubtful. (That dratted *clothing list*; the bane of Jo's life). 'And don't swear, Ben. It isn't nice.'

But the 'grey bags', as the girls called them, were invaluable, an extra layer of insulation in the draughty black building.

Sunday letter-writing was compulsory. Sitting at their desks (instead of lounging on a settee with a book and listening to her brothers squabble over the TV channels), they were required to write missives home, then hand them unsealed to the supervising prefect (to be spot-checked for *splitting*, the older girls said. Splitting about what? Jo wondered. Of course she later found out).

As it happened, Jo dipped into her Basildon Bond stationery most days anyway – for notes to Mum and Dad or Granddad, to Auntie Barbara or Ben, sometimes to Nigel and her friend Lynn from the farm next door (who she hoped wouldn't disown her for 'turning posh'). Much of her news was about the freezing dormitory and even colder prefab classrooms (she wasn't sure if that counted as *splitting*; she certainly hoped not, otherwise she was in for a *roasting*).

'If a building is colder on the inside than outside, then it is definitely haunted,' Ben wrote in reply (with an impressive sketch of a ghost). Jo thought this information was thrilling, but telling the other three girls in her dormitory one night turned out badly as they all began to cry. (Perhaps she shouldn't have embellished with sound effects. And it was pretty creepy in the dark.)

Matron appeared and flicked on the lights, hurting their eyes. 'What's going on?' she demanded.

'Jo is being mean. She says Junior House is haunted,' Kate sobbed, holding out her arms.

'Don't be such a baby,' Matron replied, stepping back. She pointed a fat finger at Jo. 'And I'm keeping an eye on you, Wragg.'

And so the days dragged. It wasn't so much the discipline, the constant *lining up* in queues, the disgusting food or the long periods of silence that bothered Jo, it was the lack of freedom and the feeling of claustrophobic imprisonment after the expanse of home.

Her older brothers had paved her childhood in Barnsley. So long as she dressed herself, pulled up the duvet on her bed and was 'on the dot' with clean hands for meals, her mum had allowed her to wander through the fields, the farms or the village as she pleased. She was astonished that she wasn't allowed to leave the junior school building and classrooms, let alone the school premises. And that was for six whole weeks until she was freed at half-term. She found herself staring out of the barred windows of the dormitory and the classroom, yearning to get away and having to dampen the frequent impulse to simply bolt in the night.

'Joanna? Joanna Wragg! Are you listening?' the form teacher asked time and again during the first few lessons. Jo soon learned to look at the exasperated woman and nod, even if she wasn't.

'Yes, Miss Holster,' she replied automatically, quickly learning that this was the expected reply to most questions. Have you finished already? Have you done fractions before? Who has read *Little Women*? *Jane Eyre* too? You do understand this is one of our rules? You look tearful. Are you all right? Are you happy? *Yes* was the truthful answer mostly, but not always. 'Yes, yes Miss.'

It was an easy trick for her to learn. After all, putting on a brave face and getting on with life was what the Wragg family did best.

Kate struggled so much more throughout those long days and weeks. The spoilt, mollycoddled youngest daughter at home, she'd been waited on hand and foot (literally, it turned out) by her mother or the current *au pair*. She'd never made a bed, let alone heard of hospital corners. She hadn't plaited her own hair, clipped her nails or tied her shoelaces. She was hopelessly ill prepared for boarding-school life, despite her older sisters having breezed through Junior House and into the senior school.

She frequently cried, too. Not just silently into her pillow at night like Jo, but during the day, at playtime or at meals, sobbing uncontrollably for Daddy to fetch her home, her eyes pink like a rabbit's.

Jo did her best to surreptitiously help her friend, patiently teaching her how to fix her laces and tie, practising with Kate's shining plaits until she got it sussed. She even learned to copy her loopy scrawl (and the way she <u>underlined</u> words she wanted to emphasise), so she could polish off Kate's geography or French homework as well as her own. But it was noticed. It was spotted by Matron, who threatened to separate Kate and Jo unless *Bayden-Jones* learned how to do things herself. Then eventually it was picked up by the older girls downstairs. One Lower Third girl in particular: Miranda Day-Carter, head girl of the junior school and Housemistress's pet.

Halfway through the first term, two new kindergarten pupils arrived, so Jo and Kate (being quite old at eight years of age) were moved downstairs to Eighteen Dorm with the more mature girls (nine years and ten; astonishingly, one or two had turned eleven!). Now, not only was Miranda head girl of the junior school, she was also head of their dormitory, so had ultimate power over Kate and Jo's lives. Two years older than them, she was well spoken, tall and handsome, with thick orange-brown hair to her waist. But any apprehension Kate might have had was soon dispelled.

'Gosh, Miranda's so nice,' she would declare. 'I wish my hair was that colour.' And with a pink face, 'I think she really likes me, Jo. You mustn't get jealous.'

Jo and Kate had been allocated beds near the draughty window at the bottom of the dorm, away from the hub of heated chatter and laughter surrounding Miranda in the middle, but with a cordial smile (not unlike Miss Smyth's, Jo thought, but knew better than to say so), Miranda would stroll over for a chat. She'd sit on Kate's silky eiderdown (from home, of course; Jo had a plain scratchy blanket because that's what the *clothing list* had prescribed) then, without asking, she'd open Kate's bedside drawer and finger her private belongings, her necklaces and dolls, her secret box and pretty stationery, her home clothes and shoes. All the wonderful items that weren't on the official list, the things Jo secretly coveted and longed to touch herself.

Of course Kate was pleased with her sudden popularity. 'I'm walking to breakfast with Teresa today, Jo.' 'Oh, Jo, you're there. I told you not to wait. I'm chatting to Pippa.' 'I'm sitting next to Heather today, Jo.' 'Why are you following me? I said I'll see you later.'

Thrilled to receive so much flattery from the bigger girls, Kate was open and trusting. She offered to share her hairbands, ribbons and bobbles. Surrounded by eager faces, she handed out sweets and chocolate from her weekly postal treat like Lady Bountiful, and promised to ask her mother to send more.

A prelude to how she behaved with her little acolyte 'minis' years later in Seniors, Kate revelled in the admiration and attention. But gradually items went missing from her locker and the parcels from Hilary were taken from her after *Post* without Kate having the chance to tug open the string first.

Then the whispers and the taunting began.

It built up slowly at first, the bullying, so insidiously that it was hard to pin down. Quiet jibes, soft name-calling, whispers, with Miranda Day-Carter at the helm. Whether actually present or not, Jo knew she was the instigator, the tyranny behind the toothy smile.

'Spoilt little Mummy's girl', 'Cries like a baby', 'Looks like a piggy', 'Eats like a piggy'. '*Fat* like a piggy ...' And it was the word *fat* that stuck; the girls in Eighteen Dorm forgot her Christian name and 'Fatty Bayden-Jones' stayed, even when Kate stopped eating.

Then there were the dandelions; no one had ever told Kate they were also known as 'piss-in-the-beds' and that if one picked the yellow flower head it meant one wet the bed. (Jo later learned from the library that this was on account of its *diuretic* effects when eaten. Diuretic meant the 'passing of urine', she also found out.)

Even as Jo rushed to prevent her from plucking a bunch on their *Sunday Long Walk*, she knew it was too late. On returning to the dorm after chapel or prep, Kate frequently found her bed stripped and when she asked why, the other girls would nonchalantly shrug. 'Must be Matron,' they'd say. 'To check your wet bed, little baby.'

Jo tried her best to help Kate. To quietly protect her from the constant barb, to tell her it didn't matter, that it wasn't true. To explain that dandelions were once eaten by the Victorian gentry in sandwiches and salads (the library again) and that the other girls were the fools if they didn't know that. But Jo was only young, she was struggling to conform, to ditch a label herself, and so at times she would stand aside and watch the devastation on her little friend's face, unwilling or unable to help, fearful that Miranda would pick on her too.

Jo understood that however bad school life became, the unwritten rule could not be breached: never *split* on the other girls, never tell a teacher and never, *ever* tell your parents. But Kate was too weak and too frightened to resist telling her mother, and so Hilary had a meeting with Miss Smyth after the half-term break.

Inevitably, it only made matters worse.

11

St Luke's

For the whole of that October, Kate had been uninhibited, friendly and generous. She'd worn her heart on her sleeve. But the tables had turned cruelly and unexpectedly. No one could have blamed her for *telling on* the older girls; the fear and the unhappiness were written on her face for all to see, if anyone had bothered to look.

Besides, that's how Kate Bayden-Jones was, she couldn't hold anything in for long, be it delight or distress. Jo had no doubt that after just one word of concern from her mother, the whole story would've come tumbling out. After all, she did the same thing to Jo day after day when they were alone on the swings or the seesaw at the back of Junior House. She poured out her anguish, relating every little detail of what Miranda and her followers had said and done, even though Jo was mostly there when it had happened. Jo understood it was a therapy of a sort, but one she never used. On the rare occasions she now talked about herself, she was always left with a nagging doubt that she'd given too much away.

The half-term break went too quickly.

'Cecil wants to see you right away. And by the way, Fatty, you're dead,' were Miranda's first words, hissed to Kate with a satisfied smile, once all the parents had gone.

Miss Smyth was referred to in whispers as *Cecil*, short for Cecily (her Christian name, so Miranda knowingly said). As Housemistress of Junior House, Cecil led the girls down to chapel each day, she presented weekly assembly in the Lower Third classroom, she took prayers in the dormitories at night (selecting her favourites to chant hymns – Jo knew she wouldn't be chosen any time soon) and handed out letters at Post in the morning, but still she seemed nebulous to Jo. One wouldn't notice her for days, and then, like a phantom, she'd appear with frightening perspicacity when anything was afoot, smelling of mothballs and lavender (Jo had finally pinned the smell down).

She had never heard Cecil shout, but with her pale, powdery face, slashed smile and piercing eyes, she didn't need to. She was terrifying, a woman most people feared (parents included, Jo suspected), but Cecil's 'pets' were the exception to the rule. These favoured few girls were allowed to travel in her shiny Austin car to the 'proper' church in the nearby village every other Sunday (rather than undertake the forty-minute walk, whatever the weather). Occasionally they were invited to take cream tea in Chatsworth, and if they were very special, they were allowed into her rooms to play the piano and sing. Best of all, they were nominated to lay out chocolate biscuits on Cecil's tea tray and, if any were broken (which was often, how surprising), they were permitted to eat them.

'*Right away*,' Miranda had said, so there wasn't much time for counselling that day.

'I'm sure it'll be fine, Kate,' Jo said, convinced that it wouldn't be. It was common knowledge that Miranda was Cecil's current favourite pet. So Jo accompanied Kate to Cecil's rooms, smiling and nodding at Kate's drawn and pale face as she lifted her fist to knock at the frosted-glass door. Then she hovered in the small library pretending to read, but really keeping an eye on the drawn orange curtains, anxious and fearful for her best friend. But when Kate eventually emerged from Cecil's room, she reminded Jo of the cockerel from the farm next door. Puffed up and beaming, her round face was a deep shiny pink.

'I told her everything and she was so nice!' she gushed. 'She says she's going to keep a special eye on me and that whenever I'm worried or frightened, I'm to go straight to her to talk about it.'

If Jo felt jealous of Kate's *special* treatment, she hid it well. After all, she knew Kate was prettier and more deserving of everyone's attention than she was. Besides, she was grateful and relieved that Kate wasn't going to leave her. She loved her dearly but would've struggled to express it in words. Now she wouldn't have to.

As Christmas approached, the name-calling continued, but Kate bore it with a head held high because Miss Smyth told her to ignore it.

'Words should never hurt a true lady,' Cecil apparently advised, and anything she said to Kate was gospel.

The thieving eased off at first because Kate no longer asked Hilary to replenish her supply of luxuries, and anything she really treasured was faithfully hidden by Jo on her behalf. But the dandelions Kate had regularly found between her sheets were replaced with clumps of grass, and one time what Jo supposed was a cat or small dog poo (she had never seen an animal on school premises; the culprit must have had it in her pocket all the Long Sunday Walk – how gross). Then small items of Kate's school uniform started to disappear; her napkins and her aprons, her tie and even her hockey stick, eventually.

Jo let Kate borrow her spares but she only had so much to lend and some things didn't fit. So Kate would be called out by the head prefect of the senior school for filing past her on the way to the dining hall without a starched napkin and ring. She'd miss domestic science for not wearing an apron and she'd be told to run repeatedly around the sports field in her heavy school blazer for not having the proper kit for hockey or netball. Kate was labelled absent-minded, forgetful and lazy by the teachers. A liar too. For when she tried to explain about the missing items, they'd be found by Matron where they should have been, in the locker next to Kate's bed or in the cloakroom.

It was only Kate's visits to Miss Smyth that kept her going. They were short at first, for just a minute or two in the lunch or tea break while Jo hung around in the library, flicking at an encyclopaedia, reading the first chapter of a novel or writing Kate's homework (Kate particularly detested précis but Jo liked the challenge, and besides, it was fun to really perfect her loopy scrawl), while she waited for her friend to emerge with a broad smile.

'I've told her everything and she says she'll sort it out!' Kate would say happily.

But Jo wondered about that; she'd seen Miranda sauntering from Cecil's room often enough, and in her view there was no sign of reprimand on her smug face. To Jo, the great observer and the people-watcher even then, things didn't add up. But she kept her head low; she'd managed to blend in and adapt to such an extent that she was no longer different to any of the other girls. She was one of them – invisible – and that's how she wanted to stay.

12

Peak District – present day

It was fun to park in the VIP space at the front of Bridge Bar and emerge from Kate's Mercedes like celebs, but the wine bar was hot with music and moving bodies, and packed so full that Jo and Kate had to push past groups of young people who were oblivious, it seemed, to anybody but themselves. Wondering if she had ever been that confident, Jo followed Kate. Long-haired and groomed, the women were stunning, but surely too much like clones with their heavy make-up, arched brows and towering heels? The men too, in their thin-lapelled tight suits and high quiffs. Why they appeared so much younger than the women, she couldn't say.

'I'm impressed!' she shouted above the clatter and sound of electronic dance music. She was dazzled too; the bar, the stools and the pillars appeared to be made of chrome and glass – or Perspex perhaps – but it gave it a minimalistic feel, a contradiction to the throng of party-goers swaying on the mirrored dance floor. It was clearly very popular, attracting what looked like the clientele Kate was hoping for, if their designer shoes, suits and handbags were anything to go by.

'I'll find Guy Voide, he's the manager. He'll sort out our table,' Kate replied. 'Stay here. I'll be back.'

Standing alone near the restrooms, Jo listened to the bass beat and peered down at her outfit. It was too bloody low or too bloody short, she couldn't decide which. Resisting the urge to pull it up at the bust or down at the knees, she laughed at the memory of Hilary's oft-given advice. 'One shouldn't do breast and leg at the same time, girls. One or the other, obviously, but never both, it looks very working class!'

Today's frock was low-cut with thin straps. Made of red silk, it was nightdress billowy. In a good way, she hoped. (Though maybe not; she had a sudden memory of the 'baby doll' nighties which had been very popular at school. Of course her mum had never bought her one, and Jo couldn't argue against flannelette when one considered the main subject of her letters home was the freezing dormitories.) After witnessing Kate's attire, she'd worried the dress would be too, well, dressy, but as she scanned the amount of skimpy Lycra in the room, she felt it was fine (albeit *working class*).

She'd bought it on a shopping trip with her *American friend* Judy.

'I can't do boobs *and* knees, Jude,' she said.

'We're not in the nineteenth century, Jo, of course you can. Besides, I don't think you really need to worry, one can hardly class them as boobs and you have fantastic pins! Your skin's a nice colour too, not as deathly pale as I expected beneath all those bloody layers, so you should show it off. How come you're so tanned?'

Jo thought of saying: 'Barnsley grime, apparently, it doesn't wash off!' (A phrase often used at school, but one which she was quick to use first, so she'd get the laugh.) But instead she kissed her friend's cheek. 'Says you with your glowing skin.'

Aware of a few heads turning in her direction, minutes passed.

Though she'd never felt pretty (an ugly duckling, in fact), she was vaguely aware she was eye-catching because people told her so.

'You look fabulous! Come on, Jo, thick dark hair, full lips and a stunning smile. And slim. Don't pretend you don't know. It's annoying,' Judy said as they'd both eyed the red dress in the changing-room mirror.

But compliments took Jo by surprise even now. A part of her still felt skinny, plain and bespectacled. In the looking glass as a child, she'd seen a goofy reflection, her mouth and her hair too big for her small face and thin frame, but she'd eventually *grown into them*, as Hilary put it. 'Aye. The ugly duckling has turned into a swan at last!' an uncle said on her fifteenth birthday (a back-handed compliment if ever there was one).

Wishing she had a scrunchie in her handbag, she raked her hair behind her ears and glanced around the room. Definitely more girls than men – they were standing in groups, chatting, laughing and drinking long icy cocktails. She snorted to herself. Bloody lucky young things. Drinks were vodka based these days; they didn't have to suffer the apprenticeship of cheap cider.

She wondered where Tom was. After dropping her back at Petersfield in near silence this afternoon, he'd driven off again. Then he'd called Kate when they were ready to leave to say something had cropped up. She had looked a touch downcast, but hadn't complained, replacing her slight frown seconds later with her trooper's smile. 'He works too hard! And because he's a perfectionist, he finds it difficult to delegate. But he's been so successful, Jo, and I reap the rewards, so I really can't protest.'

'That's because you're an angel,' Jo had replied, slipping her arm into Kate's as they negotiated the cobbles towards the garage. She felt that perhaps she should've offered to drive, but her desire to get legless was greater than her desire to be nice.

Number one complete cow, she thought.

She would most certainly have protested to Richard. Indeed, she frequently had when he was home late or work got in the way, which was more often than she'd liked, especially in the months before his death. But then again, he was setting up his own solicitor's practice.

'You'll make me think you have a mistress,' she'd occasionally complain.

A weary Richard had sighed. 'If work is a lover, then I'm guilty as charged. But it'll be worth it in the end, just you see,' he'd reply.

Worth it? Death and debt. No, it wasn't.

Tapping her foot, Jo now looked at her watch. The waiting for Kate felt familiar, but they weren't flipping school kids any more. Deciding to call, she pulled out her phone, but as though reading her mind, Kate burst through the mass with a brilliant smile. A dark-haired man followed her. Carrying a bottle in one hand and two champagne flutes in the other, he was perhaps in his late thirties, much the same age as them.

Pushing her irritation away, Jo focused on the bottle. Alcohol, at last, thank the Lord. Taittinger too, very nice.

'Jo, this is Guy,' Kate said, a little too loudly. 'He's our manager, the man who can grant your every wish.'

He gave a Gallic little bow. 'Well, for this evening at least,' he added with a trace of an accent.

Smiling politely, Jo shook his proffered hand. His fingers were slim and his handshake limp, not at all like a Brit. With his thin face and heavy lidded eyes (accompanied by remarkably long and thick lashes that the St Luke's girls would have traded their tuck for), he was certainly striking. He was wearing a wedding ring, she noticed, but then so was she.

'Guy's wife owns the fab ladies boutique in the village next to ours,' Kate said easily. 'I must take you, Jo. Beautiful clothes from France, but not too expensive, so you'll like them. Is she here tonight, Guy?'

'No, she's at home with the babies,' he replied, saying the word with a French pronunciation. Jo wondered how many *bébés* he had at home, whether he slipped in a French word every time he was introduced to a new woman, just to add a little *je ne sais quoi*.

'Oh, how old are the babies?' she asked, studying him closely as he poured the drinks. Thin and tall, his eyes were so dark they were almost black, much like his hair which was longer than that of most men his age.

'Adele is eight and Juliette is five,' he replied with a white, even smile and a twinkle in his eye. Jo found herself warming to him; he knew that she knew *bébés* sounded more charming than 'children' or 'daughters'.

She sipped the champagne. This man is a flirt! Just what the doctor ordered.

'Kate, darling, how are you?' someone called. 'I haven't seen you for yonks. Where have you been hiding? Come and say hello to Murt.'

An attractive woman in a spectacular purple sari approached, put her arm around Kate's back and pulled her away without acknowledging either Jo or Guy.

'This is what girlfriends do, I think,' he said with a small smile. 'Allow me to take you to your table.'

Lightly holding Jo's hand, he guided her through the horde, then up a spiral staircase at the back of the bar. He was attentively slow, she observed, turning frequently with a reassuring smile as she negotiated the coiled steps in her too-high high heels. Then he pulled out a chair at one of the balcony tables and topped up her glass.

Reminding her a little of a holiday in Italy, she peered over the loggia at the moving bodies below. 'Wow, what a view.' Then she laughed. 'Big Brother or what? No chance of getting up to no good without getting spotted.'

'Absolutely. But there's something appealing about being a voyeur, don't you think? May I sit?'

Guy pulled out a chair, sat, then tilted his head slightly, his dark eyes on her. 'I believe your husband died,' he said conversationally. 'Are you looking for a new one tonight, perhaps?'

For a moment Jo stilled and stared. Unbelievable! What a bloody rude and excruciating question. Straightening her shoulders, she took breath to fire out a sharp retort, but caught the glint in his eyes. The bugger knew it was an outlandish thing to say. A little like her own 'dropped dead', he was testing her somehow. And it was so bizarrely and politely asked, she couldn't help laughing.

'Perhaps,' she replied. Thinking, champagne, champagne, how wonderful you are, she leaned to his ear and breathed in the woody aroma of his aftershave. 'Is there anyone you can recommend, Monsieur Voide?' Then, after a beat, 'Someone who isn't already spoken for, of course.'

A Gallic shrug and a smile. 'Ah, pity,' he said. 'You are unusual and quite beautiful. *Petite* too.' He sat back and perused her through those languid eyes. 'French men like slim, elegant women.'

Remembering a dreadful article she had to write in her early twenties, she snorted. *Dating a French Man Top Tips*. She did some 'research' with Bella in the office. She couldn't remember most of the rubbish they concocted, but one was to make *him* chase you (a given with any nationality, surely, so they felt on safe ground). Another was not to freak out when he said he loves you after a week (true, apparently – Bella had just returned from a holiday in Brittany). They had concluded the moral was not to take French flattery too seriously.

Feeling pleasantly pissed, she decided to ignore his possibly sexist and definitely smarmy comment and just enjoy his company. Emboldened by the bubbles, she studied him again. Yes, quite attractive in a fantasy-land type of way. Hot sex with no strings? But of course there were always *strings* with married men, whether you saw them or not. She had no intention of going down that route.

He leaned forward again. 'May I at least compliment you on your dress? *Rouge* is your colour.'

Smiling despite herself, Jo lifted her flute. 'Cheers to that!'

A shadow fell on them.

'Ah, the boss,' Guy said.

'Hello, Jo,' Tom said evenly. 'I see you've met Guy. Is he looking after you?'

'But of course.' Rising from his seat, Guy flashed her a conspiratorial smile. 'I'll ask Shanice to bring up the menus. Hope to see you later.'

Tom sat opposite. 'What do you think of our manager?' he asked after a moment. He posed the question easily enough, but he seemed tense or distracted. Perhaps he was still cross about the walk. Or maybe it was his well-cut suit. She had never seen him wearing one before, albeit without a tie, at least not since his wedding.

'He's very charming, but I'm guessing that's part of the job,' she replied. The champagne was fizzing in her head and warming her chest; she wanted to enjoy herself, despite her hill-sore feet. She inclined towards him and grinned. 'Hey, I like your suit, Tom. Suit you, Sir!' she said teasingly. She wanted to forget their spat from earlier; she wanted to be friends again.

Tom seemed to loosen up too. He unbuttoned his jacket and sat back, surveying the crowd below. 'Tonight is billboard dance with the DJ, as you can see, but we do fizz, gin and cocktail nights through the week. Then it's jazz on Sundays. You should come.' He turned to Jo and grinned. 'I love sitting up here watching the world, like a king in his castle. I bet you never thought you'd see your dad's brickie wearing a bespoke suit in his own wine bar,' he said, raising his eyebrows.

The image of a shirtless, tanned and golden-haired boy flashed through her mind. Remembering that tug of attraction, she gazed at the man he'd become. Then she threw back her drink and pushed the flute towards him.

'No, but Kate did,' she replied.

13

'Tom, you didn't tell me the Shahs were moving! We could've looked at their house ... their beautiful, beautiful house ... but someone has made an offer on it now,' Kate said, moving unsteadily towards them, clutching a bottle of wine.

Jo gawped in surprise. Kate's voice had emerged even more refined than usual, and it was obvious she was trying to speak slowly. She glanced at her watch; an hour or so had gone by since last she saw her. Bloody hell! How much had she managed to drink in that time?

She turned to Tom, but his face was impassive.

'You know that I have no intention of moving from the farm, Kate,' he said lightly. 'Let's order some food. What do you fancy, Jo? Have you looked at the menu?' He scraped back his chair. 'The specials are on the board downstairs, I'll just take a look.'

Once Tom had gone, Kate thumped down heavily in the seat next to Jo.

'Kate? Are you all right? What's upset you?'

She picked up the bottle. 'I hate this place,' she replied, her voice flat.

Jo pushed the glass away. 'Well, that won't help.' Remembering Kate's elated smile from earlier, she splashed water into a tumbler and placed it in front of her. 'Drink up, Kate. Why do you hate it? I thought you were proud of it.'

'I am. It's just that ... I don't know. I prefer to stay at home, hidden away from all ...' She gestured towards the dance floor. 'From all this. I'm a home girl. You know that, Jo.'

Jo looked too. Tom was below, chatting to a couple with his hands in his trouser pockets.

'Does Tom know how you feel?'

'I don't want to be a disappointment. Besides, I wanted to come tonight to show it off to you. I wanted to show you how well Tom has done, how clever he's been.'

She took Kate's hand and squeezed. 'Look, Kate. I've seen it now and I think it's fantastic, but I'd happily go home with you. We could stop the taxi on the way back and grab a Chinese takeaway. Just the two of us.'

Tom reappeared and Kate quickly pulled back her arm. She lifted her chin. 'I've already decided. I'll have the lamb,' she said brightly, sliding the wine glass back to her place.

Minutes passed at the table, strange, awkward and loaded. Jo studied the menu yet again. 'Has Guy eaten?' she eventually asked, breaking the silence. It had become uncomfortable and she was desperate to do or say something to lift the gloom and to distract herself from watching every sip of wine Kate was taking.

His eyes steely bright, Tom stared for a moment, then he motioned to the waitress who'd appeared to take their order. 'Ask Guy if he would like to join us, would you, Shanice?' he asked, his voice low and clipped.

Jo cringed. Bloody hell, what had she done now? Perhaps inviting the manager to eat with the owners wasn't the done thing. She looked from Tom to Kate. What was going on there too? They seemed disconnected tonight, which was unusual. After all, they were the *Golden Couple*.

She smiled inwardly at the description. Ben, of course. One of several titles he had bestowed on them. As usual her brother was on point. Not just Tom's flaxen hair, but their glow, their charmed perfect life. Which was why she wouldn't dream of telling Kate. But even golden couples were allowed a night off, she supposed. Besides, if anything was really amiss, Kate would have told her. Though they only met a couple of times a year these days, they still spoke on the phone. She'd shared her excitement, her worries and concerns about Tom from the moment she'd set her sights on him at eighteen. Still did, surely?

Turning the stem of her glass, Jo vividly pictured their wedding. She'd worn *rouge* that day too, a red fitted dress to show off her figure, her nails and lips painted the same shade of crimson to match. But when she arrived for the ceremony in the dimly lit country church, she felt overdressed and painted like a ridiculous geisha, and she had longed to escape and wash it off. As for Kate, she had looked blissful in her modest ivory lace dress and veil, with only a hint of make-up, her happiness shining through her translucent skin. When Joyce glanced at Jo she'd pulled a face to express her disapproval of her daughter's appearance. Yet when she looked at Kate, it seemed that she was proud, really proud.

For a moment, but only for a moment, Jo had felt a sharp jolt of jealousy. Envious, not because Kate had it all, but that she deserved it. Yet the moment passed and she joined in with the wedding celebrations, forgetting the red dress and that vague feeling of pique. After all, she loved Kate, she was pleased her friend had what she wanted, and she hoped one day she'd learn to love Tom too.

Kate barely touched the lamb. She moved the meat and vegetables around her plate, then gave up the pretence, putting down her knife and fork and clutching her wine in both hands like a communion goblet and drinking steadily. Tom sipped sparkling mineral water and ate in silence, his jaw becoming more set with every glass Kate consumed.

It was a relief Guy was there. He was charming and affable but he seemed to resist her attempts to join Tom and Kate into their conversation, making it all the worse when Kate finally slumped on the table, her eyes closed and her mouth lolling open. At that point Tom stood quietly, his face terse and stony.

'I'd better take Kate home. Are you coming now, Jo, or would you prefer to stay?' he asked, his voice measured and mannered.

Jo sat back, surprised. 'Of course I'm coming with you,' she said. She was feeling pretty inebriated herself, but she was irked at the clear implication she'd want to stay at the wine bar with Guy rather than help her friend in this state.

Finally in the back seat of the Mercedes, Jo studied her old friend. Slumped against her shoulder, she was completely out for the count. Her mind tingling, she pulled a clump of Kate's matted hair from her cheek. How long had it been since her last visit? Definitely six months, maybe more. What the hell was going on? Did Kate have a drink problem? Or was this a one-off?

Catching Tom's glance in the rear-view mirror, she considered asking him, but he was as silent as the black countryside surrounding them. Besides, they'd never discussed Kate before, it had never been necessary or appropriate, so why would they start now? She was the bond that tied the three of them together, that kept them civilised and polite. She and Tom rubbed along with courteous friendliness for her sake, but they didn't like one another, never really had.

Kate's astonishing behaviour tonight was something she'd have to tackle in the morning, just her and Kate, and sort it out.

14

Sitting alone at the kitchen table, Jo rubbed her sore feet. She felt both despondent and disconnected. The breathtaking shock of seeing Kate in that state should still have been there, but the alcohol had numbed her too, so part of her didn't give a damn. She just hoped she'd still remember the evening in sufficient detail to give Ben a blow-by-blow account when she next saw him, though goodness knows when that would be. *Peter Pan*, Kate had called him; that was pretty much spot on.

Listlessly she stared at the assortment of empty bottles near the sink. For recycling, she supposed. She and her uni friends had got blind drunk on plenty of occasions. They'd fallen asleep in a heap at house parties, or woken up in bed next to some stranger, wondering what on earth they'd done and who they'd done it with. They probably passed out or puked on the carpet too. But that was fun and necessary. A being young, free, single and silly rite of passage.

While Kate was baking bread, reading cookbooks and sewing Tom's socks, Jo was on the pill and sleeping around. It was always a one-night stand, invariably an unsatisfactory coupling and generally forgotten a week later (or so she claimed, if anyone asked). But Kate wasn't like that; she lived in another world, a fairy-tale land of domesticity. Jo only knew it existed from Kate's frequent letters and her rare visits, but it was a life she clearly adored: 'Had to kick Tom out of the bed again, Jo. He can't get enough!' 'My Yorkshire puddings have risen at last, Joyce will be proud!' 'We have an adorable Labrador puppy. Tom's called her Custard, his first baby!' 'Made my own bedroom curtains and a cushion cover to match. Can you believe it?!'

Drinking huge quantities of wine hadn't come into it.

'Coffee?' Jo now asked, stirring herself to an upright position as Tom walked into the kitchen.

He looked at her and laughed mildly, his face considerably softer than it had been twenty minutes earlier. Kate had woken and sobbed in the car, refusing to get out when they arrived home, then she'd vomited as he carried her up to their bedroom. Trying not to inhale the sour stench, Jo had wiped the puke from the stairs with reams of patterned kitchen roll, but without any expertise or enthusiasm.

'God, no,' he replied. 'I need a proper drink. Will you join me? The night is young, as they say.'

Jo smiled in return. Yes, another drink sounded like an excellent suggestion, even though she knew it wasn't wise. Perhaps they were all turning into *middle-aged* alcoholics. And yet, when she thought about it, she only really drank to excess these days when she stayed here at the farmhouse.

'Cheers,' Tom said, lifting a tumbler of whisky in salute. 'Shame we had to leave so early, but ...' He sat back in the chair and stretched, looking more familiar in his t-shirt and jeans. 'What did you think of my latest venture?'

Remembering Guy's comment about voyeurism, she laughed.

'It's great. I particularly liked your throne. Quite fancy being royal myself, gazing at the beautiful people spending all their pocket money on expensive cocktails.' She caught his slight frown. 'I'm serious! I really could sit there all day and watch the human race.'

People-watching; her favourite hobby. A lonely pastime, but she liked to sit in the public gardens near her central Manchester flat and watch folk go by. She enjoyed guessing their names, their job, sexuality, religion; what they were feeling inside. It never ceased to amaze her how similar people were, and yet how different.

'Writing ideas?' Tom guessed.

Jo looked at him sternly. She didn't want him to start goading her again with his cryptic comments, but he didn't appear to notice or care. He gazed silently for a moment. 'Perhaps I've been unfair . . . ' he said slowly. 'I didn't stop to think that writing is a solitary occupation, that perhaps you're lonely and that's why you want to find someone new.'

Bloody hell, he was needling after all. Her cheeks coloured, but with anger this time. 'For God's sake, Tom, give it a rest, won't you!'

She glared at him. She was irked by his words but his passive face annoyed her more. He knew he was touching a raw nerve, surely?

'I'm not lonely,' she snapped. 'I don't want to find *someone new*, as you put it. Life doesn't just revolve around the male of the species, for God's sake. The last thing I want is a bloody man getting in my way at home, but . . . '

Her voice trailed off. She didn't know why she was bothering to justify her position. At that moment she had no idea what she wanted herself; she was drunk and her brain was slowing down. She needed sleep, not an assessment of why her life felt empty and pointless.

'But you want a baby,' he finished for her. 'And you need a man to give you one,' he said, folding his arms.

She was too weary to argue, so instead she stood up. Dizzy and detached, her head belonged to her, but her body to someone else. 'I don't know what I want, Tom,' she said, carefully putting one foot in front of the other and heading for the door.

Shuffling past Tom, he turned and caught her hand. His expression thoughtful and cloudy, he gazed at her. After a few seconds he nodded. 'I'll give you a baby, if that's what you want, Jo,' he said quietly. Then he released her and went back to his whisky.

15

'I'll give you a baby, if that's what you want, Jo.'

Snapping awake to the sound of Tom's voice, Jo sat up in the bed and glanced around the dark room. Empty. No Tom, just his words resounding in her head.

I'll give you a baby, if that's what you want, Jo.'

Sighing deeply, she fell back. Without washing or teeth-cleaning, or even peeing, she'd been unconscious the moment her head touched the pillow last night. Merciful sleep. But as ever the anaesthetic of alcohol had now worn off, her temples were throbbing and her throat parched.

'You only have yourself to blame!' she chided inwardly, Joyce-like.

She'd said it to herself rather too regularly over the years: not just the waking up with a horrendous headache, but the other things she wished she hadn't said or done. Her masochistic mind-voice could recite bad behaviour from years back, especially in the darkness. But last night wasn't her, it was Tom.

I'll give you a baby, if that's what you want, Jo.'

What the hell? What the hell?

Slowly, she hitched up. Resting her face in her hands, she protested out loud as the pieces of a particularly atrocious evening fell into place. Oh God. She'd flirted without even a hint of subtlety with Guy Voide, a married man. Kate's behaviour had been bizarre; she'd drunk like a fish and passed out at the table. Tom had been cross, very cross; he'd had to manhandle a struggling Kate from the car to the farmhouse.

Then his parting words when Jo finally went to bed.

Did he really say them? Closing her eyes, she drifted into dreamland for a moment. Warm hands on her skin, lips soft on hers, then the weight of his body and . . .

'Stop!'

Firmly shoving the fantasy away, the ache in her skull went from a thud to a clatter. What exactly did he mean? A test or a joke? Or perhaps he had a spare one stashed away, just ripe to be fostered. Life was suddenly and ridiculously surreal. Both Kate and Tom were behaving so strangely this weekend; she didn't know what to make of it.

She groaned with frustration. Tom Heath. Bloody Tom Heath. Save to say, 'Congratulations, Tom', before walking away with a strange sense of loss, she hadn't acknowledged him at his wedding all those years ago. She'd always struggled in his presence; she who could talk, or perhaps argue, the hind legs off a mule when roused, couldn't think what to say to Tom when they were alone. Stuck for bloody words! But as the years went by, she'd discovered he was amiable enough to chat to in company and that he was willing to have a laugh, even occasionally at his own expense. So a fragile bond existed between them. Then Richard had come along with his easy charm and the relationship seemed to relax and strengthen. There were more frequent visits between the couples, weekends away and meals out. But Richard dropped dead and the goalposts had shifted again. There was less humour, less contact, more tension. An obstacle seemed to replace Richard and the tie once again became delicate.

Climbing out of bed as quietly as her heavy legs would allow, Jo went for a wee, then ransacked her handbag for painkillers. Having discovered none, she put on her dressing gown and tiptoed down the stairs. Apprehensive she'd find Tom still sitting where she'd left him and his tumbler of whisky, turned to salt like Lot's wife, she opened the kitchen door slowly.

The room was empty, the fridge quietly humming. Jo looked at her watch. It was only three o'clock, but it felt much later. After a brief search, she took two painkillers from a high cupboard, then drank three or four glasses of tap water, wondering how on earth someone so awake could get back to sleep.

Looking around the homely room, still flavoured by the Aga, she felt an irresistible urge to cry. She'd stood in this kitchen two years ago and hadn't shed a tear, but now she wanted to stamp her feet, to throw the glass she was holding at the wall and scream at the injustice of it all.

It was so bloody unfair! Richard had been taken from her. And whatever she'd said to Tom, she was bloody lonely at times. She regularly saw Judy and Ben, but other 'joint friends' like Lily and Noah, she'd ditched. Or perhaps they'd dumped her.

She stared through the panelled window, squinting to see an orange hint of her little car parked outside. The black night and distorted fragments of her own reflection stared back. She wanted to go upstairs, pack her bag and leave. But she'd be well over the limit, and Kate might think Jo's leaving was her fault, which wasn't fair.

'It's no one's fault, it's everyone's, it's God's fault, it's mine,' she said out loud before taking a deep shuddery breath, then opening the fridge to reach for the cure of all maladies.

Rather than watch the watched pot this time, she put the drink in the microwave. Strangely troubled by the addition of a calf to Kate's collection of china animals on the top shelf of the dresser, she took her eyes off the milk. Inevitably it had bubbled over the top of the mug and she felt compelled to wipe it. She had ineffectually cleared Kate's puke, but she'd been half asleep and half spinning. She was now sober and awake; there were no excuses this time.

'Do you think that will do the trick?' a voice asked as she walked past the lounge door.

'Tom! You made me jump,' she answered crossly, the splatter of hot milk on her hand stinging in tandem with her head. 'Don't you ever bloody sleep?'

'I was asleep,' he replied dryly. 'The walls are paper thin . . .'

His words reminded her of a favourite song about making love. Mouth to mouth and limb to limb. Making love? It wasn't *love* she wanted, it was sex. Wasn't it?

She thought of walking on without responding, but she paused, transferring the mug to the other hand and licking off the milk.

She had to face him sometime.

'Sorry,' she said, looking into the room.

Why was Tom sleeping in the lounge when there were plenty of other bedrooms, including his own? It wasn't the cosiest place in the world with its original features untouched. She glanced at the low wooden beams, the slated floor and stone walls. Then she met his eyes. He was lying on the sofa where she'd napped that afternoon. Of course! The soft cushions and blanket; she hadn't realised she'd been sleeping in his bed. The idea made her squirm.

'It's hard to unwind when I've been to the bar and I keep Kate awake,' he said, as though reading her thoughts. He lightly snorted. 'Not that I'm likely to wake her up tonight.'

Jo nodded, but didn't say anything.

'Come in and talk to me, Jo. It's the least you can do now you've woken me up.'

'I bet I didn't wake you up at all.' Wincing, she lowered herself to the armchair. 'I wish those painkillers would kick in.' She curled her feet under her bum. 'I shall blame you for giving me more wine when I'd already had enough.'

'I thought it was no one's fault,' he replied with a faint smile.

Jo sipped her milk. It had already cooled. Or perhaps she was hot. She looked at her friend's husband, calm beneath the blanket, his arms behind his head, his gaze steady. Talk to Tom Heath, what a joke. She actually wanted to shout at him, really yell. But of course that would never happen; they were both too bloody polite, civilised and repressed.

'What are you thinking about?' he asked, breaking the stillness with an echo of Kate's words from earlier. They seemed odd coming from him too, and he was studying her with a strange expression. Quizzical almost.

'Oh, schooldays; china ornaments; Kate; how we never really change,' she replied, shrugging.

'Ah,' he said, looking away from her.

Jo waited for the silence to pass, then yawned, glad to feel sleepy at last. 'Back to bed, I think.' She leaned forward to pull herself out of the comfortable chair, but Tom's words stopped her short.

'I meant what I said earlier.'

She stared. His face was fixed; she couldn't read it at all. Was it a sick joke? Was he laying a trap or making some kind of point? She had no idea what to think. She intended to walk away, but found herself glued to the seat, wanting to run, but needing to stay.

The question blurted out. 'What *did* you say, exactly, Tom?' she asked, her heart pelting in her chest.

No sooner spoken, she regretted them. Oh God, oh God. She

shouldn't have asked. It was dangerous, dark territory. Opening cans of ugly worms. She should've laughed it off.

'If you want a baby, Jo, I'll father it. I'll give you my sperm. Put it however you want,' he replied, spreading his large hands but his face still impassive.

'Oh, and I suppose the turkey baster comes for free.' Trying for humour, but testing him too, trying to thrash out precisely what he *was* saying.

He lifted his shoulders indifferently. 'If that's how you want to do it . . . '

'Tom, this is some sort of joke, right?'

She could feel the searing heat, not only in her face, but pulsating her whole body. It was agonising to look at him. She wanted to hide her crimson cheeks and the tears threatening to lurch from her eyes. From anger and shock and yes, bloody yearning.

'No, it isn't a joke. I'm serious, Jo. Richard has gone. I want to do that for you.' His blue eyes were on hers. Cool? Detached? She didn't know. But they were dark, they studied her, seeming to scrutinise her response.

Kate. Kate! Why was she even giving this conversation the time of day? 'Why would you do that to your wife? Why would you hurt her like that?'

'She wouldn't need to ever know. No one would. Just you and me.'

The tears fell, splashing from her eyes and cooling her skin. She dropped her head to hide them. It was all too preposterous; it wasn't really happening, surreal, so surreal. But she still needed to know. 'Why, Tom? Why would you do it?' she asked, her voice barely a whisper.

'You know why,' he replied quietly.

She nodded and mopped the tears with the sleeve of her robe. 'That was a long, long time ago,' she said eventually.

The discordant half-hour chime of a grandfather clock pierced the protracted heavy hush.

Tom cleared his throat. 'Did you ever tell Richard?'

Jo shook her head; it wasn't something she wanted to think about. It had remained buried for years and there was nothing to be gained from resurrecting it now.

Wiping the end of her nose, she took a deep breath before meeting his gaze. 'Kate loves us both dearly. You know it's something neither of us would do to her. I'm tired, I'm going to bed,' she said, leaving the room and not looking back.

'Think about it,' she heard as she climbed the stairs.

16

Barnsley – June 1998

So thrilled to regain her privacy and freedom, Joanna Wragg returned to Moor End after finishing her A levels. Relieved to be shot of the mindless rules and disgusting food, not to mention the long minutes of pointless prayers, she looked forward to a whole summer of laziness before starting uni in Manchester.

Instead of the tedium of constant swotting, she planned to lie on her bed and catch up on her massive backlog of books. She'd been the recipient of *anybody's* cast-offs, so had amassed an eclectic collection from school – mostly trashy romance, horror and Black Lace books (for the 'erotic reader': excellent!). But there was other stuff too, ranging from *A Practical Guide to Transactional Analysis* to *Treat Yourself to Sex* (who on earth had donated that?). The latter she read several times; not that she planned on losing her virginity anytime soon – girls in sixth form had come back with graphic accounts of it after the school holidays (torn hymens and *lashings* of blood mostly) and though

Jo regularly found herself thinking about what it might *feel* like, it frightened her too.

The first week of the burning summer was great, the second OK, but by the third she was stupefied with boredom. Being a public-school outcast, there wasn't much to do. Though Lynn from the farm had stayed loyal, the poor girl only escaped her duties one evening a week (none if a heifer decided it was *time*), so their trips into town on the bus were limited.

Increasingly convinced Barnsley life was plain and parochial, she longed to travel to Barton in the Beans, stay in the old manor and feast on Hilary's fascinating pearls of wisdom about her future, as well as men, marriage and life, but the Bayden-Joneses were on holiday for a month.

Bored, bored, bored! Her own family didn't help. While it was nice to chat with Joyce in the kitchen, cooking and baking weren't really her thing (pretty dull, if she was honest), Ben was always out and about, and Nigel had started work with their dad (from their lack of communication at the dinner table, things weren't going well). The only saving grace was the construction of Stan's new double garage. She didn't like the builders' constant presence, soft whistles and comments when she went out in shorts (*coarse* comments – Hilary would not have approved). One of them, however, had caught her eye. The blond boy who worked high on the roof was unbelievably good looking. With his tanned skin and white grin he was really quite beautiful, and her heart lurched and raced when his gaze touched hers. Frequently popping outside to empty the bins or carry a tray of tea and biscuits 'for those hard-working lads', she'd straighten her shoulders and hold her breath, hoping his blazing eyes would pick her out. Which they always did.

It was nice to have a pash, a secret pash too. Though she couldn't say why, she was glad Kate didn't know. Perhaps it was because she imagined his lips crushing hers – and other more intimate things – when she touched herself at night. *That* wasn't something she'd admit to anyone. Though she had kissed a couple of boys (too protracted and too wet) at school 'socials', it was nothing like the surge of pulsating heat deep in her stomach when she imagined the blond boy's hard body invading hers. How she felt about him made her scared, if she was honest. It really didn't matter, though; Hilary's 'right sort' was hardly going to be a *workman*. The infatuation and lovemaking was only in theory and from a distance. He'd never even got close enough to speak.

No sighting of him for days, Jo had almost given up. Carrying the tea tray out as usual, she scanned the roof. Feeling the jolt of disappointment again, she lowered her gaze. Then, sloshing the drinks, she stepped back. Much taller and broader than she'd thought, there he was by her side.

For several beats she gawped – at the sheen of perspiration on his brow and those eyes, which really *were* sky blue. And his smell – an intoxicating aroma she couldn't quite describe. But the moment was broken by the sound of the boss builder's voice. 'Heath, grab your tea and stop mooning. I need you up here for the joist . . .'

'Coming.' Grinning, he reached for the blue stripy mug. 'Thanks, love.'

Heath? Oh my God! Her blond boy was a bloody Heath! The memory of his little brother's stench of pee flashed back. Though their colouring was different, the chiselled cheekbones and the accent were the same. The family lived in a council house at the 'rough' end of the village and everyone knew they were 'bad news'.

Jo returned to her bedroom and her reading pile, choosing to devour horror rather than analyse her mix of emotions. Did it really matter the boy had a local accent? It was similar to her own father's and grandfather's, after all. It shouldn't have, but it did. She stopped peeping at the scaffolding through her bedroom curtains, she deeply sighed when her mum asked her to take out the drinks.

'Don't look so surly, Joanna,' Joyce said repeatedly. 'It does you no favours. Being polite doesn't cost anything.'

Ben echoed the sentiment. He'd been in the same primary class as the eldest Heath brother and they'd remained friends over the years, despite Davy's notoriety in the village for being *in trouble* with the police. 'You should see your face, Jo. The way you suck in your cheeks and lift your chin! You're not carrying books on your head any more. Stop being such a prissy snob,' he'd laugh.

Despite her mum's reprimands and Ben's teasing, Jo didn't smile or make any attempt at friendliness on the muggy July day she reluctantly held out yet another mug of tea towards the middle Heath boy, whatever his name was. She started to turn away when he spoke again, his accent no better than it had been the first time.

'Do you fancy having a drink in The Station later?'

Spinning around in surprise, she gaped. His chest was bare, sweaty and bronzed from the sun, his torn jeans low-slung. He locked his eyes on to hers and for a moment she froze, incapable of speech. Then the penny dropped that Tom Heath was asking her out on a date.

Swamped with panic, she stared. Unable to identify anything other than risk and fear, she finally found her voice. It emerged clipped and polished. 'Thank you, but I don't think so.'

Aware of a deep crimson spread of heat, she scuttled away, up the back steps to the house, past her mum bustling in the kitchen and through the cool lounge. Ignoring the blare of *her* record from the player and Ben's inquisitive eyes, she flew up the stairs, two at a time. Finally in the sanctuary of her newly wallpapered bedroom, she lay face down on the bed.

Tom Heath had asked her out! It was embarrassing, humiliating, an outrage.

Yet dangerous lust was still there, treacherous and tingling her belly.

*

Catherine Bayden-Jones was smitten the moment she rested her gaze on Tom Heath.

'Oh my God! The blond boy, Tom. He is so handsome! Have you seen his physique, his toned chest and his arms? Do you think he likes me, Jo? Do you think I'm pretty enough? Do you really think I'm in with a chance?' she asked repeatedly when she came to stay with the Wragg family during the middle of that sizzling summer.

As the dry days went by, Kate was unable to hide her crush. Surprising Jo by wearing shorts and skimpy t-shirts, she created excuses to take things to Tom, becoming the non-surly tea taker and biscuit offerer, before giving up the pretence of being Joyce's emissary and chatting to him at every opportunity. It was to such an extent that Stan had to have words: 'He's here to work, lass, stop mithering him.'

Her friend's gushing behaviour astonished Jo. She admitted to her that Tom was 'fairly attractive', but there the appeal stopped. Didn't it? She reminded herself that the Heath family lived on a council estate with a 'reputation' (Auntie Barbara's raised eyebrows said it all). They were common. She vaguely acknowledged that she had once been *common* herself, but that was completely different. Tom was poor; he was a manual labourer, for goodness' sake! No house, not even a car. She just couldn't understand what a nice educated girl like Kate could possibly see in him. (All the reams of advice on the subject! Wasn't Kate listening to her *own* mother?)

'Oh, he's just lovely! So attractive and really gentle. I could marry him at the drop of a hat,' Kate said over and over, but Jo just laughed, knowing *that* would never happen.

'You have a snog or two with a bit of good-looking rough, but you don't *marry* them, Kate,' she replied. 'What on earth would Hilary and Harold say if you brought him home? They would be so disappointed. All that money spent on your education, too!'

'I don't think they'd mind. They want me to be happy,' Kate replied, her face dreamy.

Considering Hilary's frequent advice on lovers and husband material, Jo doubted it, but had to quietly acknowledge Kate's parents didn't seem to be unduly concerned that she had left St Luke's without any decent A levels or plans for the future. Indeed, she was staying with the Wragg family the second half of the summer to 'help out' in Stan's office ('she's a lovely lass, but I'm not sure *help* is the right word') because her curriculum vitae was blank.

Honey-flavoured August approached, Joyce's *busy* month. She won first prize at the village show for her gooseberries (she had been saving them especially, thank God; anything was preferable to *eating* them), her cross-stitching and dahlias. She also ran a cake stall at the local fete (pretty much baking all the cakes single-handed) and Stan's team won the tug of war as usual.

Jo was aware of Tom's blue gaze still on her whenever she glanced his way (what he was doing in the fruit and veg section of the village show, she had no idea). Though she continued to ignore him, she admitted to herself a slight pique that her best friend wanted him for herself. But at the end of the day, she needed Kate to be happy, so she said nothing more to dissuade her. And besides, Kate's mind was set; she knew what *that* meant.

In the September, Jo departed for Manchester with great excitement and trepidation, leaving Kate to continue her indefinite stay with Joyce and Stan, another *slight pique* Jo couldn't quite dispel. By December Kate telephoned to say she was going on her first date to the cinema with Tom.

'I decided to ask him out myself,' she said happily. 'I realised it was the only way because he's shy. But he loves me, Jo, I can tell. He really does.'

In January, Tom and Kate were engaged and in May they were married. Not the lavish event one might have expected, but a small and traditional affair at Kate's local church in Barton in the Beans with only immediate family and friends.

Kate had been right; her parents were charmed with Tom, happy that someone had brought a smile to their youngest daughter's face.

Luckily for Tom, Harold was very eager to support and invest a substantial amount of money in his son-in-law's fledgling construction business.

Perhaps Kate did *marry well* after all.

17

Peak District – present day

Jo awoke with a jerk and blew out the intense dream. She wasn't in her Barnsley bedroom, but still at the farmhouse. The sunshine was breathing through the open window and the smell of food was in the air. She bolted upright. Oh God; it wasn't the aroma of toast or even freshly baked bread, but the unmistakable tang of roast beef. She peered at her watch. Shit! It was past eleven o'clock. She hadn't slept in so late since she was a teenager.

'God, Jo, how rude!' she chided herself.

It wasn't the done thing to *lie in* at someone else's house. Her mum would undoubtedly have reprimanded her for such impolite behaviour. It was like walking away from the table without permission, receiving telephone calls after ten o'clock at night, or leaving food on her plate. Even worse: losing control or crying, making a scene in public. All the *not showing one's dirty linen* type of rules which Jo had been desperate to cast off when she left home, but which she still carried around with her nonetheless.

Like giving in to sexual abandon.

She shook her head to test the ferocity of her headache. It wasn't as bad as it might have been had she not risen in the night and drunk water.

She groaned. Oh, God, the water. And, *Think about it.* Well, she hadn't thought about it and she wasn't going to, she really wasn't.

Lying back for a few moments, she replayed the conversation with Tom in her head word for word. It wasn't even a *conversation*, she thought as she stared at the dark wooden beams. She and Tom didn't have them; they exchanged terse comments she generally found impossible to interpret. But he had made himself clear last night: *I'll give you a baby, if that's what you want, Jo.* He'd been serious. He'd offered to father a baby, a child she longed for.

She hated him for it.

Climbing in the shower, she allowed the water to assail her face far longer than was necessary. 'Fuck you, Tom,' she said out loud to the cubicle. 'Fuck you!'

There were times when she almost liked Tom, when she nearly warmed to him. But at that moment she detested him, she loathed him for playing games with her mind, whether intentionally or not.

'I'll give you a baby, if that's what you want, Jo.'

The idea was ludicrous. Silly and ridiculous, never mind unbelievably disloyal. If Tom knew anything about her, he'd understand it was something she'd never dream of doing to any friend, let alone Kate. He had no right to make such an offer, even to broach the subject. It wasn't fair of him to give her that glimmer: a baby, a child. Hope, meaning and a future.

How she wanted to confront him. To hit him, to kick out at him, to shout and scream.

'It's not fair. It's not fucking fair,' she said instead, but only to the white tiled walls of the bathroom.

*

Kate was peeling carrots when Jo turned up in the kitchen. Astonishingly, she appeared neat and fresh, with only a slight hint of lilac shadow beneath her clear eyes.

'Morning, Kate,' Jo said, feeling sheepish. 'I'm sorry for waking up so late. I hope I haven't disrupted any plans. I woke up in the night, as you do, and then I couldn't get back off.' She was gabbling, she knew, sounding lame. 'Then I couldn't wake up when I was supposed to . . .'

Kate turned away from the huge piles of denuded vegetables and smiled, but it seemed thin. 'No worries, that's what Sunday mornings are for, isn't it? Unless you have dogs and horses to feed at dawn, of course. Cup of tea?'

Aware of her threshing stomach, Jo pulled out a chair and sat down. Alcohol or anxiety? Dodgy fish or fucking anger? Her belly was churning like a thirty-degree wash and she wondered how she'd manage a full Sunday lunch with all the trimmings in a couple of hours.

The smell of meat juices hit her nostrils again. They'd had 'roasts' at St Luke's. Lamb, apparently, thin slices of grey meat with mint sauce and cabbage, the stench of which knocked her sick, even when she and her housemates were *lining up* along 'long corridor'. Clutching starched napkins, they'd file down to the dining hall to enjoy the delicacy. It bore no comparison to Moor End. Not a Sunday went by without a succulent and glistening roast: beef, pork or lamb, and of course the mandatory Yorkshire puddings as a starter. Kate had long ago learned Joyce's secret batter recipe and hers tasted just as good, if not better.

'Free-range eggs from the supermarket if you don't keep hens. It's all to do with preparing the batter early and allowing it to rest for a few hours before baking it. Not rocket science, Jo,' Kate would say, with just the slightest hint of scorn.

Gazing at her friend, Jo wondered if she rose as early as her mother used to, just to make the floury mix. Too much time and effort, in her view. But then maybe life was simpler when one concentrated on the mundane and the unimportant. It didn't leave so much time for contemplation.

'I'll give you a baby, if that's what you want, Jo.'

'Think about it.'

With perfect timing, the door was flung open by Alice, who was sitting high on Tom's shoulders. 'We've been doing a Kylie in the garden,' she giggled, the hairband from her windblown hair almost covering her eyes.

'Spinning around,' Tom muttered, as he crouched to the floor to let his daughter climb off.

Alice ran to Jo and gave her a tight hug. She smelled of clean air and cut grass. 'I've been riding on Daddy's lawnmower,' she said breathlessly. 'But not on my own because I'm not big enough yet. So I sit on Daddy's knee and turn the wheel.'

She pulled away and peered at Jo's face. 'I'm glad you're up at last. Why did you sleep for so long? When I got home from Nadia's, Mummy said I could come in for a snuggle but Daddy wouldn't let me. Can we say hello to the horses? And go for a walk, then the swings? Oh, can we read some more of that story about the elephants too?'

Jo resumed her breathing once Tom left the room. Thinking how much she loved her, she gazed at her goddaughter. She liked her pretty face, her blonde hair and her light blue eyes, but most of all she loved her willingness to bestow warmth and affection without wanting anything in return. She may have looked more like Tom, but she was just like her mum as a little girl. Loving, giving and generous. She didn't hold back. Like Kate, she wore her heart on her sleeve; she was open and sincere.

'Have you any idea how lucky your mummy is to have you?' she laughed, looking towards Kate. But Kate's face was closed. With a small frown marring her smooth forehead, she was concentrating on basting the beef joint, clearly miles away.

18

Barnsley – September 1998

It was early September, the last week of the summer holiday before Jo's departure to Manchester (or 'going over the border' as the Wragg family put it; though she'd already done that in Derbyshire, of course). The weather was unstable, swinging from stifling sunshine to pelting rain at the drop of a hat. To everyone's surprise, Joyce and Stan announced they were going away, just the two of them. Not the usual holiday to Wales, but a jaunt to the Bahamas, of all places. One of Stan's building buddies, Fred, had bought a plot of land on a small island called Great Harbour Quay and was building a luxury motel.

'Dad's persuaded me to go and I'm quite excited. Fred says there'll be non-stop sunshine and rum, white beaches and huge conch shells. Apparently they filmed some of the scenes from a James Bond film there,' Joyce said, her cheeks pink at tea-time.

Stan squeezed his wife's hand. 'My own Honey Ryder,' he commented, bringing looks of disgust from all three of his offspring.

'Fred's escape from taxes, I expect,' Ben commented, quickly changing the subject.

'From the law, more like. Fred likes to call himself an *entrepreneur*, but he's just a capitalist bastard,' Nigel said. (All capitalists were bastards or thieves, as were lawyers and accountants and bankers. Even doctors and teachers weren't exempt from Nigel's newly found *lefty* derision.)

The Wragg children couldn't quite believe their mum and dad were actually going on a foreign holiday, let alone picture Joyce in a bikini (which she had duly bought from Cole Brothers and packed in tissue paper – 'You never know, Jo, it could crease'), but Nigel returned from Manchester airport without them, so it had to be true. At that point Ben rang round all his friends (as only Ben could) and organised a party for the weekend, the official excuse, much to Jo's annoyance, being a 'leaving do' for her.

It rained all Saturday and Jo spent most of the day worrying that Joyce's pristine carpets would get muddied with footprints, but as evening came, her thoughts turned more specific. It felt as though Ben had invited pretty much everyone in the pub. Suppose anything kicked off? The house was bound to get wrecked. And what about their valuables? Stan and Joyce weren't ones for decorative indulgences like Hilary's furs and gold jewellery, but all the white goods in the kitchen were fairly new, as were the record player and tape deck.

If Kate had been there for moral support, it wouldn't be so bad, but she had been torn away from Barnsley and her quest to catch Tom Heath. Much to Stan's relief (he'd let her loose on invoices; 'a mathematician, she isn't'), she was away for two weeks, travelling by yacht to Tuscany with her parents.

The rain stopped before the party started, thank God, though Jo still worried about the gaping front door.

'Should I just put a sign on the door saying, "Brand-new microwave and Magimix available, help yourself", Ben?' she asked.

His nose crinkled. 'Magimix?' Then, lifting his hand in greeting as more guests arrived, 'Relax, Jo, have fun!' He sloshed fluorescent cider into a plastic cup and handed it to her. 'Drink, then drink more. After all, this is for you!'

'A leaving do for me? Hm. With half of the village. Gosh, you shouldn't have.' She snorted. 'You really shouldn't.'

Ben laughed. 'Yup, I should. You'll be at uni next week. No more tea and biscuits. Just alcohol and the cheapest you can find. Consider tonight as an induction.'

Jo stared at the sparkling orange liquid. Ben had bought beer and cider because it was less expensive than wine. She didn't really like either; she'd enjoyed the variety of sweet liqueurs smuggled in by a day-girl at school, and could tolerate a Babycham with Lynn or Kate in the pub (real champagne when one was with Hilary, of course), but she supposed he was right. University would be a whole new thing she still hadn't got her head around, but alcohol would undoubtedly be part of it. She took a large slug and grimaced as Ben watched with a grin.

He pulled a sympathetic face. 'Add lime, maybe?'

So Jo added lime cordial, which wasn't so bad after the third or fourth glass.

Lynn from next door arrived eventually (she'd been delivering yet another calf; she was very matter-of-fact about mating and birth, both human and animal). Pleased she had come, Jo gave her a tight hug. She loved her no-nonsense approach to life (if anything *kicked off*, Lynn would be fearless). What Jo didn't understand was Lynn's meek acceptance of her father's edict to stay at the farm when she was exceptionally bright. As Hilary always put it to her, 'You're clever, Jo. You'll go far. Never accept second best.'

'No Kate?' Lynn asked over the bass beat, and when Jo shook

her head, 'Thank God for that! We can actually talk about something other than her. Maybe even have some fun.'

She pulled Jo to the middle of the room, her hands already aloft, her body sexy and swaying. 'Let's dance! Show the boys our moves!'

The music thumped loudly and Jo found herself copying Lynn. ('See? You're not a bad mover after all, Jo.') Life was actually quite funny. She took frequent drags from Nigel's roll-up ('take it easy, Jo, it isn't just tobacco'); she grinned at Ben's stupid uni friends and belly-laughed at their jokes. She threw off her shoes and danced more. Occasionally she scanned the room for the Heath brothers and by the time they appeared she found she rather liked the taste of *lider* (as she and Lynn had named it).

Weirdly relieved he'd arrived, she kept Tom Heath in her sights. His gaze followed her, but she ignored him as usual, basking in the attention and savouring the power of rejection. Her skirt had hitched higher and the spaghetti straps of her top fell over her shoulders, but she left them. She knew that whenever she turned, he'd be there at the far side of the room, his tight t-shirt white against his tanned muscled arms, his blue eyes on her, watching her laugh, watching her move, wanting her. But as the evening wore on, she began to notice how most of the women in the room migrated towards him and his brothers.

Ready white smiles, flirtatious flicking of hair, a little finger between teeth, tinkling laughter, she observed. All the things she hated about stupid superficial girls. Ben's university girlfriends did it too; surely they should know better?

And suddenly, it seemed, Tom's attention was no longer on her.

The chatter filtered through the musty sweet air, loud in Jo's ears above the loop of the party playlist. 'Come on, Davy, you must work out. Look at those biceps.' 'What, not one of you brothers are dating? Are the girls in Barnsley blind?' 'Jimmy-from-a-rock-band. I like it.' 'Stockings, of course. And no panties.' And then,

'So, Tom gorgeous Heath, do you fancy going outside for a bit of fresh air?'

Jo didn't care; she couldn't stand the guy, so what did it matter? The whole bunch of sycophants were welcome to him, Kate was welcome to him. Besides, there were plenty of admiring glances from Ben's friends. From Nigel's too, which was pretty disgusting, the old pervs. And if the uni girls could flirt with random boys, so could she, she'd show him.

Thinking of tinkling laughter, flirtatious flicking and sexy fingers, Jo strode into the kitchen and sloshed cider with a vodka top into her plastic cup (the pervs had brought spirits, reinforcing their perviness, though Lynn didn't seem to mind; she was sitting on top of one, ready to practise her *riding*, no doubt).

'To stupid boys and lider!' Jo toasted herself, before turning to her mission.

But her exit from the kitchen was blocked. He was there, leaning in the doorway, his arms folded, his blue gaze on her.

Ha! she thought, so pleased and cheered that she grasped Tom by the hand and pulled him behind her. Out of the kitchen, pushing past the smoky glut of party people, through the lounge to the landing, up the stairs and into her wallpapered bedroom. Without saying a word.

Inhaling a musky sandalwood aroma, Jo woke to the familiar sound of the cockerel from the farm. Her throat dry and temples throbbing, she peeled back her eyelids to daylight.

'Morning.'

What the . . . ?

His head propped against his hand, Tom Heath was gazing, his eyes boring into hers. Naked and warm, his leg was slung over her thigh, his penis erect.

Reaching out a hand, he stroked a lock of hair from her cheek.

'Morning,' he said again. His gaze was so intense, she struggled to return it. Then he smiled a slow smile. 'Are we going steady, then?' he asked.

There was a beat, a pulse of astonishment, of horror. Winded and surprised, she jerked away. Before she could stop them, the words fired out. 'No! You must be joking!'

His face immediately coloured and clouded. 'I see.' Climbing from the bed, he quickly yanked on his jeans.

Breathing heavily, he glared. 'I suppose I'm not fucking good enough for you,' he said. 'Just good for fucking.'

As though it had been stuffed with sand overnight, her head felt heavy. It was difficult to focus, to bring her thoughts up to speed, but the *fucking* and the abandon she did remember. *Oh God.*

Watching him tug the white t-shirt over his tousled hair, she stared for a moment. She wanted to soften her words, to remove the hurt and anger from his eyes somehow, but the panic was still there, that delirium and danger she couldn't quite unravel. Besides, she wanted to go far, didn't she? She was clever and going to university next week; she'd meet *like-minded* people, as Hilary had put it.

Then there was Kate, always Kate.

She pulled up the duvet and turned away.

'You're right,' she muttered. 'You're not good enough for me. You never will be.'

19

Peak District – present day

The weather had cooled since yesterday and Jo felt a chill each time the sun disappeared behind a cloud. She and Alice had said hello to Kate's haughty (in Jo's view) horses, raced to the top of the first field (Jo remembering not to win), and now they were at the compact park in the village where they'd bumped into Alice's best friend, Nadia, and her father. Jo had managed to chat fitfully with the dad for a few minutes, mostly about Kate and her riding awards, but he eventually moved away for a 'guilty fag' and he asked her to keep an eye on the girls as they kicked out their feet on the swings.

Her legs pulled up to her chin and her arms around them, Jo sat on the arid grass and watched the girls fly.

'Think about it.'

Like an order: how ironic.

Jo didn't do commands, sometimes even from herself. Her instinct was to do the very opposite, a perverse wilfulness she couldn't stop at times. Like at her 'leaving do' at Moor End all those years ago.

Tapping her forehead on her knees, she scrunched her eyes and sighed at the vivid recollection. In the bedroom she'd let go of Tom's hand. Oh hell, what had she done? Then his lips were crushing hers and instead of pushing him away, she wanted to suck him in. She reached her arms around his neck and pinned her body against his, kissing and kissing and lost.

He'd abruptly pulled away. Disappointment swamped her. Oh no, was that it? Did she do something wrong? And then, with a jolt of dread, was he going to leave with a satisfied smirk and tell his mates about her eagerness, her obvious lust?

But he took a step back, tugged at his t-shirt and moved on to his jeans. Catching her breath, she just stared at his face. He was naked. He was naked! His gaze burning hers, he didn't move. Instead he stood stock still in all his glory. What now? He was waiting. Yes, he was waiting.

Oh God, she couldn't look, she couldn't touch, but with a will of their own, her fingers brushed the tight muscles in his cheek, then they moved to his broad shoulders and the hollows of his neck. Her eyes following, they travelled down the grooves of his toned chest, sweeping down to his belly button. She stopped at the tapering hair. Oh God.

Tales of broken hymens and blood, discomfort, even pain, flittered through her head, but the desire to have *that* invade her body was overwhelming – terrifying, absolutely, but uncontrollable too.

Yes, he was waiting. She could just walk away. But she knew without doubt that she wouldn't.

In the weeks following, Jo's obstinate mind thought of little else, especially before sleep. She didn't want to think about it, but she did. Constantly. She had given in to the very things that she feared – sexual abandon and raw emotion, loss of control. With

Tom Heath of all people! She was deeply embarrassed, she felt ashamed. She fervently wished she could turn back the clock or obliterate the memory of that boy, his taut body and the things he'd done to her with his lips, his fingers, his tongue and then finally his cock. *Fucking*, as he had called it. And that exquisite moment of release, the sumptuous free fall she had never expected.

It took a very long time, but she eventually put the memory in a wooden box, dug a ten-foot hole and buried it beneath layers of happiness with Richard. Yet here she was, nearly twenty years on, the recollection still fresh, like a sprinkling of topsoil.

The shadows of Alice and her friend fell like a cloud. Jo lifted her head. 'Hey, girls. Having fun?'

Little Nadia giggled and turned her huge eyes towards the ice-cream van. A woman with long ginger hair was in the queue. She looked familiar.

Alice's voice brought her back. 'Who won the race, Jo?' she asked, tittering too.

Jo laughed. It was clearly a conspiracy worked out on the swings, but cleverly done. 'I'll get into trouble with your mum. So not a word and eat every last bit of your lunch!'

Taking each girl by the hand, she headed towards Mr Whippy and his music.

Their wellies smacking the pavement, Jo and Alice strolled through the muffled village towards home. Past the thirteenth-century church, the canopied post office and greengrocer's, the farm butcher's, the newsagent and deli. Though she tried not to, with each shop window they passed, Jo glanced at the reflection of a woman with a child. But at least she felt brighter now, awake and refreshed despite her excavation of the past.

Taking in her surroundings, she ambled along the brook path which led to the farm. Set between two shallow hills in the distance, it was undoubtedly a picture-book scene. Then the sun abruptly disappeared, leaving a dank faunal smell in the air, an unsettling aroma she couldn't quite place. That or the sudden breeze made her shudder and she held Alice's hand more tightly.

Eventually stopping, Alice turned, her eyes lit by the sparkling stream. 'Look, here's the stepping stones, Jo. Daddy says it's shallow here. Can I tiptoe on them?' she asked.

Jo halted too. Feeling a catch in her chest, she gazed at the water surrounding the coppery stones and tried to snatch at a memory, but it drifted away like the pappus of a dandelion.

Shrugging off the discomfort, she went back to Alice's eager face. 'Well, we're wearing wellies. It would be a shame not to paddle a little,' she replied with a smile. 'Come on, I'll hold your hand.'

Stepping on to a large mossy stone, Jo held out her arms towards Alice. Almost like a dizzy spell, she was suddenly surrounded by more hovering white tufts. But when she shook her head and looked again, they'd gone.

Alice's gaze was concerned, so Jo swallowed and smiled reassuringly. 'Paddle away, young lady. But don't let go of me.'

Alice laughed as she waded upstream. 'Daddy thinks this is fun but Mummy says no.'

'Oops! Then we'd better not tell.'

Shining through Alice's fine hair, the sun had made a comeback, so they splashed in the glistening water for a while. Jo smiled and breathed in the special moment. How she loved her time with this perfect little girl. There was a special bond between them, more than just that of godparent and child. She would never be a mother to her, or even a real auntie, but she hoped she was the next best thing. Someone she could turn to for a bit of independent advice if she got into trouble or fell out with her parents, the sort of person Jo had longed for at times in her life. Someone who'd listen dispassionately; someone who wouldn't judge.

'Sometimes you're too quiet,' Hilary used to say from time to time, her head quizzically on one side as she studied her face. 'But you can always talk to me. You know that, don't you, darling?'

'There's nothing to tell! You'd be the first to know,' Jo would reply with a smile. And mostly there wasn't. Only once did she turn to a brother in a rare moment of crisis. It didn't end well, but perhaps not surprising. As teenagers they'd had distant relationships, separated physically and emotionally by the combination of boarding school and their upbringing. Even now her relationship with Nigel was as repressed as ever. She found him to be opinionated and self-absorbed, though it wasn't just that. It was his hypocrisy too. He pretended to be 'right-on', socially aware and concerned for people, but he only really cared for himself.

But at least there was Ben. 'Little ears and little eyes, those two,' their grandma always said when they were small and inseparable. With her cropped hair and skinny frame, people assumed they were twins. It didn't bother her. She was an honorary boy, happy to share toys and baths and friends. Eyes and Ears were inseparable until boarding school ripped them apart. But in the holidays they were back to where they'd been twelve weeks previously – rough hugs and tickling, Chinese burns and teasing; away in the Yorkshire fields and farms all day until they returned home for tea, muddy, tired and ravenous. Since Richard's death they had rekindled that intimacy.

Thank God for Ben, Jo regularly thought at the rare gatherings at Moor End. The family congregated at Christmas and the conversation over dinner would inevitably gravitate to schooldays. By the time Joyce brought out the brandy decanter (with a face of pained guilt), Jo would sigh as Nigel held forth his views about his *stifling* education and blaming their dad for it.

Though he hadn't last Christmas, had he? He'd looked strangely at Jo and announced he was taking a sabbatical, travelling to Greece to *'work things out'*.

Thank-God-for-Ben always sat on the fence and kept his own counsel. He'd smile at Jo and shrug easily. But even he never bothered to ask what her views were. They seemed to think a girl's boarding school was an easy option. Perhaps they were right. There hadn't been any beatings or physical abuse, but she had no doubt it had affected her life.

For good or for bad, she hadn't yet decided.

20

Situated at the back of the farmhouse, the dining room didn't get as much light or warmth as the other rooms and Jo felt a strange shudder like she had at the brook. Foreboding, she decided, anticipation of peril, which was all pretty silly when she'd just been served perfectly risen Yorkshire puddings at Sunday lunch with close friends.

Smiling at Alice opposite, she was surprised how hungry she felt despite the renewed cycle of froth in her belly. It had started when Tom entered the room, the sweet smell of shampoo or shower gel in his wake.

He sat at the head of the table next to his daughter. 'You look happy and windswept, Alice,' he said, gently stroking the hair from her eyes with soft fingers. 'Did you enjoy your walk, love? Have you washed your hands?'

Jo studied the oil painting of a hunt above Alice's head, searching for the fox as she tried to counter the spread of burning heat through her whole bloody body. She hoped she looked normal, whatever normal had been before her excavation of the past. She had hated the flashbacks in the first few weeks at university. They had invaded quiet moments, so she'd done her best to avoid them, replacing solitude with partying, drinking, even studying occasionally, but still the memories came before sleep, excruciating, insidious and pleasurable.

They had already done it once, then fallen asleep, exhausted, replete. But Tom woke her later, kissing and kissing until she responded. 'No more,' she said in the early hours, desperate to sleep. 'No more.' But still he stroked, kissed and licked. Gentle and firm, soft and unyielding, persistent and regular. More and more until she cried out, 'Now. Please, Tom, right now.'

The cure had seemed obvious at the time: replace unwelcome thoughts and desires by new ones. So she had slept around with anyone she found attractive during the first term in Manchester. Unless she was particularly drunk, the whole experience had felt like an out-of-body experiment which she was marking from a distance, and try as she might, it never remotely matched that abhorrent and ardent coupling at the end of the summer. It was, as she once wrote when making up the shortfall of *agony* letters for the uni newspaper, 'The fuck by which all others would be judged.'

'Jo?'

Tom's voice jolted her back to the present.

'Sorry?'

'Would you like red?'

'No, not for me, thanks.' She put her palm over the wine glass. Then smiling at Alice and trying for *normal*, 'The offal police have been and given my liver a caution.' She turned to Kate. 'The Yorkshire puds are as delicious as ever, Kate. Thanks for making such an effort.'

'No problem. The same effort I make every Sunday,' she replied, reaching for the wine and topping up her glass.

Silence for a moment, then Tom cleared his throat. 'An effort Alice and I appreciate, Kate.'

Feeling the frosty tension, Jo jumped in quickly. 'So, Alice,' she said, 'your mummy was telling me about naughty Kieran and the party yesterday. I need the whole tale! Start at the beginning and tell me everything . . .'

'Well,' Alice began, putting down her cutlery. Taking a deep breath, she launched into an impressively dramatic account of the hair-pulling incident (with demonstrations), followed by several other Kieran misdemeanour stories from the last week alone.

'What a fantastic little storyteller you are, Alice. You should be on the television! Come on, tell us another, spill the beans. Is it always Kieran, or are some of the other boys naughty too?'

Clearly enjoying the audience, Alice's cheeks were pink with pleasure. It reminded Jo of Kate again, her face flushed and bursting with delight whenever she came out of Cecil's room.

A notion took her breath. Was I jealous? she asked herself. Did I envy her prettiness, her family, her mother, her home? Did I crave all that attention? Did I want to be special? Have I spent all my life wanting something that's not mine?

Kate cleared the plates and left the room. Tom went after her, returning with a huge joint of beef which was followed by large platters of potatoes and parsnips and a variety of green veg, coloured by the carrots. Jo sat and watched, wondering how she would manage to eat more. Kate had served her four huge Yorkshire puddings and, as delicious as they were, they lay bloated in her stomach.

Kate finally returned with oval dinner plates, but instead of handing them out as usual, she stood at the end of the table, doling out the food just like the *Head of Table* prefect had served it at school.

'Just a small portion for me,' Jo said, but still Kate dished out vast quantities of food on the plate, far more than she could possibly eat.

Aware of Tom's frown and Kate's steady consumption of wine, she tried for conversation as she ate. She asked Kate about Clare and Annabelle, Hilary and Harold, receiving monosyllables in reply. She mentioned the meeting with Nadia and her dad at the park. Then, almost talking to herself, she resorted to the haughty horses, praising them for the show trophies and rosettes displayed in a glass cabinet on the wall.

Watching her daughter eat for a few moments, Kate interrupted, abruptly alert. 'I hope you haven't been snacking, Alice.' She looked from Tom to Jo. 'And that you haven't been encouraging it . . . either of you.' Then she pushed her half-finished plate away, stepped towards the sideboard and snapped open another wine.

Though Jo felt Tom's steady gaze from time to time, she avoided looking at him. Her face, she trusted, was closed. She was angry at both him and Kate for being so quiet in the presence of their small daughter, for leaving it to her to make forced polite conversation and she wanted to leave, to drive back to the refuge of her flat. But she couldn't simply stand up and say, 'I've had enough! I'm going home.' So instead she stared at the hunt painting (which, she now noticed, was missing the glass) and watched Kate drink steadily until the bottle was empty.

Kate suddenly brightened, breaking the silence. 'I think we need another Shiraz, don't we, Jo.'

'You're the only one who's drinking, Kate,' Jo replied quietly, trying to keep the irritation from her voice. She disliked it when Kate tried to include her in small deceptions. She'd done it often enough over the years and on most occasions she had been willing to oblige, but not today.

'I've only had a couple of glasses,' she replied, her voice petulant and slightly slurred. She paused for a moment and then continued, her voice shrill and surprising. 'Anyway, Jo, what's your problem? Have you become a saint overnight? I can't recall telling *you* how much to drink in your own home.'

'I think you've had enough, actually,' Jo replied, staring at Kate's face and seeing a stranger.

'Oh, *do* you? Well, I think you should leave my house if you don't like it. *Actually*,' Kate said, waving her arms towards the door.

Tom stood then. 'Come on, Kate. Alice is here with us . . .'

The shock of her friend's demeanour, let alone her words, felt like a sharp slap. But after a moment, Jo realised it was the excuse she'd been waiting for.

She swivelled to Alice. Tom was standing behind her, his hands on her small shoulders, but looking at Kate. 'Kate, Alice is here. Let's just settle down.' Then to Jo. 'Please ignore us, Jo. We're just a little hungover. Of course we don't want you to—'

But Jo had already scraped back her chair. 'It's fine, Tom. I think it's about time for me to go anyway.' She reached over for Alice's hand. 'If I don't wash my socks, they won't be dry for tomorrow. And we can't have smelly socks, can we, Alice? Will you come and help me pack? You might have to hold your nose, though.'

Alice looked up nervously towards her mother for permission, but Kate had already turned away. She was busy at the open sideboard, examining the labels on the bottles inside.

Tom cleared his throat. 'Is there anything I can do to help, Jo?'

She shook her head. 'No, Tom,' she said firmly, her eyes meeting his. 'Thank you for your offer but there's absolutely nothing you can do to help.'

21

St Luke's

The midnight feasts at St Luke's *were* fun: the mix of trepidation and adventure was thrilling, glorious – especially when treats from the girls' tuck boxes (duly padlocked in the white library cupboard until *tuck time*) were supplemented by crumbled or sticky titbits stolen from the dining room at tea.

Though exceedingly hungry much of the time, lining up in anticipation for meals didn't provide much succour for Jo. Breakfast was bearable because one could smother one's (almost wet) toast with Marmite (not provided by school, but thankfully something Joyce *did* send her in the post), but lunch and dinner excelled for their dreadfulness, with the same menu each day, or so it seemed. Limp, thinly sliced cuts of unidentifiable meat in gloopy gravy, or sausages bubbling from their intestine-like skins; mashed potatoes with lumps (acne scabs dropped from the face of a young chef, apparently) and the daily dose of translucent cabbage. The desserts weren't much better. It wasn't unknown for the rice pudding and the tinned peaches to be served with the addition of delirious ants; the Spotted Dick (more pimples, poor man) and Matron's Leg (if only) were rock hard, the custard which might have made them more palatable was cold and clotted. Occasionally the girls were 'treated' to thin cream. Jo found this quite pleasurable, not to eat, but to whip into a disgusting lump of fat (some brave soul declared it tasted just like margarine).

Still, it wasn't all bad; on a good day the increased volume of girls' clatter and chatter was a clue that 'leather' was on the menu – a hard crust of eggs, flour and milk topped with golden syrup (a prelude to Kate's early attempts at Yorkshire puddings). Tea-time food was OK too – not a lot could go wrong with a jam sandwich (upgraded to potted meat once a week). Ironically (as a lot of the school rules were), taking food out of the dining hall was strictly forbidden, so it was exhilarating to file past Head Girl trying to look nonchalant with currant biscuits (or even an iced bun on a Friday) rolled up in one's white and stiff napkin.

The midnight feasts would have been better at the beginning of term when everyone's tuck boxes were full, but it took some of the 'new girls' weeks to stop crying at night, so they were invariably later. Although tuck time was only once a day after tea, Jo's old biscuit tin was empty by then (hence the need for sticky buns *à la* napkin). Her mum wasn't one for spoiling or allowing too many sweets, preferring to fill her tuck box with home-made flapjack and Dundee cake (there was some *goodness* in them and 'because oats and fruitcake *keep*'). Kate's, on the other hand, was supplemented each week by the parcels of confectionary and chocolate treats sent by her mother, so her tin was always full.

Perhaps the weekly packages had been a forerunner to Jo's pash, but she fell for Hilary even before her eloquent tones treacled out of her red painted lips. When she climbed out of the *Roller* to collect Kate at half-term, Jo had simply ogled, finally managing to close her mouth when the glorious woman addressed her. 'You must be Jo, Kate's lovely new friend. What a tiny darling you are!'

Tall, beautiful and exotic, Hilary was always surrounded by an aura of heavy perfume. Carrying her cigarette in a long tortoise-shell holder, she wore pale fur, even in summer. She was friendly and tactile and *fun*, pulling silly faces behind Matron's back and calling Miss Smyth 'The Commandant'.

Jo loved Joyce, of course, yet she couldn't help but imagine what life would be like with Hilary as a mum. A delicious and permanent dream, she mused, picturing the scene from one of the books she'd devoured in the library. There'd be a constant stream of delicate clothes and pretty shoes, they'd go to the ballet and the theatre, they'd holiday in Corfu (who'd have thought this would happen in thirty years), and loll in the sun wearing wide floppy hats, perhaps play a little tennis and eat triangular sandwiches (crusts removed, but of course).

I'll be just like Hilary when I grow up, she determined to her-self. Rich and graceful with adorable clothes. And of course be driven in a silver Rolls-Royce. Jo ignored the fact that Kate's father was really quite old. After all, he didn't *appear* to be much older than her dad. And besides, it all added to the romance of Hilary's frequent advice. 'Do fall in love. Have clinches and passion. But remember, girls, one must marry well!'

During that first year at St Luke's, Jo was often invited to Kate's house in the school holidays and she adored it, praying that time would slow down before having to return to the 'boredom of Barnsley', as she put it (though only in her head). Kate's family lived in a small stone country manor set in a couple of acres of land in Leicestershire. The house was furnished with drapes of velvet and chintz, polished antique furniture, old portraits with gold frames and eyes that followed. There were nooks and crannies and places to hide which smelt of warm and mysterious spice. A mahogany grand piano stood in the corner of the sitting room; Jo learned to play chopsticks with her eyes closed within half an hour.

'Is there anything you can't do, Jo? You are so clever,' Hilary would say, clapping her hands. 'Isn't she, Kate?'

Kate and her sisters rode. So did Jo, but there was a world of difference between owning one's own sleek and handsome pony and all the kit, to squelching to the farm wearing her brother's old wellies and mucking out the stables with Lynn, before having a trot around a muddy field on a grumpy old mare.

'Have these, Jo, darling. They're too small for Kate,' Hilary said on her first visit to Barton in the Beans. They were real leather riding boots, black, shiny and pristine, still in the box.

She pictured her mum's face, the slight shake of her head. 'Thank you for offering, but I couldn't possibly—'

'Of course you can, darling! And I think we have a spare hat. But that's old, so your mother won't mind.'

So the girls spent most of their days in Barton in the Beans (which was as perfect and quaint as it sounded), riding around the small leafy villages and countryside, tethering the horses outside a dusty shop to buy crisps and a can of fizzy drink, eventually arriving home and changing for tea – generally thin slivers of smoked salmon on toast, topped with a sprinkling of crushed pepper.

'Oh my gosh, this tastes wonderful,' Jo declared, never having eaten it before and not quite believing Kate when she said it was raw fish.

Kate and her sisters laughed. 'It's all Mummy can cook; you get pretty sick of it after a while.'

She knew she would eventually have to ask Kate back to her home in *boring Barnsley*. She procrastinated for as long as she could, dreading what Kate would make of Moor End (which sounded far more romantic and Brontësque than it was). Her home was pretty big and had a field as a garden, but it was plain and contemporary with functional furniture and appliances. Even worse, it had been built by Stan, so there wasn't even an excuse for its lack of mystery and charm. Though still donning clothes from the Iron Age (Ben's words), Stan and Joyce were surprisingly progressive with any new-fangled gadget. A dishwasher, food mixer and tumble dryer, years before anyone else in their village. But no mahogany grand piano, heavy drapes brushing the carpet or oil paintings of ancient *rellies*.

What would she and Kate *do*? There was plenty of countryside to be had, but no elegant ponies nor curious corner shops. As Jo was a public-school outcast there would be no parties to attend and definitely no occasions to don pretty frocks. She knew her mum would make an effort with her appearance, wear a dab of lipstick, have her hair set and wear a new cardigan, but there would be no fur and frivolity from Joyce, no dressing up in her beautiful clothes.

Kate eventually arrived at the Wraggs' house with two suitcases and a side of smoked salmon. To Jo's astonishment, she immediately blended in. Like a surrogate child, she spent hours on a chrome bar stool at the kitchen island watching Joyce bake bread, make soup (from a chicken carcass, tripe and a pig's trotter – disgusting) and rich casseroles (tripe again), listening intently to household lore Joyce had learned at her own mother's apron strings. They were tips that Jo eventually wished she had listened to instead of reading yet another trashy romance in her bedroom. Years later, if she needed to remove a grass stain from her favourite pair of shorts, or write a 'Top Tips for a Perfect Quiche Lorraine' article, it was Kate she would telephone. *Sweet Savage Love* and *Love's Tender Mercy* were all very well at nine and ten years of age, but the heady excitement of reading about a passionate clinch between a fiery heroine and a chiselled misunderstood hero did nothing to assist the removal of mould from the shower curtain, red wine from a cream carpet nor the death of a husband at just thirty-six.

Part Two

Part Two

22

Manchester – ten years ago

Jo Wragg had drawn the short straw at the office again; she'd been allocated another long 'corporate crime' trial.

'Come on. I did the last one,' she'd pleaded with the deputy editor. 'We're only a small freebie paper. Does anyone really care about another chief executive caught fiddling the books?'

'I care,' her boss had dryly replied. 'How was white-collar crime once defined? One "committed by a person of respectability and high social status" or the like. Just up your street, I should think.'

It was what the deputy always said. She didn't bother to hide her distaste of Jo's *paid-for* education combined with her first-class degree. Jo wished she'd never been honest about the public school bit, but it was too late now.

The trial was in the old criminal courts at Minshull Street. Jo dreaded the thought of a month of complex legal argument over financial records, spreadsheets and data, but she was cheered by her surroundings. A modern functional complex was being built on the other side of town, but she liked the Grade II listed building, the red brick and steeply pitched slate roof exterior, which was nicely complemented by dusty floors and dark polished wood, a dank smell and brooding Gothic atmosphere inside. She enjoyed sitting on an ornate wooden bench in the high gallery, watching the defendant come up from the cells to the dock like a character from a Dickens novel. But this was a fraud trial, 'business' crime, so the defendant didn't appear from down below, but arrived in court every morning with a plastic wife on his arm, looking as though he didn't have a care in the world.

Jo endured a few days of double-dutch sheer boredom. She gazed at the suited backs of the solicitor for the Crown and the defendant and the two barristers' wigs, picturing what they might look like from the vantage point of the aquiline-nosed judge. Then, finding there was sweet nothing of interest to report, she allowed her timekeeping to slip just a little. She figured that a few lie-ins and late lunches with her new boyfriend were only fair in the circumstances, recompense for the short straw landing in her rum and coke far more than was fair.

Two weeks in and, mid-morning, she tiptoed up the rear stairs to the balcony, but the door was locked. Oh shit! She couldn't creep in and hide there as usual. Having no alternative, she dashed back to the ground floor. Taking a deep breath, she pushed the oak door (marked 'silence in court') and entered the muffled chamber. Her eyes scanned *somewhere* to sit. Shit, nowhere! So she slipped into the end of the nearest pew. Unfortunately, *silent* she wasn't, eminently clear from the disapproving eye of the court clerk. Apart from the loud batter of her heart, the door had noisily clanged and the people on the bench were loath to shift up. (They had sighed audibly and had rustled their papers. Not very sporting at all.)

Thrown back to punishments for *bad behaviour* at St Luke's, she stayed rigidly in her place and (almost) held her breath. She laughed inwardly at her own ridiculous behaviour. What was the stony-faced clerk going to do? Send her to the dock and make her face the wall for the rest of the day? Or perhaps behead her (that's how it had felt when one was *called out* at St Luke's). Yet even when the judge rose and adjourned for lunch, she stayed glued to her seat. Though her head was down to her notes, she felt the reprimand coming. It came in the form of a suited man. Dark hair with glasses, he strangely reminded her of Ben.

Instead of shouting, he grinned. 'Heads up,' he said. 'You might want to be here first thing tomorrow. The barristers must have a golf date.' His smile broadened. 'Or maybe tennis. They've agreed facts, saving days of legal argument. There's only closing submissions.' He nodded at the jury, still solemnly filing out. 'Then those poor sods have to reach a verdict.'

So pleased to be given a reprieve, Jo duly arrived early in Court Two the next day. Far too promptly, as it happened, so she settled herself on the hard bench in the empty chamber, intending to find out if she had correctly identified the murderer (first chapter, usually, she read so many) in the whodunnit she'd been devouring that week. But her deduction was interrupted by a 'shit!' from the guy who had granted her a stay of execution yesterday. He was, she now realised from the back of his head, the solicitor for the defendant, and he was scooping scattered paperwork from the grimy floor.

He looked up and grinned. He wasn't wearing glasses today, so she noticed his eyes, velvet and dark. 'The mysterious reporter. Hello again! How are you enjoying it?' he asked.

Looking to the empty jury box, she wondered if it would be very rude to tell a lawyer what she really thought of the cumbersome legal process, but he laughed.

'Not the trial, your book! *Death in High Places*. Looks a good read. Wish I could do the same. The trial is mind-numbingly boring, isn't it? Hopefully we'll get the verdict today. What do you think, guilty or not guilty?'

Surprised by his direct and friendly approach, she didn't have time to feel embarrassed or shy, but answered all his questions with humour, bantering about the guilt or otherwise of the accused in the novel, if not the dock.

'Tell you what,' the solicitor whispered as the courtroom started to fill up, 'if it's a not-guilty verdict, I'll pay for dinner. If it's guilty, then you pay. Deal?' He turned, then looked back. 'By the way, my name's Richard.'

23

Manchester – present day

Inhaling a whiff of something rotten (carrots probably – even after all this time, she still bought for two), Jo stared at her laptop and sighed. She was weary of writing articles with the same old formulas and meaningless phrases, with only a feeble attempt at changing the angle. But then again, there were only so many sides to be had. The menopause sounded horrendous whichever way you put it, birth was done to death (even with the current proclivity of having the whole family witness the pain and the cursing – *Why, oh why?*), dying was pretty much dead and sex ... well, Jo could hardly remember, or so she said to herself. She didn't want to think about that *excavation* or any other part of the *weekend horribilis* (Ben's knack of perfectly describing people and events in two words had continued); it was just too disturbing, uncomfortable, embarrassing. And the rest.

'How was the weekend with the Midas family?' he had texted during the week.

'Bloody horrible,' she'd quickly typed back. Then, picturing Kate slumped at the wine-bar table: 'Awful, really dreadful, in fact. The Golden Couple were far from golden.'

'You're joking, right?'

'No! Kate was blind drunk and I stared, open-mouthed. Tell you more when you next grace my door.'

'*Weekend horribilis*, eh? Intrigued to hear the rest, so see you very soon!'

Laying her cheek on the kitchen table, she now noticed the thick layer of dust. Lit up by the sun streaming through the wooden slats of the blinds, there were particles on the bookcase, the photographs, the lamp, Ben's old record player (he had always said vinyl would make a comeback, clever boy), on pretty much everything.

'Ashes to ashes,' she muttered, then she stood to pick up a photograph of her and Richard duly grinning on a beach in Majorca. What had Kate said before the *weekend horribilis* went pear-shaped? 'Dark and a *bit* hairy; designer stubble and all that.' Yup, pretty accurate. She studied it for a moment before wiping away the fine powder with the tip of her finger. Who on earth had taken it? Which holidaymaker had brushed through their lives that morning, a day when they'd been blissfully unaware of how transient happiness could be?

Surveying the four walls of her lounge-cum-dining area, she almost smiled. *Elephant's breath*, the emulsion was called. Richard had laughed and said 'no way, no time' when she lugged two tins of it home, but he miraculously took a day off work and they painted the room, Jo starting at one end and he the other, each quietly competing to reach the middle first. Or so she had thought. Save for the friendly rivalry he'd always had with his best mate Noah, Richard had never appeared to be driven about anything, but he always got what he wanted in an easy and charming way, so there must have been zeal underneath, surely? That's why his death had been such a shock; he just wasn't the type to let the grim reaper have his way.

Turning the photograph at an angle, she exhaled to stop the stupid tears. Alone in a flat that definitely needed a clean. Lonely, pathetic and horribly old. But she was just being silly, she knew that.

'Don't be ridiculous. You're as young as you feel, as they say,' Ben had laughed only last week.

'I don't *feel* anything, Ben,' she had wanted to reply. 'That's the problem. I should be a busy mum of two, worrying about nappies and meals, lunch boxes and school runs with my husband, rather than just existing as a sad widow.'

But she hadn't said it. It sounded feeble, needy, self-pitying and worryingly like Nigel.

The thought of her oldest brother made her turn to the post-cards. The bundle was still there by the sofa, growing weekly. She barely read them, which she knew was awful when he made such an effort, but his writing was tiny and he crammed every spare inch with his spidery scrawl. It felt odd too; strange that Nigel should be in touch, and so frequently, by postcard from the Greek Isles when they'd rarely communicated at home. She suspected it was his revenge for her unwillingness to listen to him and his constant bloody angst face to face or on the telephone. Now he could have his say, moan at her by postcard without interruption or excuses, and there was little she could do about it. Except throw them in the bin, and even she felt that would be too harsh.

Shrugging away the thought of Nigel, she stepped to the window. 'Sorry, Rich. I can't resist,' she said out loud.

She yanked up the venetian blind. Reminding her of Tinker Bell, the specks of dust sparkled in the air like a wish. Similar to parking on her street without a permit, it was against the regulations to pull up the slats during working hours. Her rules, of course. But she broke them too regularly – from this window she could see the square of grass and trees at the end of her road. As though lit by a spotlight, the gardens would tempt her from the flat and she'd waste time (far too much) observing suited workers and sleeping tramps, scruffy students and joyous toddlers take in the fresh air and sunshine.

She glanced down to the street. Twin boys were tottering along with their exhausted-looking mother, one in each hand and both crying. The sight jolted her back to Tom's words.

I'll give you a baby. Think about it.

Taking a shuddery breath, she tried to block them out. Like the yearnings, the cravings she'd had for over two empty years. Basic, powerful and impossible to ignore, they were overwhelming desires to be *with child*, to feel all the things her close friends had described – the tenderness of breasts, the movement of the foetus, even the birth itself; the pain, the pleasure, the prize.

The burning sensation pegged her nose again. At times it felt as though everyone had children and talked of nothing else, even at the book-club meetings or in the pub. From conception to birth, the excitement and worry, the ups and the downs. And then parenthood. From birth to playgroup, from there to school. The elation and the tiredness, the fun and the fears, the drudgery and the pride. There had been times she'd wanted to scream, 'I know, I bloody well know! Please just stop!'

She inhaled deeply; she was *not* going to cry.

The venetian blind would only work on one side, stymieing her attempts to yank it down with a metaphorical stamp of her foot. It looked like a lopsided grin. Babies, kids, families. She was fed up, bloody pissed off with her fixed and fond childless smile.

And 'think about it'. It wasn't fair.

It was *not* bloody fair.

24

Manchester – two years ago

It had been at lunchtime in late June when Richard had turned up at the flat unexpectedly. Despite the bowl of exotic fruit and vegetables set in front of her, Jo had struggled all morning to think of a new angle on eating 'five a day', and had finally abandoned writing for which she'd be paid in favour of her latest stab at a novel which would, of course, be an overnight sensation. This novel was dark, gothic, bloody, and surprisingly easy to write as the sun shone through the balcony doors and into the new but compact kitchen of the Manchester city-centre flat she and Richard had bought five years earlier as a temporary home until they found 'just what we're looking for.'

Her previous attempts at commercial writing had been what her agent, Lucien Du Beurre, had called 'women's relationship fiction' and even 'Aga sagas' (Jo inevitably thought of Kate). Jo hated those descriptions, especially as the agent was actually a friend she had briefly dated at university and who, she was sure, hadn't bothered to read further than the first three paragraphs of the manuscripts she sent him on a regular basis ('there wasn't a bloody Aga in sight,' she'd complained to Richard).

But Jo did have some sympathy with Lucien; she was pretty bored with the novels herself. She knew they were fairly well written and polished, but they all had the same differently named central character, a strong but vulnerable woman who was searching for the missing piece of the jigsaw. And of course, as she joked, it was impressive of Lucien to deduce what the missing piece was from the opening page.

So, on that bright Wednesday, Jo wasn't at all pleased to hear the scrape of the key in the flat door when she was on a dark writing run with a scarred hero who didn't give two hoots about jigsaws.

'Richard! What are you doing here? I'm not ovulating, you know,' she called, not bothering to turn. 'I'm busy. Go away!'

Then, because a tiny corner of her mind recollected how absent and stressed Richard had been about work, how it hadn't been that easy for him to disappear from the office for many months of quick baby-shags at inconvenient times, she reluctantly saved the document and turned her head.

'I haven't even left the flat yet, Rich, so there isn't anything to eat for lunch. Except for exotic fruit, which I still need to make me feel guilty. Richard? That is you, isn't it?'

He was sitting on the sofa, his elbows on his knees, his dark fringe falling forwards. 'I don't feel very well, actually,' he said, trying for a smile as he lifted his gaze. 'Everything feels tight and heavy. I think I've caught a bug or flu or something.'

Jo looked at him carefully, trying but not succeeding to hide her irritation. She was busy, she had a deadline for the *Good Housekeeping* article and she needed to wash her hair before meeting some friends for dinner. She hated sickness, and if Richard had a real bug, rather than man flu, she most definitely didn't want it.

She'd been asleep when he left for work that morning, but as she studied him now, she noticed he hadn't bothered to struggle with his contact lenses, that he was wearing the same red striped tie he'd worn all week and that his face seemed pallid beneath his tawny skin. He did look a bit sweaty, but, like her mum always said, *mind over matter* was the thing.

'Come on, Rich, don't be a wuss. Let's walk through the gardens to The Buttery and you can treat me to cheese and pickle on a French stick. I'm sure a little bit of fresh air won't kill you.'

She had said it crisply, she later recalled. With humour, but definitely crisply. But at least she had relented a little. She'd kissed his cheek, then taken his proffered hand as they strolled along the dusty pavement of St John Street, heading towards trees lit yellow by sunshine.

In the immediate aftermath, Jo could only remember her panic and the sound of screaming, which turned out, most uncharacteristically, to be her own. The sight of the baguettes too, laid side by side, spilling out their identical innards on the arid grass.

Richard had simply doubled up and fallen like a proverbial rag doll, a massive heart attack at only thirty-six years of age, dead on arrival at hospital.

25

Manchester – present day

Two weeks had passed by since the *weekend horribilis* and there'd been no word from Kate. Jo was surprised; she didn't think she'd done anything to apologise for, but her friend's silence weighed heavily as she ambled towards the gardens in flip-flops and shorts. (To eat her sandwich, honestly, Rich. Lunch was an exception to *the rule*.)

Her and Kate's spats were few and far between, never lasting more than a few minutes, mainly because Kate couldn't stand it. She hated any bad feeling, wanted life to be rosy and happy, and so she had an incredible ability to forgive and forget. 'Oh, that,' she'd say dismissively if reminded about something unpleasant, 'I'd completely forgotten about it.'

Jo wished she was the same, but she could never quite let go of slights or hurt, even from years back. It wasn't so much that she was unable to forgive, forgetting was the problem. And yet sometimes memories were surprisingly hazy, especially of schooldays.

Sitting on her usual bench, she chewed her panini thoughtfully. The chill of her snap with Kate was there in her chest despite the hot sunshine. Kate usually had a forgiving nature, didn't she? Hilary's influence, no doubt. 'Oh, life's too short to bear grudges! And frown lines on a young lady's forehead are most unattractive,' she would laugh. 'Come on, girls, kissing and making up is the fun part!'

Kate had even been willing to pardon Miranda and her followers to begin with. So long as the future was guaranteed to be bright, she was prepared to forgive the past. But even she had a limit beyond which she wouldn't be pushed.

Jo shook her head. God knows why she was thinking about St Luke's yet again. Leaning forward, she lobbed her tin foil in the bin (duly scoring), then stretched out her legs for a spot of people-watching before returning home to *force out the drivel*.

She was on the point of finally dragging herself away when a couple sat next to her. They were already bickering, as though she wasn't there. A mix-up with text messages, apparently. The woman had waited on one corner, the man on another. Pretty mundane conversation until mention of the wasted hotel cost (which *she* had interestingly paid for, though *he* had brought champagne, *expensive actually*). Jo wanted to turn and ogle at the lovers, but even she thought that would be rude, so instead she closed her eyes to people-*listen*.

'No reply at the flat, so I guessed I'd find you here. You're getting worryingly predictable, Joanna Wragg,' a voice said with a smile.

Jo jerked at the sound. She must have napped (though she would fiercely deny it if challenged). 'Ben! What are you doing here?' she said, sitting up and adjusting her sunglasses.

She hoped there was no evidence of sleep on her person, dribble in particular. (Sleeping in a park! Breach of Wragg etiquette and, even more worryingly, a *middle-aged* type of thing to do.) Still, she was pleased to see her brother's amiable face peering down at her.

Ben turning up when least expected wasn't unusual, but there was always that small clutch of concern in her chest. 'Everything OK?' she asked lightly.

'Absolutely.' He moved to one side. 'I've brought a mate. Aidan, meet my sister, Jo. Jo, this is Aidan.'

A dark-haired man stepped forward and held out his palm. First impressions were tricky as he was wearing dark aviator sunglasses, but he definitely had cheekbones and a lovely white grin.

Wondering what had become of the lovers, Jo stood and took his hand. All Ben's friends looked the same – late twenties, slim and chiselled, the sort of guys she quite fancied in dreamland. She wondered where he found them; they were never in short supply, these facsimiles. Smart professionals usually, with their own homes and sleek open-topped sports cars (northern English weather permitting). For a moment her mind flittered to a conversation about handsome youths on a businessman's books, but she quickly pushed the memory away.

Ben was speaking. 'We came on the spur of the moment. Thought we'd treat my little sis to a night on the town. Are you free or are you free?'

Jo put a finger to her lips. 'Hm, let me think ...' And then, 'Surprisingly, I'm free!'

She laughed, but managed to resist punching the air with her fist. She had been saved from the monotony of another Friday night in the flat with a DVD box set. An old uni friend had invited her round for drinks again, but she'd declined. The woman had three kids and a 'bastard, two-timing, snivelling ex-husband' and Jo increasingly felt like an unwilling and particularly crap counsellor.

Turning to Aidan, she smiled. 'Nice to meet you,' she said, taking a moment to have another look while shielded by her own shades. Not that tall, but taller than her (most men were); designer-messy dark hair and stubble (oh yes); fitted trendy clothes.

Very attractive in a boy-band type of way, in fact. A group of chattering young women walked past. Her long hair flowing behind, one of them turned, clearly taking a second look at the two handsome men.

Jo grinned. 'Not a chance!' she wanted to shout after her.

Climbing out of the taxi, Jo breathed in the culinary smells. Chillies, garlic, ginger and spices, aromatic and honeyed. Her idea had been inspired; she was bloody starving. Gesticulating to the long row of brightly lit eating houses and bars, she turned to Ben and Aidan. 'Which do you fancy the look of? They're all pretty good; I haven't had one bad experience yet.'

They'd strolled from her flat along the length of Deansgate, stopping at several vibrant wine bars (all newly opened, it seemed, though perhaps she hadn't been looking until now), sipping champagne, chatting and laughing, the men bickering about the talent in each bustling room.

'Do you know what I really fancy,' she had suddenly declared, slipping from the bar stool. The boys had looked at her, Ben's eyebrows raised, ready for the surprise revelation. 'A curry,' she'd said. 'Specifically a Rusholme curry.'

'Well, that's a relief. Thought you were going to do a runner with The Beard.'

'The Beard?'

'Yup, nine o'clock. Been gazing at you lustfully for the last twenty minutes.'

Jo had laughed. 'I know they're back in fashion but I don't do them.' She'd playfully touched Aidan's arm. 'A bit of soft designer stubble is nice, but not those full-on bushy things. What do they call them?' She should know – she'd done an article fairly recently (yet another piece of twaddle). 'That's it: The Honest Abe or The Viking. Or, even worse, a Lion's Mane—'

'I do them. The classics master at school. Prof Baldwin. The only reason I chose Latin. *Amor Vincit Omnia!* God he was—'

'Stop there, Ben. I don't want to know!'

They now headed for the nearest restaurant for ease. Jo looked down at her outfit as they waited for a table. On its second outing in two weeks, the red *baby doll* dress was perhaps overkill for the Curry Mile, but she felt pleasurably pissed and carefree and it had been nice to *turn heads*, as Aidan had frequently pointed out.

'Gorgeous Jo. Turning heads again.'

'What, like *The Exorcist*?' Her predictable reply.

He'd said it to be friendly, she knew. But still it was nice to be flattered, to realise there was life beyond her four *Elephant's breath* walls and thoughts of bloody babies.

Pivoting towards Ben, her eyes caught the profile of a woman at the door. Pre-Raphaelite orange hair to her waist. Bloody hell, that couldn't be her, surely? She gazed for a moment, astonished. School was many years ago, yet the resemblance was remarkable. But the moment was interrupted by a soft hand on her arm.

'Jo? Hello, Jo.'

The voice so familiar, she immediately spun round. Oh my God, it was Lily!

Stuck for words, she took in the angular face, the fair hair and porcelain skin lit by two patches of pink. 'Lily!' she finally said.

It took a moment to adjust to the shock and surprise. Her old friend looked flawless as always; perhaps a little tired. 'Lily,' she said again, 'Hello! How are you?' She looked over her shoulder. 'Is Noah with you?'

'No, I've been here on a work do.' She lowered her voice, her German accent barely there. 'Bloody clients! It has been a painful five hours. We're just leaving, thank God. I can finally go home.'

Painful, Jo thought. Such a Noah expression. She could picture him and Richard at the kitchen table, deep in conversation. Deep *competitive* conversation. The four of them had often got together at each other's homes for dinner parties, silently competing, raising the cuisine and wine stakes each time they met. But then Richard dropped dead. She last saw the couple at his funeral. Lily was heavily pregnant. That contest, they had won hand's down.

Jo shook herself back. 'Home, of course. To your little boy. Finn, isn't it? How is he?' she asked, trying to be normal, to float above the hot embarrassment which had sprung to her face.

Noah and Lily had been at law college with Richard. Lily had briefly dated him back then. They'd been his friends, not hers. That had been her internal justification when conscience prodded for not getting in touch with them after the wake. But it wasn't really true. She and Lily had been close until Richard's death, meeting monthly in Lily's lunch hour for shopping or a meal with too much Prosecco.

Lily beamed at the mention of her son. 'Oh, he's gorgeous. Though he's got chickenpox at the moment, which isn't easy with no parents around to help ...' she started. Her smile fell away. 'Sorry, Jo. How are *you*? We did try to get—'

'I know. And thank you. I wasn't in the right frame of mind to ...'

It was jealousy, of course. The green-eyed monster, pure and simple. Lily was pregnant and she wasn't; she just couldn't stomach the envy. Feeling the flush deepen, she quickly turned to Ben. 'Do you remember my brother? And this is Aidan.' Taking a breath, she smiled. 'I think this is the start of my rehabilitation and they're doing an excellent job.'

'Wonderful! Of course I remember you, Ben.' Lily looked towards the door. 'Sorry to rush off but I'd better escape while the going's good. Relieve Noah at home. Lovely to see you, Jo ... Bye then.'

Once she had left, the trio sat down at the table, the poppadoms and relishes already waiting.

Ben lifted his eyebrows. 'I remember her too,' he said, helping himself to the finely chopped onions. 'How could I not? One of the perfect Replicants.'

Jo's hands were still trembling. 'I'm not sure if that's an entirely kind thing to say, Ben.'

'Nah, they were man-made, so inevitably very beautiful.'

'Oh, that's all right then.'

'*Blade Runner*?' Ben and Jo turned to Aidan. 'The genetically engineered artificial but beautiful female Nexus-9? Yup, I can see that.'

Jo shook her head. 'Bloody hell, Aidan, you're as bad as him.' She laughed at the mental image; he was pretty much spot on.

But it had been lovely to see Lily, to break the ice so unexpectedly. She'd get in touch with her now, she really would. Feeling a surge of new energy, she picked up her glass. 'More beer, boys? I fancy another drink.'

Stuffed and pleasurably drunk, Jo sat in the back of the smooth taxi and closed her eyes. The balmy breeze through the open windows wafted across her cheeks.

This is the life, she thought, out and about, wined and dined, if a curry counted, by two entertaining and good-looking men with no expectations or preconceptions, no heavy silences or angst.

She adjusted her head on Aidan's shoulder and closed her eyes. She liked him. Apart from being pleasant to look at, he'd made her laugh all evening; his company was easy and undemanding. Like her lovely Richard, she supposed. And it was great to be herself, whoever that was, rather than the desperate sperm-seeking woman or deranged horny widow she'd almost become.

The taxi hummed and she drifted. A musky sandalwood smell. Fingers on her face, then her body, stroking and soft. The burning heat in her stomach going lower. Catching her breath, biting her

142

lip. Waiting and wanting more ... Then the cab moved, bringing her back to reality.

She flicked her eyes open. Aidan was sweeping the hair from her face. He smiled, an inviting smile that held a question.

The jolt of embarrassment immediate, she shook her head and groaned inwardly. He thinks I'm blushing at his offer, she thought, but I'm not. For a moment, just for a moment, I imagined he was someone else.

26

Manchester – two years ago

The hot summer dragged on. Jo no longer felt nor smelled the heat. She didn't notice the chalky pavements or the parched grass in the gardens at the bottom of her street. She didn't see the young people milling around the city centre in shorts, or observe how the sunshine bounced off the scorching bonnet of her unused car. She didn't hear the jangled tune of the ice-cream van nor listen to the news about the latest hosepipe ban. She just existed, a void of shock and muffled sound.

Richard is dead. My Richard is dead.

On a Thursday she sat with her mum on the balcony after dinner. Saying little as usual, they relaxed and drank tea. The evening sunshine had finally moved on from her block, but the lounge was still humid, so they sat outside as they had done every evening in the hope of 'catching some breeze', as Joyce put it.

Jo didn't catch the breeze, but a heavy bloody cold. 'Endless snot' as she described it to anyone who telephoned. She felt quite ill, but at least it was a good excuse to turn down the half-hearted offers of comfort and condolence, allowing her to stay hidden in her flat.

'I wish it would rain,' her mum commented yet again. 'Dad says the garden is suffering.'

Joyce was staying with Jo, a strange but reassuring presence after Richard's funeral, not speaking much, but making meals, washing the pots, changing linen and dusting. All the small things that seemed huge to her.

'That cold of yours is still nasty, love,' she said. 'A good job Ben's away. He's always worrying about catching germs. A man thing, I expect! Maybe a small whisky and lemon before you go to bed?'

The tumbler of whisky became two. Jo slept deeply, black and dreamless, until she awoke with a choking jerk, her lungs packed with air, unable to breathe out through her nose or her mouth. Racing and battering, her heart threatened to burst from her chest.

Oh God. Sweaty and trembling and out of control. And pain, dreadful pain. A heart attack, she was sure. An agonising coronary, just like Richard's.

Dragging herself to a sitting position, she yelped out for her mum, half expecting her to put a dry hand on her forehead, then chivvy and chide. Or, perhaps, fetch a glass of milk. But Joyce took one look at her and, with a face scored with fear, she immediately called the emergency services. Two young and handsome paramedics arrived in minutes and left in equal time, leaving Jo feeling like a time-wasting fool.

'It's just a panic attack,' they chided.

'It's all in the mind, there's nothing wrong with you. Breathe deeply and slowly, try to relax,' they chivvied.

'You don't know me. I'm not normally like this!' Jo wanted to shout. But Joyce said it for her, quietly, at the door, with minimum fuss.

'I'm sorry, but my daughter's husband has just passed away.'

Passed away. A passive expression. For someone old and ready to die, she thought as the reality of Richard's death finally hit home hard. Not my man, at his peak and in his prime, with everything to live for.

But she didn't resent her mum's anaesthetised words. 'Shall I sleep with you for the rest of the night, love?' she asked.

Jo nodded. She needed the calm of her mother's plain words and the shell of her arms through that final night. 'Thank you, Mum. And in the morning, you're to go home to Dad,' she said. Something told her that living alone with the fear of panic would be like falling off a bike. If you didn't get back on straight away, you never would.

Not a heart attack after all. Only in retrospect did she wryly smile at the poetic symmetry: she had written many articles about 'spouse death coincidences' in her magazine pieces. *Wife dies of broken heart! Daughter loses both parents within a week!* Until that moment of sheer terror, she had never quite believed the stories to be true.

And so life went on. The rain finally came and Jo sat alone at her laptop in Manchester, her mum on the phone from Barnsley. A daily quick hello, how are things, before the Radio Two news at five. The panic attack was never mentioned. Nor was Richard's *passing away*, not unless Jo raised it first. Despite both coming from huge families, Joyce and Stan Wragg didn't do vocal feelings. But that was fine. Jo knew without a doubt her parents loved their three children deeply. They were just completely unable to express it in words.

27

Manchester – present day

Jo climbed out of the warm bed and tested her head with a shake. It felt fine, despite the three beers with her chicken dhansak. As ever, the June sunshine was filtering in through the eyelets at the bottom of the roller blind. It was the one household purchase Richard had arranged all by himself after the 'why do I have to do everything just because I'm female?' tirade. The reply had been a lazy smile and a 'because a male will get it wrong, perhaps?'

Of course he had got it wrong. His purchase wasn't even a pretty Roman blind, but a plain burgundy roller, when curtains would have been infinitely preferable. To top it all, it had ugly metal eyelets at the bottom which defeated the object of a blackout blind, as the eyes let in more light than was proportionate to their size.

'I feel as though I'm being spied on,' she had complained.

'An admirer gazing at your perfect, smooth skin? Don't you like that idea, just a little bit?' he had laughed.

Shaking away the memory, Jo sat on the end of the bed, hoping there were no voyeurs today. She turned to her 'guest' and studied his soft face for a moment before standing up quietly and slipping on her robe. Although many years ago now, it was like the other times she had slept with casual acquaintances, or even virtual strangers. She didn't feel revulsion or guilt, she simply felt detached, unemotional and empty.

'He likes you, Jo. All yours if you want him,' Ben had whispered as he went to bed last night, leaving her momentarily astonished and alone in the lounge with Aidan. But she had been slightly drunk, so instead of saying something wry and dry (as befitted a nearly *middle-aged* woman), she laughed and shook her head, following Ben out of the room. 'Night, Aidan,' she called. 'See you in the morning. Hope you do a good coffee. Black and strong for me!'

She should've fallen into a deep contented sleep but she didn't. She dozed fitfully, her mind dwelling on *think about it, think about it,* her body attuned to memories of gentle stroking, rough kisses, building and building until the exquisite free fall. It had been forgotten and buried, but it was there again, torment rekindled. Those persistent memories of uninvited pleasure had annoyed many years ago; they were really pissing her off now. So when Aidan appeared in her bedroom, when he pulled back the thin summer sheet and climbed in next to her, she didn't turn him away.

Feeling achy and spaced out, Jo yawned. More sleep was the thing, but her bed was occupied, so a long soak in the bath would have to do. She turned on the taps, then remembered the new towels, still in a bag in her bedroom.

Lighting Aidan's profile, the spotlight was on her half of the bed. She'd slept on the other side last night and wondered why she'd never done it before. In Richard's place. But it felt right that she should rest there rather than allow some stranger to have it.

And she'd finally discovered why the eyelets hadn't bothered him, which made her smile, which made her sad.

'No waking light on you, Rich! The spotlight just on me. But you liked that, didn't you? You liked me to shine.'

Aidan's hair looked black against the pillow and she vaguely wondered whether he was really so dark or whether he dyed it to make his sculpted features even more striking.

God, he looked youthful. Much younger than he'd seemed yesterday. He was slim and toned, hairless on his chest. And there was the obligatory tattoo – of an ornate cross – just below his shoulder blade.

She laughed to herself despite her detachment. She had slept with one of the young and perfectly formed men she had been joking about to Kate!

A thought popped into her head, a notion of calling her to spill the beans. It was the sort of story Jo was willing to share, as she had many times over the years, because it meant nothing and didn't matter. It would be a way of breaking the ice, of smoothing things over with her friend, whose telephone chats she missed. But something held her back as she listened to the running water and gazed at the specks of dust hovering in the air. She tried to snatch at the memory, but it floated away. Not that it mattered; she knew she wouldn't because Kate was sure to tell her husband, and she didn't want to be judged by him even more.

She wanted Tom out of her head; he'd caused enough trouble already.

Her eyes caught the condom on the carpet. The first person she'd slept with since Richard died. Picking it up with the tips of her fingers, she studied its contents and contemplated the euphemism. *Slept with*, like *passed away*. Soft words. But she had slept, finally, and slept well, so that was a good thing. It had actually been fucking, a word she rather liked for its ability to encapsulate the act. The act of last night, at any rate.

Two whole years of prohibition! With company at least. Was the experience worth waiting for? Had it assuaged any of her longings or exorcised those malevolent memories? She shook her head and felt herself blush. It had certainly satisfied her immediate needs; she'd climaxed within minutes and rather noisily too. Cringing, she thought of Ben, Ben her brother, in the room across from hers, with only a bathroom in between.

'Shit, the bath!' she hissed, running from the room.

Lying in the deep tub, Jo squeezed the soapy sponge on to her stomach. Even after all these years, a soak invoked strawberry-flavoured memories of Kate. Were there bubbles that day? She couldn't remember. Just the recollection of pee-inducing fear and impotence.

Leaning over to dry her hands on a towel, she picked up her mobile to check for missed messages. Life's too short to hold grudges, she mused, as she absently stared at the screen. It's what she always thought when memory dragged her back to that time at St Luke's. Like a Knight Templar's vow (or perhaps Old Joe's sheepdog, Tip), the imperative to protect Kate as best she could was always there. But it was more inexplicable than that. After school and beyond, Kate was a constant presence in her mind, and if something went awry between them, even momentarily, she felt an acute sense of having let her down, of being *responsible* somehow.

Gazing at her overcooked toes, Jo tried to analyse why she felt guilty this time. Kate had been drunk and had effectively thrown her out of the farmhouse. Her behaviour was extraordinary. In front of Alice and Tom, too. Jo had nothing to apologise about. But there was always the other side of an argument. She hadn't been very supportive of Kate's need to get blind drunk twice at the weekend. She loathed seeing her in that state and did nothing to hide it from her face or her words. Condemning was hardly friendship. Or was it? Condoning would've been easier.

Where was the line, she wondered, the line of true friendship? With Kate, it had always been clear, but now it was blurred, inexplicably blurred, for the first time ever.

The freezer plug had been pulled and a saucepan of boiling water was steaming away on a shelf inside, but the ice was resolute, it had no intention of melting. Defrosting the freezer (which was meant to be a self-defrosting freezer, however that was supposed to work) had been on Jo's 'to-do list' for at least eighteen months. But today it seemed like a good idea. She had emerged from the bathroom, her skin resembling orange peel from excessive soaking, wondering how the conversation with Aidan was going to go, but her side of the bed was empty. It was apparent from the stifled conversation coming from the spare room and the subsequent less-than-stifled moans of pleasure that Aidan had again switched sides of the sexual divide, if not the bed.

Hanging around one's own home, feeling more than a tad embarrassed about the night before and trying to feign deafness wasn't the best start to a sunny Sunday. So pulling the freezer plug, putting on *Desert Island Discs* at a high volume and hacking at ice seemed the obvious choice.

She soon discovered that a small metal spatula was the most effective slashing implement in her cutlery drawer. During the eighth disc, Aidan appeared behind her, making her start, turn and brandish it. He backed off with a smile, lifting his hands in mock surrender and then turned to the kettle.

'Black and strong, I think you said.'

She switched off the radio and sighed. Oh God, she'd had (noisy) sex with this gorgeous, messy-haired boy. How did she feel? Was she a tiny bit miffed she hadn't turned him straight overnight with her womanly charms? That she wasn't special? A bit grossed out with the sibling thing too? He looked slightly self-satisfied, though manly smug wasn't best done in her leopard-print silky robe, which had lived in peace on the back of the spare-room door since her uni friend borrowed it several months ago.

Special. Didn't everyone want to be it? Like that eighteen-year-old girl in Barnsley. Knowing blue eyes would be on her and no one else.

'. . . and brown.'

Aidan's voice interrupted her thoughts.

'Sorry?'

'Strong and brown. Well, pretty strong and half brown. The Asian half . . . '

'Ah.' It took a few moments to adjust back to today. To Aidan, the freezer and the kettle. She hadn't realised he was mixed race – not that it mattered one bit.

'Aidan's the Irish half,' he added.

She put her hand on her hip. There was no doubt that Aidan was friendly, engaging and cute. But he'd just had sex with her brother. And he was in her way. She wanted her silent Sunday flat back. To think about Richard, to put her thoughts in order, perhaps telephone Kate. Both Aidan and Ben, she wanted them gone.

'Nice. That kettle has just boiled for me. For my freezer.'

'No problem.'

Aidan hovered and watched as she emptied a saucepan full of chilled water down the sink, refilling it with boiling, then placing it on the freezer shelf. Fascinating stuff, she was sure. But then she should've let him use it for his coffee.

Continuing her chore, she hoped that if she avoided eye contact (like she'd *finally* learned to do with the slathering Rottweiler owner in the gardens) he'd take the hint, but inevitably he started to chat.

'Last night was good . . . ' he began. His eyes, she knew, were on the nape of her neck. The very area he'd concentrated on as though he knew it was her favourite tender spot.

'Yup, the food was nice,' she replied, leaning forward to reach ice at the furthest end of the shelf.

The silk gown was too small, his erection conspicuous. It was all too surreal.

Eventually she turned. Bloody hell, no sign of movement. Hungry, she supposed. 'There's bread in the cupboard for toast if you want some.'

'Great.' Brushing her shoulder, he reached for the loaf, spending several moments trying to open the plastic tie. 'Mixed seeds. Impressively healthy. Shall I put a slice in for—'

'No, thanks.'

Tapping his fingers on the work surface, Aidan was silent for all of twenty seconds. 'Do you have—?'

'Marmite in the bottom corner. Maybe some honey or jam if you're lucky.'

'Cheers,' he said, bending to the unit.

The toast eventually popped and he snapped open the preserve. The stench of sour booze filled the air. *Preserved* it clearly wasn't. He looked at it doubtfully. 'It's . . . I don't suppose you have butter or something? I'm not really a honey or a Marmite—'

'Fine!' Stepping aside, she yanked open the fridge and glowered. 'Butter at your disposal. My bed, my bath, my brother at your bloody disposal. Don't hesitate to have your fill. When you're finally done, will you please bugger off?'

Jerking away, he looked offended and shocked.

Good, she thought, turning back to her task.

28

Jo sat on the sofa with a mug of tea, the mobile on the coffee table looking at her accusingly. She hadn't phoned Kate after her soak. She'd known the conversation would be difficult and stilted. And Richard was with her this afternoon, following her around the silent flat, more so than he'd done for months. Not in a bad way, but it threw her. He didn't visit very often any more. It made sense he'd be here today, though – her first night with someone else since he died.

Poor Aidan. She should feel guilty for being so rude, but couldn't quite summon the energy. Besides, who preferred jam to honey or marmite? Silly man.

Her gaze caught the name plaque leaning against the skirting. *Richard Sharma, Solicitor.* It was still snug in its pile nest where Noah had left it two years ago. Solid brass, of course. Perspex or aluminium just wouldn't do for Richard's new practice.

She breathed out long and hard. Money. It shouldn't have mattered but it did. Richard had been wealthy enough on paper when he died, but he'd been in the process of breaking away from his partnership and setting up on his own. 'A sole practitioner, Jo. Sounds a bit like Billy No Mates, doesn't it?' he'd quipped. 'But "Richard Sharma, Solicitor" sounds bloody good, don't you think?'

Noah tried to dissuade him, pointing out that partners were there to share losses as well as profits, but it seemed to make Richard all the more determined to go ahead. He duly gave guarantees for the premises and the equipment, he took out loans for the computers, the photocopiers and the furniture. Then he dropped dead and Noah was right; the creditors called early doors and his apparent wealth quickly dwindled to nothing, leaving her with just the flat. And a brass plaque.

At the time it felt particularly cruel. Her husband had died unbearably young and people were hammering at the door, their only concern to get their hands on his cash. But as time passed, it dawned that his death affected people other than her. Some were owed money, others were relying on him. There were employees who'd given notice and wanted to be paid, clients who were let down and didn't know where to turn.

Then there were Richard's parents. Their only son had simply *gone* and they were inconsolable. They telephoned Jo day after day, looking for answers.

'He had something on his mind, Joanna,' his mother would say, time and again. 'When he came to see us, he could only sit still for two minutes before shooting off again. Something was deeply troubling him. A mother knows this.'

What could Jo say? That she had been trying to become a mother herself; that she and Richard had spectacularly failed; that she and Abbu would never be the grandparents they longed to be? In the end they stopped any communication at all. It seemed to Jo that they held her responsible for his death. But she understood; she blamed herself too. It felt like payback for all those blithe 'cheese sandwich after tales of heartbreak' occasions.

Kate had been the best therapy when the grief slammed home. She hadn't pussyfooted around. Jo was taken aback at first, but on reflection she wasn't surprised. She had witnessed Kate's reaction to the break-up of one sister's marriage, the repeated miscarriages of the other. Though having little empathy, she was practical; she dealt with the problem head-on. 'Clare needs to talk about it and until she's ready to, there's not a lot anyone can do,' she'd say with a shrug. 'Then she needs to put it right.'

Her lack of sensitivity to other people's problems had astonished Jo at first, but she supposed Kate knew better than most what it was like to be unhappy, and it made her an expert of sorts. As a teenager she'd had counselling too, something Jo had managed to surreptitiously avoid, despite her promise to Ben.

'It isn't normal to barricade your mother out of your flat, Jo. You need help,' he'd said after *the incident*.

'OK, I know, Ben. I'll see a quack, I promise!'

Kate's brisk words belied her sympathetic soft eyes. 'You should be talking about it, Jo. Pretending Richard isn't dead won't help you feel better,' she said the day after it happened, despite Tom's warning frown. 'You need to talk it through.'

'Easy for you, Kate. You're good at it. You like it!' she wanted to retort. Instead she said the words she'd repeat ad infinitum, 'I'm fine, Kate. Really, I'm fine.'

Her questions were hard and unexpected when they came, midway through a telephone call, or during dinner when Jo stayed at the farmhouse. Interrogations about Richard's parents, his business, his finances, his health – subjects even Ben wouldn't touch. Jo never worked out whether they were intentional, unwittingly cruel or just tactless.

'Do you think Richard was in terrible pain when he died?' she asked once, blind to Tom's burning look to silence her.

That particular query had felt like a repeated stab through Jo's heart. Too awful to contemplate, it was the one thing she couldn't bear to dwell on. But once it was out in the open, she found her fear of thinking about it was diluted.

So perhaps Kate's probing was deliberate after all.

Coming back to today, Jo sighed at the memories. Kate was a good friend, a good *practical* friend. And life *was* too short (Richard had proved that, big time).

Scooping up the mobile, she quickly pressed the icon for her number. It rang out several times and she was about to give up when Kate answered in a monotone. 'Hello?'

'Hi, it's Jo! How's things? Everything OK?' she asked jauntily, trying not to sound as tense as she felt. That's when she realised what her trepidation had been. Might Kate be drunk again? Would there be a line she wouldn't know whether or not to cross? But Kate's voice was normal, clear and refined.

'Why, shouldn't it be *OK*?'

Stuck for words, Jo paused. Usually so calm and serene, it was unlike Kate to be sarcastic or hostile, and part of her wanted to say, 'Fine, be like that,' and end the call. But her friend didn't sound pissed, and what was the point of phoning to ease her own angst if she made things worse? New territory for Jo; she wasn't used to making amends when she'd done nothing wrong, but then again, perhaps she had. Whichever it was, she needed to get their friendship back on track.

'Of course not,' she replied easily. 'How's Alice? Did she enjoy school this week? Any run-ins with little Kieran?'

There was a further pulse of tension, then Jo heard a sigh.

'Sorry, Jo, I'm being a cow, aren't I? I've just cleared up lunch, one of the horses is lame and the washing machine is on the blink. I've probably got PMT too. Alice is absolutely fine and asking after you, as always. We'll have to arrange something soon.'

The conversation didn't last long. It was as forced and stilted as

Jo had anticipated, leaving her dissatisfied. She'd hoped to assuage her hazy sense of guilt and responsibility, but she'd also wanted to mention Richard in some light-hearted context, just to say his name, to acknowledge his existence.

To show that she hadn't, really hadn't, moved on.

29

Manchester – eighteen months ago

For months after Richard died, Jo left all his belongings precisely where he'd left them. *In situ.*

Even though she had been there and seen him fall, even though she'd watched with white-faced horror as the young student doctor stepped away with, 'I'm sorry, he's gone', she didn't really believe it. He wasn't really *gone.* She still walked into rooms, a sentence half hung, expecting to see him. She looked automatically to her left before switching to another television channel, she commented on the news to an empty kitchen chair and she laid the table for two. She knew he was there; she could *smell* him.

In situ helped; she knew it did, despite the glances from Ben to Joyce and from Joyce to Stan, when she said so. Richard was still there, somewhere.

His socks and his underpants remained in the bedroom where he'd dropped them on the eve of his death. The mug he drank from in the morning stood resolutely on the bathroom shelf where he'd left it, coffee half drunk. The flowers he'd bought Jo remained, dry, crisp and colourless, in a vase above the kitchen sink.

On the face of it Jo functioned quite well. She was told so often enough. Mostly by people who didn't know her at all.

'My husband died in June,' she informed people who had to know.

'Well, you're doing very well,' the doctors' receptionist, the woman from BT, the insurance man, the central-heating technician would reply.

But it seemed they were right; she did feel OK, strangely so.

It was harder with friends. She'd always played her cards close to her chest, didn't talk about her feelings at the best of times and so they didn't know how to deal with the situation. Did Jo want companionship or to be left alone? Did she want to talk about Richard or to avoid the subject? They didn't ask, of course, but she knew that's what they were thinking.

Lily and Noah too, Richard's closest friends; they did try at first. Halting calls from Lily, help with the sale of Richard's legal practice and the probate by Noah. But they had a baby on the way; they had other priorities and Jo was glad, relieved, when the contact ended. A baby, their baby, added insult to injury; it added jealousy to grief. Those emotions made Jo a lesser person; it was much easier to erase them.

In truth she didn't know what she wanted herself. She was gliding, anaesthetised. She certainly didn't want to talk about Richard's death, but she resented some of her friends treating her as though she was infectious. They kept away, they stopped calling. She understood it was fear – of saying and doing the wrong thing – but that knowledge didn't make it any easier. At times she felt alone and abandoned. But it was manageable; she was still OK.

Joyce continued to visit from time to time, appearing at the door without warning with her new vacuum cleaner, a box full of groceries and home-made food (Dundee cake and flapjack included).

'I hardly need a tuck box these days,' she complained to Ben. 'Mum doesn't need to check on me. I'm fine. And why doesn't she phone before travelling over? Ask if I'm free? I never know when she's going to appear. I might have taken on a whole platoon of Morris Men as lovers—'

'Not sure if it's a platoon, Jo. A team? A group?' Then, 'Mum knows you'll say no if she asks.'

'It's driving me bonkers, Ben. Will you have a word?'

If Ben did have a word, Joyce didn't listen. She turned up one afternoon, arriving just as Jo was leaving to babysit Judy's little boy.

'Mum, it's late, why didn't you call first?' she asked, barely concealing her exasperation. 'You've wasted a journey. I'm just going out to look after William.'

Her mum appeared unconcerned. 'Dad's busy tonight so I thought I might stay, love. Cook a meal and tidy, then go home in the morning.'

'OK, but it really isn't necessary, Mum. I'm fine. Really.'

It was late, around midnight, when Jo returned. She instinctively knew something was amiss. Perhaps it was the smell of household products: polish and washing powder, disinfectant, Toilet Duck. Or perhaps it was the emptiness, the absence of Richard, which she absolutely *felt*, even before bolting to the bathroom, the bedroom and the kitchen.

The flat had been cleaned from 'top to toe', as Joyce would've put it had she been given the chance. The coffee mug had been removed and scoured out, the flowers were in the recycling bin outside and the socks were in the wash basket.

Jo was astounded, stunned, dazed. She couldn't believe her mother had been so insensitive, so bloody, bloody stupid. Storming into the spare bedroom where Joyce was sleeping, she screamed, all sanity gone.

'What the hell have you fucking done?'

The tirade of anger and abuse was unstoppable, culminating in physically dragging her mum from the bed and pushing her out of the flat, dressed only in her brushed-cotton nightdress.

'I was trying to help, love,' Joyce whispered from the cold hallway, not wanting to make a scene. 'I was trying to help.'

But Jo was unrepentant; she sat against the door as a barricade, sobbing into her knees, her hands covering her ears to block out her mother's pleas to be let back into the flat.

Richard had left with the flowers, the flat suddenly and hopelessly empty, the grief kicking in ferociously. The arbitrary unfairness of it was the worst: no warning and no reprieve. Such an acrid grief; lonely, abandoned and missing him acutely, spiked with anger, frustration and jealousy. Mourning her missing husband. Wounded and grieving for the life and the child she'd never have.

30

Manchester – present day

He chatted, smiled and hugged, he drew stick pictures especially for her and never cried, so it was no surprise Jo enjoyed looking after Judy's little William on a Sunday afternoon. It was becoming quite a regular thing, allowing Judy a bit of what she described as 'desperately needed me-time' at the health club in town. Jo couldn't understand why anyone would waste precious *me-time* sweating buckets with a horde of other lunatics on a cross-trainer, but she was glad of the excuse to have William and his baby sister all to herself. She'd even bought a few crayons, books and toys 'to live at Auntie Jo's house, so they're always here when you come'.

William was three now and he demanded Jo's complete attention for the whole of his visit, holding tightly on to *Jo Jo*'s hand, leading her from book to toy to jigsaw, leaving thirteen-month-old Evie watching eagerly on the sidelines in her red portable playpen.

Jo liked William very much. She loved his mop of cork-screw curls, his cheeky dimpled face and his smile, and she was inordinately pleased he'd got over his initial suspicion of her. It was a delight he was so free with his hugs and kisses, but it was Evie she wanted to hold. She still looked and smelled like a baby, she was chubby and smiley, holding out her arms to Jo as she tried to manoeuvre a few steps on her own. If Jo could have ordered a child from Ocado, she would have asked for a clone of Evie, right down to her halo of golden-brown ringlets and shiny amber eyes.

The moment Jo opened the door today, William charged inside with his Disney rucksack. Judy followed with Evie in one arm, the playpen under the other.

'Evie's a bit under the weather,' she said breathlessly as she handed her over. 'But it's just a cold and I'm running late for Spin. Call if you need me.'

Taking in Evie's shy smile, Jo kissed her forehead. Judy appeared slightly anxious, but she always seemed windswept despite her neat cornrows. Her partner, Larry, commuted to London, leaving her to do the bulk of 'pretty much darn everything' and she made no secret that looking after small children 'twenty-four seven' was something of a challenge.

'You have no idea, Jo,' she would sigh. 'They eat and shit and cry all the time. And when they don't, it rains because I live in bloody Manchester! At home it would be sunny all day; at home I'd have a nanny. And Mom to sympathise. Remind me, why the hell did I come here?'

'They'll be eighteen before you know it!' Jo would reply, restraining the desire to grumble very loudly. She'd tried at first: 'Judy, you write academic texts when the fancy takes you, you have Larry who earns shed-loads of money, a huge apartment with state-of-the-art everything and two adorable kids. You're so flipping lucky!' But the eye-rolling and hand on hip were the first clues that she should desist telling her friend how fortunate she was. The inevitable scolding was the second.

'Don't even go there, Jo. You are young, free and available. You can be and do whatever your heart desires. You can travel to Tibet or Timbuktu, go scuba-diving, climb a mountain, go shopping without Kleenex ...'

But she said it with a wry and fond smile; she adored her kids really.

Jo released William from his tight (and rather snotty) hug. She wiped his nose with a tissue and ruffled his curls. 'I think we need to take special care of Evie today, don't you, Wills?' she asked, having learned pretty quickly that it was best to seek his permission so he didn't feel left out. Nodding sagely, he strode purposely to the yellow plastic box of colouring books and stickers in the corner, then carried it aloft to the kitchen table like a miniature *World's Strongest Man*.

Great! Jo thought, plucking Evie from the playpen, I'll have this gorgeous little Miss all to myself, just for a while.

Sitting on the balcony with Evie in her arms, she made sure not to sit in direct sunlight. As the warm breeze wafted Evie's downy hair, Jo watched the outer-city-centre world go by with one eye, and William with the other through the glass.

This is heaven, she mused, trying to stay focused on the here-and-now pleasure, not the what ifs of past and future which were hounding her *twenty-four seven*. But it wasn't easy. The moment she'd sat on the balcony, the memory of Bridge Bar and Tom's throne had rushed in. What did he think about when he sat there? What really went on behind those contemplative blue eyes? What had *think about it* really meant?

'Everything OK, Wills?' she asked every five minutes or so through the open patio doors. 'Tell me when you're hungry, love.'

The cars passing on Deansgate seemed muted today, the pigeons on the opposite roof fluffy and settled in the gentle air. As Jo breathed in Evie's baby-soft smell, the warm minutes passed by and her thoughts became seductive.

'This could be yours,' they said. 'You could have a baby, Tom would give you one. You could feel the child grow in your womb, feed it at your breast. You only have to say the word. You know he's a good man, and look at Alice, she's beautiful. A secret for ever, no one would know. You could do it, Jo. You can have what you want. Just say yes.'

Gently, she slipped her little finger into a coil of Evie's hair. Her mum's curls, her dad's colouring (allegedly; Larry had very little left). How would her baby fare in the gene pool? Dark with brown eyes like her or—

'I'm hungry, Jo Jo,' interrupted her thoughts.

She stood up with Evie safe in her arms. 'OK, Wills, let's see what you fancy,' she replied, heading for the kitchen.

Casually glancing at the kitchen clock, she did another take. Three-thirty already! Evie had slept solidly for well over an hour. Was that normal? And she looked very pale despite being so warm. She placed her hand on Evie's forehead. She was actually hot, her cheeks mottling red behind the pallor.

Oh, Lord, Jo thought, her heart racing, she'd made her too warm by holding her for so long. What was she thinking?

Laying Evie gently on the carpet, she called her name. 'Evie? Evie, wake up, sweetheart.'

Oh God, unresponsive. Putting an ear to her nose, she listened to her breathing. It was hardly there, but her little chest was fluttering, thank God, thank the Lord.

Think, she had to think. Evie was too hot, she was roasting.

Jo breathed out slowly, then in. 'William, I'll get you a snack in a few minutes, but can you help me?' she said, holding on by a thread to her usual voice. 'Evie's a bit too toasty, so I'm going to cool her down. Can you pass me my mobile, love?'

'She flopped like a little rag doll,' Jo later told Joyce on the telephone, the description throwing her breathlessly back to Richard.

'She didn't even wake up when I undressed her. And there was a livid rash on her chest. I immediately thought of meningitis and called the emergency doctor. I felt terrible for holding her for so long.'

'She had a fever, love, from her cold. A virus, like the doctor said,' her mum replied. 'It wasn't your fault. By rights Evie should've been at home with her mum.' Then, after a moment, 'It must have scared you. Are you all right? I can pop over if you like ...'

Jo wanted to cry then. She wasn't all right. There was that familiar metallic taste of panic in her mouth and her heart was still hammering. Her stupid, stupid thoughts. She had coveted Evie, she had allowed her mind to crave anyone's child, to dream of possibilities that were plain wrong.

It was William's distress which had helped her keep it together and focus while they waited for the medic. He'd instinctively known that something was amiss with his little sister and he'd cried inconsolably, huge tears of distress falling from his fearful eyes as he'd asked for his mummy. Then Judy had arrived, still in her gym kit, and she'd been crying too, her face puffy and wretched.

'I'm so sorry, Jo. I left my mobile in the locker so I didn't get your message until I'd finished the class. Thank God she's OK.'

'I feel so guilty,' she said as she left. 'What a bloody selfish person I am. I knew that Evie wasn't right, but I went to the gym anyway. What sort of mother does that make me?'

'Look Judy, you're entitled to a life too,' Jo replied. 'You didn't do anything wrong. You left Evie with a responsible adult who called a doctor when it was needed. You can't be with her every moment of the day and it won't make you a better mum if you do. We all need some time to relax.'

But in truth her teeth were gritted. Judy had blithely handed over her poorly daughter. How could she be so blasé when women like Jo would give their right arm to have a child?

Judy gave her a tight hug. 'Thanks, Jo, I don't know what I'd do without you. You're so grounded, so practical. You really ought to have some kids of your own, you'd be such a good mom, you know.'

Jo smiled painfully. She had to get a grip; she had to stop the obsessive thoughts about having a baby. A child was a serious business with huge responsibilities, not something to be done on a whim. She needed to fill the void, do something constructive: write a proper novel, invite friends, build bridges, get a job, go away.

'Oh, I don't think kids are for me,' she eventually replied, appearing, she hoped, to be happy with her life just as it was. 'I'm delighted to have yours to borrow. Then I can give them back!'

She helped Judy to her car, fastening William in his seat and giving him a wrapped prize for 'being so brave'. Then she kissed Evie on her forehead.

'Don't forget the Calpol every four hours,' she called, waving them goodbye, then turning back with a deep sigh to her silent, empty flat.

31

St Luke's – January 1989

It was the start of a new year, Kate and Jo's first spring term at St Luke's.

The daunting first games lesson soon came around. Each girl was required to kneel on the wooden benches of the changing rooms, nose to the wall, to have the soles of their feet checked for verrucas. Having a verruca was a sin; each child feared it. But even worse was the weighing and measuring carried out on the same day. If there was a good reason for the humiliating exercise (which Jo always doubted), there could've been a subtle and kinder way of doing it. But the muscular games mistress and her pretty young sidekick seemed to enjoy their tiny piece of sadistic power and they milked it to the full, especially with the pupils who were overweight. One teacher held the book to record the girl's height while the other dealt with the scales, calling out the number of stones and pounds, and perhaps a spiteful comment or two, so all the others waiting in their vests and grey bags could hear.

Kate, who had been blissfully unaware of her plumpness before starting at St Luke's, dreaded the weigh-in, and nothing Jo said could make it any better. 'You're skinny, Jo,' she said repeatedly. 'You don't understand.'

'Dear me, Kate Bayden-Jones, what have you been eating in the holidays?' the (not-so-slim-herself) games mistress announced to the class. 'I see you've brought a couple of your father's spare tyres and put them around your waist.'

Many of the girls sniggered almost hysterically, relieved it wasn't them this time, but Jo didn't laugh. She willed Kate to be stoical or shrug it off, but all she could see was pain, mortification and hot tears on her friend's pink face. Jo had only had a small taste of humiliation in those first few weeks, but she knew how hard it was to swallow, without weeping even harder. But the shame for Kate didn't end there. Someone told someone and before long the 'tyre' rumour had spread throughout Junior House. Whispers in queues and at chapel, in form and at night.

'Fatty Bayden-Jones eats tyres. That's why she's so fat.' 'Michelin Man's baby.' 'The fattest in the class.'

Even before starting at St Luke's, Jo had perfected the art of changing clothes or undressing without baring flesh between her neck and her knees (an absolute necessity with brothers and particularly their ogling friends), so she had no intention of getting naked like some of the other girls in her dorm. Unfortunately there was no option on dreaded bath night. Even worse, there was no privacy in the bathroom, just three white tubs on rusty legs in an open room, an area through which girls wandered to use the toilets, clean their teeth or walk to another dormitory. Jo would gladly have avoided washing at all, but Matron had a rota and a thick black pen, so there was no escape.

The doors were ajar and there was a chill in the air as always in the bathroom that evening. In the tub next to Jo, Kate continued to lather her new strawberry-shaped soap on to a matching sponge and chat happily about the holidays, listing the astonishing number and variety of presents Father Christmas had brought her (and her horse). She didn't appear to notice the sudden influx of older girls, but Jo was aware of the extra draught and stifled sniggers even before she turned her head.

Five or six of Miranda's cronies gathered around Kate's bath. 'Out Wragg and Goodwin,' one of them called to Jo and the girl next to her. 'Now.'

Her heart thumping with alarm, Jo did as she was told, grabbing her towel and retreating to a corner.

'We've come to look at your spare tyres, Fatty,' one girl said.

'No, go away!'

'Oh, what have we got here? A strawberry!' said another. 'I think I'll have that.'

'No, please don't . . .'

'Let's see how they wobble,' someone said.

'Stop! That really hurts . . .'

Listening to her friend's cries for mercy, Jo inched closer to the crowd, standing on tiptoes to glimpse what was happening. Too many taller girls to even get a peep. What to do? What to do? She spun around to the entrance where Matron had been standing, but she was turning away with a smirk.

Kate's sobs reached a shrill peak, so she snapped her head back. Oh God, what was happening? Then the whimpers became muffled. Why that felt so much worse, Jo couldn't say.

More girls had scrambled in to investigate the kerfuffle. Horribly torn between anger and fear, Jo clenched her fists. She had to help Kate and do *something*. But what could she do? Still wet and only protected by a flimsy towel, she was too small and too vulnerable herself. So she stayed to one side, full of nervous energy, trying to work out a plan while she held in the pee which was threatening to burst out.

Finally forming an idea, she decided to scream. To yell 'fire' as loudly as she could. She took a deep breath and opened her mouth, but an almost silent throat-clearing noise beat her to it, parting the waves of nighties and girls.

All eyes turned. Her neck elongated, Cecil stood poker straight at the door. Her mouth a postbox-red slit, she was wearing a pale mauve twinset today. And there by her side was a doe-eyed Miranda.

'Everyone back to your beds at once,' she said quietly. She turned to her *pet*, still demurely by her side. 'Thank you, Miranda. Please can you lead dormitory prayers tonight?'

In heavy silence, the girls filed out of the bathroom, but the hot looks of resentment in the direction of Miranda weren't lost on Jo. Wrenching her head towards Kate, she let out the breath she'd been holding. Oh Kate, poor Kate. Crouched ball-like in the tepid water, her heaving pale body was patterned by a horde of pink and red marks. Her blubbering was stifled by her knees.

Feeling a dreadful sense of guilt, Jo stepped towards her best friend.

Cecil turned a cold gaze to her. 'You too, Joanna Wragg. Bed,' she said.

The tears fell as Jo scuttled away. Clutching the towel to her skinny chest, she ran down the long echoey corridor towards her dormitory door at the bottom.

'There, there. Come to me, Kate,' reverberated behind her. 'There, there, Kate. Come to me, my poor child.'

Kate disappeared with Cecil that night for what seemed to Jo like hours. She didn't return to the dorm for prayers and songs, nor when the lights were turned out. Jo lay awake, her cold china calf in her hand, propped slightly upright and staring at Kate's empty bed.

Trying not to panic, she logically turned over the possibilities in her mind. Was Kate hurt? Had she been sent to the sanatorium? Was she in trouble? Had her parents been called for? But even reason was frightening when there was nothing but silence. Would Kate leave? Would she be expelled? Would she ever forgive Jo for standing by and doing nothing to help?

Eventually she fell asleep, and when she awoke at dawn with a horribly stiff neck, Kate was back in her bed. Turned towards Jo, her smile was soft and her eyes were bright.

'Kate!' Jo whispered, her heart squeezing with relief. 'You're back! Are you all right? What happened?'

'I cried for ages but Miss Smyth was really nice and she calmed me down. She said she's going to keep a closer eye on me now,' Kate breathed back, her cheeks shiny pink. But then her smile dimmed, her eyes brimming with tears. 'But it was horrible, really horrible. Look.' She pulled up the sleeve of her silky nightdress. Small bruises were starting to show on the top of her arms and her shoulders; some sharp scratches too. 'From pinching and scratching. She says it wasn't her, but I know it was Miranda. I won't ever forget. I really won't.' Then, after a moment, her voice barely there: 'Do you think I'm fat, Jo? I hate being called Fatty but I get so hungry . . .'

'No, you're not, Kate, it's called puppy fat, like lovely little puppies and kittens. It all disappears when you reach puberty and it turns into boobs,' Jo replied knowingly in a low voice, having researched it in the library, ready for the very question.

Holding her breath, she watched her friend's face, hoping her words would make amends for her inability to help in the bathroom. Her love for mystery and romance novels still prevailed, but she spent so much time in the library waiting for Kate that her interest had expanded to dipping into a variety of reference books. Biology was her current favourite, handy for information on puberty, puppy fat, et al.

Kate's eyes widened and she nodded enthusiastically. 'That's exactly what Miss Smyth said. But she said *she* thought I was lovely just the way I am!'

'And you are, Kate,' Jo answered, trying not to feel slighted. Everything was fine after all. She'd been of biological help and, most importantly, Kate was here and still her best friend.

Spring term eventually became true to its name. The biting wind lifted and the delicate snowdrops in the front garden of Junior House were usurped by sturdy daffodils. The girls still wrapped their arms around their chests when they were sent outside wearing flimsy airtex t-shirts by the games mistresses 'to warm up', but the heavy cloaks they had worn between the school buildings all winter were replaced by navy blazers.

Jo still looked longingly at the green Derbyshire hills from the classroom window, but the routine of school life had become perfunctory. Lining, lessons and learning, playtime and prayers, interspersed with meals in the stuffy hall.

The places at the long dining tables rotated to ensure there'd be two different girls each meal to line up and collect food from the kitchen hatch. But Jo and Kate still sat at the same bench, sometimes next to each other, sometimes opposite.

The name *Fatty* stuck, but Kate continued to eat with relish, happily tucking into lumpy mashed potato drenched with the greasy lamb gravy that Jo refused to touch. She ate three potted-meat sandwiches to Jo's one and always finished her leftover dessert. But it didn't escape Jo's observation that Kate went to the loo far too often, mostly when no one else was around.

She wondered if Kate had *worms*. Rumours had spread that

some of the second-form girls did and were given disgusting pink medicine by Matron. Jo hoped not. Worms were the devil – even worse than verrucas. She hadn't even risked looking it up in the reference section in case it was noticed. The girls in Form Two had been ostracised once their secret was out. No one wanted wriggly creatures that were *actually alive* coming out of their bottoms.

'See you in a minute,' Kate said after dinner one day. 'I'm going for a wee. You wait there.' But Jo followed a moment later, needing to go herself. The sound of retching was unmistakable and it all suddenly made sense. Kate was going to the toilet to make herself sick. When Jo casually challenged her on Sunday Long Walk, she denied it. She explained she'd been ill with a tummy bug, but Jo knew from her shifting eyes she was fibbing.

'Promise you won't say anything. About the *bug*? Promise me, Jo. You are my best friend and best friends don't tell.' Slipping her hand in her pocket, she pulled something out, then revealed it on her palm. It was Jo's china calf! Kate looked at her with a sidelong glance. 'And you want to stay my best friend, don't you, Jo?'

Not entirely sure whether it was a bad thing to make yourself sick anyway, Jo took back her ornament and accepted Kate's lie at face value. She pretended it had never happened, like a true friend should.

If the puking went on, she turned a blind eye. She stayed away from the toilets after dinner. If she had to be in the bathroom at the same time as Kate, she'd clean her teeth loudly or sing. Neither she nor Kate mentioned it again and the routine of avoidance became so firmly fixed that she almost forgot it had happened. At least not until much later in senior school, when they were thirteen or fourteen and everyone was thin. That was when Jo received an unusually shrill and clipped telephone call from Hilary during the summer holidays. Did she know Kate was bulimic and, if she did, why the hell hadn't she said anything before now? Kate was dangerously underweight. Surely Jo had noticed? How often was she sick? How long had it been going on for?

What could Jo say? On her way to becoming a sub-prefect, Kate was self-assured and confident these days. Though not close to any other girls in their form, she was popular with the younger years, thrilled to be surrounded by her *minis*.

And yet, looking back . . .

But Jo cast any doubts aside. Though the idea of Kate being ill was almost unbearable, the line of true friendship was clear.

32

Manchester – present day

As Sunday evening drew in, Jo was still sitting at her laptop and gazing at the Alpine scene on the screensaver. Once Judy had left, she took a deep breath and tried to squeeze out some positives, hard though it was. She'd delve into her cookery books and invite Lily and Noah to dinner, just like old times. She'd look into a new hobby; perhaps even the dreaded gym. She'd read through the flipping India manuscript to refresh her memory and see whether it was as brilliant as she had secretly believed at the time.

Best foot forward, woman. No more seductive thoughts about babies. Ever.

Picking up her mobile, her finger had hovered over Lily's number for some time. But she didn't know what to say. They had been close once and, on reflection, she felt bad about abandoning her to Herr Noah (who was all right in small, *painful* doses) and motherhood without offering to help. After all, Lily had no other family in the UK. She didn't know if she should apologise or explain. She could hardly say, 'You got what I so desperately wanted and I blamed you.' That was the ugly truth, but some things were better not said, surely?

She chickened out of making the call, but sent a text message instead, suggesting a get-together, progress of a sort. Then she looked up the price of gym membership (extortionate) and dismissed it immediately (a positive too, surely?). But as she now gazed at the screen, ready to open the India file, she felt it wasn't the time to look back. Looking ahead was the thing. To an actual Alpine skiing holiday rather than a photo, perhaps. Maybe it was simple procrastination, but reading the novel would be emotional and tiring, and the taste of the panic attack she had experienced earlier was still with her.

Taking off her glasses, she closed her eyes and rested her cheek on the table. Her dark ponytail flopped over like a mask. She was weary but not sleepy, her thoughts still whirring with all the mixed emotions of the afternoon. The overwhelming broodiness, the sensuous pipe dream of doing something about it, then the paralysing terror when she realised Evie was ill.

She'd put on a brave front for Judy, but she'd actually felt like jelly and was still tremulous inside. That instant she realised Richard was having a heart attack was in technicolour, fresh in her mind. The sudden change from happy wellbeing to a fearful realisation that something was horribly wrong, an appalling moment slowed down and then frozen. Like the damned freezer. Like all the bad moments in her life. Set in her head, unwilling to melt, refusing to dissolve.

A young medical student had been passing through the gardens that day. He'd heard her screaming, turned his head to look, then bolted over in his football kit to help. He'd taken command of the situation, immediately carrying out CPR, leaving Jo to stand and watch with powerless dread, abandoning all control.

Like an instant snap, the image of the medic's face was there too. Desperation, sweat and sheer despair. He'd known Richard had gone and she could see the weight of that responsibility etched on his youthful features.

Much later it occurred that the episode must have affected his life too, one way or another. Perhaps he'd gone back home, or to his student digs and said, 'A man died in front of me today and there was nothing I could do'. A lesson for life, maybe, that sometimes there *is* nothing we can do. Or perhaps the shock reality of becoming a doctor.

Had he seen it through? She'd written to the medical faculty to thank him, a note *To Joseph*, his name only remembered because he was a Joe. She'd shared the greatest intimacy of her life with Joseph. She'd relinquished capacity to him, a stranger who'd been unable to help.

Sighing, she closed the laptop lid. That was the trouble with Joanna Wragg. Everyone save for that stranger assumed she had cool self-possession. But nothing could be further from the truth.

33

Jo watched the sun finally disappear behind another block of flats. The longest day, of course. And it had been a *very* long one, the onset of dusky darkness finally giving her permission to retire.

Too tired to lift her legs, she shuffled to her bedroom but stopped abruptly. Someone was knocking. Was it really *her* flat door? What the hell? She glanced at her watch, wondering who would be calling so late.

Aidan, oh bugger. Despite her rudeness this morning, he'd sent a couple of comical *bad food stench* GIFS already. He'd clearly taken her apology as more encouraging than she'd meant.

'Everything OK, Jo?' Ben had asked before leaving at lunchtime. Nicely put, but he meant her deranged outburst, she knew.

She could have said a hundred things in reply – that she missed being *special*, that she was tired, confused, mortified by her own behaviour. That sleeping with the first person since Richard was a huge thing, actually.

'Oh, nothing . . .'

'I thought you liked Aidan.'

'I do! Well, sort off. I just want you both to leave me in peace.'

'Well, why didn't you just say!'

But she had felt awful a couple of moments after freaking out with Aidan. So she tried to make amends by being a tad more friendly when he and Ben left. The *tad* had clearly been too much, she now reflected with a sigh. He had lingered at the door before leaving, as though he had something to say. Looking at her for a few seconds longer than was necessary he'd said, 'See you soon, Jo Jo,' and now here he was, far sooner than *soon* should be.

She flung open the door. What the? Not Aidan but Tom bloody Heath! Putting a hand on her chest, she stared open-mouthed at his unexpected large presence. Then concern set in. Why was he here? Had something happened to Kate or Alice?

He immediately lifted his palm. 'It's OK. Nothing's wrong. Can I come in?'

'Seeing as you're here,' she replied curtly, stepping back to let him in. She was both shocked and irritated that he should turn up unannounced. He'd never done it before and he'd caught her at a bad moment, her face still waxy from night cream and wearing an oversized t-shirt, ready for bed.

Astonished, she stared at his back fleetingly. Then, shaking the disbelief from her mind, she followed him to the lounge. There he stood silently, looking towards the patio doors, presumably seeing nothing but his own reflection in the glass.

Though she hated herself for it, the quickening was there like cold hands on her skin. Dislike and delirium, that involuntary tug.

Walking past him to the kitchen, she automatically lifted the kettle to test the weight of water, flicked its switch and took two cups off the rack. She stood tense and speculating as she waited for it to boil, then returned to the lounge, the mugs of tea steaming in each hand. Tom's face was still averted, his body erect and soldier-like, his hands in the pockets of his jeans.

'What are you doing here, Tom?' she asked, not wanting to mask her annoyance, but apprehensive of what the answer might be.

He turned and studied her for a moment before spreading his arms.

'I wanted to talk to you . . . ' he replied evasively.

Slowly pacing around the room, he picked up random objects: *Mslexia* magazine, still unopened; an ashtray from Spain full of drawing pins; her granddad's antique silver snuff box. He replaced each item with a frown, as though searching for the answer. Jo watched mutely, questions popping inside. Then she sat down. She felt sapped from standing, sapped from a rubbish day, sapped by his silence.

'Does Kate know you're here?' she asked eventually, her eyes burning somewhere between tiredness and hostility.

'No, I've been . . . out.'

She pushed Tom's mug across the coffee table, then hitched to the far end of the sofa, lifted her legs under her bum and sipped her tea. 'I didn't have any decaf, so it'd better be good.'

He stopped walking and turned. 'I wanted to know if you'd thought about my offer.'

She was angry then, the heat rushing to her face. 'Have I thought about it? Have I fucking thought about it? I've thought of nothing else!' she wanted to shout. But that would be confrontation, emotional and embarrassing. She would be revealing too much of herself, losing control. And it felt dangerous, bloody dangerous.

'No, and I'm not going to,' she said instead.

He smiled a small smile, a puff of air through his nose. 'That's a lie, and you know it.'

Said so bloody evenly, his blue eyes on hers. 'Fuck off, Tom!' she replied, unable to contain her exasperation any more.

As she stared, the anger bubbled. She'd been living a dull but ordered life until he had started asking his pointed questions and making his stupid, stupid suggestion. It was as though she had emotionally regressed years after last seeing him, and it wasn't bloody fair. She'd put that part of her life firmly behind her; she didn't want to be plagued by it again. Yet here was Tom, unemotional and detached, barging into her home and presuming to know how she felt.

She stood. 'Go on, Tom,' she repeated. 'Fuck off! Get out of my home!'

Tom didn't move. His face was implacable, the only sign of distress in the clench of his jaw. 'I'm not going until we've talked,' he replied evenly.

Any sense of reason left at his words. Jo strode towards him, pushing hard at his large frame with the flat of her hand; when that didn't move him, she curled her fingers into fists, battering his chest.

'Get out, Tom, get out of my flat. You have no right to be here,' she yelled. But he caught her wrists in both hands and held them so tightly that they stung, bringing tears to her eyes.

'I have every right,' he replied, his voice staccato and harsh. 'I have every right because you killed our baby.'

From the street below, a sudden blare of car horns broke the moment.

'You're hurting me, Tom,' Jo muttered. Her anger was spent. Despite his cruel words, she felt exhausted. She ached to lie down and sleep. She didn't want to think about the abortion. She could never describe to anyone, let alone him, what a painful, debilitating and lonely experience it had been. She wanted to bury it again, along with the rest.

'Not half as much as I want to,' he replied quietly, releasing her arms and looking at his hands. 'You have no idea. No idea how many times I've wanted to put these around your neck and ...'

Jo glanced at him in surprise. She didn't understand what he was rambling about, whether he was referring to her or to some invisible person in his mind. The situation was strange and dream-like. She felt no fear of him, despite her aching wrists. Tom Heath still looked the same, but everything was different. Life had shifted somehow.

He lifted his head, his stare icy cold. 'I hate you, Jo. I loathe and despise you,' he said softly. He shook his head, his smile bitter. 'You have no idea how much time I have wasted hating you.'

She wanted to laugh. He means me, she mused, how utterly bizarre. Whatever emotions she'd ascribed to him over the years, it was never hate. 'But I thought . . .' she began, her musing involuntarily finding sound.

His voice hard, he snorted. 'That it was love? Don't flatter yourself,' he replied. 'What was there to love, Jo? For all those months at your dad's place you could barely look at me, never mind acknowledge my existence. I was like shit off a shoe as far as you were concerned. Then Kate arrived. She wanted me, she had time for me; she realised I was a human being with feelings. She could see beyond my pretty face and thick accent. And you couldn't stand it, could you? You couldn't bear the competition, so you decided you'd have me and like a pathetic fool I couldn't resist.'

She stared at the floor, saying nothing. There was nothing to say. His harsh words were true. But it was a long, long time ago and she had been punished.

Putting his hand to her face, he lifted her chin until her eyes met his. 'You were so wanton, Jo, so dissolute. You loved it. Like a bitch on heat, you wanted me again and again. But did you give anything at all except your body? Did you connect with me as a person with feelings and emotions, even for an instant? No, you didn't. Because you only take; you're self-centred and cold.'

'No, no. That's unfair, Tom,' she answered slowly.

Her cheeks were burning but her thoughts were sluggish as she pulled away from his touch and sat down. There was something therapeutic in his words, in hearing them out loud. Like a confessional, part of her was glad they'd been said. There was a feeling of release, of freedom. But she didn't think that his accusation of *only taking* was fair, certainly not so far as Kate was concerned. And of course she was willing to love, she was willing to give. Wasn't she?

Always on your terms. Having to win. Complete selfish cow. You know that, don't you, Jo? flashed through her mind. But they were her own descriptions. No one else had said them.

Except Tom, here and now.

'What's unfair, Jo?' he asked quietly, crouching down and peering into her face. 'Tell me, I really want to know.'

There was a breath through his nose and the faintest of smiles. 'Oh, you mean Kate, I suppose. The one person you don't take from.' He gazed at her thoughtfully. 'What's that all about, then? Why was she the exception, Jo? Were you in love with her at school or something?'

Jo shrugged. She didn't know whether Kate had ever spoken to Tom about St Luke's and she wasn't going to talk about it now. As for her feelings for Kate, it was complicated; she didn't know the answer herself. There had been times at school when she'd worried about being a lesbian, but it wasn't that. It had never been sexual. Even now she didn't know whether it was love, envy or even hate, or simply that enduring desire to be in her shoes, to be someone other than *'the ragamuffin from Barnsley'*.

'You've said what you wanted to say, Tom,' she replied wearily. 'Will you leave now, please?'

Tom shook his head as he stood. 'I haven't even started,' he said.

Jo spent some time in the kitchen recess. Her arms on the cold granite work surface and her head down, she inhaled slowly through her nose and exhaled through her mouth. As though that would help, she thought wryly. Deep breathing from her diaphragm wouldn't make Tom disappear. Or the past. And anyway, she was not, absolutely not, going to have a panic attack in front of *him*.

Lifting her chin, she opened a corner cupboard. There were the dregs of ancient sherry and port in sticky bottles, but further back she found three tiny flagons of whisky left over from hampers created by Joyce. Every Christmas, a wicker basket full of unlikely little luxuries, put together with love.

She pictured the last pannier and sighed, hoping she wasn't quite as self-centred as Tom described. Or, if she had been, that she was becoming less selfish and more appreciative of those around her, especially her mum. Pulling out a glass tumbler, she emptied one miniature, noting with surprise how little a measure was, then adding two more, mixing the malts. She didn't usually drink Scotch, but she liked the idea of its sourness, the way it took her breath like a shock. Besides, she guessed from Tom's demeanour she was going to need alcohol-induced sleep tonight.

Sitting in the armchair, he had one hand on each arm, his head back, his knees spread. 'Is that what you do to deaden the pain?' he asked, nodding at the glass. 'Or am I right, do you feel nothing at all?'

'That's a bit cryptic for you, Tom,' she answered with a faint smile as she sat.

He knows nothing about me, she thought, nothing at all. Though overwhelmingly exhausted, she sipped her bitter drink, wondering where this crazy little drama was going.

'How about this then?' he replied savagely, sitting forward. 'How do I know it was my baby? You shagged everyone in sight at university according to Kate. Why didn't you fuck up some other mug's life by telling him you intended to get rid of his baby? Why pick on me? Why didn't you leave me out of it?'

'Because it was yours, Tom. You were the first; it was the only time I didn't use . . .' she started, trying to stay calm. She could feel the burn rising, a combination of anger and whisky. 'Do you think I wanted to be pregnant? Do you think I wanted it to be you, of all people?'

'As if you gave a shit! There you were, calm and collected, the educated young lady. No emotions, no feelings. Forcing out tears when you weren't getting exactly what you wanted. You had a baby, a life growing inside you. My baby, my life. Didn't that mean anything?'

'Not at first, but then ...' she started, searching for the right words as she thought back. 'It was a terrible mistake, a dreadful shock, and I couldn't dwell on it. Perhaps I wasn't *emotional*, as you put it, but I couldn't let it in because ... Because I was so bloody petrified. I was only eighteen, Tom. Young, inexperienced, frightened. I didn't want to screw up my life.'

'And having my baby would have screwed it up?' he asked, spitting out the words.

She lifted her chin. 'Yes, it would. And yours and Kate's.'

Tom clapped his hands slowly. 'Well done, Jo. Full marks for remembering other people.'

'You two were waltzing into the sunset, as I recall.'

His face colouring, he stared. 'You know that isn't true. Not then, not yet. I offered you ... I offered you a choice, but still you decided to remove the small inconvenience—'

Jo stood and glared. 'You self-absorbed, sanctimonious bastard!'

She was no longer tired. It was all too unfair. 'You know nothing about it. Nothing.' She roughly pointed her finger. 'It takes two, Tom. Two people to make a baby. Where were you when I travelled alone to the clinic on the bloody Number 92 bus? Where were you when they scanned me and showed me the foetus with their disapproving eyes? Not an ugly lump of cells as I imagined, but a human. It was perfect: a baby-shaped head, arms and legs, a beating heart, lungs and a liver. And toes. It moved, Tom, it looked at me and begged me not to do it. What was I to do? Don't you think it ripped me apart? I had second thoughts, a whole week of agonising second thoughts, knowing I was doing the wrong thing.

But who could I turn to? My mother? My dad? There was only you, and I tried ...'

She closed her eyes. The appointment one week later, the terror, the sharp agonising cramp, the blood, the vomiting. They hadn't said much at the first consultation about the procedure or what to expect. For seven whole nights she'd tried not to imagine what it might be like. 'We'll help you with the pain,' they'd said on the day. What pain? she'd panicked. They put you to sleep, didn't they? And when you woke up it was over, all gone.

'Have you any idea how lonely and frightened I was?' she now asked, her voice low and hoarse. 'Did you ever consider what an abortion at nearly twenty weeks involves? They made me give birth, Tom. They induced labour because it was too late to scrape it away. You were there when Alice was born, you know what it's all about. Can you imagine what it was like, all alone? There was no one there to hold my hand, to help with the suffering, no one to comfort me, to help me grieve. I've lived with the guilt and the regret. Don't you dare to presume otherwise.'

She fiercely wiped her face with the back of her hand and glared at Tom. 'Like every other woman, it was my right to choose, but don't think for a moment any of it was easy. I hope you're satisfied. Now go. Leave me alone.'

Tom stood up and gazed at her for a moment, his look inscrutable, before turning away and walking to the door. With his hand on the handle he looked back. 'My offer remains open,' he said simply.

Jo sighed; she was so tired, emotionally and physically. 'For God's sake, why, Tom?' she asked quietly.

'If you have a child, I want it to be mine, nobody else's. You owe me that much,' he replied, letting himself out to the warm early hours.

34

Barnsley – December 1998

Joanna Wragg didn't realise she was pregnant for several weeks. Her periods still appeared every month and, although her face became less bony and she put on weight around her stomach and boobs, she assumed it was the inevitable result of student life – the beer and takeaways, the crisps and Mars Bars, the ready meals and all the other processed *junk* that Joyce denied her at home. But her breasts remained tender even after her period ended and she started to experience a faint fluttering sensation in her pelvis. Then, in a flash of understanding when she woke up one night to pee yet again, she knew without a doubt it wasn't just wind and that she was pregnant with Tom Heath's child. She'd slept with several other guys by then, but she'd gone on the pill and she used condoms too to protect herself from STDs, unless she was really too drunk.

At home for the Christmas holidays, the light-bulb moment occurred when she was sitting on the loo in the family bathroom.

Joyce had recently renovated it from an olive-coloured suite to pink, and Jo slipped down on to the matching shag-pile mat, ready to weep. The tears burned her eyes but they were paralysed like she was, refusing to fall.

Pregnant. Oh God. Pregnant, really? No, surely not. And yet, and yet ... The stench of toilet cleaner was almost making her heave. Then there was the peculiar taste of tea and beer, her sudden dislike of the old stalwart Marmite, her constant need for catnaps.

It was a terrifying experience; up until that moment she hadn't realised what a comfortable and closeted life she'd lived. There had been no real trauma, no serious illness, no one had died. Despite being away at university, she'd been cosseted in a hall of residence; she hadn't had to stand up for herself or make any real decisions. She'd eaten crap, drunk too much alcohol and slept around, but she hadn't missed many lectures, done drugs or shoplifted to supplement her grant like the other girls on her floor. She wasn't a bad person.

Her gut reaction was to run to her mother, to beg for her understanding and help, but she was too afraid of the consequences. It was untrodden territory. Suppose her parents threw her out, suppose they refused to pay for her university fees and accommodation? Even worse, what if they made her keep the child? The thought filled her with horror. It wasn't a baby, a human. It was something growing inside against her will, something freaky and alien like the film. And even in the lucid moments when logic kicked in, she knew she wouldn't confide in Joyce; she couldn't bear to see the inevitable look of disappointment on her face.

The numbness and shock eased eventually, replaced with an awareness of her freezing surroundings. It had been snowing all night and the bathroom windows were glazed with ice. She tiptoed back to her bed, and with a thrashing heart she tried to walk through a mental list of options. It was hard to concentrate. Each time she started, her mind flipped back to the paralysing reality.

Pregnant, God pregnant. This *couldn't* be happening.

Another deep breath, she tried again. There was Kate. But Jo couldn't possibly tell her; she was madly in love with Tom. After inviting him to the cinema, there had been a couple more dates and she was already pally with his mum; the news would devastate her, break their friendship for ever. The doctor in the village was no good: he'd known the whole family since childhood; he'd even delivered Nigel in this house, for God's sake. Practical and down to earth, Lynn would've helped, but she'd astonished everyone by packing her bags and flying to Switzerland to work as a chalet maid. Grasping at straws, Jo went through her new uni friends one by one, but she knew they would be as clueless as she was.

'I'm pregnant, I'm pregnant. This can't be happening, it can't!' hammered through her head. The overwhelming urge was to get rid of it as soon as possible, but she had no idea how. An abortion clinic wasn't something she could look up in the *Yellow Pages* downstairs. So, having discounted all the other possible choices, she decided to tell Tom. He was the one person who wouldn't breathe a word of it to anyone else as he had too much to lose. Not only had Kate ingratiated herself with his mum, he had already begun his first renovation – a small terraced house, bought with a loan from her father.

Barely breathing, Jo knocked at the white door the next day. The beige-rendered council house was in what Auntie Barbara described as the 'rough' end of the village. She waited for seconds, then rapped again, fearful Tom wouldn't be in. But eventually it was opened with a warm blast by his mother, still wearing her dressing gown.

Jo remembered Mrs Heath from primary school. She was one of

the mums who looked scary and sharp, wearing her work uniform and reeking of cigarettes when she bothered to turn up to collect Jimmy. Jo and Lynn had been alarmed when she glared in their direction. 'Like the witch in "Hansel and Gretel", only blonde,' Jo once whispered to her. But on that bitterly cold December morning she was surprised to see that Tom's mother had a good figure and that she was still fairly young. Though her face had a hardness about it, she was a good-looking woman.

'Thomas. You're wanted,' she called over her shoulder. She looked Jo up and down with indifferent blue eyes before turning back into the house without another word.

Looking ruffled, Tom appeared at the door. His curious expression was replaced with surprise. 'Oh, right. Are you looking for—'

'Can you get your coat? I need to talk to you,' Jo interrupted, stamping the snow from her wellies.

Nodding, he said nothing, then he sat on the bottom stair, silently pulling on his boots and yanking at the laces. Jo stared at his hands, those bloody, bloody hands. It didn't take long, but the waiting was unbearable. Finally he grabbed a jacket from the banister and came out.

Ignoring the Christmas lights winking in the windows, Jo stalked ahead, past the row of identical, dingy houses, down the slippery hill to the bus terminus, then up the lane towards the fields, afraid of them being seen together.

Her old wellies chafed her calves but Jo walked as briskly as the softening snow would allow. Eventually she stopped halfway down a stile. Despite her thick parka, gloves and scarf, she was unable to control the shivering when she turned. Tom was wearing a beanie hat, from his pocket presumably, and his handsome face was quizzical.

'So, what do you need to—'

'I'm pregnant and I need to know how to get rid of it,' she blurted.

'What?'

'I'm pregnant, Tom.'

He looked stunned, dumbfounded, a knockout blow. Whatever he had been expecting, it clearly wasn't this. 'What? Are you sure?' he asked, gazing at her features, his face open with surprise.

'Of course I'm bloody sure,' she replied, trying to hold back the tears threatening to explode – from embarrassment and agitation and sheer bloody terror. She took a deep tremulous breath. 'Look, I don't want anything from you except a name of someone to go to. I don't know, a clinic or something. I'm not after money or anything like that. I just need to get rid of it.'

He looked at the ground, silent for a time, his feet shuffling the snow. Then he lifted his head, his eyes burning, his voice cold. 'Oh, I see. I suppose you think I go around getting girls pregnant all the time? That I'll have a few names and numbers of abortionists in the back pocket of my fucking jeans?'

But she was crying by then. She was cold, she was afraid, and she was more humiliated than she'd ever been in her life. She hadn't spoken a word to Tom since the summer party morning. On the few occasions they'd met, she'd completely blanked him. Yet here she was having to face up to the shaming reality of what she'd done with him, to admit that night of intense lust and abandon really had happened. But most of all she was scared; petrified that he wouldn't help.

Lifting her chin, she brushed the tears away. 'Yeah, well maybe you do. And if you don't, then someone you know is bound to.'

The anger showing in his cheeks, he stared for a few moments. 'I'll have to think about it,' he said, turning around and striding away.

35

Barnsley

As Christmas approached, Tom left Jo on tenterhooks, the waiting agony, her energy and appetite clean gone. In contrast, the Wragg family were cheery. Moor End smelled festive, an intoxicating mix of pine tree (their first real one *ever*) and holly, mince pies and chutney, fruitcake and Ben's crystallised ginger sweets. Her mum replaced their jaded childhood decorations with sparkling new ones, even splashing out on exterior lights which twinkled on the furs at the front like a grotto. And, as always, carols from King's filled the air.

Astonishingly, Stan and Joyce invited the neighbours to a drinks party (more bottles of Mateus – Joyce liked to keep them for candles) and her brothers asked her to the pub every night. But Jo was too distracted to listen or smell, notice or join in. She picked up the telephone receiver repeatedly, staring hard at the green casing before replacing it with a deep sigh. She played out ridiculous scenes in her head of hammering hysterically on the Heath front door and demanding to see Tom, or dying in childbirth like Fanny Robin, deserted and alone.

Tom Heath was punishing her, she was sure. She pictured him in The Station with his brothers and his mates, laughing and relaxed, bragging about his *loaded* catch and kindling business.

She loathed him then, more than ever before. He knew she was helpless. For the first time in her life she had asked for help, she had cried with desperation, and this was how he responded. With silence: vindictive, spiteful silence. What to do? What to do? She needed to get it sorted as soon as possible; she wanted to get on with her life, pretend it hadn't happened.

To make matters worse, Jo's waistline was increasing. Conscious of Joyce's occasional glances at her stomach, she borrowed Ben's jumpers to cover it. Did she know? Did her mum suspect? Perhaps she did, or maybe she didn't want her daughter to be fat. Or perhaps Jo was paranoid. Without a doubt she felt slightly crazy with anxiety, struggling to act normal, whatever normal had once been.

Armed with a Santa sack, Tom finally appeared at the house on Christmas Day morning. Looking awkward and uncomfortable, he extracted the beautifully wrapped gifts one by one. Though they were labelled, *From Kate & Tom, with love*, in her loopy handwriting, 'From Kate,' he said repeatedly as he doled them out to all the family.

As he handed over hers, she avoided his eyes, but couldn't help notice he was wearing a dreadful Pringle golf jumper beneath his smart jacket. In another life, she would've grinned and made an eye-rolling comment to Ben about Kate having scrubbed him into a respectable middle-class young man, that soon she'd be polishing his accent too. But this wasn't another life; today's was the only stomach-churning one she had.

After the gift unwrapping, the tiresome toasts and pleasantries,

Tom finally looked her way. 'I'm off home to telephone Kate now. Do you want to come too? Say hello?'

It was his turn to stride ahead this time, his face set and his hands dug in the pockets of his donkey jacket. Still wearing her party shoes, Jo followed until they were again in the frozen, snow-covered field beyond the village. When she finally caught up, her feet were saturated and freezing. Her heart thrashing with both agitation and exertion, she looked up at Tom. His back was to her, his foot raised on a stone.

He turned, his face pale and serious. 'We could get married, you know,' he said. Then, looking at her intently. 'Marry me. We could be good—'

'Oh, don't be ridiculous, Tom,' she snapped. Her mind cramped with fear that he wouldn't help. Oh God, oh fuck. Was he going to put a spanner in the works? Would he somehow force her to keep the bunch of alien cells taking over her body? 'I don't love you, I don't even like—'

'I get the picture,' he interrupted coldly. He held out a folded piece of paper. 'Season's greetings, Jo. I hope it's a Christmas gift you'll never forget.'

And with that he spun around and stalked away.

Wearing the large woolly hat Ben had given her for Christmas, Jo caught the Number 92 bus into town and walked the slushy mile to a newly built clinic on the outskirts of Barnsley. She felt as frozen as the weather, the only issue on her mind being an overwhelming and urgent need to get rid of whatever was inside her.

She hadn't asked questions when she made the appointment from the red telephone box in the village. When she let her mind dwell, she supposed they'd take her into an operating theatre there and then, put her to sleep, then hoover the cells out, job done. But when she arrived in the bright clinic, she was told by the plump girl on reception that her appointment was for a scan.

'Oh, right.'

Though Jo had determined to keep her vision strictly *tunnel*, she noticed the girl's hair bobble looked like mistletoe. Perhaps it was. Maybe she'd had a jolly Christmas snogging boys, rather than meeting one in secret for all the wrong reasons.

Her ponytail swung. 'It's to work out how far you're gone, love.' She smiled. 'Won't take long. Have a seat.'

There was definitely a smell. Layers, in fact, the top one being as artificial as the sparsely decorated pine tree in the corner. Not that she could see it in full. Like her fears and her terror, it was on the periphery.

Threading her fingers like crochet, Jo waited until a uniformed woman called her name. 'This way,' she said briskly. She gesticulated to a side room. 'Strip to your underwear, lie down and lower your knickers.'

Wondering how low *lower* should be, Jo undressed to her undies. Tense and shivery, but keeping her eyes strictly forward, she climbed on the narrow bed.

The woman pulled out a clipboard. 'A few questions first,' she continued, apparently oblivious to Jo's trembling. She took details and dates. 'Last period?' she asked eventually.

Jo found her voice. 'I'm not sure. A couple of week ago, maybe?'

Wrong answer, clearly. 'Right,' the woman sighed. 'Stay there.'

Really? It was biting outside; Jo was hardly going to abscond in this state.

Aware of equipment surrounding her, she stared doggedly at the ceiling. Much like her, a fly was trapped in the strip light, buzzing to get free. But *she* had to be patient. She just had to get today over with and everything would be fine.

A different woman finally appeared. Without introducing

herself or giving a warning, she squirted icy jelly on to Jo's exposed tummy, then pressed firmly with a probe. The combination made her jerk and turn her head in surprise. The woman was clicking a computer mouse, but her eyes were on a screen.

Her face stiff and reproving, she filled in a form. 'Nineteen to twenty weeks' gestation,' she stated. She handed Jo a wad of rough hospital tissue. 'Sort yourself out, then hand this file in at reception to arrange an appointment in a week's time for the procedure.'

No smily girl at reception, so Jo sat down, the folder hot on her knee, waiting. *Waiting.* Waiting for Godot, waiting for someone to take over, to tell her what to do, to say, 'You're not bad. It's just bad luck.' But she'd read the play. There was no Godot.

The tears didn't come then. She was dry-eyed with shock, her emotions frozen solid from the bombshell of what she'd just seen on the monitor.

'Would you like some company, love?' a thin voice asked.

A bird-like older woman with sixties spectacles and slate-grey hair perched on the chair next to her. Holding a tray of small jars, she peered, her eyes huge and hazel through the lenses.

She smiled. 'I'm a volunteer from over the way, but I was passing through and . . . well, you seem to be alone. Would you like a chat? It's a bit of a shock, isn't it?'

Unable to speak, Jo shook her head; the woman's kind tone was threatening to splinter her strained emotional hold.

'Well, you don't know me, but chatting helps. It really does.' She put a bony hand on Jo's. 'Before you decide, love . . . the first decision isn't always the right one.'

'Are those urine samples for me, Bernadette?'

Carrying a mug of ten o'clock tea and a biscuit, the receptionist was back, this Tuesday the same as all her Tuesdays. She nodded at Jo. 'An appointment in a week? Tuesdays OK? I'll just take that file.'

When Jo turned her head to Bernadette, she'd gone.

Retracing her steps from the clinic to the terminal in town, the tears finally came. A rush of water that wouldn't stop even as she stood in the queue for the Number 92 bus, a horde of cheery shoppers surrounding her with their chock-full 'Winter Sale' carrier bags.

Her glance at the scanner hadn't been what she'd expected. The bunch of alien cells had turned into a baby before her eyes on the screen. A fully formed baby with limbs and a heartbeat. One with fingers and toes, a mouth and a nose. A baby which moved. Yet she had known, really. All those school hours with reference books in the library hadn't been for nothing. She'd been good at biology, had taken it for A level, she wasn't a fool.

But of course she had been a fool. She'd had unprotected sex at the end of the summer. Intercourse with Tom Heath, for no good reason at all.

The third day was up, the third out of seven. As each day slowly passed, Jo became more and more sure she was doing the wrong thing.

The irreversibility of death, she mulled repeatedly. There must be another way.

She thought of nothing else, her mind like the reference books, scanning every possibility, which were ultimately few. There was adoption; the baby could be taken by new parents at birth. But that would involve coming clean, confessing to her parents, embarrassment and shame. Then there was keeping it and becoming a mother, a whole other world she couldn't begin to imagine. She occasionally allowed herself to entertain the idea of secretly retaining the baby for herself, like a Polly Pocket toy. Something she could hide from the world, from university life, friends and family. Bringing the baby out to love and enjoy, to feed, to kiss and to dress, but only in private. Pure fantasy, of course.

'You can't have your cake and eat it, Joanna,' she heard her mother's voice in reply. 'Everyone knows that.'

Subjective, claustrophobic and repetitive, the thoughts were exhausting. Keep, kill, adopt. Keep, kill, adopt. And, *The first decision isn't always the right one.'* Mentally picturing the scanned image, her heart crumpled. A baby, her baby. Perhaps she could be a mother after all. She needed to talk to someone. That someone could only be Tom.

Ten days on and she was staring at the dial of the green telephone again, willing him to call her, knowing with certainty that he wouldn't. She had to make the first move, swallow her bloody pride and ask him for help.

The receiver at the rough end of the village was picked up almost immediately, the voice settled, where it belonged. 'The Heath residence. Can I help?'

It was Kate.

Kate knew immediately. She hadn't seen Jo for weeks and the change in her appearance, together with the tears, must've made it obvious she was pregnant.

They met in town and had a coffee at Greggs. And it was so simple for Jo. Kate made it easy for her, she didn't have to lie.

'Oh my God, you're pregnant, aren't you? All those boys at uni, Jo. I warned you to be careful! Have you any idea who? I bet you don't. Oh, poor you. What a disaster. You have to get rid of it, obviously. You can't let Joyce know. She'll be so disappointed.'

Listening to her friend's voice, Jo felt the tension drain from her body. The sound of reason. An echo of her own thoughts before a scan and emotion got in the way.

'Of course, we'd all be there to support you if you decided … But what about university? You love it! And your career as a journo? Adoption sounds kind, but really, Jo, if you think about it, it has all sorts of consequences. The child might come looking for you one day. They'd want to know about their father. What on earth would you say?'

Thank God, oh, thank God. Kate was there for her. Her eyes huge and concerned, her hand tightly around hers.

'I know I sound harsh, Jo, but you know I'm right. A single parent? That isn't you. You're so bright and clever. And one day you'll meet someone fabulous and have his beautiful babies!'

The tears were of relief. And gratitude.

'Don't worry. I'll be here on Tuesday, Jo, absolutely. I'll drive you to the clinic and hold your hand. I promise.'

36

Manchester – present day

The telephone rang, but Jo was so deeply asleep and woozy from whisky that it became part of her underworld. Still a teenager and at home in Moor End, the old-fashioned green receiver was blaring. Then an echo of her brother's voice: *'No. Don't put this on me. No, Jo. This is down to you. I have enough problems of my own.'*

Scrabbling out of the darkness, she tried to shake herself awake. What the hell? A dream about Nigel, of all people. Ah, that was right, he'd found a new love in Corfu. Had Joyce told her? Was it a glimpse from a postcard or was she still dozing? But the shrill peal continued and with a sudden throbbing alertness, she realised the call was for real. Whoever it was would continue to shout until she roused herself and answered it.

Staggering to the lounge, she snatched up the handset. 'Hello?'

'Thank God!' It was Kate. 'Jo, it's me. I'm in trouble and I need you,' she said in a rush. 'I'm in Buxton. You have to come straight away.' Then, after a moment, 'You are listening, aren't you, Jo? Why was your mobile off? I've been ringing for ages.'

'Was it? Sorry. Yes, I'm listening. What's happened?'

After listening to the instructions, Jo put down the phone and steadied herself on the sofa arm until the dizziness passed. Lifting her head, her gaze caught the empty mugs on the coffee table. No, don't think of that now. Kate said it was urgent; she pledged to leave immediately. A promise is a promise. Immediately means now. Come on, girl, time to move.

Trotting back to her bedroom, Jo pulled on underwear and a t-shirt, then fumbled with the buttons on her jeans for several seconds before giving up. Roughly dragging a brush through her hair, she made for the bathroom and threw back water from the grubby toothbrush glass. She cleaned her teeth at the same time as popping two painkillers, grabbed a water bottle, a banana and her handbag, finally slamming the door in the space of twelve minutes.

She climbed in the car, tugged on her seat belt and looked at the time. Ten o'clock. Would she be over the alcohol limit? She'd gone to bed as soon as Tom left, but there'd been too much confusion darting around her head, so she'd climbed out of Richard's side and found one last miniature at the back of the cupboard, brandy this time.

Mixing, more mixing, she had thought as she drifted. Mixing emotions, mixing memories, mixing metaphors. The word sounded strange after several goes. 'A jumble,' she decided as unconsciousness sucked her in. 'My life is a catastrophic jumble.'

Her throat raspy and head pounding, she reversed from her space. Though paying for it now, the brandy had, at least, done the trick. An image of Kate slumped against her rattled in. Oh God, she should have been more sympathetic during the *weekend horribilis*, shouldn't she? Everyone boozes for a reason. Hers was to sleep last night, to be oblivious to the mental chaos hounding her. Perhaps

Kate had needs too. She should've asked; she should've listened at the farmhouse or later, tried to understand and sympathise.

She'd been a crap friend.

The smooth voice of the satnav and the swish of windscreen wipers keeping her company, Jo drove steadily, deep in thought. In truth she hadn't been attentive to Kate for a long time. But for years she *had* listened to her every woe and worry, she'd been her constant crutch, her steadfast companion. It was only when they finally left St Luke's that she realised how entrapped she had felt by Kate's demands, her dependency. The feeling of freedom and escape had been immense and surprising. Tinged with guilt too. But Jo was coming now, at a moment's notice, hurtling down the busy A6 as fast as the heavy traffic would allow.

Because Kate had asked her to; because she was needed.

It was only when she hit the saturated Derbyshire countryside that a thought occurred to her. The one time she had asked the same of Kate, to drop everything and come because she was desperately needed, Kate had let her down.

Jo parked the car and looked up to the building. It was as handsome as one would expect of the grand spa town. She and Kate had often come here on trips for inter-school competitions: singing, individual and choral-verse speaking. Joyce had kept all Jo's Guildhall School of Music and Drama certificates in an envelope, along with St Luke's bills and other memorabilia. She doubted Hilary would have done the same.

Picturing a golden-haired Kate on the stage, she smiled wryly at the memory. Speech, singing and drama. They were the only things she excelled in. Did she remember? Would she see the irony?

Taking a deep breath, she pushed open the door. She hadn't been in a police station for many years, not since trying to eke out information from surly desk sergeants at various grotty bases in the northwest for the newspaper. In fairness a bright smile had gone a long way in those days. She doubted in her current state she'd get far today.

This station sergeant wasn't surly; indeed he had a tug at the corner of his mouth which suggested the contrary. 'Ah, you're the friend Mrs Heath called,' he said, lifting his eyebrows. 'This way. Had to put her into an interview room to calm her right down.' His lips twitched again. 'She was in a bit of a state, to put it mildly. I'll show you through, shall I?'

Kate was sitting at a metal table that was attached to one wall. Concerned though she was, Jo couldn't help seeing the comedy of putting Catherine Bayden-Jones, of all people, in a room designed for dangerous criminals.

'Thank God you've come,' she said tearfully, rising from her plastic seat with open arms like a child.

Jo gave her friend a quick and tight hug, then led her back to the bench and sat opposite. Covering her shaking fingers, she examined Kate's ashen face. The information she had imparted on the telephone was brief – she'd had an accident in the car and was at Buxton police station. When Jo had asked for more, her voice became tetchy and tearful. 'Are you coming, Jo, or do I have to ask someone else?'

'What's happened, Kate?' Jo now asked, glancing around the functional bare room (the smell of stale pee took her right back to working at the paper, to primary and little Jimmy Heath too). 'Kate?' she repeated. The officer had given his version of events with a judgemental sigh, but she wanted to hear it from the horse's mouth. Only then would she believe it to be true. 'And where's Tom?' she added.

Kate finally spoke. 'I haven't telephoned him yet.'

Jo sat back. 'Why not?' she asked, Tom's unannounced visit last night suddenly large in her mind.

'I don't know. He might be cross with me. And when he gets angry . . .' Kate replied, her eyes flickering, evasive.

Jo felt her own wrists and pushed the notion away. 'I'm sure he will be cross, Kate. You were over the limit apparently. Well over, according to the sergeant. He could smell it on your breath. That isn't normal at half past nine in the morning.'

Looking at the ground, she tried to assess her willingness to obey Kate's command, even now. It was uncomfortable for sure, but there was something else too, that vaporous feeling she could never quite grasp. When she looked up, Kate's face was wet, those silent large tears Jo remembered.

She leaned forward and took Kate's hand. 'Hey. It isn't that bad, no one was hurt. That's the important thing. I expect the insurers will pay for the damage to the other car—'

'And the fruit shop,' Kate blurted. 'The car hit the stalls at the front. The fruit was everywhere, on the pavement, in the road.' She gazed, her mortified expression throwing Jo back in time again. 'Oranges were everywhere, Jo. They'll all be laughing at me. Everyone in the village. I can't bear it.'

'No, they won't, and if they do gossip a little, it'll blow over in no time.' She squeezed Kate's palm. 'Thing is, Tom's going to find out sooner or later. Obviously! Come on, Kate, you need to call him, before someone else tells—'

Kate rose abruptly. 'I can't!'

Covering her mouth as though to hold in the words, she leaned towards Jo's ear. 'I can't tell him, not yet,' she said quietly. The sergeant was right, the sour stench of alcohol was still on her breath. 'He'll be angry, so angry. He'll ask me about Alice.'

Jo pulled back to examine her face. 'What about Alice? Please don't tell me she was in the car when it happened?'

'No, Jo, she wasn't.' Kate flicked a glance before whispering again. 'But . . . well, we were running late, so I drove her to school today. I was on my way back through the village and the other car pulled out. Just ran out in front of me and there was nothing I could do. It wasn't my fault.'

Her chair clattering to the floor, Jo stood. She needed to shout very loudly. 'What the fuck!' she wanted to yell. 'Your daughter is six years old! She's a precious, beautiful child. What the hell were you *thinking*?' But she needed time to absorb it. This was Kate, for God's sake. Calm and composed and sensible Kate. She couldn't quite believe she would do such a reckless thing. It was crazy.

Kate was watching her. 'I only had one little glass this morning to keep me going, Jo. To get me out of the house. And it really wasn't my fault. Honestly. The other driver just darted out of nowhere.'

'Well, one *little glass* is all it takes if you went to sleep drunk. You must know that!'

Kate's voice became petulant. 'But Tom wasn't there last night. He'd gone somewhere and turned off his mobile. It was late and I was worried, so I just had one or two to calm my nerves. You see, Jo, it really wasn't my fault, was it? Tom wasn't home when I needed him. And this morning the other driver was in the wrong. Really, Jo, you have to do something.'

Jo sighed and sat down, that familiar surge of responsibility and entrapment leaden in her chest. There was no point reasoning with Kate in this state. Besides, she was here, she was already *caught*.

And, of course, she knew where Tom had been.

'What am I supposed to do about it, Kate? What on earth could I possibly do?' she asked wearily.

'I don't know; you're the clever one, Jo.' Kate traced a finger along a deep scratch on the table top. 'But I thought that maybe you could drive to Alice's primary before Tom hears anything. You could have a chat with her about this morning. Tell her that going to school in the car is our little secret and not to tell Daddy. She's to say that we walked as usual if he asks. Then he won't need to know . . .' She lifted her head, her eyes bright with entreaty. 'You know how Alice loves you. She'll do anything for you, Jo! And it won't happen again ever. I promise.'

Almost dumbstruck with disbelief, Jo gaped, but she was saved from replying. A brisk knock and the door was opening.

'Your husband is here, Mrs Heath,' the sergeant said, his twitch turning into the smallest of smiles. 'I'll show him through, shall I?'

Leaving the stink of urine behind, Jo slogged down the corridor, brushing past Tom without looking his way. In the waiting room she stopped and perched on a chair to catch her breath. Her mind jerked from thought to thought. What now? Should she hang around or leave? Neither prospect felt as though it would have a good outcome, not for her anyway. And what the hell was going on? Kate's suggestion that she 'silence' Alice, a six-year-old child, was astounding. Kate's whole reaction to the arrest, her failure to tell Tom, her apparent fear of him, was bizarre. Tom was a 'darling'. Kate had told her so for the last twenty years; there'd never been anything to suggest otherwise.

Not wanting to talk, she tried not to meet the eye of the officer, but he had other ideas.

'Mr Heath didn't look very happy, did he? I'd like to be a fly on that wall. One thing you learn in this job is that nothing's a surprise. Nice-looking lady, your *fine* friend. Butter wouldn't melt. But she can't half stand up for herself. Dutch courage, eh? Not the first customer we've brought in morning drunk and it won't be the last.' He chuckled. 'Face like thunder, he had. A major bollocking is my guess. What do you reckon?'

Jo had no idea what to *reckon*, but she needed to escape from the oppressive room and his curious gaze. 'Fag break,' she said, as though she needed an excuse to get some fresh air, to inhale the Buxton drizzle.

Losing count of how many times she'd circuited the car park on foot, she suddenly realised her hair was inordinately wet. Ah, layers of drizzle, she thought as she glanced in the wing mirror of a police van. She looked dreadful too; layers again, of alcohol this time, which had accumulated under each eye and turned a purplish grey.

Sighing, she walked back to her car and sat inside, drumming her fingers on the steering wheel. A song about *staying* and *going* and *trouble* looped through her head as she waited. Then eventually she saw them emerge from the building, a golden couple indeed. Kate was smiling at her husband and leaning against him, her arm slotted tightly through his.

Jo watched, fascinated. Bloody hell! What had Kate said to Tom? How had she wriggled out of doing something so irresponsible? His face was fixed, but there was no sign of reprimand. 'No bollocking, then,' she said quietly to herself.

She continued to gaze. Tom opened the passenger side of his Range Rover, helped Kate in like an invalid and closed it gently with the flat of his hand. She turned away then, pulled on her seat belt and pressed the ignition, but her door was abruptly wrenched open.

'Who the hell do you think you are?' Tom demanded, his face blanched with anger, his words staccato. 'I find out from some random woman in the village post office that my wife is in police cells, I drive like a lunatic to Buxton and find you here with Kate, without a fucking word to me.'

Her heart thumping with shock, Jo took a rapid breath. 'I'm sorry, Tom, but Kate telephoned me first thing this morning and I came. It's as simple as that.'

'And you'll do anything for Kate, right? Or at least you like to go through the motions to make you seem less selfish, to ease your conscience,' he said, tight-lipped.

She took her hands off the wheel and stared for a moment. His words were unfair and hurtful, but then again, she understood how annoyed she would be if a whole village knew her private business before she did. But this was more than irritation; Tom was barely keeping himself together and he looked close to tears. His fingers were on the enamel, white and knotted. She touched them lightly. 'What's going on, Tom?' she asked gently. 'With you and Kate?'

Recoiling, he pulled back and stepped away. 'Don't you dare,' he said, pointing. 'Don't you dare. Just leave us alone.'

The rain spattering in, Jo watched through the mirror as he climbed into the Range Rover, reversed it smoothly, then accelerated away with a purr.

'It's not my fault!' she wanted to shout, an echo of Kate's words. But a feeling of culpability was there, a tug from the past. Damp grass and dandelions? Flowing water and stones? She strained to reach it, but the memory fluttered through her fingers like the wispy flower's seeds.

She shook her head. Not her fault? Perhaps in some way it was.

37

St Luke's – April 1989

Still wearing grey uniform, but with stripy dresses duly packed (as per the *clothing list*), the girls arrived at Junior House to start the summer term. Same bed, same dormitory, same smell and routine. (Same disgusting *silverfish* infestation in the Eighteen Dorm loo.)

Jo wasn't aware of Kate's nocturnal visitor at first, but one night she woke from a frightening dream to glimpse a figure at the foot of the bed. The shock of seeing a looming dark phantom on top of the nightmare was so fierce that she nearly screamed out loud. But the lavender aroma was undoubtedly there, so she managed to hold back, watching intently as Cecily Smyth moved forwards and quietly lay full length on Kate's bed.

'What on earth was Cecil doing last night? I woke up and she climbed on your bed!' she said to Kate when they were finally alone the next day.

'She's keeping a close eye on me, like she said she would,' Kate replied easily, skipping ahead. 'She's been doing it all week.'

Jo frowned. It seemed a very odd thing. 'What does she do?' she asked, running to catch up.

'Nothing,' Kate replied, shrugging. 'Sleep, maybe? She's gone in the morning.'

Jo was still spending a great deal of time with the reference books. For some reason, perhaps their weight or their smell, and the fact that one wasn't allowed to remove them, they made her feel important. They even figured in the plot of the romance story she developed each night before sleep.

'Oh, I've been in the library reading a reference book,' her wise and bespectacled (but not yet very pretty) heroine would casually mention to the handsome and chiselled hero. (He had a scar, as one would expect, but a tasteful one. He also smelled of sweat, but nothing like either of her brothers.) He, of course, would eventually fall in love, not with her slow-growing beauty, but with her exquisite mind. Biology books were (not surprisingly) the heroine's current favourites, diagrams of the male of the species especially (which included a *penis* and *testicles* – she knew about the former, but the latter was a shock), which held both her and Jo in thrall.

Later that day, Jo spent time with several tomes, her finger denting each index momentarily as she dragged it down the page, making sure not to miss anything obviously connected with 'close eye', but with no success. She also tried staying awake, several nights on the trot, just long enough to review the visit and inspect it at close hand. But she was exhausted at bedtime and wanted to progress her story plot (from flirting to *actual* kissing), so if Cecil continued to visit, she was asleep by then. In any event, she lost interest after a while. But one morning Kate was bursting to tell her some news as they filed down to the dining hall for breakfast.

'Guess what?' she hissed.

'What?'

'You have to guess!'

'It could be anything, Kate. Unless you give me a clue, and we're nearly there.'

'She gave me a cuddle last night!' Kate announced, her face flushed with pleasure.

'Cecil gave you a *cuddle*? What do you mean?' Jo asked, trying not to feel miffed that Kate was so pleased with herself yet again.

Kate shrugged as they joined the (stomach-turning) scrambled-egg-flavoured queue. 'It was just like Mummy, really. I'll show you later ...'

Kate dragged Jo into the music room at break.

'So do you want me to show you?' she asked.

'Show me what?'

Putting a hand on her waist, Kate tutted. 'You know perfectly well.'

'Sure ...'

Jo flinched at the thin kisses Kate planted across her forehead and cheeks. She wasn't used to anybody getting so physically close, only her mother, and that was when she was ill or upset. But after a moment or so, she experienced a nice warm feeling which spread through her skinny chest like a Fisherman's Friend.

'Hm, I see what you mean,' she said, pulling away. She didn't want to be too enthusiastic about her best friend's popularity with Miss Smyth, and she was more than a little worried someone might look into the glass door and see them. 'It's OK, I suppose.'

Kate took a step back and looked at Jo, her eyes like cat slits. 'You're just jealous, Joanna Wragg! You wish it was you!' she said, sitting down at the piano in triumph.

Jo didn't reply, but nudged Kate up the stool and began to practise the latest tune she'd picked up by ear. This 'keeping a close eye' was all very strange and she needed time to mull it over.

*

213

'Jo, darling, can we have a little chat about Kate?' Hilary asked.

It was a *vizzy day* and Kate was in the tearoom toilets. Jo's parents never came for afternoon visits on a Saturday, even though they lived closer than Kate's. But that was fine; Jo loved spending time with Hilary, Kate and her sisters. Besides, it wouldn't have been the same with her mum twitching over the 'extortionate price' of the cakes and scones, when she could've rustled them up in ten minutes.

Hilary leaned over, her new perfume intoxicating. 'Is Kate eating properly at school?' she asked easily, holding the teacup in her right hand, a cigarette in a ruby-red holder in her left. 'Leaving a nice clean plate like Matron says?' she added with a conspiratorial smile.

Tensing, Jo wondered how to reply. Logically speaking, Kate *was* eating properly. Perhaps she sicked it back up again, but she didn't know that for certain.

'Yes,' she replied, trying to ignore her mum's face in her mind's eye. ('A lie by omission is still a lie, Joanna. You know that.')

'You would tell me if Kate was unhappy, wouldn't you?' Hilary asked, peering intently, as though she *knew*.

Savouring a last teaspoonful of Devon clotted cream, Jo nodded. It was too delicious to waste, albeit rather sickly on its own. As she swallowed it down, she felt safe on that score. Kate was happy; she'd been as cheery as a cherry since Cecil started *keeping a close eye* on her. Indeed her position as Form One favourite pet had been upgraded. Not only was she still visited at night, she was occasionally invited into Cecil's rooms before bedtime to pour tea from a gold-rimmed china pot into a matching delicate cup (with a saucer, of course) and to share a chocolate biscuit or two. (A wafer base, a thick layer of orange fondant cream and an even thicker layer of chocolate covering *and* wrapped in gold foil. Jo's mouth had watered – Kate had been very descriptive.)

214

The bullying had all but stopped, not least because Kate was no longer fat so the name 'Fatty' seemed silly.

Kate was definitely content. For now, at least. Watchful as ever, Jo had noticed that Miranda's green eyes still stared malevolently at Kate for longer than was comfortable. There was no doubt in Jo's mind she was simply biding her time. But she wasn't going to tell Hilary about that; Kate was far too perky and pleased to unsettle.

38

St Luke's

Kate's visits to Cecil's room become so commonplace that Jo barely noticed them. She was busy herself on the sports field most afternoons. She still doted on Kate but reasoned there was no point hanging around uselessly in the library or the playground. She'd discovered a competitive streak. It turned out she was good at games, a demon with sticks, bats and racquets in particular, and she could run faster than girls two or three years older.

Alert to the lardy games mistress's reluctance to select her for anything, let alone for inter-school competitions, Jo persevered until the woman had no choice. Then she spent much of her time after lessons running and jumping, catching and thwacking balls and best of all winning. Very quietly coming first.

She still received detailed reports from Kate if anything unusual or special had occurred; if the foil wrappers on the biscuits changed colour or if Miss Smyth bestowed any particular praise. She already knew Kate had graceful hands and uniquely shaped eyes.

She agreed that her singing voice was exquisite and that she had the best deportment in Junior House. Though the description of her handwriting as 'elegant' was a stretch (more than a stretch – it was loopy but really quite scruffy, and she should know), she was aware Kate would marry well and make everyone proud.

Jo accepted these things as truth, not because Cecil told Kate and Kate eagerly related it, but because she could see for herself and wholly concurred.

In the evenings she sat alone in the library, occasionally glancing at the closed orange curtains, but mostly immersed in the (still higgledy-piggledy) array of books. Even now, she loved their smell (vanilla and almonds, she decided), especially if one was new and she was the first person to open it (glue? she wondered when she was older).

Dipping in became a favourite game. With her eyes closed, she'd bump her finger along the spines on a shelf before stopping at that day's given number. Then she'd read a section from it, from a paragraph to a chapter, depending on her fancy, and if it was a romance or a mystery she'd skim-read the whole novel through at one sitting.

It was only when she looked back that she realised books and the library were her escape and her freedom, her way of coping with the claustrophobia. But at the time the best part was no one bothered her there. She was quiet, nondescript and unimportant, and thus invisible, which was useful at times, particularly when there was gossip to be learned.

The first 'summer' at St Luke's started earlier than usual. The headmistress gave the order from her rooms in the ghostly senior block (which Kate and Jo had never seen and didn't want to) that pupils were to switch over from winter uniform to dresses. Out went the grey skirt and cardigan, the blouses and ties and brown lace-up shoes. In came the striped frocks, white socks and sandals, even though it was only May. Ditching their grey bags, the girls enjoyed the draughty freedom of wearing just one pair of knickers.

The feeling of elation rippled through the whole school. Never having worn summer attire before, Jo and Kate were particularly excited. There had been four choices of frock colour at Cole Brothers: yellow, green, blue and red. Joyce had chosen blue for Jo, three of the same in the next size up so they'd do for this year and next. Kate had one of each colour with hair ribbons to match. But Jo didn't mind blue, she was more excited about her cardie and socks. She'd never had a white cardigan before in her life and her mum had astonishingly allowed her one with some embroidered embellishment on the front. With white pearl buttons too! It was the equivalent of Hilary's fur; it made her feel fabulous.

Jo was *dipping in* one evening, indiscernible as usual, when a group of girls from Lower Third bustled into the library. Tall and worldly, their dresses were belted tightly, their white socks rolled down and their boob bumps were starting to show.

From the reference books, Jo knew that some girls started puberty at eleven, some even earlier, and that it involved bosoms and bleeding. Jo and Kate's year had watched a film about menstruation in the dining hall, but it was ancient, from World War II someone said, so most girls were none the wiser, save for whispers that it was known as *the curse*. But it was clear from their new-found confidence and size that the Lower Third girls knew all about it; perhaps they had even *started*.

They stood in a huddle near the door. Jo recognised them as part of Miranda's entourage so she kept her head low in the book.

'Have you heard about Kate Bayden-Jones?' one of the girls asked.

'Ssh. Keep your voice down. Cecil might be listening.'

'It's fine, I saw her walking to her car . . .'

Her ears pricking, Jo pushed her new glasses up her nose. They were National Health and she knew they made her look even uglier than before. She had begged her mum to buy pretty pink frames, like the ones Hilary had bought Clare, but she said Jo was bound to break them and that she could have *nice* ones when she was older.

'Kate Bayden-Jones is a lezzy,' the girl whispered to the others. Her eyebrows were raised, her gaze huge and knowing. 'She does things with Cecil ...'

'It's true, it really is,' another said, nodding her head with conviction. 'Barbara Hawkins saw it with her own eyes!'

'Really?'

'Yes. They snog and stuff. And apparently she left her grey bags in Cecil's sitting room. They were found by the cleaner.'

'Oh my God, that's disgusting! Does Miranda know?'

'Of course, it was Miranda who told me.'

Jo glanced at the frosted door of Cecil's room with dread. She knew she'd have to break this development to Kate. She had no idea what a *lezzy* was, but she was certain it wasn't a good thing.

The hissing and hushed chanting began almost immediately, 'Lezzy, lezzy, lezzy,' whenever Kate walked by, if there was no teacher in sight. Even the younger girls joined in, participating in the fun without the slightest realisation of what it meant. Although Kate was slightly surprised that the lull in hostilities had ended, she took no notice at first, supposing it was just another name to ignore, another complaint to discuss with Miss Smyth at their next meeting. So she held her head high with Jo resolutely at her side.

Miranda said not a word, her face patiently malevolent. Biding her time, Jo guessed, waiting for the question to come, which inevitably it did, quite soon.

A loud whisper from a small girl at the toilet end of their dorm. 'Miranda, what's a lezzy?'

The lights were *out* and talking was forbidden, so the sound resonated through the long room, allowing each little ear to prick up and hear clearly.

'What did you say, Belinda?'

'What's a lezzy, Miranda?'

'Lezzy is short for lesbian. L-e-s-b-i-a-n.' Miranda spelt the word out, her voice ringing with clarity as she mimicked the elocution mistress. 'You can look it up in a dictionary in the morning. No more talking now, girls, lights are out.'

39

Manchester – present day

The July rain, then procrastination. Jo had found herself at the top of St John Street without an umbrella (or a flipping coat), so she decided to sprint to the tram station and take the one stop to Central Library (without a ticket – who said she didn't live an exciting and dangerous life?). But the tram was just leaving without her (story of her life) so, on a whim, and to dry off, she jumped on a carriage going the other way. In for a penny, she thought (not that she'd paid one). She might as well get hung for a sheep. And besides, it was Saturday, there were damp people to watch.

A young woman immediately caught her attention. Not because of the small child sitting on her knee, but the noise coming from her mobile phone. *Peppa Pig* was on full volume, far too loud for the coach, let alone the poor child.

Jo scanned the blank faces of the passengers around her. Would someone say something? Ask for the sound to be turned down? A woman with red hair was turned to the window. She did another take. Not again, surely? She leaned for a better look, but the baby cried out, so she quickly snapped her head back.

'What?' the mum said flatly, picking up a bottle and thrusting the teat into the child's mouth.

Irritation rising, Jo gazed at the baby. A girl, she assumed, with blonde downy hair rubbed and knotted at the back. She was gazing at the screen, the fingers of one chubby hand in her mouth, the others softly threading through her mum's long hair, a gesture of love which made Jo turn her attention to the mother. A young mum; too young, probably. Her face seemed unbearably sad, sorrow and tears near the surface. She wanted to reach out then, to ask if she was OK. Perhaps *she* was an eighteen-year-old who'd had to make a choice; maybe she regretted the one she'd made.

Was it possible Joanna Wragg hadn't made the wrong decision after all?

A loud 'quack' from the programme and an exquisite peal of laughter cut through her thoughts. The baby was chortling, the mum kissing her head and smiling with pride.

Taking a deep breath to combat the tears, Jo closed her eyes. She had to move on; she had to get out there, make new friends, build those bloody bridges with the old ones. She took out her mobile. Lily hadn't yet replied to her text suggesting a get-together. Who could blame her? Jo had blanked her after the funeral. And bringing up a kid was demanding.

'Hope little Finn is over the chickenpox,' she texted. 'I fancy dusting off the old cookbooks. Are you and Noah free to come for dinner one Saturday soon?'

She hit send, sat back and blew out. There, that was easy. And the rain had eased. Time to stop dithering and get to the library.

The bloody English summer, she mused, as she gazed from a window of the newly refurbished building. It fools me every time!

She had supposed that the balmy June sunshine was set for summer, but since turning the calendar it had pissed down intermittently like a miserable February. She was glad to be indoors, but the library was just that touch chilly, the weather obviously having fooled it too.

So there! she thought. I'm not the only fool here.

But it very much felt like it. Unlike the Midas family, everything she touched seemed to crumble and die. Or so it seemed. No one, not even Ben or Joyce, had been in touch all week. Nothing but bloody postcards from Nigel, two arriving on the same day. But in fairness to him, now she'd taken the time to actually read them, she found they were interesting, intoxicating almost. A travelogue of escape, with quirky descriptions of all the places he'd visited. From ancient monuments to white sandy beaches. From bustling markets to wiry hiking terrain. She was half minded, but only half, to contact him and suggest a book of some sort. It would have to be fleshed out, of course, but the postcards already formed the bare bones.

The reading room was surprisingly full for a Saturday. After her tram diversion, she had tried her best to knuckle down and work. She was there to peruse and research for an article, 'The Libido of Men Over Sixty'. She had found herself people-watching again, but this time she had an excuse.

Though age was often difficult to judge, she gazed at another man in the bracket. Not bad looking, she thought, though a good head of hair made all the difference. Perhaps she should ask him; she could do it to a stranger and it would save a lot of time swotting. Slip him a little note along the bench. *How many times a month would you like to shag? How many times a month* can *you shag? If ever?* Or maybe she should ask her dad. He'd be sixty-six next month. 'All the sixes', as he put it.

The Bahamian snaps popped into her head – her mum's shoulder coquettishly forward, smiling for the camera and wearing that floral bikini. She snorted inwardly. Not only would such a direct question be a breach of Wragg etiquette, it would be acknowledging the possibility that even her mum and dad were at it (*not* a nice image at all!).

Ready for another stroll to break the monotony, she stood up and stretched. She wasn't thinking about sex *per se*. It was just that today her emotions were jumbled. PMT probably. She felt slightly envious of everybody. Small minded and pathetic, she knew, but after her attempt at positivity on the tram, she felt dejected, morose and ridiculously sorry for herself. Even Nigel was having more fun than her; life was that bad.

Some mums had brought in toddlers and were reading quietly to them in the kids' section of the library. Jo tried for her indulgent smile as she passed, but the truth was that God, or whoever, had dealt her a shit hand. Would she and Richard have conceived eventually? Or was their 'failure' related in some way to the termination? Unlikely, she knew, but the notion was always there, deeply hidden at the very back of her mind.

Tom Heath had made it topical, though. Well done, Tom!

She shoved the thought away. She hadn't heard anything from the Golden Couple for over two weeks. But that was fine, absolutely. A bloody good thing, in fact. The whole episode of Tom and his offer was ridiculous. She was over it.

Well, if she repeated it enough, she would be.

Jo's promise to herself (or perhaps *command*) had been a whole day of hard research at the library before a relaxing evening at Judy's. She'd taken nuts to snack on and a large bottle of water, but the almonds became repetitive and tasteless, the Evian even more so. So she surrendered by three, lured by the thought of a toasted bagel soaked in a specific brand of butter. Not that she was fussy, she just knew what she liked.

The rain was on a break, the sunshine making a valiant attempt to peek through the nimbus clouds, so she walked home the long way round. Past the tram station, GMEX and the glossy Bridgewater development, down the newly cleaned arches, along the canal towards the back end of Deansgate, avoiding the Saturday shoppers.

Her backpack bouncing behind, she studied her surroundings as she strolled. What would she write on a travelogue postcard? It was difficult to imagine, the mundane was hard to describe. Yet she knew this city centre was far from ordinary. The buildings were spectacular, from the revamped library and the glassy office blocks opposite, to central station and the Bridgewater Hall. The 47-storey Beetham Tower had transformed the skyline and more was to come. Then there was the financial centre, bars and posh shops at Spinningfields. Even the Arndale Centre was hugely improved from her student days.

But one got used to the everyday. Which was why, she supposed, she spent too much time obsessing over what she didn't have.

Like an evil wink, the answerphone was flashing when she returned to the flat. Same as the post, a message was rarely something nice. She was minded to get rid of it. Of course she had a mobile, but Joyce didn't, and Jo still liked to give strangers her landline number; it felt less intimate. And some people used a mix of mobile and home.

Like Kate, she thought with a sudden clutch of apprehension, Kate used both.

She pressed the button and stood back, involuntarily holding her breath as she listened. There was just one message, from Aidan.

'Hi, Jo Jo. I'm in Manchester this weekend. Do you fancy another night out on the town? Call me back.' His voice sounding a touch Irish.

She couldn't help feeling a smattering of pleasure. At least someone liked her company, at least there was somebody who didn't think her *selfish and cold*.

Cheered by Aidan's message, Jo ate her bagel, sang along to the Stereophonics and took her time getting ready. She showered, put on make-up, a fitted dress and leopard-print heels. Then she sprayed herself with (overly expensive) perfume. It was only a casual get-together at Judy's apartment half a mile up the road, but it felt good to make an effort.

Jo wasn't entirely sure what turned a *flat* into an *apartment*, but in fairness Judy and Larry's penthouse *whatever* was spectacular. On the sixth *and* seventh floor of the renovated building, the huge balcony overlooked the River Irwell and the Lowry Hotel.

The sun had finally won, gently warming her back as she cradled Evie. Her pretty eyes were drooping as she drifted into sleep. Completely clear of the livid rash, her skin was now perfect. Time, Jo thought. Time heals.

'I'll pop Evie in her cot,' she said, though no one seemed to hear.

Larry, his father and brother were sitting in a semicircle. Each holding a glass of red wine in one hand and gesticulating with the other, they were deep in conversation. The discussion, it seemed, was about the economy. As though taking it all in for when he grew up, little William was gripping his own drink and avidly watching.

'You will come, won't you? For my sanity?' Judy had asked in the week.

She always invited Jo to any family occasions – Larry's family, that was, hers being tucked away in Sacramento. They seemed nice enough to Jo, but she could see why Judy needed moral support. Larry's clan were sharp and intense people, only appearing to discuss dry and serious issues, generally politics or finance. She suspected they considered Judy to be a touch below them intellectually; it was the way they spoke slowly to her, carefully enunciating their words.

'I'm not a child, I'm American!' Judy laughed with Jo. But the irony was that she was clever, very clever. She'd met Larry at Oxford on a Rhodes scholarship.

'See what I mean?' she now whispered to Jo in her spacious kitchen. 'Dull, dull, dull! Thanks for coming.'

It was on the tip of Jo's tongue to say it was fine, that she had nothing better to do, but she held back. She didn't want Judy to know quite how lonely she was. Instead she accepted the proffered glass of wine with a smile. She'd already told her about the flirtation with Guy Voide because that didn't matter, but the other surreal events of the past few weeks had got stuck in her throat.

She inwardly sighed. Why couldn't she confide? She wished she could say, 'I slept with my brother's lover, the first person since Richard, and I don't know how I feel.' Or, 'My best friend was over the limit at nine o'clock in the morning driving her kid to school. She asked me to lie and I haven't heard a peep since. Oh, and her husband offered to father me a child, something I long for. What would you do?'

But she knew the answer. That person would say, 'No, you can't possibly do such an awful thing. Why are you even thinking about it?'

That's how they would respond, wouldn't they?

Feeling a bit tipsy and content from the vino, Jo strolled home through the gardens. She rather liked family events and found herself increasingly invited to them (like a spinster-aunt character from an Austen novel) because she was willing to chat to the guests and was good with children.

And because I'm always available, she thought. But still, not completely selfish, surely?

She smiled as she walked. She suspected Judy was grooming her as potential wife material for Larry's brother. He wasn't bad looking, albeit with thinning fine hair. And definitely wealthy enough; he'd bought both himself and his ex a five-bedroomed house in Hale. He was president of both his local golf and tennis clubs (so presumably had a reasonable body), he already had kids (so his sperm count was up to scratch) but, as Judy herself put it, was *'dull, dull, dull'*.

But then again, Jo mused, still trying for upbeat, Judy had often alluded to her incredible sex life with Larry (mind-blowing, surely, if she was trading Californian sunshine for Mancunian rain). Perhaps sexual prowess ran in the family, so if all else failed . . .

Turning into St John Street, Jo stopped. Her stomach contracted and lurched. Between the cherry trees, a Range Rover was parked next to hers, like kippers in a packet. The evening was dimming but she could clearly see Tom in the driver's seat, his head forward on the steering wheel, resting on his arms.

Her heart thumping, she slowly approached. The window was open, the breeze lightly wafting his hair. His eyes were closed, his face stony still. Like death, she thought, struggling to find the image of Richard on the grass, to see how they compared.

'Tom? Wake up, Tom. Are you all right?'

No response, so she reached for his shoulder and touched it, light and hesitant, like one might stroke a sedated lion – wanting it to be soft and warm with life, but fearful of its bite.

Opening his eyes, he gazed, a moment's confusion passing through them. Then he rubbed his face. 'Can I come in?' he asked.

40

Barnsley – January 1999

Relieved and thankful Kate would be at the clinic to give sympathy and support, Jo felt she could survive days four, five and six. The decision had been made; the hard part was over. She just had to get past those final minutes and hours, then through it. *It* being the procedure, the abortion. A gritty girl with gritted teeth, like a hard-hitting sixties chick flick. Only Joanna Wragg wasn't a working-class girl *up the junction*. Her family was *nouveau riche*, this was the nineties and these days it was called a termination.

But it all added up to the same thing.

She spent New Year's Eve at home with her mum and dad, absently watching the television until she could escape from the bagpipes to her bedroom at midnight. Though Nigel hardly made eye contact, she'd felt Ben's inquisitive gaze when she'd turned down the offer of a party. 'She's very quiet. Do you think it's boyfriend trouble?' she'd heard Stan ask Joyce.

Hiding in her bedroom as much as possible, she read and studied the text for her course. Anglo-Saxon poetry, James Joyce and Milton, none of the trash she usually devoured to relax. She'd never read romance again; it didn't exist in reality. Real life was a bitch.

'Are you all right, love? Scones are just out of the oven and I've bought Lurpak just for you. Or how about a mince pie? There's plenty left. Cup of tea?'

Joyce's face appeared around the bedroom door at regular intervals, lined and worried. But Jo didn't realise her mum's intuition then. Only as a proper grown-up did she wonder what she suspected during those agonising days.

'I'm fine, Mum. Not really hungry. Uni reading. I'm behind, so . . .'

Pushing her away. Always pushing her lovely mum away.

'Oh, and Mum? Kate's driving us to Sheffield on Tuesday. We're shopping for stuff in the sales, and you know what she's like, so it'll probably be all day. No need to set a place for me at dinner.'

Tuesday came with a jerk, suddenly, it seemed in retrospect. The farm rooster woke Jo at five, the dawn of just another day. But it was happening too soon and she didn't feel ready. And she was scared; she'd had stitches at a hospital before going to St Luke's, but Joyce had been there clutching her hand as the doctor sutured her soft flesh, and when she'd come home (after showing herself up by weeping and whimpering during the *procedure*), Stan had been waiting with a brand-new pair of red roller skates from a toy shop in Leeds because she'd been 'such a brave lass'.

She was dressed for eight o'clock and didn't feel brave at all. Though needing her mum's hand more than ever today, she stayed in her bedroom, fearful of questions.

'Oh, you're wearing the skirt I bought you for Christmas! Looks lovely, love,' Joyce said when she popped into Jo's room with steaming tea and hot toast.

A sensible skirt around her stomach for modesty. A nice skirt to show she was a nice girl, not some slag who'd done what she'd done. Not a killer.

The disbelief still intense, she stared through the window at the snow-covered hills, the cows in the next field and sheep freckled beyond. A blood-orange glow lit the horizon. *Red sky at night, shepherds' delight.* What of the morning? Oh, God, *shepherds' warning* . . . She pinched the top of her nose. She was just a child herself. This couldn't be real. But a fluttering in her belly told her otherwise. Pacing the bedroom, she willed Kate to be early. Oh God, she needed a hug, someone to hold her, to say the decision was still the right one. Absolutely the right one.

'Jo?' A muffled voice beyond the door. Thank God, she was here. Lifting her chin, she opened it.

'Jo! Did you hear me? Kate's on the phone,' one of her brothers hollered up.

The *phone*? Scrabbling down the stairs, she ran to the hall and snatched up the receiver. As though they knew the words before she did, her hands trembled uncontrollably.

'Hello?'

'Oh, Jo. I'm so sorry,' Kate said breathlessly. 'I can't get away after all. Tom's asked me to drive him to look at another property. It's in the middle of nowhere, so he can hardly catch a bus. He did mention it and I'd forgotten and it's really important to him and it would look odd if I said shopping was more important. I'm really sorry. You do understand, don't you, Jo?'

41

Manchester – present day

Tom sat in the armchair, silent and staring ahead. Jo closed the curtains this time, blocking out his reflection. And hers. Switching on the small table lamp, she went through to the kitchen trying to focus on drinks. Hot or cold? Coffee or wine?

She came back with tea, which looked too strong in the dim light.

'More milk, maybe,' she muttered, wondering if Tom would ever speak or whether she should leave him to sleep. Or perhaps shake him and shout, 'What the hell is going on, Tom? Why are you here? I don't understand!'

But he took the proffered mug, looked at it briefly and spoke, his voice distant. 'Looks fine. Thanks.'

Perching on the coffee table, she scanned his face. It was completely at odds with his usual composure. Squashed on one side, his hair appeared unwashed and he hadn't shaved. His dull eyes were smudged with dark shadows beneath them. Clearly shattered, he looked as though he hadn't slept for days.

'What's happened, Tom?' she asked quietly, thinking of little William and his wretched face when Evie was ill. It was hard not to reach out, to offer comfort and love.

'Kate's gone to Barton in the Beans with Alice.'

'What, for ever?' she blurted in amazement. The Kate she knew would never leave Tom.

He shook his head and smiled faintly. 'No. Just for a few days.'

'Oh.' There was a flip inside her chest she didn't want to acknowledge. 'So . . . everything's OK?'

Not replying for a moment, he turned the cup in his hands. 'I don't really know,' he said slowly, placing it on the floor. 'But I can't work and I can't sleep. I suppose I need somebody to . . .'

He fell quiet again, then abruptly stood, making Jo flinch on her perch. He paced for a few seconds, then turned.

'No, that's a lie,' he said savagely, resting his burning eyes on her. 'I don't need somebody, I don't need anybody, I need you, Jo. I've driven miles today, the first weekend for years without my wife and my child. I've gone in every direction, I've tried to fight the impulse, but like a bloody pigeon I've come home to you.'

He stopped and laughed, a small dry laugh. 'It's ridiculous, Jo. I'm ridiculous. I know that.' Crouching down, he gazed, then put his fist on his chest. 'You fucking bewitched me,' he said quietly. 'Twenty bloody years ago. And I need you to break the spell, to release me, set me free.'

Lifting a hand to her cheek, he held it there carefully. 'I want you to want me. Still, after all this time.' He rose again and tapped his temple. 'It has to stop, in here.'

Looking distractedly around the room, his hair spiked as he raked fingers through it. 'Sorry, Jo. I've lost it, I know. Ignore me, I'm just tired, so tired.' He felt his pockets. 'I have to go. My car keys. Where did I put them?'

Jo stood up. Her body was trembling, her mind trying to quell the warm surge in her chest, to dampen and expel it. The words *Kate and Alice, Kate and Alice*, thumped in time with her heart.

Lifting his keys from the sideboard, he made for the door.

'Don't go, Tom,' she murmured. 'You can stay here tonight. Things will look better in the morning. You're in no state to drive. You need to sleep and then . . .'

Holding her breath, she kept her distance, watching and waiting as he turned. *Something* seemed to seep through his face, his body, his expression. Doubt, uncertainty. Temptation?

'No, no. I really should get going. There are the dogs and the horses. It isn't far, I'm fine to drive . . .'

Richard's prone body flashed through her eyes. 'No, Tom, you're not.' Sudden fear setting in, she quickly stepped forward, put her arms around his chest and pulled him close. 'Please, Tom. You're scaring me. It's dark now. I really don't want you to drive tonight.'

His head rested on her shoulder; she could *feel* his hesitation.

'You just need sleep, Tom. That's all. Come on, the spare room awaits.' Smiling a small smile, she took him by the hand and tugged lightly. 'This way.'

Sighing, he followed, then sat on the bed. Almost swaying with fatigue, he reached down to his laces.

'I'll do them, lie down,' she said, pulling back the duvet.

His eyes half closed, he watched as she knelt by the bed, slipping off his shoes and socks, then moving on to his shirt, button by button.

'You've bewitched me,' she thought, the notion fluttering in her belly like an unopened gift.

He continued to gaze sleepily, his face expressionless, but as she moved from the bed, he turned and caught her hand.

'Go to sleep, Tom,' she said, gently pulling away from his fingers, turning off the light and closing the door.

The tears already falling, she briskly walked away. It had taken

234

so much self-control not to climb in beside him. She'd wanted to touch him, to feel the warmth of his skin on her lips, to stroke the soft hair on his chest. Oh God, and more, so much more. But she hadn't done it; she hadn't done it. She'd resisted the desire to take something not hers.

42

The peal of her mobile thrust Jo from sleep. Remembering Tom was in the flat, she snatched it up quickly. Well, that was interesting. She'd known he was there without having to shake herself first. It had taken many weeks of *shaking* before she was used to Richard's absence. That terrible waking up, thinking life was fine and dandy and then remembering it was not. But then again, Richard wasn't absent at first; he stayed, a cushion of comfort, for months.

'Jo? Are you there?'

Dizzy from the sudden movement, it took a moment to place the voice.

'Yes—'

'Darling, it's Hilary. Have I woken you?'

'No, it's fine—'

'Can we have a chat about Kate?'

Her heart sinking, Jo turned to the clock. It was actually half past ten, it just felt very early. She'd managed nine and a half hours of sleep without stirring. 'Because you knew Tom was there,' a small voice said. She batted it away, trying to concentrate on Hilary and the spreading dread at the mention of Kate's name.

'Of course,' she replied, almost from habit. This wasn't the first time Hilary had called for such a *chat*.

'You probably don't know, but she's here with Alice. Which isn't odd, *per se* . . .'

A pause. Dramatic effect, perhaps, but more likely for a drag of her cigarette. Joyce had never smoked and had deep smoker's lines above her lips; Hilary smoked twenty a day and didn't. Life wasn't always fair.

'But it's the first time without Tom since they were married,' she continued. 'He drove them down here but he didn't say much before going off again. But then Tom never does, does he? Of course, we all love him to death, but he's always been the strong silent type, hasn't he? Have you any idea what's going on, Jo? Kate's staying tight-lipped for now. I know she'll spill it all out sooner or later, she always does, but if you give me the *heads-up*, as the young people say, it'll save a lot of time and energy.'

Falling back on the pillow, Jo stared at the ceiling. She usually felt on safe ground when it came to Kate's mother. Over the years, when the *line* was so vividly clear, she'd told several white lies for her friend, or fudged the truth – even blatantly lied, she supposed. But today she was stuck for words because she genuinely didn't know what was going on.

The *strong silent type* in question was asleep in the spare room. A man who had said things last night. Exciting, wonderful and inappropriate things, now covered in gold tissue, then wrapped in brown paper and kept secure in a box somewhere deep in her heart. Or perhaps he had just raved, a crazy, sleep-deprived lunatic who'd clearly lost the plot.

Hilary was still speaking. 'Is it the drinking, do you think? For the last two nights Kate has consumed wine as though it's going out of fashion. It's been quite horrible to watch, especially for Harold since he went on the wagon. We'd already sent Alice to bed, thank goodness, but it wasn't nice, *she* wasn't nice, arguing like a fishwife when I said she'd had enough. I think she needs professional help, Jo. Of course, it's not up to us. We're just the old fogeys. Do you think Tom will agree?'

'I really don't know,' Jo replied. 'You'll have to ask Tom.'

'Good idea, darling. Oops, Kate's up, better dash.'

'Who will have to ask me what?'

Tom's voice made her start. 'Oh, I didn't know . . .' Lifting her head from the pillow, she looked to the door. Wearing his unbuttoned shirt and boxers, he was towelling his hair dry.

Suddenly she felt shy; this was the man she'd apparently *bewitched*. He'd *needed* her. She'd assumed he was sleeping, but he'd been in the shower, lathering her soap and shampoo, rubbing himself dry with her towels.

It felt ridiculously intimate.

'Yes, the call . . .' she started. Inwardly she sighed. She didn't want to discuss the *old fogeys*, Kate and her drinking; she didn't want to think about reality. What she *wanted* was to open her present very slowly and peek, before sealing it again.

Those exhilarating words, secret and rousing.

' . . . It was Hilary. She wants to talk to you. About Kate,' she finished.

Lying back down, she hid her hot cheeks. Tom's large presence in her bedroom made her uncomfortable, the subject matter even more so. They hadn't mentioned the dreadful Buxton episode last night, but it was there, Kate was there, looming large like a phantom.

Her eyes half closed, she watched him above the top of the duvet. Running fingers through his fringe, his face was thoughtful. Still in good shape, he most certainly was not a *balding, fat, middle-aged* type. More like his old self this morning, the sleep had done him good. The stubble was interesting, though. She'd never seen it before yesterday, and why would she? He was a stranger, a person she hardly knew.

Seeming to make up his mind, he tossed the towel aside and sat by her on the bed.

'We need to talk about her, Jo. About Kate. She's my wife, the mother of my child. I know you don't want to be disloyal or involved, but . . . ' He spread his hands. 'You are involved, we're all involved, that's why it's so difficult.'

His voice was tender, too tender. She couldn't say why, but disappointment hit her chest like an unexpected thump. Trying to fend off the need to cry, she put her hands to her face, but he took them in his own, gently turning them over and inspecting them, as if to remember. She closed her eyes to stop the tears, but they fell anyway.

'Don't cry, Jo. If you cry, we're all doomed,' he said, his voice hoarse with emotion.

He wiped the tears with his fingers, then moved them to her neck, resting his thumbs in the hollow of her throat.

'Do you trust me, Jo?' he asked softly as she opened her eyes.

She nodded, then his lips touched hers.

Tom's head was on her chest, the room silent save for the sound of a distant train and their heavy breathing.

'It was different from how I remembered,' he eventually said, almost to himself. Then with a rueful smile. 'Probably out of practice.'

Touching his face, her fingers traced his bone structure, his nose, his jaw and then his lips. She remembered how he'd described her as wanton. Perhaps she was more restrained these days, but for her the exquisite peak had still been as intense.

239

'It was lovely,' she said quietly, wondering if she had disappointed him in some way.

'I can do better, last longer,' he said wryly, lifting his head to search her face.

'I know. I remember.'

Propping his head on his arm, he looked at her intently. 'Do you really remember?'

'Of course I do. Why wouldn't I?'

'There's a thousand reasons why, Jo,' he replied, with an edge to his voice. 'Where should I begin?'

What the ...? Where should he begin? Anger flaring, she flounced from the bed. Though embarrassed by her nakedness, her cheeks burned with indignation. Scooping up the towel, she covered her modesty and took a sharp breath.

The compulsion to put the record straight sizzled through her body. 'Of course I've thought about that night, Tom,' she snapped. 'No, I've relived that night time and again, like an old movie. Christ, I've wanted you, I've yearned for you, but I still don't know if I would have lived my life any differently.'

He was staring at her, but she couldn't read his expression. '*I need you, Jo. You bewitched me*,' he'd said last night. She wanted those words, nice words, words of enchantment, of desire. Not the ugly ones, 'where should I begin?' implied.

No reply, no reply. Just a small shake of his head.

Needing to punish him, she shrugged. 'Well, it hardly matters either way. I'm sure you're spot on. I am a cold, selfish and unemotional bitch, but that's the way I am. Clearly, I must like it.' She glared. 'Have I broken the spell? Can I send you home fully cured now I've done my duty?'

Turning away to hide the threatening tears, she heard him climb from the bed and gather his clothes off the floor; she felt his anger behind her, his eyes burning her back.

'Fucking duty,' he said eventually. 'Sounds a pretty apt description to me.'

Staying perfectly still, she listened for several moments, even minutes. Oh fuck, there it was – the thud of the fire door. Letting out the trapped breath, she flung herself down, clutching the towel to her face.

Oh God, the mattress was still warm from his body. He was meant to say that she wasn't cold and unemotional; he was supposed to say sorry, to whisper tender words of adoration and love. Say that he needed her. Instead he'd just left. And she was fed up of crying; she was too, too pathetic.

Then a wry voice from the doorway. 'Perhaps I should murder you and have done with.'

Returning to the bed, he gently pulled her over and enveloped her in his arms.

'You make me so angry,' he said into her hair. 'But you make me feel alive. What the hell do I do?'

'Love me again,' she replied.

43

Glad to escape the alarming dream, Jo jerked awake to the aroma of fried eggs. Tom was standing at the bedroom door, a plate in each hand, looking at her quizzically.

'Are you OK?'

Her heart was still thrashing. 'A bad dream. I don't usually have them at all.'

He passed the dishes and climbed in beside her. With gentle fingers he raked a lock of hair from her forehead and tucked it behind her ear. 'What happened in the dream?'

'I don't really know . . .' She shook her head. It had almost dissolved, but she'd been wearing her school blazer and her pockets were stuffed. She'd slipped out a red glove but, like a popped cork, it was followed by a spray of dandelions. The more she pulled out, the more there were. Same as the gruel in 'The Magic Porridge Pot' story, they just kept coming, rising like water until she knew she would drown.

Breathing away the vague alarm, she came back to Tom's offering and the yellow-spattered toast. 'Eggy bread – fantastic! I haven't had it since I was small. Thank you.'

The hair, the breakfast. Small gestures by Tom, bringing on another wave of emotion. She wanted to cry. She was ridiculous, too ridiculous. Instead she tried for a smile.

'Hidden talents, eh, Mr Heath?'

He took his portion and began to eat. 'I could've done better, something a bit more creative, but eggs and bread were all you had in.'

A man she hardly knew. 'You can cook?'

'Course. A dab hand at anything pasta- or potato-related. Rice too. As well as improvising with eggs, milk, cheese, the basics. As kids we pretty much had to fend for ourselves.' He snorted. 'No meat. A treat saved for Easter and Christmas . . .'

Thoughtfully chewing her delicacy, Jo pictured the *rough* end of the village. And little Jimmy's face as he stared at the classroom door whenever parents were invited. The Christmas fair, carol concert or nativity play, even a special assembly, the disappointment was always there.

And Tom's words, 'I could've done better.' Again. He was doing fine, much more than fine. But of course today was a glitch; she was just borrowing him. She had to give him back to Kate and Alice.

Her stomach clenched. Oh God, Kate and Alice. But not yet, not yet; she wasn't ready to let go.

'Alice likes eggy bread,' Tom said, as though reading her thoughts. 'We make it together on Saturday mornings, then go for a long walk.' Pulling Jo to his shoulder, he absently stroked her arm. 'I'm still hungry, are you? I can offer toast or toast.' He paused for a moment. 'I've asked a neighbour to sort the animals. Fancy getting some fresh air?'

Lifting her head, she pecked his lips. He wasn't leaving yet. 'Might not be fresh air as you know it, country boy,' she replied with a beam. 'But yes, a ramble's an excellent idea.'

*

Side by side, they strolled up St John Street, turned right on to Deansgate and headed for Castlefield, in companionable silence mostly. Jo was conscious of Tom's long strides, aware he turned from time to time to study her face with a pensive half-smile.

How did they appear to people driving by? Did they look like friends; did they look like a couple? Or strangers, struggling to speak? She had always been the first person to dive into a silence or fill an embarrassing void with a joke, but this stillness felt warm.

'This way to the canal,' she eventually said. Shading her eyes from a shaft of sunshine, she grinned. 'Best I can do for your fresh air request.'

'No complaints so far,' he replied, taking her hand.

The breeze balmy on their faces, they strolled along the tow-path. Though the ground was hard and dusty beneath their feet, the week of rain quaffed and forgotten, the sandstone in the walls sparkled and the trees were the brightest of greens.

The sun broke through fully, lighting Tom's hair. Aware of his fingers softly moving between hers, Jo pointed out the Manchester wildlife (a large dragonfly hovering over the murky water, her usual grey and green heron and several families of ducks), strangely proud to show him her patch.

'Even geese,' he commented, looking up to the sky.

'Yes, we have them too. Though they seem malevolent in their air-strike format. And, look, we also have graffiti. Pretty fabulous artwork, it has to be said,' she replied, gesticulating to the brightly embellished bridge ahead.

'Ah, a bridge. I'm glad there's a bridge.'

Tom propelled her forward with a firm hand. Drawing her into the dusky arch, he softly pushed her against the wall, cupping her bum with his palms and pulling her firmly against him. Then he kissed her and kissed her; hard on her mouth, soft on her neck, moving to her breasts.

'Say you want me, Jo.'

He slipped his hand down her shorts, his fingers warm and rhythmic.

'I want you, Tom.'

'And you want only me.'

'Only you,' she replied, putting her hands on his belt, aware they were probably about to commit an act of gross indecency in a public place, but not giving a damn.

He brushed her fingers away. 'No. Just you. I want to watch you come,' he said softly.

Afterwards, she held his proffered palm again, her legs like jelly as they retraced their steps. Past the ducks, the walkers and dogs, only releasing their grip when the whiff of food and the hubbub of outdoor lunchers flurried over.

Jo's heart finally slowed as they turned down St John Street, but at her flat entrance, Tom peered ahead to the gardens, then to her with a soft smile. 'It's nice to be outdoors,' he said. 'Stretch out the day?'

As though reserved just for her, the usual bench was empty. 'I must sit here three times a week,' she said, flopping down. 'Watching the world go by.' She snorted at the memory of her recent eavesdropping and nap. 'Listening too.'

Tom stayed standing and looked around, his hands in his pockets, his eyes matching the sky. 'Is this where Richard died?'

She smiled wryly; his question was more like the old Tom, direct and to the point, so she knew where she was with this one.

'Straight behind you, just in front of the big oak.'

Contemplative, she paused for a while. 'For a couple of months after his death, someone laid flowers there – exquisite pink lilies – a fresh bunch every week.' Taking a quick breath, she continued. 'Richard's parents, I think. They walked right past my flat to get here, but never let on.' She caught Tom's steady gaze. She didn't

245

know why she was telling him; she'd never told anyone else. 'His mum, Richard's mum, she used to nod at his father and whisper to me, "Please give him a grandson, Joanna. Give Abbu a boy."'

Shaking away the emotion, she reached for humour, the expected quip. 'I watch people walk over the spot where he died all the time. Some even picnic on it. Sausage rolls, Scotch eggs, strawberries, couscous and carrots, the lot.' She chuckled. 'Perhaps they should've drawn a white body-line, as they do in those old spoof police movies. I wonder what the hamper folk would think if they knew?'

Tom glanced at the tree with a faraway expression. 'Like walking on graves, crouched behind the headstones with a fag. But we all did it, didn't we? Cutting through the graveyard from school?'

Aware of a spread of discomfort, Jo wished she'd remembered her sunglasses. 'Yes, sometimes I forget we're from the same village, the same primary,' she replied. The subject was dangerous. She felt a prickle on her neck, a need to lighten the conversation quickly. 'But even a bad girl like me didn't smoke at age eight.'

He looked at her then, with a frown. 'Was that when you went to boarding school? At eight years of age. I didn't realise you and Kate ... Too young, far too young. Alice is nearly there, that's cruel. Your parents, they must have—'

'They thought they were doing the right thing. You know, the best education and all that.' She gazed back, the sentiment tight in her chest. 'You're not that much older than my dad when he left me there. I can still see his face that first day. It was ...' She pictured it. 'It was broken.' Remembering the desolation, she quickly changed the subject. 'How about your parents? How are they?'

He turned back to the oak. 'I drive over occasionally. To Barnsley. See them both, take Alice with me. They're in the same house, didn't want to move. But it's theirs now, at least I could do that.' He took a breath. 'I wish I could say we were poor but happy, but that wouldn't be true. I spent my childhood hating my home, my parents and my poverty. And myself – wishing I could have been born someone else.'

Winded, Jo stared. Tom's long speech was surprising, but there was a feeling of synchronicity too. She hadn't hated her parents, far from it, but she understood him exactly. Pretty dresses and triangular sandwiches, furs and frivolity. *Marrying well.*

'Perhaps we're not so very different after all,' she said. 'Sounds like me at ten, bursting with wild dreams of what I would like to be. Anything other than I was.' She stood and took his hand. 'And not just at ten. At eighteen.' She thought back to those first few weeks at St Luke's. That ragamuffin from Barnsley. 'I had to conform to survive, but I took it too far for too long. Oh, God, what a cow I was, Tom. I'm so sorry—'

'Hello, Jo Jo. In your favourite spot again?' a voice intruded.

She spun in surprise. Oh God. Perfectly turned out all in black with the mandatory sunglasses, it was Aidan. His expression clearly inquisitive, he turned from her to Tom.

Aware of her crimson face, she pulled back her hand. 'Aidan. Hello!' she replied, not knowing how to introduce Tom, so saying nothing.

Taking off his shades, Aidan flashed his white grin. 'I tried the flat. No reply, so I guessed you'd be here.'

Wondering what to say, her mind raced. Should she pretend she and Tom had just bumped into each other? Say they were going somewhere? Or invite Aidan to the flat for a drink?

Tom's voice cut in. 'I was just on my way.' He said it easily but, from the clench of his jaw, she knew he was angry. 'So, I'll say goodbye.' He pulled the car keys from his pocket.

'Was that your Velar outside Jo's flat?' Aidan asked. 'HSE model? I wouldn't mind sitting in it. I'll walk along with you.'

So they strolled to Tom's car, the three of them silent in a row.

Then Aidan sat in the driver's seat, chatting to Tom about fuel economy and performance, technology, design. Already swamped by desperate sadness, Jo dumbly waited and watched. Something irrevocable had just happened and there was nothing she could do about it.

Conscious of Aidan waiting for her at the flat entrance, she spoke to Tom eventually. Her breath was stuck high in her chest. 'You don't have to go,' she said through his open window.

His eyes icy, he turned from the windscreen. 'You've fucked him, haven't you?' he asked.

Oh God, how to reply? She inhaled quickly, but Tom had already turned away, slipping the car into gear and driving off without a backwards glance.

44

Aidan lay on the sofa with his feet up. He'd taken off his shoes at the door and was wearing black socks with a designer logo. Jo had no doubt his undies would match.

'Did I interrupt something? He was very attractive,' he said casually as he leafed through a magazine. 'In a mean and moody sort of way, if you like that sort of man,' he added, seeming to enjoy her obvious discomfort.

She was sitting where Tom had sat only yesterday. *I need you, Jo.* Batting that thought away, she folded her arms. 'You're wearing eye-liner,' she replied, changing the subject. 'And you've gelled your hair differently.'

'Is this your article?' he asked, turning the page to show her. '"Ten Menopause Misconceptions".' He laughed. 'Thank God I'm a man. Well, mostly. Not a man at all, if you ask my dad.'

He continued to flick as she watched, her mind frazzled. Life had taken a strange turn, but it felt too much like a collision, completely out of her control. That was the frustration; the uncertainty and, she supposed, the excitement of it all.

Aidan tapped a glossy advert for perfume. 'He's nice. But then so is she.' He threw the publication aside. 'Look, I'm sorry if I interrupted or whatever. But you should reply to your messages, Jo Jo! Anyway, I'm here now. So let's go out for some food, maybe a club in the Northern Quarter later. I'm already glammed up, as you can see, and you're pink and windswept. Maybe a change of clothes, though? But keep on the Docs. They'll look fab with a dress.'

Thinking how rapidly life could oscillate, she glanced at Aidan absently. High and low, like the double swing in her Barnsley garden, the one she played on for hours with Kate. Kicking up and reaching for the clouds, always needing to get that little bit higher than her best friend.

Best friend, oh God.

She looked down at her boots. They were dusty from her walk, their walk. The stroll with Tom. Heady, erotic. One she'd never forget.

'A penny for them?' Aidan asked.

'You really don't want to know,' she replied. 'Besides, we must be up to a pound these days for thoughts. You have to pay a pound to pee at some places.'

'It's worth it as a tip, though. Standing in the bog all day can't be fun,' he replied. 'The Savoy Grill is the best – they polish the sink as soon as you've turned off the tap. Makes you give them a good wash. You know – knowing you're being watched.'

She lobbed over a piece of paper she'd been idly folding with her thoughts. 'A *good* wash, eh? Lucky Savoy diners!'

He picked up the bundle of postcards from the coffee table. 'Come on, Jo Jo, cheer up. I'm starving! You choose. Italian, Greek, Turkish, Spanish, Nepalese, Japanese, Chinese . . .'

'OK, I get the drift.'

She was actually hungry; she hadn't eaten since the toast. Tom had brought a heap back to bed. He'd taken a bite of the top piece, then he'd brought it to her lips, quickly pulling it away before her teeth made contact. So then she'd snatched another buttery half and stuffed it all in her mouth so he couldn't have any. Puerile fun. And so unexpected.

She thrust the memory away. *You've fucked him, haven't you?* Who was he to judge? He was married. She wasn't.

The sense of loss was slowly being replaced with anger, which was a good thing, a very good thing. Anger was easier to manage; it was productive, it galvanised her. Not always into doing the right thing, but still. Action was better than inaction. She didn't want the paralysis that sorrow and anxiety produced.

'Whose handwriting is this?' Aidan asked, now sitting cross-legged on the sofa and working his way through the postcards. 'I can't make out a word.' But he studied each photograph intently.

The greetings had kept coming, two or three every week. But Jo read them now, almost looking forward to reading her brother's tiny scrawl of news. Not that she'd admit it to Ben. She almost liked this Nigel. This Nigel who found pleasure in everything from lemons 'the size of melons' to the deep wrinkles on the leathery brown skin of the old lady who sold them.

Was it normal, she wondered, to like this postcard brother, but not the real flesh and blood? It was a one-way conversation too, which suited her. And she had an excuse to keep it that way.

'Nigel is on the move, Mum,' she'd replied when quizzed by Joyce, who wanted all her children to be friends. 'I don't know where he'll be, so I can hardly reply.'

But Joyce had recently telephoned asking for her email address. 'What do you want it for, Mum?' she had asked.

'For Nigel, of course. He said that he wants to send you photographs. Proper ones from a camera. To go with the postcards, he said.'

Jo had been irritated then, annoyed that somehow, between

them, Nigel and her mum were encroaching, getting under her skin. She'd determined not to open the emails when they arrived. She would put them in a folder marked 'Nigel' and forget they existed. But the postcards had been so evocative, so descriptive, that she hadn't been able to resist opening the first attachment, just for a peep at the melon-lemons. They and the leather-faced lady were there, but only one or two. The other snaps were of a dark-haired young woman, whose bright eyes clearly adored the person behind the camera.

'Mao, my girlfriend. Isn't she beautiful?' The last message had read.

'Right,' she now said, standing up. 'Let's do it, Aidan. Let's eat, get stoned, be outrageous, whatever. But no sex.'

'Fine by me. As gorgeous as you are, Jo Jo—'

'You prefer boys. Touché.' She leaned forward to kiss his cheek. 'Give me half an hour and you'll be begging me to change my mind!'

'Fucking Tom,' Jo declared as she stripped off her t-shirt and shorts. 'Judge and bloody jury.' He was in no position to criticise. Bloody hypocrite. It took two and he instigated it, coming *home* to her like a bloody *pigeon*.

She stood in the shower feeling angry and impotent, but she wasn't, she most definitely wasn't going to cry. But the hurt was there; he'd wounded her again, and so easily.

I wish I didn't care, she thought, the onslaught of water stinging her eyes.

I wish his opinion of me didn't matter.

She wrapped her wet hair in a towel, opened a bottle of Prosecco, poured Aidan a glass and carried the rest to her bedroom. It reminded her of the evening at Kate's – the chat and the tights and the embellished secret box. Everything had been fine then. Or had it? She wasn't sure any more; her mind was torpid when it came to Kate and memories of the past.

Sipping the chilled wine, she put on *You Gotta Go There to Come Back* and blow-dried her hair. The Stereophonics were bloody spot on! And she was *alright*.

Her journalist friend, Sara, had called on Friday.

'Got a new man yet?'

'Nope.'

'Right. We're going to a rave. Meet some new men.'

'Tricky when you're in Milan.'

'And get blind drunk.'

'Will you hold back my hair when I puke?'

'Yup. I'll be back before you know it. Get shaving!'

Sara was away on a six-month contract. But the rave would happen, she decided. Or she'd go to flipping Milan and do it there. New man was just the thing. New *single* man, in particular. There was no future with Tom, or any married man, just misunderstandings, pain and guilt. And tonight she was going out to have some fun.

She looked in the mirror. 'I'm going to get a life,' she declared to the person gazing back with newly blown hair.

Leaning closer to her reflection, she studied herself carefully. She'd dressed in bright colours and made up her face, but she didn't look right. A bloody clown, she thought after a moment. Like the song, she'd painted on a smile to hide the loneliness beneath.

Thumping down on the chair, she put her head in her hands. Who was she kidding? She was thirty-eight years old and trying to have a good time with someone eight or ten years younger, a person with whom she had nothing in common, save for a brother.

'You are really pathetic,' she said out loud as the tears spoiled her make-up. Weeping at the drop of a hat. She never used to cry. Just weak and feeble these days.

Knocking softly before opening, Aidan put his head around the door. He was still holding the bundle of postcards. 'I take it our night out is off. Can I come in?'

'I'm sorry. I'm really not in the mood to go out.' Turning, she glimpsed his made-up eyes and sighed. 'Besides, we haven't really got anything in common, have we?'

He shrugged, then lay on the bed. 'Apart from being lonely, you mean? Look at us. We're both lost and single, on a hiding to nothing.' He raised his dark eyebrows. 'Mind you, I'm not in love with a married man.'

Laughing, he lifted his hands in mock surrender. 'Don't glare at me like that; he's obviously married. The moody, misunderstood ones always are. Nice-looking ones too. It's bloody annoying and I should know.'

He switched the lamp on and off, then picked up a book. 'Do you love him?' he asked.

She wiped her face with tissues. 'I have no idea.' Answering straight, like a breath of fresh air. 'How can you tell when you're *lonely*, as you put it? Perhaps it's just because the person is there and they want you. Or so they say.'

'I'm here and I want you, but you don't love me.' He shrugged. 'I don't make you happy and sad at the same time. I don't fill you with passion and loathing, with joy and with hate and all that other clichéd crap, which just happens to be true. Am I right, or am I right?'

'You're very wise for someone so young and so pretty, Aidan.'

'Yeah, wisdom comes with suffering, or something like that.' He grinned. 'Or maybe I'm wrong. A hunky chunky blondie, with Hemsworth brother eyes. Perhaps it's just lust.'

'Oh, it's that all right!' she replied with a smile, wondering why she was being so frank with him, but enjoying the freedom. 'But it's more complicated than that.' She glanced at the chest of drawers and the photograph on top. Kate and Alice. Not with Tom, but a horse. 'Maybe it's simply a case of wanting something you haven't got.' She sighed. 'But there's no point having it if you can't have it all, is there? Living half a life is worse than having no life at all, don't you think?'

Aidan smiled a sad smile as he played with the bedside clock. 'I'm not the one to ask. I'm Muslim, I'm Catholic, I'm gay and I'm straight. Loved by my mum but Dad can't bear to look at me. Seems I'm living double, triple lives and it doesn't make me happy, so I'm going to drift and see where the river flows. You know, abandon all control and see where fate takes me. Like your brother and those pictures. They've got me thinking. Even if I'm not happy, it'll be an adventure not to know what's around the corner. Am I making any sense?'

'Perfect sense!' she replied. 'Though letting go is the hard bit. You know, of control. That's pretty scary. I don't think I could.'

Shrugging, he shuffled the postcards like a pack of cards. 'You don't know until you try. Pick a card, any card.'

She smiled, blew her nose hard and caught her face in the mirror. 'What about Ben?' she asked.

'Just friends. Anyway, you know Ben. Too many men, too little time.' He paused for a moment and glanced at her. 'I didn't mean that literally.'

'I know.' The thought of her brother made her smile. Naturally gregarious and tactile, even as a small child, he made friendships wherever he went. From the village, from football, holidays down south, then Interrailing and university. Boys, girls, waifs, strays: he was never alone, always turning up with somebody and offering them refuge in Joyce and Stan's spare room. Not a lot had changed. And though he'd had a setback at school, he'd done his own thing, he was determined to embrace life and be happy.

Taking a leaf out of his book, she nodded at her reflection and stood. 'I'm bloody starving. Sorry about being such a party pooper, Aidan. Tempt you to a Chinese takeaway and Netflix? But you'll have to get it; I couldn't possibly be seen in this state. Deal?'

'Deal,' he replied. 'Let the party begin!'

45

Jo shared her bed with no sex. Which was nice. Companionship and chat with no wet patches. Aidan on her side, her on Richard's.

'Why can't your dad bear to look at you?' she asked. It had been quiet and dark in the bedroom and they hadn't spoken for some time, but she could sense he was awake even though her back was turned.

'I think that's pretty obvious.'

'Is it?'

'He's Muslim and strict. Even my mum, who was as Irish as they come, went through the motions.'

She turned to make out his expression. He was lying on his back, staring at the ceiling, his dark eyes glinting. 'The motions of converting to Islam. Though she was still Catholic inside, obviously.'

Jo propped her head on her hand. 'So, just because you're . . .' She searched for the word. 'Fluid?'

'Adds insult to injury, I think you'll find is the expression. Dad's a neurologist, a consultant no less. Carries his work ethic around with his stethoscope, which they don't use any more, by the way.'

He turned towards Jo. He had beautiful dark eyes, the shape of almonds, but his face, lit by a shaft of dull streetlight through the eyelet, was pale Irish.

'So recruitment isn't good enough for Dad?' she asked.

His lips tight, he smiled and rocked his head. 'No. *I'm* not good enough,' he said eventually. 'The wrong brother died.'

'Bloody hell, Aidan, what happened?'

He didn't speak for some time. Jo assumed he didn't want to elaborate and she'd started to drift when his voice broke the stillness.

'We were named after our grandfathers. Hassan after Dad's dad. Firstborn and all that shit. Perhaps that's why Dad loved him the best. His name set the tone; I was just Irish.' He paused. 'I'd just started high school, private of course. Mum drove us: Hassan in the front, me in the back. And that day I was complaining, moaning about it. Nothing new, just the usual – I hated school, only scraped through the entrance exams with tutoring, didn't understand most of the lessons, wasn't clever like Hassan ... Mum soothed from the front, her voice soft and kind. Telling me it'd get better, I just needed to be patient.'

She heard a sharp intake of breath, then he continued: 'She said she'd bought me a treat for when I got home.'

He stopped speaking. Fearful he might think she wasn't listening, Jo squeezed his hand.

Clearing his throat, he spoke again. 'But I still moaned. The other boys were bullies, the teachers didn't help. The school food was disgusting. Why couldn't I go to the same secondary as my old friends? I was so, so unhappy. Then Hassan butted in, "It would help if you weren't such a lightweight. They all think you're a gay boy."'

He sighed. 'Mum didn't like to take sides, but sometimes he went too far, "That's enough, Hassan," she said.'

His voice cracked. 'She met my eyes in the rear-view mirror and smiled. Soft and loving. Then everything went black.'

Oh God, poor Aidan. A car crash, Jo assumed. A moment's inattention, that's all it took. She shuddered – a child's death – it was dreadful, too dreadful. 'Hassan died?' she eventually asked, filling the silence.

Aidan nodded. 'I finally woke in hospital two or so weeks later, crying and desperate for my mum.' Completely immobile, he stared at the ceiling, tears sliding from his eyes. 'But she didn't come then. She didn't come ever. She had died too.' He took a shuddery breath. 'My dad instructed solicitors to sue her estate for my injuries. Her fault apparently, though I knew it was mine. I refused and kicked up a fuss, but I was a minor so I didn't have a choice. I got the blood money at eighteen. Lucky me.'

Despite Aidan's complaints about the light from the blinds, they slept in.

'I suppose I'd better go to work,' he grumbled from the pillow. Then, when Jo looked at the clock and gasped at the time: 'Don't worry, Auntie Jo. It's recruitment. No one knows or cares where you are. I appear at an office in the north of England before the day's out and all is cool.'

He left at some point, but definitely late, after noon.

Jo stayed *in the sack*. There were three missed calls from Ben by the time she turned on her mobile. Still she didn't get up. She knew how the conversation would go. Besides, she was having one day to wallow. She knew it was indulgent given Aidan's devastating story last night, but she was having a last afternoon of sex and sunny strolls, of buttered toast and touching, behind her closed eyes, before ditching Tom for ever.

If the headache or heartache, or whatever it was with him, was really to end, it had to come from within herself. It was a cliché, she knew, the type of *purple* answer she and her journalist colleagues used to snigger about when standing in for 'Dear Elspeth' at the paper (who in fairness was actually a real person and counsellor to boot). But as Aidan had said, hackneyed phrases were so often true. As she had put it (in *extreme* purple) to the anguished letter-writer: 'you have to find a way to loosen the knot in your heart, to let it unravel and fly far, far away.'

By the evening she couldn't ignore Ben any longer. He wasn't Nigel, after all. And it would be weird to alienate everyone. Kate included. Oh God.

'What's going on with you and Tom Heath?' the call began.

'Hello, Ben. How are you? I'm fine, thank you,' she replied, stalling for time, even though she'd suspected those very words were coming. Ben didn't call six times within the space of half a day for no reason.

News travels fast, she mused as she hitched up the bed. Like their mum, Ben had always possessed that silent *knowing*, but on this occasion she guessed it was hands-free chat. 'Phone me when-ever,' Aidan had said on his way out. 'For our mutual agony-aunt society. I'm hands-free in the car. Breaks the boredom of driving.'

Reminding herself to programme the washing machine for a towel, bedding and anything-else-Tom-might-have-touched wash, Jo took a breath. 'What makes you think it was Tom?' she asked, filling Ben's loaded pause.

Bloody Aidan! What had he said? She hadn't asked him to keep their chat a secret, but she hoped he hadn't been too indiscreet. She sighed. Her own bloody fault – she'd been too frank with him, uncharacteristically open. Tom was a one-off mistake, best brushed under the carpet, or piled into the washing machine with the towels and the bedding for a really thorough purgation. Still, her honesty had been reciprocated by Aidan during the night. And that felt good, really good.

She came back to Ben's voice. 'The description was fair-haired, good-looking, thickset and angry. Sounded like Tom to me.'

The hairs on her arms stood erect. 'Why do you say angry?'

'He's been angry for years,' Ben replied evasively. Then, 'You're not sleeping with him again, are you? He's married to Kate, one half golden, for goodness' sake.'

'What do you mean *again*?'

'Oh, come on, Jo, we all knew you two were together at the leaving party. He stayed all night in your bedroom and I don't suppose you were playing rummy. You gave him the heave-ho in the morning and he left with a face like thunder.'

'You never said anything.'

'Well, we didn't talk in those days, did we? If I'd said anything you'd have run a mile with embarrassment. We all knew he had a massive crush on you and married Kate on the rebound. But that's not the point; it was a long time ago. The crux is what you're doing with him now.'

You've fucked him, haven't you? 'Nothing,' Jo said, feeling winded. 'We're not doing anything. We're not even friends.'

Ben's voice softened. 'Look, Jo. I'm not bothered about Tom or Kate, they can look after themselves. I don't want you to get hurt again, to love someone then lose them. You deserve to have somebody who'll make you happy, a guy who'll make you laugh again, not one who's—'

'Who's what?'

'Well, he's not exactly a barrel of laughs, is he? Jimmy and Dave think he's clinically depressed.'

The toast popped in her head and she wanted to defend Tom, to say he was funny. And tender. But then she thought of his erratic behaviour at the police station and felt a lurch in her chest as the (purple) knot in her heart tightened. Knowing that her day of bedded self-counselling was for nothing, she shook her head.

'Oh, God,' Ben said after a few moments. 'I shouldn't have said that, should I? All those injured creatures you brought home.'

'Yes, and they all died on me, didn't they?'

261

The goosebumps stayed after Ben ended the call, so she slipped under the duvet, feeling the chill even though the evening sun was still loitering outside.

She'd forgotten about the wounded rodents. They'd been shrews mostly, traumatised by the cat who was 'only playing', as Stan pointed out. 'Survival of the fittest, I'm afraid, love. That's a fact,' he'd say when the small creature soon died. But it was kindly said and he'd dig a little grave with his large rough hands in the rose bed, not afraid to really dirty them, but careful not to unearth the previous tiny mouse.

Hilary dragged Jo out of bed eventually, not in person, but by mobile, the cold shivers soon turning to sweat.

'Hello, Jo, darling. Do you have time for a chat?'

Watching TV in her bedroom for distraction, Jo had been channel-flicking for a while (another form of *dipping in*; it matched her erratic mind, so was surprisingly therapeutic) and she'd found an old Hitchcock movie starring one of his 'icy blondes'. It was still on, the sound blaring.

Hilary didn't pause for an answer. 'Thought I'd give you an update as I knew you'd be worried.'

Struggling to hear over the sound of the crescendo, Jo got up, searched for the remote and pressed mute. The muted blonde, she observed, looked a little like the younger Kate. The one who married Tom. Pale, fair and pretty 'but not particularly sexy'. Ben's words, not hers, but what did he know?

'Sorry, Hilary. Start again. I had to turn off—'

'Thought I'd give you an update on Kate. Tom came to collect her and Alice a few days early. Must've been missing his girls. Sweet of him, wasn't it?' she said before the usual cigarette pause.

'Are you still there, Jo, darling?'

Hilary was shouting, the way she spoke to poor Harold these

days. 'A salutary lesson,' Kate often commented, 'for marrying someone your own age.'

Which, of course, Kate had done: her *little investment*.

'Yes, still here.'

'I thought you might like to know Kate eventually spilled the beans. She won't admit to drinking too much, although Lord knows why, she polished off at least a bottle and a half last night, but she did confess to a fear of leaving the farmhouse unless Tom is with her. She says she panics without him. She hasn't even gone riding for weeks. Did you know that?'

Kate loved her horses only marginally less than she loved Tom and Alice, so Jo was surprised, but then she thought back, remembering her apprehension when they were getting ready to go out during the *weekend horribilis* and her words at the bar. 'I'm a home girl,' she'd said.

'But the good news is that we've persuaded her to see Madden-Michaels. He was at school with Harold, so he's ancient, but top drawer, obviously. Says he'll refer her to one of the sympathetic women on his team so she can talk it through. I don't think Tom minds. I did have a little chat on the QT, but he never says much. Love him to bits, but never really known what he's thinking. Still, it can't be fun for him, can it, poor man? Having to be at Kate's beck and call all the time – it would drive me to distraction. Good job I had girls, isn't it, Jo? We can all have screaming tantrums and get it off our chests! Anyhow, expect a communiqué from Kate. She said she wanted to talk to you. Rather you than me. Had enough of her just for now. Oh Lord, there's the doorbell. Bye bye, darling!'

Feeling febrile, Jo ended the call. Stepping to the chest of drawers, she turned the photograph of her old friend face down. Oh God. Kate couldn't possibly know about her and Tom, could she? No, surely not.

So what did she want from Jo now?

46

The communiqué from Kate didn't come until a Thursday evening. Jo was halfway through her version of a Spanish omelette. Onions, mushrooms, pancetta, cheese, a touch of fresh root ginger (*waste not, want not*, as Joyce would say) and of course eggs, but no potatoes. Opening the fridge to take out the ingredients, she had inevitably thought of Tom and his *basics*. That had led on to the usual mind jumble: *I need you, Jo*; *you've fucked him*; *do you trust me?*; *clinically depressed*. The graphic stuff too, from toast to his toned torso. And the rest. So she'd picked up her mobile to call Aidan, her regular diversion technique.

'Today's headline news is that I'm just about to make an omelette for dinner. Of the Spanish variety. Very tasty, though I say so myself. I'll treat you to the delicacy next time you're in Manchester.'

'Sounds nice, Jo Jo. If I'm not away with the postcards by then,' he replied. 'But remember, no pig! And I'm on your side of the bed.'

Which, of course, was Richard's, strictly speaking.

She spoke to Aidan on the telephone most days and, when she

didn't, he was often in her thoughts. The revelation about his devastating childhood had stopped her self-pity, or reduced it at least. A moment's inattention for a glance of reassurance and love had killed a mother and one son, emotionally crippling the other who'd survived. When she caught herself in the mirror looking soulful, she chided her reflection: 'You're alive; you're lucky. There are so many people worse off.' Sounding Joyce-like. But that wasn't so bad. Her mum was a good person, thoughtful and kind, doing her best to love her dysfunctional offspring equally.

'Still mooning over Blondie?' was Aidan's first opening line.

'I don't *moon*. And anyway, no comment. You blabbed.'

'Ben twisted my arm!'

'Hm, hands-free?'

'I hardly said anything, but he worries about you. He wants you to be happy and all that elusive crap.'

Jo didn't say much about Blondie to Aidan any more, but it helped that someone else knew about the *knot* and she could speak about it if she wanted to. Not that she was convinced talking really helped. One had to be brutal, to exterminate indulgent thoughts of babies and sex and *you bewitched me.* Besides, it clearly hadn't been a very effective enchantment as Tom hadn't been in touch. He was back home with *his girls*, as Hilary put it.

But a small voice would creep in. Small voices always do. 'Clinically depressed. Tom's clinically depressed. Perhaps he needs help; perhaps he needs you.'

Singing along to 'Maybe Tomorrow', the onions were nicely softening when Kate's call finally came. 'Jo, it's me, Kate,' she said, as though her name hadn't been pulsating from the mobile screen for several seconds before Jo steeled herself to answer. 'Can we meet?'

The tone of her voice took Jo back in time. Conspiratorial and intimate, with suppressed excitement.

'I really need to see you; I want to talk about something . . .'

'Yes, of course!'

Jo's immediate response was relief. And if she was honest, pleasure. Kate sounded exactly like the old Kate, not the one married to Tom, but the girl before that. The one who was animated by something secret and delicious that could only be shared with her.

'Tomorrow morning at the farmhouse then? Tom will be out and Alice is going to a friend's house.' Then, after a moment, 'You're not doing anything else, are you?'

Suddenly feeling as hot as the frying pan, Jo removed it from the hob. 'I work, Kate, and you don't!' she wanted to declare. Or, 'Yes, actually, I'm busy.' Or, 'Why don't you come here for once? Why does it always have to be on your terms?'

But she knew she was being *number one selfish cow* (and far, far worse when she let herself ruminate). Hilary had telephoned with regular updates. Kate had been to see the 'nice lady psychoanalyst' who'd made an initial diagnosis of agoraphobia. She had felt 'just awful' for not taking Kate more seriously.

'Poor Kate must have suffered terribly keeping it all to herself,' Hilary had said only this morning. 'All the family – and of course that includes you, Jo, darling – must pull together and help in every way possible.'

'No, that's fine, Kate,' Jo now replied, a beep from her mobile notifying her of a new message. 'I'll see you tomorrow at ten.'

Trying to blow away her irritation and apprehension, Jo went back to the fresh ginger aroma. She'd done an article on its benefits only this week – powerful medicinal properties that could impact conditions ranging from period pain to osteoarthritis – but right now it smelled rank. Sighing, she cracked three eggs into a glass jug and beat them with a fork. It prompted the memory of Catherine Bayden-Jones's tearful pink face as she struggled to remove a piece of shell before the domestic science teacher descended.

Another flash of anxiety jolted her stomach. Oh God. What

would tomorrow's meeting bring? Listening to the song, she snorted. Would *she* find her *way home*?

The disappointing omelette half eaten (yup, too much ginger), Jo remembered the messages and picked up her phone. The first was from Lily. She had already accepted Jo's offer of food and was suggesting a date. (Why, oh why hadn't Jo suggested a meal out? She was already fretting about the menu. So out of touch, she hadn't even caught up with *Masterchef*, and *Bake Off* got on her pip. What on earth would she cook? Clearly not a *tortilla española*.)

The second was from Nigel. Jo was missing the postcards, but found herself looking forward to the email updates from him instead. He and Mao had settled in Corfu. He missed the internet cafés, he'd told her, but they now had regular Wi-Fi in their new home.

'So here it is,' today's message read.

A photograph was attached – a block of deserted-looking flats standing alone on a dry dusty road. The white render had peeled away in parts, showing the grey breezeblocks beneath, but two shades of blue met on the horizon beyond.

'We're on the second floor. I know Dad would call it a slum, but Mao is a genius, she's made it like home already. We can see the ocean from the bedroom window and of course the lemon trees! It's only temporary, though. We're looking for something with our own front door. Then you can visit. Or stay. For as long as you want. You will come, won't you?'

Putting down her mobile, Jo absently moved the omelette around her plate. She hoped her brother's relationship with Mao would last. He was a good-looking guy. He never had difficulty attracting women; keeping them seemed to be the problem. They'd always had nice names – Bridget, Zelda and Geraldine – but the flings didn't last long. Not that she had met any of them in recent years. The women's names and descriptions had come from Joyce, which made her all the more intrigued about Mao and the invitation to visit.

Stretching her arms and yawning, she looked to the weak light filtering in through the window. The idea of Greek sunshine was lovely, but if she did trek all the way to Corfu there'd be no escape. Nigel would nag and justify the moment she arrived, lemon trees or not. An analysis of his childhood, his parents, the world at large. Still, the thought of escape was appealing; there'd be no more small voices, disappointing tortillas or updates from Hilary.

Aidan and his 'river flow' sounded tempting.

47

There were other ways to drive to the Hope Valley from Manchester, but Jo chose the Snake Pass. From habit, she supposed. She'd always taken this route to drive past Ladybower Reservoir and take in the 'Lake District of the Peaks' picturesque alpine view. Sometimes she even parked up and spent a few moments breathing in the forest and moorland smells and revisiting fond childhood memories of picnics and playing. Even after all this time, she still hoped to glimpse the village submerged beneath the dam if it had been a very dry period, or watch the water gallop into the overflow if it had been particularly wet.

She had come this way the night Richard died too. It was only when she parked on Petersfield's cobbled drive that she realised she hadn't thought of him during the journey, not even once. Instead she'd fretted about the pending dinner date with Lily and Noah, what delicacies to eat (Nigella? Noah was definitely more a Heston man), which fine wines to drink (no idea), whether she still had matching cutlery for more than one course (where *had* the dessertspoons gone?). Then there was the need to clean the flat from *top to tail*, including the flipping toilet. But most of all she'd admired the sunlit view and contrasting countryside. Steep hills and sunken valleys; green fields and purple mounds; brown and red woods, shimmering streams and blue sky.

As ever, she thought about Old Joe. In the 1950s, he and his sheepdog, Tip, had gone to tend his flock on the frozen moors. Fifteen weeks later, the shepherd was found dead with faithful Tip by his side. The story had always made her cry, not because the dog had died, but because she'd lived.

Peaks and troughs; perhaps one had to weather the lows to fully appreciate the highs.

Rolling down the sleeves of her blouse and buttoning them at the cuffs, Kate was waiting at the farmhouse door.

No one else was there but she spoke in a dramatic hushed tone. 'Victoria wants me to talk about school,' she said the moment Jo stepped into the kitchen.

Though her apprehension had returned in droves once she hit the village, Jo couldn't help but smile at the dogs beneath the table. Knowing they were in the farmhouse without permission, they were thumping their tails with muted delight.

Studying Kate's face, she was catapulted back in time. Her colour was heightened and it made her appear young, plump and pretty. After interrupting Jo's dinner yesterday, she had continued to call intermittently throughout the evening. The iciness between them had melted, Jo supposed, so there had been nothing to stop her flow of information, from what Victoria the psychoanalyst liked to wear, to the art on the walls of her rooms at the private clinic in Derby.

She had given a blow-by-blow account of all the questions Victoria asked and how she responded. Was Kate's marriage happy? Of course it was! Never mind successful, Tom was loving and kind, she was incredibly lucky, she'd never even wanted to look at another man. Was the pregnancy difficult, any postnatal depression? No, it went like a dream: little Alice was a dream too. Her relationship with her parents, her siblings? Well, as Jo knew, they were lovely people.

Jo had found the telephone calls pleasant and warming; Kate was happy and clearly enjoying the attention she was receiving from her sessions. It reminded her of schooldays when they'd sit on the swings in the playground, whatever the weather, Kate talking and her listening, honoured and proud to be Kate's confidante, pleased to be in the rays of her love. But as she now sat in the fragrant farmhouse kitchen, having travelled thirty plus miles to be there, she found herself irked that Kate had insisted on a personal visit rather than discussing St Luke's on the telephone, along with everything else.

Kate was peering at her now. 'Did you hear what I said, Jo? Victoria wants me to talk about school.'

'We could have spoken about it on the telephone,' she replied, trying to keep the impatience from her voice as she pulled out a chair.

Her eyes caught the row of china animals high on the dresser. Why they caught her breath whenever she looked at them, she didn't know. There was something else too; a feeling of discomfort or danger she couldn't quite grasp.

Kate frowned. 'How can you possibly say that?' she protested.

'Sorry, you're right.' Jo put her hands on the table and waited for her friend to begin.

Sitting opposite, Kate leaned forward. 'So, should I tell Victoria about Junior House and being a *pet*?'

'Yes, of course you should.'

Kate looked at her intently. 'But are you sure? You weren't one, so you don't really know how it felt.'

'You're right, I don't know, but I can imagine.'

Could she though? Certainly not at school; she wasn't anyone's favourite. Possibly not even Kate's. In Seniors, when Kate had grown both in height and confidence, she'd gathered her own little troop of minions, or 'minis', as she called them. Sycophantic girls from the lower years who would do her bidding in return for sweets, stationery or make-up. Their constant presence had really irked Jo, but Kate had loved her *entourage*. Like Cecil's *pets*, she supposed. She'd never thought of it like that before this moment.

Was Joanna Wragg ever anyone's pet? Tom's at eighteen? But that was long, long ago. And how easily the dazzle of *bewitched* and *need you* had been tarnished.

Kate's tut interrupted her thoughts. 'Jo, you're not *listening*. Should I tell Victoria about the ...' She lowered her voice, an adult in her beautiful kitchen thirty years later, still whispering. '...the lesbian stuff?'

'Ah, sorry, of course.'

Examining her flushed face and bright eyes, Jo paused before speaking. Yes, of course – Miranda's pronouncement in their dormitory that night. As if Jo could forget. She could still remember being the first person out of bed the following morning, the first to be washed and dressed. The first in the chilly library, the very first to read those words from the dictionary and thinking: Is this me? Am I someone who is *sexually attracted by persons of one's own sex*?

She'd hurriedly unearthed all the relevant books and cross-referenced the description and information for as long as she could before the other girls were rising and yawning and lining up for breakfast. What she discovered defined how she felt for the first time since meeting Kate, and she kept the knowledge close to her heart, knowing it was a secret she could never tell anyone, ever. Only as an adult did she realise she was wrong. She had been *attracted* to Kate, enormously so, but even now she couldn't quite put her finger on why.

'Jo? Did you hear what I said? Should I tell Victoria about the lesbian stuff?'

Jo hauled herself back from the memories. How she'd longed to be that special sunny and golden-haired girl. 'I think you ought to tell her everything,' she replied. 'I imagine a therapist needs to know all about your childhood and school years to get to the root of the problem.'

Feeling wistful and sad, she focused on the Kate of today. 'You have to remember that you did nothing wrong. Nothing at all. You were only a young child.'

'But it was wrong, it was all wrong!'

'You know that now, but you didn't know it then.'

Absently playing with the buttons on her cuff, Kate drew Jo's eyes to her slim wrist. Like before, it was bruised, even more discoloured than last time. And now that she looked, there was a smudge of purple on her brow bone.

'Oh, but I did know, Jo,' she said. Her eyes flickered, unusually shifty and sly. 'I knew it was wrong then too, yet I welcomed it, I wanted it, I rejoiced in it. I needed the love and attention. I was so lonely and isolated. I had no one ...'

You had me, Jo thought, but she remained silent as she gazed at her animated face.

'She made me feel unique, Jo, better than everyone else. She could see all my strengths when no one else could; she encouraged me with compliments and flattery. And I loved seeing their jealousy, all eyes on me because they knew I was special. Especially *her*. She hated it the most.'

Discomfort and danger. Jo sensed it again. Copper hair and green eyes. She'd seen her recently, hadn't she? Somewhere, she was sure.

Looking beyond Jo, Kate's eyes became glassy. 'When she called me *Fatty* there was something I could do about it, but when she said the other thing, the other name ... It spoilt everything; she spoilt everything. Cecil dropped me, but the name stuck and there was nothing I could do because ... Well, it was true in a way.'

'Come on, Kate, it wasn't true, you can hardly choose something at eight or nine. You were only a child. It was abuse, unforgivable grooming by an adult, which you thought was love.'

The dogs shifted under the table as they fell silent.

'You did nothing wrong, Kate. You were only a child,' Jo repeated eventually, remembering how unsettled she'd been when Kate finally confessed to 'the *special* cuddles'. Two years had passed, their junior days were behind them and they were enjoying the last of the summer holidays before going into senior school. They were talking about boys and snogging; Jo had tried it with the back of her hand, but couldn't imagine what it was like in real life.

'Oh, special cuddles,' Kate said dismissively.

'What are they?' Jo asked.

'Did I never say? Well ...'

Jo hadn't been so much stunned with what had gone on in Cecil's room, shocking and disgusting though it was, but that Kate, *her* Kate who told her everything, hadn't told her about the special cuddles already.

Now feeling a shiver pass through her, Jo gazed at her old friend. 'It *was* abuse, Kate. Pure and simple.' She rubbed the table top thoughtfully. 'Have you thought about reporting it to the police? I know years have passed and some people make loaded comments about the time delay, but historic abuse is taken really seriously these days.' She reached for her hand. 'It might help. I don't know, I'm no expert, but involving the police might give you closure.'

With a peculiar expression, Kate cocked her head. 'Why would we do that, Jo?'

Flummoxed by the *we*, she wondered how to reply, but Kate stood and clapped her hands. 'Lunch!' she said brightly, as though the last fifteen minutes hadn't happened. 'Are you hungry? French onion soup and baguette?'

Jo shook her head. 'Thanks, but I need to shoot off.'

Both the soup and the bread would be home-made and delicious, but she felt sapped, exhausted from the different emotions Kate brought out in her. Fondness and guilt, sympathy and exasperation. And the bruises; she didn't want to think about them. 'Do you trust me, Jo?' looped through her mind. She had trusted him, trusted him completely, but where else could they have come from? Then there were the memories of school, some so clear and others hazy and hidden. It was a long drive home too and she had deadlines to meet. She picked up her car keys.

Kate smiled. 'Tom's such a sweetheart. Did I tell you he's bought me a new mare? She's a little frisky but she's beautiful,' she said. 'You must see her before you go.'

Remembering a time when she loved her so, Jo held out her hand. 'Come with me, Kate, and show me,' she replied. 'Show me how beautiful she is. You're a wonderful cook, but you can't stay in the kitchen for ever.'

'I know.' She held back in the shadow of the door. 'I'm going to start riding her in a few days. When Tom's here to ride with me, but not yet.'

'Phone me,' Jo said as she left, thinking how well Kate looked. Her hair was silky, her cheeks pink and she'd put on some weight. However low life became, she always seemed to bounce back. Jo supposed one had to. Like Aidan, like her, life trundled on.

The August sunshine had turned to drizzle. Prepared to be unimpressed with yet another 'posh pony', she headed for the stables. The new horse's white mane wasn't plaited like the others. A chestnut brown and white skewbald, she looked spectacular, wild and free. So she stayed and admired her for a few minutes, talking to her softly and stroking her handsome head.

'What the hell are *you* doing here?'

She swivelled to the sound. Tom was climbing from his car and striding towards her. Though wearing a white shirt and smart jeans, she immediately noticed he was unshaven again, unkempt and thin, a stark contrast to Kate's glow of health.

Taking a step back, she thought of Kate's bruising. 'Kate asked me to come; she wanted to talk about things,' she replied with a shrug. She wanted to feel alarmed or angered by his aggression, but instead there were hammers of concern at his appearance. 'Didn't she mention it?'

Deeply scowling, his face was dark, almost menacing. 'No, she didn't. Don't come again. You only make things worse.'

Remembering the sleeping lion in the car, she held out her hand. This beast was awake, his eyes burning with anger, but still she rubbed his arm. 'Tom, you look terrible, are you all right?'

'Don't,' he replied, flinching away. 'Just go. You're not wanted here. You're not wanted at all.'

'Fine. Whatever. I don't really care,' she responded, her words tumbling out. 'But you need to see a doctor or someone to talk to, Tom. Take a look at yourself. You look dreadful. You're ill or stressed, I don't know what, but you need help. Just take a look in the mirror.'

But he was gone before she finished, so she stood there alone, the tears wrecking her face as the mare calmly looked on.

48

The Replicant dinner date had arrived. The door buzzer shouted at six-thirty, but it was thank-God-for-Ben.

Jo gave him a hug, but a quick one (despite everything, they *were* still Wraggs). 'Thank you so much for coming. And miraculously early too! You get Brownie points for that. Oh God, I have dreadful butterflies. No, furry fat moths bloody battering my stomach. Is that normal?'

'Never had a dinner event, so I wouldn't know. If it was a *party*, however . . .'

Jo snorted to herself. Bloody hell, twenty years on and the mention of a Ben party propelled her mind to *that* one like a magnet on a fridge. Still, there would definitely be no cider, ridiculous arm-bopping nor sex today. Apart from lack of fizzy alcohol, dance music or appropriate man, she was on her best behaviour.

'I'm going to be so well mannered tonight, you won't believe it,' she said. 'You are going to be debonair and charming, aren't you?' she asked.

'When am I not?' he replied with a smile.

She had chickened out of facing Lily and Noah alone, though why she'd thought the get-together was a good idea in the first place, she didn't know. Lily was lovely, but Noah could be hard work at times. Or *painful*, as he always put it. He'd been Richard's best mate for years, but the friendship had seemed to thrive on competitiveness. He had been the only person who could provoke or rile Richard: salary, status, car, house and holidays, Noah generally winning. Including, of course, haute cuisine (oh hell!).

In fairness Noah wasn't a bad person; it was he who'd advised Richard to think carefully about leaving his partnership; it was he who helped Jo with the sale of the practice and the probate; it was he who made sure to reclaim Richard's brass nameplate and return it to her with tears in his eyes. Still, having Ben there would even the numbers and smooth things along tonight if Noah became prickly, which wasn't unknown after too many drinks.

'Let's look, then.' Ben peered over her shoulder to inspect the food she'd started preparing at noon. 'Wow, what a feast. So, remind me. Why are we doing this?'

She was glad of the *we*. 'Best foot forward, being positive, looking to the future, building bridges. Have I covered all the clichés?'

She had already told him about her last visit to the farmhouse, albeit loosely. She hadn't wanted to get bogged down in the whole school thing, or her concerns about Tom. Just that her relationship with the Heaths felt finally over.

Reading her mind as usual, he lifted his eyebrows. 'Getting over the Golden Couple and moving on to Nexus-6 models?'

She shook her head and laughed wryly. 'Something like that.' She often found her thoughts roaming towards the Midas Family, but tried not to dwell. She didn't expect it of Tom, but Kate hadn't been in touch either. Their lives were none of her business. As he had said clearly, she wasn't wanted.

Ben was sampling the chowder. 'So, why the long hiatus with

these guys? You always liked Lily. Prosecco at lunchtime, then buying something frivolous at Selfridges just for the yellow bag, as I recall.'

Jo frowned and thought back. She still felt guilty about dropping Lily after the funeral, but in truth there had been a bit of a stand-off before then, for Richard even more so than her. 'They scored the baby goal first,' she said, surprising herself that she'd said it out loud.

'Ah,' he replied. He turned to the table, neatening the cutlery like the butler from *Downton*. 'Anything I can do to help?'

'Unfortunately not,' she muttered to his back.

She'd never discussed the whole broody thing with Ben, but like everything else, he seemed to instinctively know. And even better than that, he understood when to push things, when to leave them alone. She was bloody lucky to have such a fantastic brother; not just a sibling but a friend. Impulsively she caught him from behind, wrapping her arms around his chest and clutching tightly.

He turned when she released him. 'What was that for?' he asked with a quizzical smile.

'For being you,' she replied, sniffing the emotion away. 'Thank you for coming.'

The meal was going pretty damn well, Jo thought as she topped up everyone's glass. The initial meet and greet had been fine; Lily and Noah had sat on the sofa drinking gin and tonic (with an inspired dash of pomegranate juice and a few pretty seeds) in the new goblets she'd bought; the conversation had flowed about work and the weather, their new house in Didsbury and their plans for an extension. (Five bedrooms, Rich? Who needed *five*?) Then they'd sat down at her kitchen table, an intimate foursome, boy, girl and boy, girl.

Lily had been complimentary about the soup and Noah had asked Jo to go through the steps for the starter. Had she prepared the pea purée earlier? How long in the pan for the black pudding and scallops? The pancetta was an interesting twist, he'd said.

A compliment of sorts, she now thought, feeling quite jolly from the effect of the vino Noah had brought. She'd never been convinced about spending a lot of money on alcohol, but this went down very easily – too easily, in fact. Lily had thrown off her initial reticence and was flirting pretty outrageously with Ben.

'I had forgotten just how charming and handsome your brother is, Jo,' she said, as though he wasn't there.

Ignoring his wife, Noah continued to look steadily at Jo, his pale eyes on hers. He'd been expounding on wine for some time. 'So, yes, this red is from California. The Napa Valley; people don't realise, but it produces considerably more wine than Australia . . .'

Jo nodded and listened. He'd called her in the week and asked what they'd be eating. She'd been startled when his name appeared on her mobile screen, then a little thrown at his request, concerned that the menu would now be set in stone; there'd be no chance of binning a course if it went horribly wrong. But the reason had become clear when he and Lily arrived at the flat. He'd brought a different bottle for each course, from a very pale pink to white to deep red, then a yellowy dessert wine and finally a ruby port. It was really quite sweet of him.

Though his tone was slightly lecturing, it was interesting to hear a description of each wine, every country and region; the aromas she should detect before drinking, the different tastes when she drank. He seemed to be enjoying her attention; he hadn't said 'this is painful', not even once.

With an unusually strong Germanic twang in her voice, Lily was persisting with her description of Ben. 'He's a good listener too, Jo.' She put her head to one side and studied him. 'I love his wavy dark hair, but I think it's the cheekbones, Jo. He has such a sculpted face.'

Jo turned to her old drinking pal. She had a chiselled face too; so did Noah. Both pale and blonde, they could have been twins.

Though in personality, they were very different. It had always been the same – the less inhibited Lily became, the more Noah buttoned up. It reminded her a little of Tom and Kate at the wine bar all those weeks ago. She snorted to herself. Hopefully Noah wouldn't offer to father her a child later on in the evening. She pushed that memory away; digging up Tom wasn't good for her.

Conscious of Noah's tightening jaw, Jo tried for flippant before changing the subject. 'Yeah, very true. Shame he's my brother. Did you know Nigel was in Corfu? And guess what? He has a girlfriend who has put up with him for more than three weeks. They've just found a beach-fronted cottage apparently . . .'

Ben taking the lead, the conversation drifted to the Greek economy. Noah joined in, but when it came to this year's holiday plans, he pushed his plate away, emptying and replenishing his glass without contributing. Eventually he left the table, heading unsteadily for the bathroom.

'We called him Freddie at law college.'

Everyone turned to the voice. Noah had returned holding something. He placed it on the table. Jo stared. It was a photograph of her and Richard from their wedding day. What the? He must have been in her bedroom. Had she not been on *best behaviour*, she would have protested.

He sat down and tapped the image with a finger. It was a close-up, one she didn't particularly like, but Richard had framed it because it wasn't posed and had 'captured a moment'.

'Yes, we called him Freddie at college,' he repeated, his voice clipped as usual but a slight mumble creeping in. His smile didn't reach his eyes. 'Not because he had those . . . *unfortunate* teeth, I hasten to add. But they looked similar, him and the young Mercury. Slightly exotic around the eyes, don't you think? Like wearing eye-liner. You remember, don't you, Lily, my sweet?' He turned to Jo. 'Our very own Freddie. Did he tell you that?'

Smiling stiffly, she nodded. Richard had told her; she'd never seen the similarity herself, but apparently he'd had long hair back then.

Noah snapped open the dessert wine and sloshed it in his glass without finishing the red. 'Did he always tell you everything, Jo?' he asked, but before she could reply, he continued to speak. 'Dying too young. Very tragic.'

Feeling a pulse of alarm, Jo glanced up from the pink swirling through the sweet yellow liquid. His tone was definitely off. And was he speaking about Richard or Freddie? Either way, it set her teeth on edge.

'Of course he sought it himself,' he carried on. Turning to Lily and Ben, he guffawed. 'I'm talking about Freddie, the genuine Freddie!' He paused for a moment. 'Though that wasn't his real name, was it?' He took a gulp of wine, then continued, his voice slurry. 'Well, whoever he was, he was a bloody promiscuous ... *person*. What did he expect? He fucked everyone, apparently. And so he was brought to book, taught a bloody lesson!' He wafted a hand in Ben's direction. 'People should be punished. Not just men. God's curse, if you ask me.'

A leaden stone in her chest, Jo put her hand on Ben's knee to stop him from standing. 'That's a very personal opinion, Noah, one I most certainly don't agree with,' she said, her voice clipped.

She glanced at Lily's mortified face. She wanted to let out her outrage and shout very loudly, but it was better to smooth things over. Noah was drunk, extremely drunk, that was all. Taking a deep breath, she stood. 'Anyone ready for pud? Or we could have a coffee break first ...'

Pretty inebriated herself, Jo flicked on the kettle and returned to the table. Ben looked close to tears and no one had spoken. Oh God, this was much more than *painful*. A change of subject was needed, something light-hearted to pull Noah back from whatever was clearly eating him.

Looking from him to Lily, she tried for a smile. 'How is little Finn? Fully recovered from the chickenpox, I hope.' Then, with a genuine grin: 'Have you got any snaps? I'd love to see what he looks like. Beautiful, no doubt, with you two as parents.'

Lily opened her mouth but the clatter of Noah's chair made her jump. He glared at his wife. 'Why did we come? This is too fucking painful,' he snapped. 'Are we really going to do this happy family shit? Are we, Lily? Are we?'

She stood too. Her eyes were huge with alarm. 'Noah, stop, please. Please don't—'

But he had already stomped off, returning moments later with his jacket. Jo watched, transfixed. She assumed his plan was to storm out without Lily, but instead of putting the bomber on, he took out his wallet, fumbling through its contents with trembling fingers. Apparently finding what he wanted, he threw them in front of Jo where they scattered on the table.

Photographs; there were three or four snaps. Astonished and perplexed, Jo lifted one from her soiled plate and gazed at the smiling toddler looking back.

'There, Jo. Are you satisfied? You wanted to see my son. My *Pakistani* fucking son.'

She squinted and stared. The similarity was remarkable, the cold realisation immediate. Dark-haired and dark-eyed, the boy was a replica of the child on his grandparents' mantelpiece.

A beat of silence, then she spoke, her croak barely a whisper. 'No, Noah, you're wrong. *Indian*,' she replied. 'Richard's father is Indian.'

Still gripping the image, she was unable to move.

'Lily, Noah. Please leave now,' she heard. Ben's voice. Winded, tremulous. Shocked. 'There'll be taxis at the top of St John Street.'

Then movement around her. The scrape of chairs, the shunted table, the clink of cutlery and glass. The sound of footfall, the departing aroma of sweet perfume. The breeze blowing in.

Sudden sobs pierced the silence. Lily, of course, Lily. 'Jo, I'm sorry, so sorry.'

She turned then. Noah was trying to manhandle his wife out, but she was holding on to the doorjamb, pulling herself back in. 'I'm so sorry. Jo, please forgive me. I'm sorry, so sorry.'

With no idea of what she would do, whether she'd slap, shout or scream, Jo found herself walking to her *friend*, then opening her mouth. Words fell out without thought. 'You have to contact Richard's parents, Lily. You have to tell them they have a grandchild. Promise me that.'

White-featured and dumb, Lily nodded and followed Noah, leaving Jo alone with her brother.

Ben raked his hair. 'Oh my God. What the hell? Oh God Jo, I'm so—'

'Did you know?' She stared at his face. Pulsing through her body, hurt and anger consumed her. And pain, physical pain, bubbling and busting in her head.

'Ben. Did you know?' she repeated.

'No, of course not.'

The room was tilting and swaying. His expression wasn't right. 'I don't believe you. You knew, didn't you?'

'You're being ridiculous, Jo. Why would I know that?'

'Because you know everything. You've always known everything.'

Humiliation and betrayal. Bitter, bitter anger. Uncontrollable rage. Whipping up her right hand, she cracked his face. Then she lifted the other, indiscriminately smacking and striking and slapping until his hands caught her wrists and his voice finally broke through.

'Stop it, Jo. Just stop. I'm leaving the flat now. I'm really sorry, but I can't take this.'

49

Jo suddenly stirred. She was still propped up on the sofa, holding the wedding photograph. She had thought of hurling it against the wall, then watching the glass shatter and spread, but she'd fallen asleep.

She shook herself awake; she didn't have the energy or the anger right now. It reminded her of the horse and hounds painting at Petersfield. Glass there one visit and gone the next. Had Tom smashed it? Had he bust glass, then moved on to Kate's face? She used to think not, but she no longer knew. People were capable of anything. The ground under her feet had irrevocably moved; nothing was certain any more.

Richard's devotion, the one thing she'd been absolutely sure of, had been taken away.

Looking towards the door, she picked up her mobile to check for messages. Nothing. A couple of hours had passed. Oh God, Ben, poor Ben. Her loss of control, her appalling attack. What the hell had she done? He'd been her rock since Richard's death.

On her insistence after the panic attack, Joyce had reluctantly packed her case and returned to Moor End, and that was when he'd taken it upon himself to be her *Big Brother*. ('Well, that's what I am. Strange, isn't it?') He'd driven from Leeds to Manchester most weekends and tried to persuade Jo to *talk*.

She'd found it intrusive at first; she wanted him to go away, to let her grieve alone, but he persisted. 'You have to let it out, Jo. You've got to talk about it or it'll cripple you . . .'

'You can't say that!' she managed to splutter. 'No, thank you. I don't want to bloody well *let it all out*, as you put it. Richard's death is no one else's business. Besides, blabbing is demeaning, embarrassing for everyone.'

Then, when she'd recovered herself, 'Breach of an unwritten Wragg rule, Ben. Bottling is best! I'll report you to Mum if you're not careful.'

But Ben was unrelenting and gradually Jo learned that their new-found intimacy didn't involve just talking, but *listening* too. The truth of what she'd always believed was his *rugby injury* at school was unburdened – the badly fractured cheekbone, chipped front teeth and two broken ribs.

Outwardly the bruising had faded, but clearly not inside. Perhaps an explanation for Ben's need to be constantly surrounded by friends, the sheer dread of any conflict had remained.

The shame now burned in her chest. How could she have behaved that way to Ben, of all people? With violence, unjustified violence. She pictured him at fifteen. At half-term she had dived into the house, eager to see him after his injury. He was still black and blue; his teeth hadn't yet been fixed. And there had been a look in his eyes as he gazed at her, the same expression as two hours ago. Of fear, cowering terror.

Placing the picture face down, she sighed deeply. Then she stood on heavy legs and dragged them to the kitchen table. Mechanically lifting the plates, the cutlery and dishes, she slotted them in the dishwasher. But her mind was busy, leaping from one notion to the next. Finn was Richard's son; he'd had sex with Lily: a one-off or an affair? Deeply troubled, his mother said. Rushing off after two minutes. The late hours at the office, the stress. The cooling of relations in the weeks before he died.

Then the lilies in the gardens, for months. Of course. The lilies from Lily.

How had she not noticed anything amiss? How had she been so completely blind? *'Because you only take; you're self-centred and cold.'* Tom's words. Oh God.

Moving on to the glasses, she automatically filled the sink with soapy water because that's what she did when Richard was here. He thought the dishwasher made the glassware cloudy. Richard, her husband and *soul mate*.

Cloudy? Fucking cloudy? Trying to focus, to think, she stared at the bubbles. Did she know? On some level was it not really a complete surprise?

Breathing in the sickly 'apple' detergent smell, she thought back to a house party she and Richard had once had. What was it for? When they first moved in together they had them quite often – casual affairs where people turned up, drank too much, put the world to rights and danced. But this was more recently, maybe a year before he died. Astonishingly, Kate and Tom had appeared. Jo always invited them in passing and they never came, but this time they did, Kate talkative and bright, apparently on a high. Not drunk, though; Jo couldn't recall that.

By the end of the gathering, the numbers had worn thin. Much to Judy's chagrin and raised eyebrows, Kate had commandeered Larry, chatting to him animatedly all evening. In fairness, she listened too, wide-eyed and laughing a tinkling laugh in all the right places. Clearly in a huff, Judy was smooching with Noah, of all people. He'd melted against her curvaceous body like an invertebrate. Wondering how on earth Lily would peel him away, Jo laughed to herself.

'That's a nice smile.'

She turned to Tom's voice. They were the only ones sitting at the table.

He turned his glass. 'People-watching?' he asked.

'Caught me red-handed.'

He gestured to the small group of boppers. 'I guess it's you and me, then.'

Jo laughed. 'God, I don't dance!'

'Me neither.'

He held out his hand, guided her to the 'ballroom', drew her towards him and moved. It was somewhere between a rhumba and a waltz. And he could dance.

Fairly pissed like everyone else, she listened to the music and let herself be led in his firm and smooth grip. The next thing she knew, Kate was tapping her shoulder.

Reminding Jo of her excitable tone at school when something was afoot, she spoke quickly. 'I think Lily needs to go home.'

Jo pulled away from Tom. 'Oh right.'

Kate's cheeks were pink, her eyes shiny with intrigue. 'You mustn't worry, I'm sure it was nothing.'

She had to shake the inebriated fudge from her head. 'Oh right,' she said again, wondering why Kate was so interested in Lily after barely speaking to her all evening.

'In your bedroom,' she pressed.

Jo finally twigged. Lily must have been sick on her bed or carpet or something. Bit gross, but not the end of the world. She opened her mouth to say it, but Kate was still talking, her expression now filled with concern.

'Loads of people kiss at parties when they're drunk. It's nothing to worry about.'

That's when she lifted her gaze to the door. His eyes catching hers, Richard was shaking his head and smiling wryly. Noah was helping Lily into her coat and they were shuffling out.

Richard joined Jo when they'd gone. He hung his arm around her shoulders. 'Lily and sambuca. She's going to have a very sore head tomorrow,' he said easily.

She didn't think about it twice. Lily was a tactile person. Yes, she could picture her giving Richard an affectionate drunken hug or a peck. But it meant nothing because she trusted him absolutely. And besides, only minutes earlier, she'd had a moment with Tom, hadn't she? A surprising and arousing one. If he had leaned forward and brushed her lips with his, what would she have done?

The incident came and went. If anything, she'd thought ... What did she think? That Kate was, what? Causing trouble where there wasn't any? Being malicious, even? Did she really think that? More likely her feelings were confused between two people she loved, so it was better just to shelve and forget it.

Stepping backwards, she sat down to let the wave of nausea pass. Oh God. That kiss had been real and had meant something. She'd misjudged Kate, hadn't she? She'd always had a sixth sense, somehow. Almost knowing things before Jo knew herself.

Suddenly needing to puke, another thought hit, more wounding than any other. Quickly stepping to the sink, the realisation, the pancetta and the bile propelled out.

Richard had fathered a child. He wasn't sterile. It left only one nagging terror. She was.

50

Jo stirred from time to time, forcing her eyelids open to peer at her mobile, but Ben hadn't replied to her apologetic texts. She couldn't blame him; she'd lost all control; she'd directed her shock and anger at him.

Because she couldn't take it out on a dead man, she supposed.

Finally alert in the morning, the realisation she'd burned every bloody boat in her life hit instantly. Kate and Tom, Ben, the friends she'd dropped after Richard's death. And, of course, Lily and Noah. Strange though it was, she couldn't summon anger against them. Perhaps it would come, but at that moment all she could detect was overwhelming grief, that old feeling of heart-rending abandonment. She'd lost everything; the certainty that she was loved by Richard, the hope she would have a baby one day. And she'd destroyed friendships, hurt her brother, jettisoned her bloody self-respect.

Forcing herself out of bed eventually, she was momentarily surprised to see the cleared table, the pans from last night neatly stacked on the drainer. Like the *Elves and the Shoemaker* – making things right in the dead of night. If only; if only. She flicked on the kettle, but she wasn't thirsty; she peered in the fridge, but she wasn't hungry. A yawning day lay ahead and she had no desire or energy to eat, drink, dress, shower or shit. No, not just a day: a week, a month, a whole bloody empty, pointless life.

She washed her face, cleaned her teeth, put on jogging bottoms and a t-shirt, her thoughts mercifully shallow, then the memory of *all the sixes* abruptly popped in her head. Of course! It was her dad's sixty-sixth birthday today. She had spoken to Joyce in the week saying she'd put a card in the post, making her excuses for not delivering it in person: she'd invited Lily and Noah for dinner; they were pretty heavy drinkers; it would be a late night and she wouldn't be in a fit state to drive; she'd drop off his gift another time.

'Oh, don't worry about a present, love. Dad would rather forgo one to see you,' her mum had replied.

The thought of her solid, unshakable dad brought tears to her eyes. Of course she hadn't bought him a damned birthday offering. Her forecast for heavy drinking and a late night had ironically been true, but she could give herself as a gift, in fact more than anything she wanted to. Like the little girl who'd stared longingly through Junior House windows, she desperately needed her parents. And she was a grown-up now; there were no imprisoning bars; she was free to go to them straight away.

Having showered and drunk what felt like gallons of water, Jo arrived at Moor End at half past one. Taking a steadying breath, she rang the bell. 'Who on earth is that calling at this time?' she imagined her mum saying with a frown. 'We're halfway through dinner!'

But when Joyce opened the door, her face was a picture of delight. The aroma of Sunday roast billowing out, she put a finger to her lips and led Jo through to the dining room. Her dad was sitting in his usual place at the head of the table, gazing out of the large window to the green picture beyond, a wistful expression on his handsome face.

'Happy birthday, Dad,' Jo said, her voice cracking with emotion.

He turned, his cheeks flooding with colour. 'Joanna! Hello, love. What a lovely surprise.' Recovering himself, he cleared his throat. 'Do we have another plate, Joyce?' He nodded to the serving dishes, stuffed with an array of vegetables, and far too much for two. 'Sit down and tuck in. There's plenty left.'

'You look a bit peaky, love,' Joyce said later on the sofa. 'Is everything all right?'

'No, not really, Mum,' she replied. She wondered whether to let it all out, but she couldn't have spoken if she'd wanted to; her throat was clotted, her eyes shedding tears.

Joyce took her in her arms, rocking her like the child she was still inside. 'Stay for a few days, love? Dad and I would be delighted. Your bedroom's all ready as usual.'

The television mute in the background, her mum talked about Stan's latest property acquisition, Mrs Brown's new grandchild, the bakery in the village which had served cheesy rolls for the very last time, the death of the local gossip (alcohol poisoning, apparently; 'Some say poison for poison,' she said, raising her eyebrows), and her fancy for a fish pond in the garden. But Joyce didn't pry. She didn't probe about Kate or how the dinner party had gone; she didn't ask Jo what was wrong or why the rush of tears wouldn't stop. As though she *knew*, Jo thought, her mum's rare talent for caring and comforting, for understanding and empathising, without saying the words.

Trying to ignore her reflection, Jo gazed through her bedroom window. The fields and rugged hills, the cows beyond the white fence, the cotton-wool sheep dotted on the horizon. The dry-stone walls, the stile and broccoli-like clumps of trees. Everything the same, her childhood frozen. But she was a grown-up now, had been for a long time.

Turning her head to the right, she observed the roof of the double garage. How many times had she longingly peeped at the golden-haired boy from here? Then changed her mind and refused to look at all.

She deeply sighed. How she wished she could turn the clock back and do everything differently. Would she, though? *Could* she? Self-centred and cold, apparently. Only making things worse. Was it possible to be anything other than herself? And anyway, her 'life' had irrevocably changed in the space of twenty-four hours, crumbling and collapsing without any input from her. Moving and sliding, beyond her control.

Hearing the opening door and clink of crockery, a tiny flame of hope flickered. Mum with four o'clock tea and love. Some things didn't change, thank God.

'Thanks, Mum,' she said, turning.

It wasn't Joyce, but her dad. Handing her a mug of tea, he joined her at the window.

'How's it going, love?' he asked.

Afraid of crying, she didn't reply. Instead, she rested her head on his shoulder.

He kissed the top of her hair. 'The same old view, eh?' he said. 'Nothing wrong with that, not at all. But ...' He paused for a while. 'I'm set in my ways, I know it. But I'm learning that sometimes I need to be a bit more flexible. Bend a little with the wind.' Dipping his head to hers, he lifted his eyebrows and smiled wryly. 'Not easy, though.'

Jo laughed. 'You're right there, Dad.'

'Aye.' He kissed her head again before stepping away. 'Come on then, love, all the sixes birthday cake is calling. Not at all sure about *red velvet* sponge, but I'm going to give it a go.' He grinned. 'You never know, I might even get a taste for it.'

Sitting on a high kitchen stool, Jo watched her mum spread the fat from the roast on to a bread cake. She followed it with stuffing and shiny slices of pork, including a few strips of crackling.

'There you go. Just as you like it,' she said, handing the plate over.

'Thanks, Mum.'

Jo wasn't in the least bit hungry and she hadn't had a sandwich made with *dripping* for donkey's years, but she took a huge bite to please her. Despite its questionable health benefits, the blast from her pre-boarding-school past was actually delicious.

Absently listening to the clang and clatter of her mum at the sink, she chewed and contemplated Ben's text.

Joyce interrupted her thoughts. 'Nigel says he's invited you to Corfu,' she said, wiping her hands on her pinny. 'A bit of sunshine might do you good.'

'That's true,' she replied absently.

'Well, what's stopping you, love?' her mum asked.

Her guilt blurted out. 'I've offended Ben,' she replied.

The two subjects weren't strictly related, but Ben had finally responded to her profuse apologies: 'I know last night was devastating for you, but I need some space right now,' it read. 'Took ages to get home safely last night and I don't feel well.'

The surge of culpability smacked her again. Of course Ben didn't feel well. Noah's suggestion that a person should be *punished* for his or her sexuality would've brought the old terror to the forefront of his mind.

Not a rugby injury but a homophobic attack. Sent to the showers alone by the games master, he had been ambushed while naked, abused verbally, then punched and brutally kicked by a gang of older boys.

Listening to him relate the story, she had watched each booted assault painfully pass through his eyes. She had behaved no better – pummelling him like that.

Shame, she felt deeply ashamed.

Joyce took her hand. 'Give him time,' she said.

51

Listless and tired, Jo existed as another week trundled by.

Rock bottom, she mused when she allowed wallowing in. At least it couldn't get any worse.

It was the only good thing she could think of in the stony terrain of her existence. That and Aidan's phone calls, which raised a small smile between her random dull thoughts and deadlines. Like a human-shaped target on a shooting range, she felt peppered and punctured and wounded. Tom, Richard and babies. Kate and Lily, Richard's parents. Even little Alice. But the biggest hole was Ben's absence. Of all the missing parts, the loss of his constancy was the worst. He hadn't been in touch, and though she had acknowledged his last text, she'd respected his request for space by not chasing him. Objectively she knew she had to do something to change her life and move on from the past, but until he got in touch, she couldn't focus on the future.

Life was on hold.

A text from Lily had arrived, saying she'd written to Richard's parents and was awaiting a response. Despite the message almost ripping out her heart, Jo had replied and thanked her. It was a good development, undoubtedly, but focusing on the honourable was difficult at times. Too easy to dip into self-pity, she tried to float above it with her mum's mantra of *time.* But at least she slept well. Working hard at her laptop, she was exhausted by ten, sleep impersonating death until the alarm rattled her awake every morning.

The peal of her mobile prodded her too early on Friday. She peered at the screen. Aidan, of course. Who else? But she was glad of their strange friendship. Save for Joyce, he was the remaining *brick* in her life.

'Put on your dancing shoes, girl, I'm coming over tonight.'

'*Me* dancing? Really?'

'Fair enough – a meal out. I have something to celebrate.'

'Oh brill! So, spill the beans . . .'

'Tonight. Let's meet somewhere nice first. I'll send you a text.'

'I can't wait that long.' She laughed. 'Besides, you're gagging to tell me. I can tell from your voice.'

'I've just told my MD to fuck off. Five minutes ago, actually.'

Jo looked at the time. She'd overslept again – it was flipping ten o'clock.

'Stop. Rewind. You've done *what*?'

'I've just ditched my job. Your fault, Jo Jo.'

'And that's because . . . ?'

He put on an accent. 'It's the Irish in me, to be sure . . .'

'Really? You're going?'

'Yup, starting there and see where the river takes me. Fill you in later.'

Falling back on the pillow, she smiled. Good news, finally! Last time they met, she and Aidan had talked about his Irish relatives (over an improved Spanish omelette – without pig. Or ginger) and how he'd lost touch with them.

'They travelled over for Mum's funeral, apparently. I didn't see them. I was still in the coma,' he explained.

'So why no contact since?'

'Something happened at the wake. Dad never elaborated. He just muttered that my gran said unforgivable things and that the family were no longer welcome in his home.'

'Bloody hell. I wonder what was said,' she replied. And then, 'Why don't you track them down yourself? It's where it all began. Their daughter's child. Their grandson! You've got to do it, Aidan. They'll be thrilled to see you. Why don't you give it a try?'

He snorted. 'Hm. Visiting family you're not sure about. Sound familiar, Jo? I will if you will . . .'

Wearing the red dress yet again (but this time with the zippy biker's jacket she'd forgotten about – a bit creased, but what the hell), Jo walked towards the railway arches. Taking a deep breath at the door, she sniffed away the last iota of self-indulgence. She'd miss Aidan, that was all.

Absorbing the mix of perfume and juniper, she lifted her chin and searched the busy bar for Aidan. Despite him being the last standing brick, she was still absolutely delighted for him. The break would be the making of him, she was sure. His only close living relative was a father he didn't like. He was lonely. He was haunted by what ifs and maybes. And what was the point of feeling unfulfilled, hanging on in a job he didn't enjoy when there was a whole world out there? Family who wanted him too!

They sat in a corner. Sipping his Whitley Neill rhubarb gin, he said the same himself. He'd even planned the route.

'Cairnryan to Belfast crossing, returning via Rosslare to Fishguard or Dublin to Holyhead. So Ireland to start, which may seem lame, but as you pointed out, it's where it all began.'

'Finally!' she said, rolling her eyes. 'I'm so pleased you've decided to go.' She prodded him playfully. 'What took you so long?'

'Hark you!' He put a finger on his chin. 'Let's see. Feeling lost and unfulfilled and lonely. An open invitation to escape. An opportunity to take a break, to stop the day job for a while and focus on writing. You're ... what did my mum always say? Yeah, you are the pot calling the kettle black. Come on, Jo, what about you?'

She tasted her 5th Gin Fire and grimaced. It was a pretty apt description. 'Well ...'

'You could go island hopping like your brother did. God, that's a thought – you've got to do Santorini, it's stunning.' He laughed. 'And you don't even have to tell your boss to fuck off!' He peered at her carefully. 'We made a deal. I don't understand why you're hanging on. Has something happened you're not telling me about? Has Blondie been in touch?'

'Nope.' Not a chance. Tom was with *his girls*. Kate had regained her confidence, was out riding again and doing 'amazingly well', according to Hilary's latest update.

His eyebrows knitted. 'There's something else. What's wrong?'

Unable to speak, she shook her head. She didn't want to rake up the whole Richard and Lily saga, and how could she begin to explain her terrible behaviour with Ben?

As though reading her mind, he continued to gaze. 'What does big brother think? Does he say you should go?'

'It's not that simple, Aidan. It's a massive decision.'

'Well, if Ben says you should absolutely do it, would you?'

She shrugged. 'I guess.'

Looking to the door, Aidan stood and waved his hand. 'Late as bloody always,' he commented. He came back to her questioning frown. 'Ben. He's finally arrived. Still, it's perfect timing: your new life, Jo – we can ask him.'

52

Like the start of a new school year, Jo decided on September for the break, the rupture from life as she'd known it for over two years. In her mind she compared that time to living with a single kidney. One could do it perfectly well, but one wasn't on full blast. If there was no danger of losing the kidney one had (God, she hoped not – control kicking in to some extent; this was Joanna Wragg, after all), but infusing life into the other, then what did one have to lose?

That was the theory, anyway.

Everything was packed, a few clothes, sunglasses and her laptop, but she felt anxious, her mind jumping from thought to thought. She had a nagging doubt there was something she'd forgotten, a feeling which seemed to creep in increasingly these days.

I'm turning into Mum! she chided herself, but in a kind way. It wasn't so bad being Joyce Wragg, something positive she'd learned from the *one-kidney years*. She'd miss her mum and dad, their plain Yorkshire ways, their steady, calm love and their constancy.

Staring at her suitcase, she wondered what had become of her blue school trunk. She could picture the skinny, sharp-faced child flying out of Junior House in her boater to greet Stan at the end of each term. So pleased to see him, yet worried the other girls would notice how he was dressed, even worse hear him speak. She'd implore the school porter to bring her trunk outside rather than allow her dad into the dormitory. 'Our chauffeur,' she even once said, like the denial of Peter. She recalled it with shame in the dead of night when sleep escaped her, along with the host of other cock-crowing reprimands.

Perhaps we never grow up, she mused as she gazed, maybe that's the problem. We get moulded by our parents as infants and then shaped, or perhaps stunted, by circumstance as we age. Boarding school in her case, her brothers' too. By the time puberty arrived, they were set hard like rock and there was little they could do to change it without help. Without a total demolition and rebuild.

She shook her head at the building metaphor. Tom Heath was still in her thoughts; too often, probably. She hoped he'd found help, and happiness too. The unwrapped gift was still firmly there, rousing and painful when she allowed herself to dwell, but at least the obsessiveness had diminished – not by any miraculous self-help, but that old chestnut of *time*.

Aidan had set off on his travels. She missed knowing he was *around the corner*, but his comical postcards made up for it. The first one was a sepia picture of Blarney Castle.

'Still on my way!' he had written (in impressively neat handwriting). 'Waylaid by a gay club in Galway. Two days of passion with an Irish pig farmer, can you believe! Now making tracks to Cork to meet the clan. Wish me luck!'

The second was a photograph of St Fin Barre's Cathedral. 'You won't believe this,' it read. 'After my interlude, I finally reached Cork and guess who was there? Dad!! Impressed with my sheer spunk (ha!) and determination, he decided it was time to seek peace with the Irish. A lot of hugging, tears and reminiscing, but in a good way. Right now I'm happy, Jo. You should be too.'

Imagining the look of astonishment on Aidan's face when he arrived, she felt a warm spread. 'I hope Aidan was quick on his feet with an excuse for being late,' Ben had said, laughing, when she told him.

She had wished Aidan *luck*. She needed it too. Sadly it (and happiness, for that matter) wasn't just something one could order from Amazon. Too agitated to sit, she paced the length of the lounge. Twenty flipping years on and she was dressed and ready too early for a life-changing decision again.

Her heart raced. Of course life altered all the time; fine lines and fate. Husbands dropped dead, deep betrayal was exposed, friendships turned sour. But grandparents discovered a grandchild to fill a void and, against all the odds, a brother had found love. These things happened, out of one's control. But going to a Greek island (not even to Tibet or Timbuktu, as Judy had put it) on a one-way ticket was an active decision, a commitment which felt enormous.

She snorted. Her anxiety was silly. She wasn't emigrating, for goodness' sake.

'It feels like severance,' she had said to Ben, the best she could describe it.

'Isn't that a good thing?' he'd replied.

He was right, of course. Just for the hell of it, she'd looked the word up. *The state of being separated or cut off*, it said. She wasn't sure if she liked that. The second definition was even worse: *division by cutting or slicing*. She'd had to remind herself about swimming every day, hummus and halloumi, lemons and melons, sun, sand and sea. Exploring other islands, particularly Santorini (she'd always wanted to go, as it happened, but it would be fun to send Aidan a postcard saying I DID IT!). Then there was the writing, *proper* writing.

She glanced at the new laptop bag Joyce had bought her (not really her thing – it had a cat wearing shades on the front, but she had said, 'You like things that are a bit different, so I knew this would be perfect' with such pleasure that Jo was determined to embrace the whole *cool cat* thing). This isn't just a holiday, she reminded herself. She'd sent the first few chapters of the India manuscript to Lucien Du Beurre.

'No word for months. I thought you were dead,' he replied in his editor's scrawl. 'But this looks very promising, Jo. Send me more chapters and keep at it!'

Pulling her hair into a ponytail, she wondered what Mao would be like. She hoped they'd get on. Flying out to a brother she didn't even like, let alone understand, was all very scary. But she'd made a promise to herself, to Aidan and Ben.

'Go to Corfu,' they had both insisted in the gin bar. 'If you don't expose yourself to possibilities, then nothing will change. You'll just stay as bored and lonely as you are now. Nothing ventured, nothing gained.'

They had sounded like someone's grandma. God, she loved them!

A long and insistent buzz interrupted her thoughts. Oh shit, the lobby bell. The taxi had arrived early.

The nausea she'd felt all morning rose from her stomach to her chest. 'I'm not ready,' she whispered. 'I'm not ready to move on.'

Staying frozen for moments, she stared at the cool cat, examining the possibility of hibernating in the flat and not telling anyone she'd completely chickened out. But the taxi driver had come up to her floor and was politely knocking.

'He's too early,' she muttered. Knowing she needed more time, she opened the door and gesticulated to the room. 'Sorry,' she said, 'but you're twenty minutes early. I still have things to do. Could you wait?'

'I know it's taken far too long, but I've come to say sorry.'

She spun back to the voice. Wearing a smart jacket, his hands folded at his crotch like a football player in line, Tom Heath was on the threshold. 'I won't shout, I won't bite, I won't lose the plot.' He smiled faintly. 'I promise. Can I come in?'

Her instinct was to say, 'No, go away! You can't do this to me now!' But she knew she'd regret it for ever. 'I'm going somewhere,' she said instead, letting out the breath she'd been holding and focusing on Tom who looked tanned, fit and well, his face heart-rendingly handsome.

'Sorry,' he said, suddenly appearing young and uncertain. 'Have I chosen a bad time? I was on my way to Lancaster. I should've phoned first.'

She sighed at the surge of emotion inside. 'Come in, Tom,' she said, opening the door wide and letting him past.

53

They sat either side of the kitchen table on the turquoise chairs Jo had bought at great expense from the furniture shop across the main road. A rare whimsy, a year or so previously.

Richard never sat on that seat, she mused irrelevantly, her mind refusing to focus on Tom's steady stare. She'd never thought about it before; she'd assumed he had, because he'd 'visited' so often. Of course his presence had gone completely once his guilty secret was out. Perhaps he'd needed *severance* too.

Tom was silent. She knew his gaze was on her, but she couldn't meet it. Was she really going to jump into a taxi and travel to Terminal Two, eat an English breakfast on the aeroplane and a Greek dinner outside? And was everything packed? The fridge emptied, plants watered, heating off? And why did she want so badly to cry?

'Jo?' He was dipping his head to reach her eyes. 'I wanted to—'

'How's Kate?' she interrupted, fearful of his words, of the hope and the dread colliding in her chest.

Lifting his arms behind his head, he sat back, pausing as though to reorganise his thoughts. 'Fine. She's fine. The magistrates were reasonably sympathetic when they read the medical reports, but it was a mandatory driving ban, so . . . '

She nodded. She had almost forgotten about the drink-driving, her ridiculous race to Buxton police station and the confrontation with him in the car park. All that strife had become hazy, put into perspective by losing things she held dear, sweet memories of a happy marriage and a warm friendship, amongst other things. Almost a brother too, but that relationship was back on track, thank God.

She came back to Tom's voice. 'She's riding again. Just in the paddock, but still good news. The fearfulness is the same as before, though. She won't leave the farm without me. I've arranged for a young girl from the village to help out with the school run and shopping, but she prefers to have me around.'

She looked carefully at Tom. There was something in the tone of his voice, something unexpected and out of place.

'It must be hard for you,' she said.

She understood how tough it was to be the one on whom someone was utterly dependent, even if you loved them. Though when she thought about it, his account of Kate's progress was strange; it differed from Hilary's – hers was far more upbeat.

He laughed without humour. 'Suffocating, actually,' he said, rubbing his face. 'Which is why I almost welcome the drinking, it gives me a rest for a few hours. But I'll live with it, I always have. I should be used to it by now.'

Her skin tingling, Jo nodded but said nothing. It was the first time Tom had implied anything even approaching a criticism of Kate. But she wasn't surprised; she'd always felt that suppression, his need but his inability to let it all out, and she wondered if he had taken her advice, if he'd talked his problems through with someone, maybe seen a doctor or a therapist.

'Have you spoken to her recently?' he asked. 'I never really know if the two of you are in touch.'

'No, we haven't talked for quite a while.'

She must be happy, Jo reflected, she must have what she wants, for now.

'Did she always tell you everything?' he asked, looking at his palm as though studying his wedding ring.

'No,' she replied thoughtfully, remembering the *special* cuddles. 'I always thought she did until—'

'Until what?' he interrupted, lifting his chin and looking at her quizzically.

'Oh, nothing, just a school thing.'

He sat back, the muscles tight in his cheeks. 'A school thing? Are you sure? She didn't tell you about her ... her *liaison* with Guy Voide?'

'No!' she responded with surprise. She searched his face, looking for a joke. 'When was this? Are you sure? You must have that wrong.' She was shocked, absolutely stunned that Kate would be unfaithful to Tom, *her little investment.*

'Last year, apparently. I was surprised too, Kate's never been that keen on ... Well, she likes her beauty sleep, put it that way. But she told me herself about Guy.'

'You're joking! You must be wrong. Kate wouldn't do anything to threaten your happiness.'

Tom smiled a soft, tired smile and shook his head. 'Jo, we haven't been happy for years. I'm not sure if we were even at the beginning. Did you never notice? Were you so blinded by Kate's pretence, her fantastic acting? That me, me, me, in-your-face-all-the-time personality? That incessant cheerful talk?'

He put his hands on the table and spread his fingers. 'But I was fooled too, Jo. I thought I had married a paragon of virtue, an angel who'd save me from oblivion. But Kate's a masterful

307

manipulator and she knows precisely how to get her own way. I'm never quite sure what the next trick will be.'

Mesmerised by his countenance, Jo stared. The handsome features of the reasonable, reliable and reticent Tom. He was back and he was talking. Not with anger or rage but with a calm weariness that she recognised as truth.

A masterful manipulator. The words were so simple and so clear.

And you knew it, Jo, she thought. You knew it all, but you chose not to see.

The words felt so transparent, but distant memories were hazy. Quoting from *Hamlet*, a field full of dandelions. Red gloves. The sound of running water. He loves me, he loves me not. Every time she reached to touch them, they floated away.

Tom was still speaking. 'She was clever, fully aware I wasn't in love with her, but she knew the right buttons to press. Money, of course. I was desperate to escape, to make something of my life and she gave me the means and the opportunity. I was filled with intense gratitude, which almost felt like love. I thought that I was lucky, Jo, blessed that something good had come out of something so bad.'

Smiling ruefully, he touched her fingertips with his. 'So I vowed to make it work and it was fine. My indebtedness to Kate went far! But eventually it wore off, the scales fell from my eyes and I saw her for what she was – cunning and snide – playing innocent and dumb, but constantly insulting and criticising and blaming. Always those half-truths ... She knew it; she must've seen the recognition in my face, so the guilt trip began – the illnesses and anxieties, the poor helpless victim. And of course the unspoken blackmail. It didn't help that she and Harold were – and still are – the majority shareholders in the company.' He snorted softly. 'Or that a couple of planning applications were pushed through by less than conventional means.'

Tom rubbed his eyes; he suddenly looked exhausted, as though this strange confession was taking its toll.

'Then as the years went by and I got used to her tricks, she moved up a gear and she threatened me with having affairs, with harming herself, even suicide. And of course the spitefulness, destroying the few possessions I loved, eventually poisoning Honey.'

He lowered his forehead to the table while Jo looked on, silent and gobsmacked, the hairs sharp on the back of her neck. Surely not Honey? Pregnant Honey? Actually killing a dog?

She found her voice. 'Kate had bruises. On her wrists and her temple . . .'

He looked up and smiled wearily. 'Oh, she likes those. Plays with her cuffs to draw attention to them when people are around. Caused occasionally by me when I've had to restrain her from doing something stupid, but mainly self-inflicted.

'But she knows I won't leave, they're just little reminders to keep me in line. No, she handcuffed me when she got pregnant with Alice.' Glancing briefly, he sighed. 'I always wanted kids, she didn't. Then out of the blue she was expecting, a trump card she played just as I finally realised she had no intention of hurting herself.'

His jaw tight, he paused for several moments. 'I'd worked bloody hard to create a thriving business, I knew I could do it again. With my own money this time. So I summoned up the courage to leave. Then she announced her news. Wonderful but double-edged. Her timing was impeccable.' He frowned. 'Didn't she tell you any of this?'

She shook her head slowly, a distant dream nagging the back of her mind. 'No, I thought you were incredibly happy, like the smiley families in the adverts. I thought you had it all.'

The Golden Couple, the Midas Family; we all did.

Tom breathed through his nose. 'And so we have. Until death do us part.'

Falling silent, Jo looked back to the Kate she'd adored.

'Can we play hopscotch now?' she would ask.

'Can't we finish this game first?' Jo would reply.

'I won't be your friend then!'

Said time and time again, until Jo didn't even bother to object.

'Carry my satchel, Jo. It's too heavy,' she would demand.

'Mine is too. I can't carry both,' Jo would reply.

'But I have a tummy ache. Maybe I should ask someone else.'

So Jo would carry both.

'Why are you playing with her?' she would say, her eyes narrowed.

'Because you were with Cecil,' Jo would reply. 'I was lonely.'

'You're just to be my friend or I'll tell Daddy I want to leave.'

So Jo had no friends other than Kate.

Then her dear china calf on the dormitory floor. Smashed into a thousand pieces when Jo, just the once, said no.

But we were only small children, she now reflected. All kids are like that. There must have been more, but I can't remember. It's too late to summon it now.

Vaguely aware of a beep from her phone, she came back to Tom. *She knows I won't leave.* The words had been said. With desperate resignation, but clearly spoken.

As though reading her mind, he looked at her intently before dropping his gaze. 'My priority is what's best for Alice. I know that isn't necessarily having both parents living under the same roof – God knows, I only need to look at my mum and dad to see that. But I have to be around.' Inhaling with a shudder, he looked up. A jolt of pain passed through his face. 'Look what she did to Honey ...'

'No, Tom, absolutely no. She wouldn't hurt any child, let alone her own.'

He hung his head again. 'I know, I know. It's crazy. But she's said things, cryptic things – parental suicides and the mum or dad taking the kids with them. Other stuff too.' Squinting, he seemed to search for an example. 'If there's been a tragic drowning in the news, she'll look at me with those innocent eyes and ask how I'd feel if Alice *accidentally* died. I understand it's just talk, but I can't take that risk.' He cleared his throat. 'Look, I didn't actually come here to speak about Kate,' he said, standing up. 'Can I get a glass of water?'

She nodded and motioned to the cupboard. Though her whole body was crawling with goosebumps, she felt weak and winded. But she had to move; the taxi would be here any minute.

Stopping in his tracks, Tom appeared to register the suitcase for the first time. 'Are you going away?' he asked.

The queasiness flooded back. 'Yes. To Greece, to Corfu, to stay with Nigel. I thought you were the taxi.'

He sat down again. 'God, I'm sorry. I shouldn't have gone on about Kate. I came here to talk to you, to say sorry and explain.'

She watched him ruffle his hair and take a deep breath. Then she gazed at the gold wedding band moulded to his finger, that old feeling of abandonment surfacing.

'You visited the farm that weekend and talked about dating. Back in June. Do you remember? Richard was a great guy, but when he died, I never thought you'd . . .' His expression was earnest. 'I'd been numb for years and I was used to it. But suddenly the idea of you with someone else was unbearable. I was racked with jealousy and hurt and my behaviour was inexcusable. But the offer of a child, I want you to understand why—'

He was interrupted by the sound of the buzzer downstairs. 'When are you coming back?' he asked, his voice urgent.

'I don't know. It's a one-way ticket. That'll be the taxi.'

Standing up, she started towards the door, but Tom blocked her way and held her tightly by her shoulders. 'Jesus, Jo, you can't just walk out. Tell the taxi to go, get a later flight, talk to me, tell me why—'

Jo shook her head as the bell rang again, a long, impatient peal. 'There are things I discovered about Richard, but it's too complicated to explain now. I've decided to go, Tom. It's best for everyone.'

'Then let me drive you to the airport. Don't just disappear before I have time to talk to you. I've spent years avoiding it; I've been too repressed, too afraid to be honest, a bloody pathetic coward. Because my fear of your rejection and derision was so fierce and so raw, I couldn't just say it. I was too proud, so I tried to . . . hurt you, I guess, which made me as bad as *her*. And the things I said about the termination . . . well, my emotions were unbelievably confused. I knew it was your right to choose, but it felt so personal – you were stripping away a part of me, I suppose. But the offer of a baby was genuine, because . . .'

He seemed to realise his grip was too strong, so he let go, his arms dropping to his sides.

'Because I knew it was what you wanted so badly. Something I could give to you freely. A part of me, with love. I've loved you from the moment I set eyes on you, Jo, and though I cloaked it in indifference, even hate, it never wavered, not even for a moment.' He stepped back, his eyes blazing. 'That's it. That's everything.'

Hearing the sharp rap of the knocker, Jo gazed one last time. The word *love* was exquisite, but it wasn't enough. *'If only'* and *'she knows I'll never leave'* and *'half a life is worse than none at all'* beat through her mind. She understood Tom had nothing more to offer, so with strength she hadn't known she possessed, she strode to the door.

'Sorry for the delay,' she said to the driver. 'I'm ready to go now.'

Part Three

54

Corfu – present day

God knows what the taxi driver made of it, Jo mused as the Greek sun brushed her skin through a cloudless blue sky. She'd mostly napped during her first week at Pink Cottage, treacly dark sleep she couldn't escape, but in her waking moments she thought constantly of Tom. His huge presence in her flat, the tips of his fingers against hers, his tender parting kiss. But especially his face, scored with profound despair as he watched her leave. Though dry-eyed then, she'd cried later and couldn't stop, a stream of heavy tears which lasted until she started her endless slumber under the watchful gaze of Mao.

Physical severance it might have been, but not emotional. As the taxi pulled away and Jo stared through the rear window, she would've given anything to make it all different because she knew then she loved Tom, truly loved him. Looking back, she'd always known it on some level, though she'd denied it and fought it. But at least she had told him, a parting shot as she clutched his hand, pointless but true. 'It's hopeless, Tom, but I love you too. I really do.'

Speaking to Mao was easy, too easy. 'Talk to me, Jo. Tell me what's wrong,' she asked after a few days of silent tending. Even as the words poured out with her tears, Jo couldn't help but smile. A woman who listened without making judgements; Nigel had chosen well.

'I'm in love with a married man,' she replied, the words sounding a terrible cliché from the *Dear Elspeth* column, but true nonetheless.

'Does he love you?' Mao asked.

'Yes, I think he does.' Another torrent of tears. 'I *know* he does. But he has a child; he can't leave.' Then a sigh. She had to be fair. 'And he's married to my . . .'

How to put it? She used to say 'best friend' without hesitation, but that hadn't been the case for years. What was Kate to her now? She touched her cheek and felt the sharp sting. The one and only flash of anger behind that calm and reasonable façade.

'Jealousy, Jo, you were just jealous, not a nice trait at all.'

Coming back to Mao, she tried to shake the words away. 'His wife is someone I've known for a very long time.'

Mao nodded. Like the counsellor she'd never had, she was asking all the questions Jo needed to answer, to figure it out for herself.

'When did you realise you loved this man?'

Jo fell silent, trying to work it all out. Her mind was foggy, cluttered with so many thoughts and memories about Tom, about Richard and Kate, about bloody everything, it was difficult to concentrate.

'I've known him so long, I don't know . . .'

Did she ever love the Barnsley Tom Heath? She deeply fancied him, for sure. But that was part of the problem. She couldn't handle the burning desire, the way he made her feel out of control.

A boy from the *rough end of the village* hadn't fitted into her plans. Was it just his accent, his poverty? Or was it also his steadfastness, his adoration, his plain Yorkshire ways? It made her think of the denial of Peter again, a cock crowing twice. Which it had; it really had – on conception and death.

She came back to Mao's green gaze. 'It was clouded with ... lust, I suppose, and preconception. No. Bigotry in a way, though I hate to admit it.'

It seemed important to tell her the truth, to let it all out, to be honest at last. Like Nigel and his need to talk; ironic though it was, she was beginning to understand him a touch. 'He reminded me of what I was trying to escape,' she continued. Barnsley, her parents. How could they be bad things?

Falling silent and looking back, she remembered a conversation with Tom in the gardens. *'Perhaps we're more alike than we think.'* Of course that was it.

Smiling weakly, she shook her head. 'Too like me, I suppose. If I couldn't love myself, how could I love him? He was everything I hated about myself – aloof, constant, ordinary.' She pictured his face at the police station, the farmhouse, her flat, the sheer anger and emotion blistering out against his will. 'Repressed – terrified of losing control. Does it make any sense?'

Mao smiled. 'You're no ordinary, Jo.' She cocked her head. 'You love him, he loves you. Then why you leave? He could divorce, yes?'

Her eyes stung then. 'He'll never leave Kate, Mao. He says it's because of Alice, but perhaps it goes even deeper than that.' She pictured Catherine Bayden-Jones still wearing her boater, her pretty pink face and her tears. 'There's a fine line between love and hate and an even finer one between carer and dependent, the lover and the loved. You wake up one day and find the roles have been reversed. It's so hard to escape, it's frightening. No one understands it better than me.'

She put her fingers to her lips, remembering the last kiss as the taxi driver looked away in embarrassment. Tom had never kissed her like that before. It had nothing to do with passion or lust, hatred or anger. It wasn't a prelude to sex; it was simple pure emotion tinged with terrible sorrow.

Nigel and Mao rented Pink Cottage in the village of Kalami, a holiday – let on the beach, but at a reasonable rent because he was teaching the owner's kids English. He'd brushed up his Greek to near fluent and word had spread he was patient and amiable (really? – was this the same bloke as her brother?) and so the job had grown to teaching pupils ranging from six to sixty in the local village hall.

Jo was beginning to understand that parental pressure and unhappiness had tainted his life, but she and Nigel weren't up to teasing yet. He'd lightened up enormously, in her view, but the prickles were still there. *Her* thorns, she knew, but she couldn't completely let go. Still, it was interesting to see his sole possession from Moor End was a framed photograph by his bed – one of Joyce and Stan drinking rum from half a Bahamian pineapple.

She liked Mao very much. Short, chunky, homely and much older than Jo had assumed from the photographs, she was tactile and attentive, her warmth and affection beaming out with her ready smile. And she was pregnant, something Nigel hadn't mentioned in his emails.

Despite Jo's resolve to put the number one complete cow behind her, the sight of Mao's huge belly had knocked her badly on arrival. *A baby, a baby; someone else's, not mine*, played like an earworm before sleep engulfed her the first night, but when the warm rays of sunshine woke her, she thought of her mum. How thrilled she would be by the news (if she didn't already know – that was something she parked). So she had a last smarting weep, picked herself up and dusted off the envy. Nigel was her brother; she was pleased for him. He'd swung from denial (apparently – there was no trace of it now) to attentive delight at the prospect of becoming a father. As for Richard and his child, she thought about them sometimes, but only loosely. Idle pondering: were Richard and Lily a long-term thing, a one-off, or was it just part of the competitiveness with Noah? Did he know he was the father of her baby before he died? Was that the 'deeply troubled' man his mum saw? How had his parents reacted to the news they had a grandson? Joyfully, she hoped. As Tom had said, something good from something so bad.

It would've been easy to be hurt and angry and jealous, but she was sapped mentally and physically; she didn't have the energy for further turmoil. Richard was dead, and besides, those emotions were corrosive, they bubbled and burned inside. Like Noah, poor Noah. Giving his name to a child he knew wasn't his. A selfless act of love he couldn't quite carry through.

Her laptop stayed in its case and her mobile lost its charge. She had no desire to be creative, she just needed quiet time, reflection and calm.

Pink Cottage gave Jo peacefulness during the day. It squatted on the beach-front of the bay and she strolled for miles along the shore, the sand pliant in her toes, the wind soft in her hair. As the sun burned above, she'd think empty thoughts before stopping off at the mini-market for a bottle of chilled water and a treat for Mao, or at a taverna for a syrupy Greek coffee and baklava on the way home. She found Nigel's mute, leather-skinned and toothless lady on a dusty back street and she'd empty every coin from her purse into her weathered hand for a polished lemon. On other days she'd walk with Mao to the White House in Kalami with its tavern, where Lawrence Durrell had once lived, thinking, I ought to be writing, I really should.

Even reading was a struggle; flicking through the English local paper as she sat in the garden pretty much covered it. She was distracted, happily so, by the simplicity of her new life. The look, the smell and the feel of her surroundings. The bouquet of lemon and orange trees at the rear of the cottage. The colourful flowers and plants in the front yard; the bougainvilleas, aromatic herbs and fragrant roses. And the pleasure of eating outside; small, delicious meals on the shaded Corfiot bozo, gazing at the yellow evening sky, alone or with Mao.

But night-times were different in her small cool bedroom at the back of the cottage. It felt as though her sleep was cursed. Strange merging visions – her dad and Tom, the shrill warning sound of the cock, a lawn carpeted with dandelions, a woman looking through her rear-view mirror, baguettes bleeding on the ground, copper stones in a fast-flowing brook. But mostly they were about Kate. Hostile and violent dreams, anger, disbelief and shouting, always by Jo herself. She'd sweep the china ornaments from the top of Kate's dresser on to the hard floor; she'd slap her head repeatedly, just like she'd struck Ben. Screaming and screaming until she shook herself awake to break loose from the nightmare. Then she'd sit up in her bed, soaked in sweat and burning heat, wondering if the howling had escaped to reality. As her heartbeat slowed and her skin gradually cooled, she'd listen to the crickets beyond the shutters and remember Tom's face.

'Before you go, there's just one more thing I need to know,' he'd said, the morning drizzle fine and wet on his face as the taxi waited.

He held her hands firmly in his. 'Back then, in Barnsley ... Is it true you told Kate about the baby, the pregnancy?'

Thrown by the question, she nodded. 'I did. Sorry. I hadn't intended to, but yes, I told her. A couple of days before the ... appointment, I'd changed my mind. I wasn't sure what to do.'

She took a breath to steady her voice. 'It was so long ago, Tom. But I needed you. I needed to talk to you. So I telephoned you at your home.'

He nodded, his expression dark and stony. 'But Kate answered?'

'Yes, and we met for a coffee in town. She knew I was pregnant; she could tell as soon as she looked at me. I'd put on weight and looked pale and distraught, I suppose. But it was fine, Tom. She didn't know ... who. She immediately assumed the father was some random boy from university.' She paused, thinking back. 'To be honest, she helped me. You know, objectively. I was wavering, seriously thinking of going through with the pregnancy, but she helped me see the sense of ending it, going ahead with the termination. She was there when I needed her.'

His arms folded tightly, Tom turned and looked away towards the gardens. Then eventually he came back, his eyes hard and shiny. He put his hands on her shoulders, but softly, a feather touch, as though he was trying very hard not to crush her.

'Kate knew it was mine, Jo. She knew. She encouraged you to *kill the little bastard*, as she put it. She informed me quite conversationally when I told Alice that she'd always be my little baby. Said something like, "Though not your first, Tom. But Jo killed the little bastard. I made sure of that." With a serene bloody smile over Sunday lunch.'

Jo gazed at his face, watching the anger and hurt in his eyes as she tried to make sense of his words.

'But I didn't think you'd told anyone, Jo,' he continued. 'I didn't think she really knew about the pregnancy, about us. I thought she was just speculating, that it was one of her spiteful little games.'

Lifting his head, he stared into the cloudy drizzle before looking at her. 'And when I looked back, I remembered that day because it was strange. Just after the New Year she'd gone out with you in the morning for coffee in town, then had to hurry back unexpectedly to Barton in the Beans *to see Daddy*. She came back a day or two later with a cheque from Harold. A huge amount of money, in my name. "We all believe in you, Tom," she said. So I asked her to marry me. A devil's contract. Such a greedy, blind fool.'

Jo closed her eyes and remembered Kate's words: *Of course, we'd all be there to support you if you decided . . . But what about university? You love it! And your career as a journo? Adoption sounds kind, but really, Jo, if you think about it, it has all sorts of consequences. The child might come looking for you one day. They'd want to know about their father. What on earth would you say?*

So calm, so sensible and so supportive, knowing exactly what to say.

'She knew.' Jo nodded, her mind blurry, a tumbleweed of thoughts.

Of course Kate had known.

55

The fitful sleep and sweaty nightmares in Pink Cottage continued. Lack of closure, Jo supposed. The need to confront Kate about the termination of her and Tom's baby had pounded through her head and her chest the moment she'd closed the door of the taxi. The desire to stand up to Kate had increased over the years, but she'd never quite sustained it. She'd always been talked around and blindsided by Kate's innocence or neediness or her reasonable calm.

She was the *master manipulator*, of course. All the traits Tom had described were so utterly true. Like those old Scooby Doo films, the mask had been ripped off and Jo could recognise it quite clearly now. But that wasn't enough. She had to face Kate and tell her; it had to stop. For once she would say her piece and see it through. Make Kate acknowledge it and say sorry, even beg for forgiveness.

But that hadn't happened. Of course not.

'It's hopeless, Tom, but I love you too. I really do.'

Her own words still tolling in her ears, Jo had taken in a last glimpse of her lover's broken face before the cab joined the busy traffic on Deansgate. A million thoughts were battling for dominance, but one stuck out a bloody mile.

Kate knew the baby was Tom's, she bloody knew. She'd made sure that Jo *killed the little bastard*.

Dry-eyed for now, she was certain the tears would come, she could feel them swelling her body like a corpse fished from water, but she *would* hold on, the anger was shielding her.

The driver's eyes caught hers through the mirror. 'So the airport's on hold. Now we're driving to Hope. As in the Hope Valley. That's in Derbyshire, right?' Then, turning from his seat and looking at her quizzically. 'It'll cost minimum seventy-five quid. Are you sure?'

He was called Sohail, she remembered from the booking. Sohail was the start of her new one-kidney life. *Not going to plan* was an understatement. 'Whatever it takes. Just get me there, please.'

After the last fifteen minutes, he clearly thought she was crazy, but Jo didn't mind. She felt a little deranged, actually. No, not a little – she was consumed with rage; gut-wrenching fury.

Aware of Sohail's occasional glances of curiosity through the mirror, she sat stone still and watched her adopted handsome city turn into a busy dual carriageway, then a motorway before hitting the soggy hills. Her thoughts were thankfully shallow and pragmatic as she gazed at the familiar countryside through the rain-smattered windows: she didn't know the postcode for the farm, but she could direct the taxi from the village. She needed to stop at the cashpoint anyway. Maybe she should get out there – the walk would clear her head, help her shape what she wanted to say. But she was still going to Corfu. No last-minute reprieve, despite the stupid hope. So she'd still need Sohail to drive her back to the airport. Course she'd miss her flight, but they had standby seats all the time. She'd text Nigel when she knew what the times were. The cost of the booking was down the pan, but what did that matter? She had a mission.

Though what *was* the plan? She didn't know, she didn't know. All she understood was that she'd never forgive herself if she didn't challenge Kate and say *something*.

Kate was in the wet yard. Her back turned, she was holding her riding hat and bolting the stable door. Clearly hearing the car, she turned with a scowl and watched it bump along the shiny cobbles until it came to a standstill.

Feeling queasy with nerves, Jo climbed from the cab.

'Oh, Jo, it's you!' Quickly recovering herself, Kate smiled. 'Sorry, you surprised me. I was just . . .'

She'd clearly been riding. Only in the paddock? By the state of her muddy boots and jodhpurs, Jo doubted it. And the dogs were in the kennels, not running free as they usually did when she was around the farm.

Jo swallowed the threatening bile. 'Can I come in?'

Kate's eyes flickered to the stationary taxi.

Anger flashed. 'Unless you'd like Sohail to join in the conversation about the abortion,' Jo snapped. She glared at Kate's passive face. 'You know, the termination you encouraged me to have when—'

'Oh, poor Jo.' Her expression gentle, she rubbed her arm. 'Why are you thinking about it now. It was years ago!' She studied Jo's face before nodding. 'Of course, you must come in. You're so pale, you don't look very well. I can see you need to talk.'

Handing her a key, Kate beamed. 'So lovely to see you. I'll rustle up some lunch. Maybe slivers of smoked salmon on toast like Hilary! Remember? Do let yourself in, I'll open the kennels and be back in a mo.'

Holding on to her resolve, Jo opened the side door and stepped in. How did Kate do this? How did she pretend that everything was normal and fine, when she must know, surely know, that it wasn't.

Watching Kate remove her riding boots, Jo thumped down at the table and breathed in the usual patisserie smell. Too honeyed and sticky, it almost made her retch. Why hadn't she noticed it before? Heavy saccharine sweetness, nauseous and false like her *friend*.

Stuck for words, she stared at the china ornaments but Kate sat opposite and immediately filled the silence.

'It was such a hard decision for you. But we talked about it then, didn't we? We looked at it from every angle and it was the right thing to do.'

Through clenched teeth, Jo found her voice. 'Right thing?'

Kate reached for her hand. 'Yes, it was at the time. You were at university, you wanted a career. You—'

'I will never have a baby because of you.' So, there it was, the real root of the anger. 'The one thing I want I can't have.'

Kate frowned. 'How do you know that?'

Jo thumped her chest. She wasn't going to give this woman the satisfaction of learning about her failure to conceive and Richard's two-year-old offspring. 'I know it right here.' The emotion bubbling, she stood up. 'I was undecided. You knew I was wavering, but you—'

'No, Jo, no.' Kate looked at her calmly. 'It was your baby, your decision. And whatever advice I gave, I was doing it for you.'

I was doing it for you. Thrown for a moment, Jo mouthed the words. She'd heard her say the exact ones before. But Kate was still talking, her voice smooth and eloquent.

'And let's be honest, Jo, you didn't even know who the daddy was. Having a baby is hard work – believe me, I know. There wasn't exactly a knight in shining armour wanting to whisk you off into the sunset like in one of your funny little stories.'

Her heart thudding loud in her ears, Jo stared at Kate's implacable face. Tom, Tom. He was married to this woman *until death do us part*, she didn't want to get him in trouble. But what was the point if she didn't say *something*? Besides, she wanted to smash Kate's smug and rational façade. 'There was a *daddy*. You know there was.'

'Was there? I can't recall you ever mentioning it.' She scraped back her chair and headed for the sink. 'Do you have time for a coffee, or do you need to get back to—'

Jo spat the words. 'You knew Tom was the father. He wanted me to keep it and he asked me to marry him. He asked me first. Did you know *that*?'

Kate slowly turned. 'That's a lie.'

'It's the truth. You know it's the truth.'

The searing slap came from nowhere, jolting Jo back against the table. Her face a deathly white, Kate looked at her trembling hands, then she raised her cold eyes.

'Truth? You want to talk about truth?' Suddenly laughing, she sat down. 'It was right from the start, wasn't it, Jo? From the moment you met me, you wanted what was mine. Don't think I didn't see your greedy eyes on my belongings at school, your sweaty little fingers touching everything in my home. How you hated it when anyone else wanted to be my friend. How you loved it when I was bullied. Because that meant I was all yours, didn't it? I'd still take you to Barton in the Beans where you could covet my mother and lavish her with your adoration like a puppy. And she just couldn't abstain.' She mimicked Hilary's voice. *'Isn't there anything you can't do, Jo? You are so clever.* Clever Jo! Always having to be the best at everything, needing to win. Who even said there was a competition?' She snorted. 'Not me. Jealousy, Jo, you were just jealous; not a nice trait at all.'

She took a deep breath. 'And as for my husband ... Well, you couldn't bear he was mine, could you? Still can't. But don't bother even trying. He'll never leave me or Alice. He wants to keep us happy and *safe*.' She smiled her serene smile. 'You love Alice, don't you, Jo? You should want it too.'

She looked at the window. 'I think we've covered everything. Time to dash off, Jo. Your taxi is waiting.' Then finally, with a nod. 'And wherever you're going, don't come back.'

56

October came and daytime temperatures fell, but the Greek weather remained balmy and soft. The sun was lower with mellow rays, the sky a clear light blue. Rain appeared sporadically and the evenings became cooler, Jo resorting to a jumper for warmth. But she still swam, the salty sea warm from the punishing dry summer. Walking further afield, she discovered olive groves and hills, fascinated to see how time changed and healed the landscape. Like her, it had slowly recovered from a stripped emotionless dusty yellow to a hopeful lush green.

Christmas soon approached, December cold for Corfu, and there was rain, heavy downpours most days. Jo thought of Joyce and Stan and, for the first time, she felt homesick. But surprisingly not for St John Street, or even for England. Just for them, her lovely mum and dad and her childhood home, that feeling of dejection and abandonment at the surface again.

'I want to come home,' she said to Ben on the telephone. She was almost in tears at the idea of her first Christmas somewhere other than Moor End. 'Do you think I should? Just for Christmas?'

'I know you do, Jo, but I think you should stay,' he replied. 'Be there for Mao when the baby comes. She'll need you. I'll be at home with Mum and Dad. They do understand.'

Of course Ben was right. *Number One Complete Cow* was well in the past, and though paralysed by concern and impotence during Mao's long and painful labour, it was a joy to be at her side when her son was finally delivered, to see the tears in Nigel's eyes, the look of astonishment and love on his face when he first held his baby.

'Congratulations, big brother,' she said in the ward, holding him tightly for the first time in many, many years. 'Right, I need to stop crying! I'll leave you two with your beautiful son and see you later. Call if you need anything.'

Her legs felt leaden. Like post-traumatic stress, the film of Mao's labour was still playing through her head. Yawning widely, she wryly wondered what it would be like to give birth to a baby that size. She had only watched the agony, the puffing, the pushing, and she was totally wiped out. Almost through the door and into the cold night, she heard Nigel's voice and turned.

'Jo.' He looked at the ground before lifting his head. 'That day when you asked me for help . . .'

She dropped her gaze; over the past three and a half months she'd lived with a brother she'd grown to appreciate and love again. Now wasn't the time to talk about it. It was all in the past.

He spread his hands. 'I'm sorry.'

Tensing, she closed her eyes. There was no point going there; no one could change it. Remembering that freezing December day, she shivered. Her scarf damp and her eyes swollen from crying, she'd trekked from the bus terminus to Moor End, inordinately relieved to see her mum's car wasn't in the drive. The image of her scanned baby was still vivid in her mind. Its fingers, its toes, the upturn of its nose. Without glances of concern or questions, she could go to her bedroom and sob her heart out, thank God.

The tears already dripping, she unlocked the front door, but the moment she stepped in, Nigel's Audi screeched up behind her. Slamming the car door, he charged into the house, stomped through to the lounge and slumped down on the sofa.

Picking up a tea towel, Jo wiped her face and followed him in. Her brother was wearing the usual shirt and tie. 'Shouldn't you be at work?' she asked him.

His arms folded, he snorted. 'Couldn't bear it a moment longer.' Then, scowling at her, 'You have no idea, do you? You just go around with your important little nose in the air, getting everything you want, just when you want it. Mum waiting on you hand and foot, everyone indulging you. You have absolutely no clue about the real world, have you?'

'What's that supposed to mean?'

'Your *lovely* Dad, for starters.'

'What about him?'

'I fucking hate him, that's what. He's a bully, Jo. Everything on his terms. No communication, no compromise. His way or the highway. Making me feel like a stupid idiot.' He glared. 'Did I want to work for the fucking *family* business? Taking a degree in languages might have been a clue, but they were both at it, *her* as well as him. Constant bloody pressure. *When Nigel joins the family business . . . Just imagine how nice it'll be working with your dad . . . When it's you and Stan . . .*' He snorted. 'I wanted to do something meaningful, look out for people, maybe social work or counselling, even go abroad, but I'm turning into him, a bloody inflexible fascist, the sort of person I fucking loathe.'

Suddenly twigging her wrecked face, he frowned. 'What's up with you? You've been crying.'

And there it was, salvation. A person who cared about people, someone Jo could confide in, open up her heart to. The words tumbled out with the tears. She was pregnant. She'd just come back from a scan. The clump of alien cells had turned into a baby before her eyes. She was so very torn and there was no one to talk to. Should she tell Mum and Dad and have the baby or go through with the abortion? She was scared, unbelievably scared of making the wrong choice. She only had a week to decide. What should she do? What the hell should she do?

Needing a hug, human contact and warmth, she found herself holding out her arms, then scrabbling at her brother's chest and his shoulders, desperate for his love, for his *help*.

But he pushed her away. 'What the hell, Jo?' His expression shocked, he stood and rubbed his palms. 'No. Don't put this on me. No, Jo. This is down to you. I have enough problems of my own.'

Though stunned by rejection and hurt, she stupidly assumed he'd have second thoughts, that he'd knock on her bedroom door later to talk it through, but the days hurtled on. No chat nor eye contact. Nothing. But she remembered his hands, the way he'd smoothed them together as though washing them. Like Pontius Pilate, she thought. Despite all his right-on wisdom, by default he'd sent her baby to its death.

'In my own way I've tried to show it,' Nigel now continued, as though reading her mind. 'But I need to say the words. I'm sorry, Jo. I should have listened. I should have helped. I was just so unhappy and ... ' He looked over his shoulder to the ward door. 'I didn't understand the enormity of what you were going through, not until ... ' He sighed. 'Until Mao got pregnant; until I saw my own baby's scan.'

She nodded in acknowledgement. Perhaps today was the time after all. She put a hand on his shoulder. 'You'll be a fantastic dad, Nigel. Go back to your new family. The past is the past.'

Outside the hospital, Jo took a fresh and crisp breath. Today's planet was sparkling. Nigel had a son, the palm trees outside the

General Clinic were brightly lit by fairy lights and an orange glint of dawn coloured the sky.

The past was indeed the past. No more raking at what ifs and maybes. A future was before her. She would damn well embrace it.

57

Listening to the hungry bleat of little Spiros (the nickname had stuck), Jo stared into the black, balmy night. Though she couldn't stop yawning, she knew sleep was nowhere near, so she breathed in the musky aromas from their evening meal, identifying each one. Olive oil, herbs and tomatoes, feta cheese and chorizo sausage. Like a thermos flask, Pink Cottage seemed to retain all the flavours. Or perhaps it was her, absorbing every sound and smell, trying to bottle these special moments.

The distraction didn't last long. Her mind circled back to her dream. Almost like drowning, she'd popped from it with a shock, swimming to the surface and gasping for air. Kate and extreme anger, as always. Yelling the millions of retorts one only thinks of afterwards. Like her failed confrontation at Petersfield back in September. She always came back to that, picking away at Kate's statement about keeping Tom and Alice *safe*. Her strange stare from the door too, when Jo finally climbed into the taxi to leave. That *cat's eyes* squint she remembered from school. And she hadn't stood up to her, at least not effectively. Perhaps it was that.

She snorted wryly at the memory. Say her piece to Kate and see it through? *Of course* it hadn't happened. The feeling of entrapment had been almost overwhelming. Then, 'The airport?' Sohail had asked. She'd blown out the panic and smiled. She was off to find lemons the size of melons, sit in the sunshine and write. She was escaping, thank God. She was breaking free of Kate Bayden-Jones at last.

Corfu was certainly freedom – paradise, too – but Jo knew she couldn't drift on for ever. When Nigel's baby was born she was able to help Mao and repay some of her love and hospitality by changing nappies, making meals and cleaning (even brandishing a feather duster and donning rubber gloves). But she felt the time had come to leave the new parents alone with their baby. Besides she had promised her mum she'd come home very soon (via Santorini – she was determined to do that). Truth was she needed to focus on her own future. Get back to Manchester, water those long-suffering houseplants and carry on earning a *crust*. She just needed the driving force to *get off her fat arse*.

After a night of particularly vivid nightmares which had repeatedly sucked her in each time she tried to escape, the impetus came out of the blue early on Cheese Eating Sunday (a redolent name, if ever there was one). On her phone when she woke, there was a text from an unknown sender.

'How are you, Jo? Just caught up for a coffee with Joyce and heard all the Corfu news . . .'

Oh God, it was from Kate.

'Alice says hi. Sure Tom would too but he's just gone off for another two weeks – scouting for a new bar down south. Another one in the <u>chain</u>, so can't complain!'

Her heart racing, Jo stared at the message, then read it again. Kate's chirpy voice shone through it, as though their last meeting and the hostility hadn't happened.

She read on. 'I've been going through some old school things. Guess what? I found a few of your stories. Can't believe how good they are. So incredibly <u>realistic</u>!'

Jo's whole body tingled. Stories, her old stories. Why mention them? Something was tugging and nagging in her mind. What was it? What the hell was it?

She blew out a long breath. It was just the shock of hearing from Kate, that was all. Fresh air was the thing to shake it off. Mao was sleeping, so she'd put little Spiros in his papoose, walk towards the village and show him the preparations for the approaching Lenten festival. Yesterday she'd watched the locals adorn brightly coloured floats; the singers and dancers had been practising for the parade too. More of that would distract her febrile mind.

Like an English November, there was a chill in the air. It had rained through the night, diluting the usual eggy smell of the seaweed but highlighting the aroma of shrubs and trees. The streets were silent, still and damp, but the sun was peeking through the pale, cloudy sky.

Inhaling a salty tang, she strolled along the promenade and idly chatted to the baby. A sole woman with red hair brushed by her shoulder, but Jo's eyes were on the sea. It moved silently, the ripples winking and glinting like glass. And there it was. The recollection had been seeping through her consciousness for weeks, but as the breeze buffeted her face, it was there, complete and transparent.

As clear as the river.

58

St Luke's – November 1991

A chilly Sunday afternoon in November, the late bloom of bright dandelions the only reminder of summer. Joanna Wragg and Kate Bayden-Jones sneaked from the dormitory in their new school house. Pulling on wellington boots at the side door, they checked the all-clear, then trotted with a mix of excitement and trepidation towards the river.

Rubbing her arms to keep warm, Miranda Day-Carter was already at the bottom, the copper of her glorious hair glowing in the reluctant sun. Pulling out a bag of crisps from her blazer pocket and holding them aloft, Jo waved. Miranda did likewise and laughed. They were almost friends by then, the three of them in Kemp, a school House down the road from the main building. Jo and Kate had gone up to Seniors in September and had immediately been greeted by Miranda on the first day back at school.

'You two! Thank goodness, friendly faces I know! Last year it was all new girls from other schools and they were such hard work.

Welcome to Kemp. Best House ever,' Miranda had said with a friendly grin.

Wondering how Kate would react, Jo had glanced at her face, but she was smiling and animated, her eyes shining, her cheeks pink. She'd developed over the summer months, was as tall as Miranda now and had the confidence too. 'Agreed! We both wanted Kemp, didn't we, Jo? You won the choral verse speaking last year and I can't wait to join in. The House play too. If you'll have me!'

'Course we'll have you. Everyone said your Lady Macbeth soliloquy at Buxton was brilliant. You've got a great singing voice too. And we *so* need a soprano for the House choir.'

Away from the school and classrooms, there was more freedom in Kemp House. A small dark stone manor in its own grounds, the manicured gardens sloped down to the water. Of course the river was forbidden. It was dangerous, Matron warned, a local boy had died, caught in the fast flow of the weir at the bottom of the ravine. But none of the pupils really believed it. They knew Kemp House was haunted (some girls had seen the ghost for themselves) and that mice (possibly rats) scratched the floorboards at night, but the river at the bottom of the hill was shallow, clear and stony, more like a stream.

Country girl that she was, Jo was desperate to explore it. Preferring the indoors, her plethora of *home* clothes and magazines at a weekend, Kate had firmly declined, but over the sickening stench of scrambled eggs, she'd relented at breakfast that morning.

Though the girls were required to rotate their places at the dining benches, as *Head of Table* Miranda was sitting between them that day.

'Have you ever been down to the river?' Kate asked her in a low voice. 'Jo wants to cross it and see what's on the other side. She's such a daredevil but I'm a complete wimp.'

She'd continued to whisper, her eyes glowing and wide. 'But I'll feel safe with you, Miranda. We'll have to keep it a secret, but I'll do it if you will. Matron always naps on a Sunday afternoon. We could do it today!'

The three girls now gazed at the shadowy stream.

'It looks deep. Are we really going to do it?' Miranda asked.

'Of course we are,' Kate replied.

But neither of them moved. Instead they linked arms and giggled.

Inhaling the delicious wild aromas around her, Jo frowned. She'd been excited all day, she wasn't going to abandon ship now.

'OK, I'll test it,' she said.

Holding on to Kate with one hand, she dipped a foot in, searching for ground. Though nearly at the top, the water didn't spill over her wellies.

'Not too deep if we fall, but let's keep to the stepping stones.'

Taking a breath, she stepped forward, quickly dancing across the mossy boulders in a zigzag, stopping briefly with a grin on the other side before heading back.

'Simple! Your go.'

Miranda went first, slightly wobbling halfway, then eventually Kate followed.

'Gosh, it is easy,' she declared. 'Let's do it again! Faster this time!'

Laughing with nervous exhilaration at their daring, the girls continued to cross the dappled water, the mix of delight and fear making them howl more loudly each go. Slimy with limp grass and algae, the rocks were slippy and, despite stretching out their arms for balance, they nearly toppled several times, risking wet legs and damp uniforms.

Feeling carefree and reckless, Jo tested a sturdy branch that bowed over the stream. It was slithery too, but they'd come prepared with woollen gloves. Jumping to catch it, she pushed her legs forward, watching the ripples glinting like glass as she swung.

'Gosh, do you dare?' Kate asked Miranda.

'Course I do,' she replied, taking her turn. 'How about you, Kate? It's your go.'

Kate narrowed her eyes and watched for a while. 'Maybe later, you can show me. I'm starving! Let's eat.'

Finding a felled bone-like tree trunk, Jo hitched along it and quoted from *Hamlet*. '*Think it no more. For nature crescent does not grow alone . . .* '

Miranda's nose crinkled. 'What?'

'Laertes. Miss Havenhand always chooses me to read him in lessons.' She shrugged. 'A boy as usual, of course.' She bowed flamboyantly. '*Farewell, Ophelia, and remember well what I have said to you.*' She patted the bleached seat and pulled out her squashed packet. 'Which means you may now eat your crisps, dearest sister!'

Miranda laughed. 'Why thank you – I think. Didn't she drown?'

'Yes, but she was very beautiful. My mother took me to see *The Story of Ophelia* at the Tate in the summer.' She eyed Miranda's mane. 'You know, it's a painting.'

Falling silent, the girls munched their snacks. Then Miranda pulled the stem of a white and grey dandelion. Blowing its delicate clock softly, she chanted. 'What time is it, Mr Wolf? One o'clock, two o'clock—'

Wondering if life could be more perfect, Jo watched the tiny helicopter seeds fly away on the breeze. 'Let's predict our futures!' she said, plucking one for herself. 'Let's see. When will I marry? Does he love me or love me not?'

'How many children will I have? Will I be rich or poor?' Miranda suggested, selecting another.

'Or how long will we live?' Kate added with a laugh.

They washed their sticky hands in the water, then scooped palmfuls to their mouths, slurping greedily to wash down the salty residue of crisps.

'Hide and seek now,' Kate announced, pulling on her pink gloves. 'Let's run to those shrubs. More hiding places there.' And so they charged towards thorny bushes and almost naked trees, the ground squelchy and soft as the taller girls ran ahead holding hands, taking them further downstream.

Time had passed; the sky had turned moody and raindrops speckled the air. It was Jo's turn to seek before going back to Kemp House. Inhaling the dank, grassy smell, she settled on a low wall and shut her eyes tightly.

'One, two, three, four, five . . .' she slowly counted.

A sound caught her short. The sharp and clear peal of a scream and a splash. Snapping open her eyes, she jumped from her perch, hurtling down the slippery path towards it, her wellies sliding and squeaking. She rushed to the stream's edge; so much deeper here and galloping fast like tiny white ponies. Her eyes scanning the water, she glimpsed copper hair. Oh my God, it was Miranda! Dragged down the river, her body was bobbing under by the weight of her blazer.

Hot with adrenaline and alarm, she snatched up a dead branch, intending to do *something*, to pelt along the river bank, even jump in, but gloved hands on each arm firmly held her back.

'No,' Kate said simply. 'It's what she deserves.'

Spinning round, Jo gaped at the placid face of her friend, her heart torn with uncertainty and impotence, then she hauled her gaze back to the river. Only the pappus of dandelions skimmed the surface.

Miranda had gone.

'Jo, listen. Are you listening? It's getting dark. We've got to go back now or we'll get into trouble,' Kate said evenly. Her gentle eyes were on Jo's, her features calm and relaxed.

Seeming to notice Miranda's red glove in her hand, she lobbed it into the water. 'You're trembling, Jo, poor thing. Let me give you a hug. Whatever would you do without me?' she said, smiling.

But Jo couldn't move. Dragging her eyes back to the river, she searched the dusky surface. Nothing. Desperate to spot the Pre-Raphaelite image in the water, she blinked and stared again before turning to Kate.

'What have you done?'

Kate lifted her eyebrows. 'What have *we* done.' Then with a tut, 'We planned it together.'

'No, we didn't.'

'Yes, we did. For years. You came up with some jolly good ideas but it was always going to be drowning. That's why Kemp House was perfect.'

Jo gaped. She was referring to her stories, whispered to Kate on the swings or the seesaw at Junior House. 'They were just tales to cheer you up when you were—'

'Oh Jo, you know that's not true. You even wrote them down for me.' She gave a sidelong glance. 'I kept them, actually.' Then, after a moment: 'Don't look so worried, they're in my special box with a key.' She held out her hand. 'Come on, we have to go now. You and me. Best friends for ever.'

Back at Kemp House, Kate carefully washed their rubber boots at the outside tap.

'We haven't been near the river at all, if anyone happens to ask,' she said. 'We just went for a walk. After all, the river is out of bounds.' Her face pink and pleased, she smiled softly. 'Don't look so worried, Jo. We'll put these back on the shelf in the cloakroom. No one will notice.'

She finished her scrubbing, then placed a single finger to her lips. 'It was just an accident, but they might not believe us, so I'm doing this for you, Jo. I'd hate you to get into trouble, but it *was* your idea to go down to the river.' She lifted her eyebrows mean-ingfully. 'And the rest . . . You even crossed first. And swung on the branches. Everyone knows I'm a wimp. I wouldn't have done *any* of it without you.'

No one asked where Jo and Kate had been that day. The two of them joined in the tears, the horror and the grief when it was announced that Miranda Day-Carter was missing, and then dead, inexplicably drowned in the river, which, as they all knew, was absolutely out of bounds. A beautiful and talented pupil gone for ever: someone's baby, someone's child, lost for no reason at all. As the days and the weeks went by, Joanna Wragg came to believe it was true.

59

Manchester – present day

Still stiff from so much walking, Jo adjusted her position on the turquoise kitchen chair, reread her piece and sighed. She'd only been in Manchester for two flipping minutes, but it felt as if she'd never been away. It was bloody freezing and raining heavily outside; she was back to writing drivel about food and death. Today's article expounded the benefits of cottage cheese. If you ate it before bed, the low-calorie snack would boost your metabolism and help shed the pounds. Yeah, right. Though in fairness there was some *scientific* research about it.

Feeling a sudden chill, she reached for her hoodie, but the peal of her mobile cut short her struggle to get it on. She looked at the name of the caller. Result. Ten pots of cottage cheese were lined up on the table, ready for the *taste test*. She never had liked the blinking stuff – she could defer a little longer, or perhaps tempt her brother to sample it for her.

'Ben! How do you like cottage cheese?'

He snorted. 'Not, hi Ben, I'm back in one piece with a case full of raki and ouzo for my beloved brother.'

'Sorry, I was going to call you and Mum later. Thought I'd force myself to get stuck into the old routine straight away, otherwise I'd dream of lazy sunshine and procrastinate for ever.'

'So, go on. How was Santorini? As beautiful as they say? What did you decide about the hot springs—'

'Hold on.' Another call was waiting. She peered at the screen. 'Oh, it's Mum.' She glanced at the clock. Not her usual time for a chat. Best take it.

'Hi, Mum. Everything OK?'

No reply for several beats, and then, 'Are you sitting down, love?' she asked.

'Yes . . . why?'

Quickly and breathlessly, Joyce's words toppled out. 'Oh Jo, I'm so sorry but I've just heard some terrible news from Hilary. Really dreadful. I'm afraid Kate has died, love. Sorry to put it so bluntly but I don't know how else to—'

Until death do us part immediately flashed through Jo's head. Then the question was out before she could stop it. Not 'Sorry' or 'How dreadful' but, 'What happened?' she asked.

Her mum's intake of breath was heavy. 'Oh Jo, it's so awful, I can hardly say it. She drowned, love. She fell into the reservoir at Ladybower. From the viaduct probably. Well, somewhere near there apparently because—'

'Oh God, not her new mare,' Jo replied. 'I knew she was frisky, but Kate is such an experienced . . .' Her voice shaky, she corrected herself. 'She *was* an experienced rider. How on earth—'

'She wasn't riding, love.'

'Then how . . . It's a pretty long walk from the farm – probably five or six miles.'

'She drove, took her car—'

'But she'd been banned!' Then, more quietly, 'She was barred from driving a while back, Mum. Why would she ... Oh God, had she been drinking? Did she lose control and and ... ' Feeling sick, an image of Kate being swallowed by icy water flew into her head. So vivid, she had to breathe the nausea away. 'A crash, oh God, poor Kate. The sheer panic, the terror, I can't begin to imagine ... '

Joyce didn't comment, she seemed far too silent. 'What else, Mum? There's something else, isn't there?'

'There wasn't a crash. The car was parked up, undamaged.'

'So how did she—'

'She jumped, love.'

Until death do us part, until death do us part thumped through her head. The image rising again, the words caught in her throat. 'No, Mum. That can't be right.'

'Sorry? What was that?'

'You must be wrong. Kate would never kill herself.'

'I'm afraid she did, love. There's no doubt. She left a note in the car.' The sound of Joyce loudly blowing her nose cut through her quavery voice. 'Poor Hilary. It's taken her a few days to get over the shock. She said to apologise for not phoning you herself, but she was worried it would be too difficult with you girls being so close. As devastated as she is, she says it's not a complete surprise. Well, you know about Kate's drinking. Then there were her other problems. I'd heard about the agoraphobia, but Hilary said they went even further than that. The poor girl had been seeing a psychiatrist for some time, apparently, and ... ' Joyce's voice trailed off.

'And what?'

'Well, she'd threatened to do it before. Many times, love. Tom was so shell-shocked, it all came tumbling out at Hilary's. He never for a moment thought she actually meant it. But, well, clearly she did. Waited until Alice had gone to school, then drove to Ladybower. Seems she was intoxicated. Very drunk, apparently. But perhaps that was a good thing because—'

Feeling another swell of queasiness, Jo interrupted. 'Sorry, can I call you back, please, Mum?'

She needed time to think, a breather to control and dampen the feverish, conflicting emotions which were running through her head. The realisation had finally hit. Catherine Bayden-Jones was dead! The pretty little girl in the boater was gone, gone for ever. It was horrifying and strangely liberating. But there were also feelings of guilt. Kate was dead. What about Tom and Alice? Oh God, Alice, poor child.

Her mum didn't reply. But after a moment she spoke swiftly, like ripping off a plaster. 'She was sucked into the plughole, Joanna.'

'What?'

'The plughole. You remember it, don't you?'

'The overflow?'

A sob and then, 'Yes. So dreadful. I suppose there might have been a chance for her to change her mind, but getting caught up ... Well, you can imagine. I can't get it out of my head.'

Her chest tight, Jo stared through the window. Yes, she and her brothers knew the bell-mouth overflow well. On picnic days to the reservoir with their parents, they used to gaze at the spiral shape of the 'plughole', mesmerised by the fleecy foam and the thudding, insistent din of fast-flowing water.

God, she'd loved it there. The dam had been built in the war years and the hamlet of Derwent flooded to create it. She'd search the tranquil surface for a sighting of the submerged church spire, or even more, allegedly, in a drought. Her fascination with the *village beneath the water* had been the source of countless tales in her head. A piano teacher had refused to move and she'd imagined the water lapping at her front garden steps, getting higher and higher until she and her house were swallowed. Before swamping, they'd dug

347

up the consecrated bodies from the church graveyard and moved them. It gave her an endless source of ghost stories. They were all murdered, of course, but how was the crime executed? She could still remember sitting on the seesaw at the back of Junior House and regaling one graphically to her golden-haired best friend. That death was by drowning.

Scrunching her eyes, Jo blocked out the memory. Fighting the panic, she breathed deeply, in and out, in and out. The muffled sound of a baby's cries broke the moment. Looking down to the pavement, she nodded to herself.

Kate was dead now, she had gone. It was time. Time to forget and finally move on.

60

It was an unusually sunny day for February, far too hot for a
funeral, and it was a cool relief to slip in at the back of the old
village church. Jo had promised Ben she'd come, but she wanted
to do it alone. Besides, he was bringing Joyce and Jo knew she'd
be devastated to lose Kate and would need his support.

The dank church was full, the sun brightening its dusty
stained-glass windows. Many of the women were wearing hats,
Jo noticed. She involuntarily touched her hair. The idea of a head
covering hadn't occurred to her, but then she wasn't one of them,
never really had been. Today she was just an ordinary girl from
Barnsley who wanted commonplace things; a girl who was happy
to be just herself.

Familiar hymns from schooldays floated by her consciousness.
Prayers too, her lips moving with the words deeply ingrained from
each morning's service in the chapel at St Luke's. But her thoughts
were shallow, they didn't mull on Kate, or the past, during the
short ceremony.

Standing in the shadows of the arch, she watched the mourners file out, led by Tom, his face inscrutable and his jaw set. He was holding Alice's hand. Oh God. Alice, poor Alice. Jo wanted to reach out and brush her shoulder, but she didn't.

She followed at the rear, her eyes catching the ancient gravestones of people long dead. Elsie and Mildred, Ada and Pearl, Abel and Tobias. Young children too. Five, ten and twelve, tragically drowned.

Someone's baby, someone's child.

The graveside was packed with some faces she knew. Along with Hilary and Harold, there were Kate's older sisters, Guy Voide and his wife and the Shahs, but mostly people she didn't recognise. An older generation mainly; Hilary and Harold's friends, she guessed. The cluster of ancient ladies who'd sung the dirges with shrill voices stood slightly back and there was a woman holding a small boy's hand, naughty little Kieran, perhaps; but there was no one she recognised from St Luke's.

It was funny, she mused, how funerals attracted all manner of people. 'Funeral groupies,' Richard had whispered at his grandma's. 'Don't know them from Adam! And they always sing the loudest, have you noticed?'

Her dead husband still popped into her mind from time to time, but in a dispassionate way. She could picture him in snapshots like a photo album, but struggled to remember or *feel* the living Richard. But that wasn't surprising; when she looked in the mirror, she no longer recognised the Joanna who had loved him.

Standing a little away, Ben and Joyce were at the graveside, so she joined them quietly from behind. Joyce took her hand, then tucked it under her arm. 'Oh, Joanna. Look at you! You do look lovely.' And then with a sigh, pulling her closer. 'Thank the Lord it wasn't either of you.'

It sounded harsh, but it wasn't, Jo knew. More born out of love for her children, from shock and the transience of life.

The mourners milled at the front of the church. Blinding light after hours in the dark, Jo thought. It felt like Kate's wedding day – smartly dressed people, pleasant faces and nods, but no one really sure what they were supposed to do next. She still wanted to shrink away and hide, but she knew she couldn't conceal herself for ever, so she edged into the brightness, greeting Kate's family and neighbours with a sad smile and a kiss or a handshake. And suddenly there was Hilary, holding both Jo's hands in hers, a genuine look of pleasure on her face.

'Oh, Jo, hello! Don't you look radiant? Joyce told us Corfu suited you. But thank goodness you're here now! I'm so pleased to see you. And after months of constant rain, you've brought the sunshine, darling. It's been a terrible two weeks. Kate gone just like that and Harold not talking to any of us. He just shut himself away in the study and wouldn't come out. Then Annabelle was in Scotland and I couldn't get hold of Clare for two days, which still hasn't been explained, and I so needed to talk, to scream and to shout, which is always the best medicine, as you know.'

She kissed Jo's cheeks. She looked as elegant as ever, her hair still auburn, her face hidden behind a marvellous purple hat and sunglasses.

Barely taking breath, Hilary continued to talk. 'Then poor Tom, it was awful. To lose a wife so suddenly is bad enough, but to be questioned by the police as though he was a common criminal is just terrible. I know they have to look at every angle even when there's a . . . ' She lowered her voice. '*Suicide*. Such a terrible word. But he was away in London so couldn't really add much. I'm sure he feels dreadful for going and not knowing what Kate was planning, but work called. As I said to Harold, being a busy man isn't a crime. And a whole horde of people were with him. Then of course they found the car and the note.' She squeezed Jo's hands. 'She was my daughter, so of course I loved her dearly, but she'd been unstable for a very long time. I think poor Tom was blind to it, but you and I have always known, haven't we, Jo?'

Pausing for a moment, she fumbled in her handbag and took a drag of an e-cigarette. 'Of course they came to the house asking all sorts of questions. Was the handwriting definitely Kate's? Had she said anything in the days leading up to it? How was her mood? Did she have an alcohol problem? Well, I could hardly deny that. And anyway, they were the ones who'd charged her with drink-driving. But that's the last of it now. Harold finally came out of his den, told them to back off and have some respect. And poor Tom. Dashing from London to collect little Alice from us. I don't need to tell you how taciturn he can be, but he was white with shock, then all sorts came out and suddenly everything made perfect sense. But how could he know she *meant* all those things? How he'll miss her. He loved her so. Oh, but what am I telling you for? You know that better than anyone, don't you, darling?'

Hoping the thrashing heat in her chest hadn't spread to her cheeks, Jo nodded. *Until death do us part?* But it was fine, really fine. Tom didn't do anything. He was working away. Hilary said he had an alibi.

A shadow fell, blocking her light, so she knew he was there before lifting her head. His gaze was constant, blue and even. 'Thank you for coming, Jo,' he said. 'You look beautiful.' Then he stepped back, his expression clearly shocked.

For a moment he didn't speak, then he rallied. 'I didn't know congratulations were in order. Congratulations!'

Feeling a surge of emotion, Jo waited for the question.

'When is the baby due?'

'In just a few weeks. An unexpected summer conception.'

'So, it's—'

She nodded and spoke quietly. 'Yes. Only you.'

Studying her intently, he was silent for several seconds. Then slowly he smiled. 'It suits you. I knew it would.' His eyes glistening, he swallowed. 'Can I . . . ?' he asked, nodding at the great swell of her stomach.

'Of course,' she said, smiling and smiling, hoping no one was witnessing her inappropriate joy.

He nodded thoughtfully. 'March. Yes, March sounds perfect. I'll be there this time,' he said, 'I promise,' before being called away by Harold.

'You're huge, Jo! I never thought I'd say it but you are!' Ben said as he approached, trying but failing to get his arms completely around her. He glanced at Tom. 'So, not a little Spiros after all, eh Jo?'

Trying to dampen her beam, she shook her head and thought back. Convinced she was infertile, she hadn't clocked her lack of periods, her fancy for salty food or her gradually changing shape. Not until the lemon lady had put a gnarled hand on her stomach. '*Moró*,' she'd said with her toothless grin.

Jo's pleasure at seeing her after an absence of several weeks was replaced with surprise that she could speak. Then she mentally translated the word and the smile fell with the shake of her head. But the old lady persisted by rocking her arms. '*Naí, naí. Koritsáki*,' she said, and in that moment Jo knew she'd been blessed, truly blessed.

Joyce had been unable to conceal her delight on the telephone. 'I'm so excited, I can't tell you how much, love. My Joanna having a baby on St Patrick's Day of all days! It's wonderful, just wonderful. I know I'm being selfish, but you will come home, won't you? Home for good. Not to Moor End, of course, but back to Manchester and the flat. Ben's missed you and so have I.' Jo heard a big sniff. 'And your dad. I know he doesn't say much, but I think he suffers the most. He'd go in a black cloud the moment we left you in the school dormitory and he wouldn't come out of it until

353

he collected you again. You were his special little girl. I think he regrets not showing it more. Can you imagine how he'll make up for it with this one?' Then, after a moment, 'I can't wait to tell Barbara and everyone . . . '

'Yes, Barbara and the family, but maybe not everyone yet, Mum, I'm still getting used to the idea myself.'

Now catching her breath, she watched Tom's retreating back. The sun was lighting his blond hair like a halo. He didn't know; he didn't know. Thank God he was happy.

Kate had, though. The text, that message out of nowhere. *'How are you, Jo? Just caught up for a coffee with Joyce and heard all the Corfu news . . . '*

Inhaling deeply, Jo closed her eyes. The nightmares had been about babies, her baby and Kate. She was always there in the dreams, a midwife in uniform, smiling, benevolent and kind. But the infant died every time. 'Sorry,' the nurse said, with tears in her eyes. 'The baby is dead. Poisoned, how sad.' Or, 'Sorry, the baby drowned. But she deserved it.' Or, 'Sorry, my dear, but you murdered her. It's your own fault.' And Jo would scream, 'I don't believe you! Let me see her. You're lying, you're lying.'

But on the eve of Cheese Eating Sunday, the baby had lived, sleeping and safe in the nurse's arms. She'd leaned forward to pass him to Jo, and Jo saw him, her child, perfect and beautiful and *alive*. But the Kate-midwife had looked at her with narrowed eyes, then she'd sharply pulled back, opened her arms and dropped him to the floor, his head smashing into a thousand pieces of china.

Yes, Kate's text. *'How are you, Jo? Just caught up for a coffee with Joyce and heard all the Corfu news . . . '* it had started. Then it had continued: *'So thrilled about your pregnancy. Can't wait to be next to you every step of the way!'*

Sighing, Jo shook the graphic images away. The story had

a happy ending, so she wouldn't think about them any more. Turning away from the guests, she strolled along the side path, looking again at the names on the headstones. So many to choose from! The lemon lady had said a girl, but she didn't know for sure. And, of course, she'd have to agree it with *Daddy*.

Reaching Kate's flower-strewn grave, she lowered her heavy body and carefully kneeled down beside it. No monument yet. What would it eventually say? Beloved friend, perhaps?

Taking a scoop of loose soil, she let it slip through her fingers. Excavating the past.

'Why they think you killed yourself, I have no idea,' she said in a whisper. 'You of all people would never do that, would you, Kate? Still, they don't know you like I do. And besides, you wrote a note.'

Rubbing her bump, she smiled. 'My baby. Poor Mum – did you drag the news out of her?' Picturing Kate's *cat's eyes* stare at the farmhouse, she thought for a moment. 'Though perhaps you suspected much earlier, when I looked *so pale*. Just like all those years ago.'

She cocked her head. 'Did you know it was Tom's, Kate? Did you want to look me in the eye to find out? Like you looked me in the eye and told me to abort our other baby? *Every step of the way*. What did that mean, exactly? Was I going to have a tragic accident and die like poor Miranda?'

Seeing Kate's guileless face, she quietly snorted. 'Not a chance. I know you too well, Kate. I had to play you at your own game. Maybe I am *so clever*, as you put it, but the heavy rainfall for all those weeks helped.'

Saying she was spending those few days in Santorini, she waved Mao and Nigel goodbye. Instead she flew straight back to Manchester. She'd heard all about the downpours from her mum, but the fine weather had felt like a good omen as she drove to the Hope Valley and parked in a deserted ramblers' car park. Carrying the wine, she turned up at the farmhouse. Not one bottle, but two of Kate's favourites, opening it right away to let the bouquet breeze out. Kate just couldn't resist. Guzzled the whole lot as Jo smiled and smiled *like a villain*, pretending to bond over the baby and be friends again.

'Shall we have a drive out, Kate? Get some fresh air?' she asked later. So sloshed, Kate didn't ask why they were in her car, where they were going or what for.

Hearing a squabble of birds, Jo now glanced across the grave-yard to a sturdy yew tree. She took a shuddery breath. Kate had climbed out at the reservoir to help Jo look for the elusive Derwent spire. So sweet, so docile and compliant, Jo had almost changed her mind. She'd had to remind herself why they were there. The lies, the veiled blackmail and manipulation, the abortion and the sheer terror about the safety of her baby. And for Miranda, of course.

Like the yew tree, Kate was poisonous. She had to go.

Now steeling herself again, Jo pulled a wry face. They wouldn't have seen the steeple anyway. It was actually demolished with explosives many years ago. And besides, the water was too high, so swollen it had to run into the overflow, the *plughole* which had featured in Jo's *funny little stories*, as Kate had scornfully put it.

She rubbed her back. In her condition she'd been a little worried, of course, but it only took one sharp shove before Kate teetered and fell.

Closing her eyes, Jo pictured the moment. After the initial ripple, the water had seemed so smooth and undisturbed, she'd held her breath and scanned it for an age. Her chest almost burst and her body shook with fear that somehow Kate would swim and make a comeback like always. That she'd *never* be free. But suddenly her body popped to the surface in the distance, already bobbing its way to the plughole as planned.

Jo had finally stood up and done *something*.

Then there was the letter in the dash of Kate's car. She had to be careful when she wrote it in Kate's loopy scrawl, which had changed very little from schooldays. The impulse had been to create one of her compelling dark stories. After all, her best friend had given her plenty of ammunition over the years. But she'd contained herself and kept the note simple: 'I'm so sorry, Tom and Alice. I love you both <u>dearly</u> but I think you'll be better without me.'

Which was very true.

Now feeling a sudden shiver, Jo lifted her head. A copper-haired woman was standing a few metres away and lifting her hand. Miranda, of course, appearing from time to time and asking for closure or exposure or maybe revenge. Jo nodded in acknowledgement. The ending of Kate's tale was a drowning too, but *this* one, she felt, was for the greater good.

Going back to Kate, she reflected for a moment on that fine line between love and hate. At times she had almost despised Catherine Bayden-Jones, and yet adored her too.

'Would you really have done anything to hurt Tom or Alice?' she asked quietly. 'Or my baby and me? You loved and needed me just like I loved and needed you, didn't you? Chalk and cheese, we always said. So different and yet . . . yes, so alike too.'

Almost tasting that corrosive bubbling and burning of envy inside, Jo sighed. 'And you were right, Kate, absolutely. I *was* jealous.'

Hearing a stream of sound, she turned towards the pretty lych-gate. Tom was saying a few words and shaking mourners' hands as they slowly filed out. Inhaling the fragrant smell of spring and hope, Jo gazed at her man. As though he knew she was watching, he looked towards her. His smile was soft, his blue eyes on hers, his hair lit by brilliant sunshine.

Still feeling that intense and delirious tug that had never really gone, she went back to the conversation with her old friend.

'But you were wrong about one thing, very wrong, Kate,' she said. 'It *was* a competition and I won.'

ACKNOWLEDGEMENTS

So much heartfelt thanks to:

My wonderful girls Elizabeth, Charlotte and Emily, and my hubby Jonathan, for your brilliant company, loyalty and love.

All the fantastic people I've mentioned previously. You are still much loved and appreciated friends.

The Piatkus team, especially my fabulous editors, Anna Boatman and Hannah Wann, for gently guiding me in the very best direction.

My literary agent, Kate Johnson, for your continued dedication and encouragement.

My early readers Elizabeth Ball, Hazel James and Robert Peett, for your insightful feedback. And not forgetting you, my Liz Lanigan!

My special friend Belinda Goodwin – not least for your spectacular book-themed carrot cakes.

The eclectic mix of writers I raised a glass with at the crime writing festivals and HarperCollins' parties. I had such fun with all you guys!

Katie Gammon, for a lovely author photograph, Steve Rouse and my Charl Lanigan, for fantastic launch photographs.

My local bookshop, E J Morten Booksellers of Didsbury, for your book-stocking support.

Anna and Ed at Wilmslow Waterstones, for two brilliant book launches.

My 2018 writing journey was a little bumpy at times, but what shone through was the kindness, generosity and goodwill of so many people I met along the way. Thank you to:

The wonderful authors who gave their time to read my novels and offer brilliant quotes – Teresa Driscoll, Rachel Sargeant, Amanda Robson, Helen Fields, Roz Watkins, Elisabeth Carpenter, S.D. Robertson, Sanjida Kay, David Stuart Davies, Jane Isaac, Faith Bleasdale, Petrina Banfield, Kate Ellis, Katerina Diamond, Sarah Jasmon, Louise Beech. A special thank you to Martina Cole – what a big-hearted lady!

All the hard-working bloggers who championed my books. There are too many to list, but special thanks to Nicola Smith of Short Books and Scribes for choosing *My Husband's Lies* as one of her Very Special Reads of 2018.

The folk who kindly invited me to do author talks, interviews and readings, or chat at their book clubs. You were all incredibly welcoming – my dear friend Liz Ball and her Saxton book club, Dale Gilligan of Didsbury Library, Joanne and Susanna of Trafford Libraries, Mike Madden and Dave Hailwood of Ex-Pat Radio, Sally Penni of Didsbury FM, Sue Jenkins of DAC Beachcroft, Repton Literary Festival, Millie Sarin of All FM 96.9 Radio, Poynton Writers' Group, Women in the Law UK, Liz Norris of Alderley Edge Inner Wheel Club, Cheshire Book Connectors, Write Club, Anne Guy's Didsbury book club, my lovely neighbour Sandra Ellis and her book club, Sue France,

Emma Truelove of Radio Royal, Gin and Phonics Book Club, Tracy Carley's Bramhall book club, The Fiction Café, Melanie Roach's Nassau book club (I'm coming in person next time!), Hannah Kate of North Manchester FM, the Didsbury WI.

Those who gave me space in their magazines, newspapers and groups – Deborah Grace of *Open Up*, Beverley Waring of *Didsbury Magazine*, Claire Hawker of *Inside Wilmslow*, Sally MacDonald of *The Sunday Post*, Lizzie Hayes of Mystery People, Angela Rose of *Roqueta Magazine*, Yakub Qureshi of *Manchester Evening News*, Ian Ross of *Wilmslow Guardian*, Jan Cobb of *The Arch*, Kate Houghton of *Living Edge Magazine*, Andrew Hill of *Shots*, Julie and Karen of UK Gossip Girls.

The lovely people who helped by introducing me to their colleagues and friends – Adam Lanigan, Mike Whalley, Donna Barnard, David Beckler, Malcolm Hollingdrake, Paul Finch

Last, but not least, the fabulous reading public! It was so exciting – and incredible – to watch *My Husband's Lies* climb the overall kindle chart and become a top ten bestseller! Thank you so much.

Don't miss the next gripping psychological thriller
from Caroline England . . .

TRUTH GAMES

Family is everything to Ellie Wilson. She tries hard to
be the perfect mother, the perfect partner, the perfect
daughter – but she can't always seem to get it right.

When an old friend from university re-enters their
lives, dark memories from Ellie's past begin to
resurface. Memories that have been buried for a
long time.

As Ellie starts to unravel some shocking and sinister
realities, she realises that she must choose between
keeping the family she loves – and facing the truth . . .

Coming soon

Available now to pre-order